YOU HAVE NEVER BEEN HERE

YOU HAVE NEVER BEEN HERE

New and Selected Stories

Mary Rickert

Small Beer Press
Easthampton, MA

You Have Never Been Here: Stories copyright © 2015 by Mary Rickert. All rights reserved. Page 329 is an extension of the copyright page.

Small Beer Press
150 Pleasant Street #306
Easthampton, MA 01027
smallbeerpress.com
weightlessbooks.com
info@smallbeerpress.com

Distributed to the trade by Consortium.

Library of Congress Cataloging-in-Publication Data

Rickert, M. (Mary), 1959-
 [Short stories. Selections]
You have never been here : stories / Mary Rickert. -- First edition.
   pages ; cm
 Summary: "Mary Rickert writes hard, political stories that yet encompass the gentle wisdom of the ages. Here are cruelty and love. War and regeneration. She has long been an undiscovered master of the short story and this survey collection, including new work, will open the eyes of a wide, astonished audience."-- Provided by publisher.
 ISBN 978-1-61873-110-4 (paperback) -- ISBN 978-1-61873-111-1 (ebook)
 I. Title.
PS3618.I375A6 2015
813'.6--dc23
                2015029660

First edition 1 2 3 4 5 6 7 8 9

Set in Centaur 12 pt.
Cover photo "Angel" © 2015 by Emma Powell (emmapowellphotography.com).

Printed on 50# Natures Natural 30% PCR recycled paper by the Maple Press in York, PA.

TABLE OF CONTENTS

For Gordon Van Gelder

Memoir of a Deer Woman

Her husband comes home, stamps the snow from his shoes, kisses her, and asks how her day was.

"Our time together is short," she says.

"What are you talking about?"

"I found a deer by the side of the road. It was stuck under the broken fence. Hit by a car. I called the rescue place, but when the animal rescue man saw it, he said it had to be shot. The policeman shot it."

He looks through the mail while she stands there, crying. When he realizes this, he hugs her. Already she feels the hard shapes forming at the top of her head. Later, she will tell him she has a headache.

He will hold her anyway. He will sleep with his mouth pressed against her neck. She will think of the noise the deer made, that horrible braying.

At midnight she wakes up. The sky is exploding with distant fireworks. From past experience she knows that if they stand and strain their necks, they can just barely see the veins of color over the treetops. It is mostly futile, and tonight neither of them rises. "Happy New Year," he whispers.

"What do you think animals feel?" she says.

He mumbles something about Wally, their dog, who sleeps soundly at the foot of their bed.

"That deer was frightened. Today, I mean. It made the most horrible noise; did I tell you that? I never heard such a noise before. It was really mournful and horrible."

The fireworks end in a flourish of tiny explosions. She knows what she should have done. She should not have waited for the policeman, who took four shots before he killed it. She knew that deer was dying; why did she pretend otherwise? She should have smothered it and put it out of its misery.

New year's morning is cold and crisp. Wally wakes them up with his big, wet tongue. Her husband takes him out to do his business. When they come back inside, she listens to the pleasant sounds of her husband talking in soft cooing words to Wally, his food dish being filled. Her husband comes back into the bedroom alone, carefully shutting the door behind him. She knows what that means. He crawls in beside her. He rubs his hands up and down her body. "Happy New Year," he says. She sinks into his desires until they become her own. Who knows how long they have? Maybe this is the last time. Later, he fries maple sausage and scrambles eggs, but she finds she cannot eat. He asks her if she feels all right. She shrugs. "My head hurts," she says. "Also my hands." He tells her to go to the doctor. She nods. Well, of course. But she does not tell him that she already knows what is happening.

She takes down the ornaments, wraps them in tissue paper, circles the tree, removing the lights. The branches brush her cheeks and lips and she nibbles on the bitter green. Her husband is outside, splitting kindling. For a while she stands at the window and watches. Wally lies on his bed in the living room. He does not like the loud noise of the axe. She raises her face to the ceiling. She feels trapped and the feeling rises inside her like bile. She brays. Wally slinks past her, into the kitchen. She brays again. It is both deeply disturbing and a relief.

When her husband comes in, carrying kindling, he'll ask her if she's all right. He'll say he thought he heard a strange noise. She'll shrug and say that she thought the tree was falling. He'll accept this as reasonable, forgetting that she is not the sort to scream at falling Christmas trees, forgetting that when they met she was at least partly wild. He drops the kindling into the box next to the wood-burning stove. "Come here, help me with the tree," she says. He holds the tree while she unscrews the stand. Dry sap snakes from the holes; she cannot help but think of it as blood.

They dump the tree in the forest behind the house. There is a whole graveyard of Christmas trees there. They walk back to the house together, crunching across the snow. A green truck is parked in the driveway. "I wonder who that is," he says. A tall man wearing camouflage clothes and a Crocodile Dundee hat steps out of the driver's side. He nods as they approach.

She knows just what her mother would have said about all of this. She would have said, "You are never going to be tame. You will regret trying. You will hurt others if you deny yourself."

"Hope I'm not disturbing you. I've got an owl that needs to be released. It was found not too far down the road. You know the Paterlys? They're in Florida now. I thought I could release it in your yard. You could keep an eye on it."

"This is Kevin," she tells her husband. "He came to help with the deer yesterday."

Her husband stares at her blankly.

"You know, the one I found? That had to be shot?"

"Can't believe that guy couldn't shoot between the eyes," Kevin says, shaking his head.

"Oh. Right," says her husband.

"Where's the owl?"

"I was just passing by. I'll come back tonight. If that's all right?"

"Tonight?" her husband says.

She tells Kevin that it would be great if he came back later, with the owl. He doesn't look at either of them. He nods at the snow, gets into the truck. They watch him back out of the driveway.

"He's kind of strange," her husband says.

She shrugs. Her bones ache, her head, her hands and her feet, and it takes a lot of effort for her to understand that her husband is not being mean, just human. They walk back to the house, holding hands. Who knows, she thinks, maybe this is the last time. Already by nightfall she is wearing mittens. She tells him her hands are cold. Again he tells her to go to the doctor. She tells him that she has an appointment the next morning. This is love, she reminds herself. She smiles at her husband while he turns the pages of his book.

———

"Stage three," the doctor says.

"There must be some mistake."

"You can get a second opinion."

"What are my options?"

"I say we hit this with everything we've got."

"Are you sure that's my report?"

"I know this comes as a shock, but I recommend that you address it quickly. The sooner the better."

"Chemo and radiation?"

"Yes. And then chemo again."

"The magic bullets."

"You could think of it that way, but you might want to choose a different image. Something soothing."

"Like what?"

"I have one patient who thinks of the treatment as flowers."

"Flowers?"

"It soothes her."

"What kind of flowers? Flowers that'll cause my hair to fall out and make me throw up? What kind of flowers would do that?"

"This is your disease, and your body. You get to decide how you want to treat it."

"But that's just the thing, isn't it, Doctor?"

"I'm sorry?"

"This isn't my body anymore."

"Why don't you go home? Take the weekend to think about your options. Get a second opinion, if you'd like."

She rises from the chair, stomps out of the office on her sore, hard feet. The waiting room is full of women. One of them looks up, her brown eyes beautiful in the soft pelt of her face. She nods slightly. She smells like salt.

When her husband returns from work she is sitting at the kitchen table, waiting to tell him the news.

"Oh my God," he says.

"It hardly hurts at all."

"How long?" he asks.

"Nobody knows, but it seems to be happening sooner rather than later."

He pounds the table with his fist, then reaches for her hand, though he recoils from the shape. "But you're a woman."

She is confused until she sees where he is looking. She touches the antlers' downy stubs on the top of her head. "It's rare, but females get them too. Nobody knows why. Kind of like men and nipples, I guess."

"What are you going to do?" he asks.

"I'm thinking of writing a memoir."

His mouth drops open.

She shrugs. "I always did want to be a writer."

"What are you talking about?"

"I think I should start with the deer being shot, what do you think?"

"I think you need medicine, not writing."

"You make it sound dirty."

He shakes his head. He is crying and shaking his head and all of a sudden she realizes that he will never understand. Should she say so in her memoir? Should she write about all the places he never understood? Will he understand that she doesn't blame him?

"It isn't lonely," she says.

"What?"

She hadn't meant to speak out loud. "I mean, okay, sometimes it is."

"I don't know what you're talking about."

"There's a memoir-writing group that meets every Wednesday. I e-mailed Anita, the leader? I explained my situation and she was really nice about it. She said I could join them."

"I don't see how this is going to help. You need medicine and doctors. We need to be proactive here."

"Could you just be supportive? I really need your support right now."

He looks at her with teary blue eyes that once, she thought, she would look at forever. He says, his voice husky, "Of course."

She is sniffling, and he wipes her nose for her. She licks his hand.

———

She continues to sleep with him, but in the morning he wakes up with deep scratch marks all over his body, no matter how thickly they wrap her hooves in layers of cloth and old socks and mittens. "They're like little razors," he says. "And it's not just the edges, it's the entire bottom."

She blinks her large brown eyes at him, but he doesn't notice because he is pulling a tick out of his elbow. That night she sleeps on the floor and Wally crawls into bed with her husband. He objects, of course, but in the end, they both sleep better, she facing the window where she watches the white owl, hugely fat and round, perched on the bough of a tree, before she realizes it isn't the owl at all but the moon.

Near the end she stops trying to drive; instead she runs to her memoir-writing workshop. Her husband follows in the Volvo, thinking that he can prevent her being hit by a car or shot. He waits in the driveway while she meets with the group.

Anita tries to make her comfortable, but lately she feels nervous coming all the way into the house. She lies in the doorway with only her nose and front hooves inside. Some of the others complain about the cold and the snow but Anita tells them to put on their coats. Sometimes, in the distance, they hear a mournful cry, which makes all of them shudder. There have been rumors of coyotes in the neighborhood.

Even though they meet at Anita's house, she herself is having a terrible time with her memoir. It sounds self-pitying, whiny, and dull. She knows this; she just doesn't know what to do about it; that's why she started the workshop in the first place. The critiquers mean well, but frankly, they are all self-pitying whiners themselves. Somewhere along the way, the meetings have taken on the tone of group therapy rather than a writing workshop. Yet, there is something, some emotion they all seem to circle but never successfully describe about the pain of their lives that, Anita feels certain, just might be the point.

After the critique, Anita brings out cakes, cookies, coffee, tea, and, incredibly, a salt lick. Contrary to their reputation, and the evidence of the stories told in this room, people can be good.

The deer woman hasn't shared what she's written yet. She's not sure the group will understand. How can anyone understand what is happening to her? And besides, it is all happening so fast. No one even realizes when she attends her last meeting that she won't be coming back, though later they all agree that she seemed different somehow.

She is standing at the window, watching the yard below. Six deer wait there, staring up at her. He weeps and begs her not to go. Why does he do this, she wonders, why does he spend their last moments together weeping? He begs her not to go, as though she had some say in the matter. She does not answer. The world shatters all around her, but she is not cut. He shouts. She crashes to the ground, in a flurry of snow and hooves. He stands at the window, his mouth wide open. He does not mean to hurt her, but she can feel his breath pulling her back. She runs into the forest with the others, a pounding of hooves and clouds of snow. They do not stop running until they are deep into the night, and she can no longer hear her husband shouting.

After she is gone, he looks through her basket of knitting, projects started and unfinished from the winter, before her hands turned into hooves: a long, thin strand of purple, which he assumes is a scarf; a deep green square, which he thinks might be the beginning of a sweater for him; and a soft gray wasp nest, that's what it looks like, knitted from the strands of her hair. Underneath all this he finds a simple spiral-bound notebook. He sits on the floor and reads what she wrote, until the words sputter and waver and finally end, then he walks up the stairs to the attic, where he thrusts aside boxes of books, and dolls, cups, and papers, before finally opening the box labeled "writing supplies." There he finds the cape, neatly folded beneath deerskin boots, a few blades of brown grass stuck to them. The cape fits fine, of course, but the boots are too tight. He takes them downstairs and splits the seams with the paring knife, laces them on with rope. When he is finished, he makes a strange sight, his chest hair gray against the winter white skin, the cape draped over his narrow shoulders and down the skein of his arms to his blue jeans, which are tied at the calves, laced over the deerskin, his feet bulging out of the sides, like a child suddenly grown to giant proportions. He runs into the forest, calling her name. Wally, the dog, runs beside him.

There are sightings. An old lady, putting seed into the bird feeder, sees him one morning, a glint of white cape, tight muscles, a wild look in his eyes. Two children, standing right beside their father waiting for the bus, scream and point. An entire group of hunters, who say they tracked him and might have gotten a shot. And an artist, standing in the meadow, but artists are always reporting strange sightings and can't be relied upon. What is certain is that wherever the strange man is sighted, words are found. The old lady finds several tiny slips of paper in a bird's nest in her backyard and when one falls to the ground she sees that it is a neat cut-out of the word "Always;" she can't fathom what it might mean, but considers it for the rest of her life, until one afternoon in early autumn she lies dying on her kitchen floor, no trauma beyond the business of a stopped heart, and she sees the word before her face, as though it floated there, a missive from heaven, and she is filled with an understanding of the infinite, and how strange, that this simple word becomes, in that final moment, luminescent; when the father searches the bushes where the children insist the wild man hides, he finds nothing but scraps of paper, tiny pieces, which he almost dismisses, until he realizes that each one contains a word. Frightened of leaving the children too long with madmen about, he scoops some words up and returns to the bus stop, listening to the children's excited chatter but not really hearing anything they say, because the words drag his pocket down like stones, and he can't believe how eager he is to go to work, shut the door to his office and piece together the meaning. He is disappointed at what he finds, "breath," "fingers," and "memory," among several versions of "her." It is nonsense, but he cannot forget the words, and at the strangest times catches himself thinking, "Her breath, her fingers, her memory," as though he were a man in love; the hunters follow the trail of words, but only the youngest among them picks up and pockets one torn paper, which is immediately forgotten, thrown in the wash and destroyed; the artist finds a neat little pile, as though the wild creature ate words like sunflower seeds and left these scraps behind. She ties each word to colored string and hangs them as a mobile. Sometimes, when the air is just right and the words spin gently, she believes she understands them, that they are not simple nonsense; but on other days she knows that meaning is something humans apply to random acts in order to cope with the randomness of death.

Anita, from the memoir-writing group, goes to the house, uninvited. She doesn't know what motivates her. The woman wrote nothing the whole time she'd attended, had offered no suggestions during the critique; in fact, Anita began to suspect that her main motivation for coming had been the salt lick. But for some reason, Anita felt invested in the woman's unknown story, and feels she must find out what has become of her.

What she finds is a small house in the woods, by all appearances empty. She rings the doorbell and is surprised to hear a dog inside, barking. She notices deer tracks come right up to the porch, circling a hemlock bush. The door opens and a strange man stands there, dressed in torn boots, dirty jeans, and a cape. Anita has heard rumors of the wild man and doesn't know what to say; she manages only two words, "Memoir" and "writing," before he grabs her wrist. "Gone," he says, "gone." They stand there for a while, looking at each other. She is a bit frightened, of course, but she also feels pity for this man, obviously mad with grief. "Words?" he says. She stares at him, and he repeats himself ("Words, words, words, words, words, words?"), until finally she understands what he's asking.

"She never wrote a thing." He shakes his head and runs back into the house. Anita stands there for a moment, and then, just as she turns to walk away from this tragic scene, the man returns, carrying a handful of words. He hands them to her as though they were ashes of the deceased, gently folding her fingers over them, as though in prayer, before he goes back inside.

She shakes her head as she walks away, opening the car door with difficulty, her hands fisted as they are. Once in her car, she drops the words into her purse, where they remain until a windy day in early fall, when she searches for her keys in the mall parking lot. A quick breeze picks the tiny scraps up and they twirl in the sky, all the possible, all the forgotten, all the mysterious, unwritten, and misunderstood fragments, and it is only then, when they are hopelessly gone, that Anita regrets having done nothing with them. From this regret, her memoir is written, about the terrible thing that happened to her. She is finally able to write that there is no sorrow greater than regret, no rapture more complete than despair, no beauty more divine than words, but before writing it, she understands, standing there, amidst the cars and shopping bags, watching all the words spin away, as though she had already died, and no longer owned language, that ordinary, everyday, exquisite blessing on which lives are both built and destroyed.

Journey into the Kingdom

The first painting was of an egg, the pale ovoid produced with faint strokes of pink, blue, and violet to create the illusion of white. After that there were two apples, a pear, an avocado, and finally, an empty plate on a white tablecloth before a window covered with gauzy curtains, a single fly nestled in a fold at the top right corner. The series was titled "Journey into the Kingdom."

On a small table beneath the avocado there was a black binder, an unevenly cut rectangle of white paper with the words "Artist's Statement" in neat, square, handwritten letters taped to the front. Balancing the porcelain cup and saucer with one hand, Alex picked up the binder and took it with him to a small table against the wall toward the back of the coffee shop, where he opened it, thinking it might be interesting to read something besides the newspaper for once, though he almost abandoned the idea when he saw that the page before him was handwritten in the same neat letters as on the cover. But the title intrigued him.

AN IMITATION LIFE

Though I always enjoyed my crayons and watercolors, I was not a particularly artistic child. I produced the usual assortment of stick figures and houses with dripping yellow suns. I was an avid collector of seashells and sea glass and much preferred to be outdoors, throwing stones at seagulls (please, no haranguing from animal rights activists, I have long since outgrown this) or playing with my imaginary friends to sitting quietly in the salt rooms of the keeper's house, making pictures at the big wooden kitchen table while my mother, in her black dress, kneaded bread and sang the old French songs between her duties as lighthouse keeper, watcher over the waves, beacon for the lost, governess of the dead.

The first ghost to come to my mother was my own father, who had set out the day previous in the small boat heading to the mainland for supplies such as string and rice, and also bags of soil, which, in years past, we emptied into crevices between the rocks and planted with seeds, a makeshift garden and a "brave attempt," as my father called it, referring to the barren stone we lived on.

We did not expect him for several days so my mother was surprised when he returned in a storm, dripping wet icicles from his mustache and behaving strangely, repeating over and over again, "It is lost, my dear Maggie, the garden is at the bottom of the sea."

My mother fixed him hot tea but he refused it; she begged him to take off the wet clothes and retire with her, to their feather bed piled with quilts, but he said, "Tend the light, don't waste your time with me." So my mother, a worried expression on her face, left our little keeper's house and walked against the gale to the lighthouse, not realizing that she had left me with a ghost, melting before the fire into a great puddle, which was all that was left of him upon her return. She searched frantically while I kept pointing at the puddle and insisting it was he. Eventually she tied on her cape and went out into the storm, calling his name. I thought that, surely, I would become orphaned that night.

But my mother lived, though she took to her bed and left me to tend the lamp and receive the news of the discovery of my father's wrecked boat, found on the rocky shoals, still clutching in his frozen hand a bag of soil, which was given to me, and which I brought to my mother, though she would not take the offering.

For one so young, my chores were immense. I tended the lamp, and kept our own hearth fire going too. I made broth and tea for my mother, which she only gradually took, and I planted that small bag of soil by the door to our little house, savoring the rich scent, wondering if those who lived with it all the time appreciated its perfume or not.

I did not really expect anything to grow, though I hoped that the seagulls might drop some seeds or the ocean deposit some small thing. I was surprised when, only weeks later, I discovered the tiniest shoots of green, which I told my mother about. She was not impressed. By that point, she would spend part of the day sitting up in bed, mending my father's socks and moaning, "Agatha, whatever are we going to do?" I did not wish to worry her, so I told her lies about women from the mainland coming to help, men taking turns with the light. "But they are so quiet. I never hear anyone."

"No one wants to disturb you," I said. "They whisper and walk on tiptoe."

It was only when I opened the keeper's door so many uncounted weeks later, and saw, spread before me, embedded throughout the rock (even in crevices where I had planted no soil) tiny pink, purple, and white flowers, their stems shuddering in the salty wind, that I insisted my mother get out of bed.

She was resistant at first. But I begged and cajoled, promised her it would be worth her effort. "The fairies have planted flowers for us," I said, this being the only explanation or description I could think of for the infinitesimal blossoms everywhere.

Reluctantly, she followed me through the small living room and kitchen, observing that "the ladies have done a fairly good job of keeping the place neat." She hesitated before the open door. The bright sun and salty scent of the sea, as well as the loud sound of waves washing all around us, seemed to astound her, but then she squinted, glanced at me, and stepped through the door to observe the miracle of the fairies' flowers.

Never had the rock seen such color, never had it known such bloom! My mother walked out, barefoot, and said, "Forget-me-nots, these are forget-me-nots. But where . . . ?"

I told her that I didn't understand it myself, how I had planted the small bag of soil found clutched in my father's hand but had not really expected it to come to much, and certainly not to all of this, waving my arm over the expanse, the flowers having grown in soilless crevices and cracks, covering our entire little island of stone.

My mother turned to me and said, "These are not from the fairies, they are from him." Then she started crying, a reaction I had not expected and tried to talk her out of, but she said, "No, Agatha, leave me alone."

She stood out there for quite a while, weeping as she walked among the flowers. Later, after she came inside and said, "Where are all the helpers today?" I shrugged and avoided more questions by going outside myself, where I discovered scarlet spots among the bloom. My mother had been bedridden for so long, her feet had gone soft again. For days she left tiny teardrop shapes of blood in her step, which I surreptitiously wiped up, not wanting to draw any attention to the fact, for fear it would dismay her. She picked several of the forget-me-not blossoms and pressed them between the heavy pages of her book of myths and folklore. Not long after that, a terrible storm blew in, rocking our little house, challenging our resolve, and taking with it all the flowers. Once again our rock was barren. I worried what effect this would have on my mother, but she merely sighed, shrugged, and said, "They were beautiful, weren't they, Agatha?"

So passed my childhood: a great deal of solitude, the occasional life-threatening adventure, the drudgery of work, and all around me the great wide sea with its myriad secrets and reasons, the lost we saved, those we didn't. And the ghosts, brought to us by my father, though we never understood clearly his purpose, as they only stood before the fire, dripping and melting like something made of wax, bemoaning what was lost (a fine boat, a lady love, a dream of the sea, a pocketful of jewels, a wife and children, a carving on bone, a song, its lyrics forgotten). We tried to provide what comfort we could, listening, nodding; there was little else we could do: they refused tea or blankets, they seemed only to want to stand by the fire, mourning their death, as my father stood sentry beside them, melting into salty puddles that we mopped up with clean rags, wrung out into the ocean, saying what we fashioned as prayer, or reciting lines of Irish poetry.

Though I know now that this is not a usual childhood, it was usual for me, and it did not veer from this course until my mother's hair had gone quite gray and I was a young woman, when my father brought us a different sort of ghost entirely, a handsome young man, his eyes the same blue-green as summer. His hair was of indeterminate color, wet curls that hung to his shoulders. Dressed simply, like any dead sailor, he carried about him an air of being educated more by art than by water, a suspicion soon confirmed for me when he refused an offering of tea by saying, "No, I will not, cannot drink your liquid offered without first asking for a kiss, ah a kiss is all the liquid I desire, come succor me with your lips."

Naturally, I blushed and, just as naturally, when my mother went to check on the lamp, and my father had melted into a mustached puddle, I kissed him. Though I should have been warned by the icy chill, as certainly I should have been warned by the fact of my own father, a mere puddle at the hearth, it was my first kiss and it did not feel deadly to me at all, not dangerous, not spectral, most certainly not spectral, though I did experience a certain pleasant floating sensation in its wake.

My mother was surprised, upon her return, to find the lad still standing, as vigorous as any living man, beside my father's puddle. We were both surprised that he remained throughout the night, regaling us with stories of the wild sea populated by whales, mermaids, and sharks; mesmerizing us with descriptions of the "bottom of the world" as he called it, embedded with strange purple rocks, pink shells spewing pearls, and the seaweed tendrils of sea witches' hair. We were both surprised that, when the black of night turned to the gray hue of morning, he bowed to each of us (turned fully toward me, so that I could receive his wink), promised he would return, and then left, walking out the door like any regular fellow. So convincing was he that my mother and I opened the door to see where he had gone, scanning the rock and the inky sea before we accepted that, as odd as it seemed, as vigorous his demeanor, he was a ghost most certainly.

"Or something of that nature," said my mother. "Strange that he didn't melt like the others." She squinted at me and I turned away from her before she could see my blush. "We shouldn't have let him keep us up all night," she said. "We aren't dead. We need our sleep."

Sleep? Sleep? I could not sleep, feeling as I did his cool lips on mine, the power of his kiss, as though he breathed out of me some dark aspect that had weighed inside me. I told my mother that she could sleep. I would take care of everything. She protested, but using the past as reassurance (she had long since discovered that I had run the place while she convalesced after my father's death), finally agreed.

I was happy to have her tucked safely in bed. I was happy to know that her curious eyes were closed. I did all the tasks necessary to keep the place in good order. Not even then, in all my girlish giddiness, did I forget the lamp. I am embarrassed to admit, however, it was well past four o'clock before I remembered my father's puddle, which by that time had been much dissipated. I wiped up the small amount of water and wrung him out over the sea, saying only as prayer, "Father, forgive me. Oh, bring him back to me." (Meaning, alas for me, a foolish girl, the boy who kissed me and not my own dear father.)

And that night, he did come back, knocking on the door like any living man, carrying in his wet hands a bouquet of pink coral which he presented to me, and a small white stone, shaped like a star, which he gave to my mother.

"Is there no one else with you?" she asked.

"I'm sorry, there is not," he said.

My mother began to busy herself in the kitchen, leaving the two of us alone. I could hear her in there, moving things about, opening cupboards, sweeping the already swept floor. It was my own carelessness that had caused my father's absence, I was sure of that; had I sponged him up sooner, had I prayed for him more sincerely, and not just for the satisfaction of my own desire, he would be here this night. I felt terrible about this, but then I looked into my suitor's eyes, those beautiful sea-colored eyes, and I could not help it, my body thrilled at his look. Is this love? I thought. Will he kiss me twice? When it seemed as if, without even wasting time with words, he was about to do so, leaning toward me with parted lips from which exhaled the scent of salt water, my mother stepped into the room, clearing her throat, holding the broom before her, as if thinking she might use it as a weapon.

"We don't really know anything about you," she said.

To begin with, my name is Ezekiel. My mother was fond of saints and the Bible and such. She died shortly after giving birth to me, her first and only child. I was raised by my father, on the island of Murano. Perhaps you have heard of it? Murano glass? We are famous for it throughout the world. My father, himself, was a talented glassmaker. Anything imagined, he could shape into glass. Glass birds, tiny glass bees, glass seashells, even glass tears (an art he perfected while I was an infant), and what my father knew, he taught to me.

Naturally, I eventually surpassed him in skill. Forgive me, but there is no humble way to say it. At any rate, my father had taught me and encouraged my talent all my life. I did not see when his enthusiasm began to sour. I was excited and pleased at what I could produce. I thought he would feel the same for me as I had felt for him, when, as a child, I sat on the footstool in his studio and applauded each glass wing, each hard teardrop.

Alas, it was not to be. My father grew jealous of me. My own father! At night he snuck into our studio and broke my birds, my little glass cakes. In the morning he pretended dismay and instructed me further on keeping air bubbles out of my work. He did not guess that I knew the dismal truth.

I determined to leave him, to sail away to some other place to make my home. My father begged me to stay "Whatever will you do? How will you make your way in this world?"

I told him my true intention, not being clever enough to lie. "This is not the only place in the world with fire and sand," I said. "I intend to make glass."

He promised me it would be a death sentence. At the time I took this to be only his confused, fatherly concern. I did not perceive it as a threat.

It is true that the secret to glassmaking was meant to remain on Murano. It is true that the entire populace believed this trade, and only this trade, kept them fed and clothed. Finally, it is true that they passed the law (many years before my father confronted me with it) that anyone who dared attempt to take the secret of glassmaking off the island would suffer the penalty of death. All of this is true.

But what's also true is that I was a prisoner in my own home, tortured by my own father, who pretended to be a humble, kind glassmaker, but who, night after night, broke my creations and then, each morning, denied my accusations, his sweet old face mustached and whiskered, all the expression of dismay and sorrow.

This is madness, I reasoned. How else could I survive? One of us had to leave or die. I chose the gentler course.

We had, in our possession, only a small boat, used for trips that never veered far from shore. Gathering mussels, visiting neighbors, occasionally my father liked to sit in it and smoke a pipe while watching the sun set. He'd light a lantern and come home, smelling of the sea, boil us a pot of soup, a melancholic, completely innocent air about him, only later to sneak about his breaking work.

This small boat is what I took for my voyage across the sea. I also took some fishing supplies, a rope, dried cod he'd stored for winter, a blanket, and several jugs of red wine, given to us by the baker, whose daughter, I do believe, fancied me. For you, who have lived so long on this anchored rock, my folly must be apparent. Was it folly? It was. But what else was I to do? Day after day make my perfect art only to have my father, night after night, destroy it? He would destroy me!

I left in the dark, when the ocean is like ink and the sky is black glass with thousands of air bubbles. Air bubbles, indeed. I breathed my freedom in the salty sea air. I chose stars to follow. Foolishly, I had no clear sense of my passage and had only planned my escape.

Of course, knowing what I do now about the ocean, it is a wonder I survived the first night, much less seven. It was on the eighth morning that I saw the distant sail, and, hopelessly drunk and sunburned, as well as lost, began the desperate task of rowing toward it, another folly as I'm sure you'd agree, understanding how distant the horizon is. Luckily for me, or so I thought, the ship headed in my direction and after a few more days it was close enough that I began to believe in my life again.

Alas, this ship was owned by a rich friend of my father's, a woman who had commissioned him to create a glass castle with a glass garden and glass fountain, tiny glass swans, a glass king and queen, a baby glass princess, and glass trees with golden glass apples, all for the amusement of her granddaughter (who, it must be said, had fingers like sausages and broke half of the figurines before her next birthday). This silly woman was only too happy to let my father use her ship, she was only too pleased to pay the ship's crew, all with the air of helping my father, when, in truth, it simply amused her to be involved in such drama. She said she did it for Murano, but in truth, she did it for the story.

It wasn't until I had been rescued, and hoisted on board, that my father revealed himself to me. He spread his arms wide, all great show for the crew, hugged me and even wept, but convincing as was his act, I knew he intended to destroy me.

These are terrible choices no son should have to make, but that night, as my father slept and the ship rocked its weary way back to Murano where I would likely be hung or possibly sentenced to live with my own enemy, my father, I slit the old man's throat. Though he opened his eyes, I do not believe he saw me, but was already entering the distant kingdom.

You ladies look quite aghast. I cannot blame you. Perhaps I should have chosen my own death instead, but I was a young man, and I wanted to live. Even after everything I had gone through, I wanted life.

Alas, it was not to be. I knew there would be trouble and accusation if my father were found with his throat slit, but none at all if he just disappeared in the night, as so often happens on large ships. Many a traveler has simply fallen overboard, never to be heard from again, and my father had already displayed a lack of seafaring savvy to rival my own.

I wrapped him up in the now-bloody blanket but although he was a small man, the effect was still that of a body, so I realized I would have to bend and fold him into a rucksack. You wince, but do not worry, he was certainly dead by this time.

I will not bore you with the details of my passage, hiding and sneaking with my dismal load. Suffice it to say that it took a while for me to at last be standing shipside, and I thought then that all danger had passed.

Remember, I was already quite weakened by my days adrift, and the matter of taking care of this business with my father had only fatigued me further. Certain that I was finally at the end of my task, I grew careless. He was much heavier than he had ever appeared to be. It took all my strength to hoist the rucksack, and (to get the sad, pitiable truth over with as quickly as possible) when I heaved that rucksack, the cord became entangled on my wrist, and yes, dear ladies, I went over with it, to the bottom of the world. There I remained until your own dear father, your husband, found me and brought me to this place, where, for the first time in my life, I feel safe, and, though I am dead, blessed.

Later, after my mother had tended the lamp while Ezekiel and I shared the kisses that left me breathless, she asked him to leave, saying that I needed my sleep. I protested, of course, but she insisted. I walked my ghost to the door, just as I think any girl would do in a similar situation, and there, for the first time, he kissed me in full view of my mother, not so passionate as those kisses that had preceded it, but effective nonetheless.

But after he was gone, even as I still blushed, my mother spoke in a grim voice. "Don't encourage him, Agatha."

"Why?" I asked, my body trembling with the impact of his affection and my mother's scorn, as though the two emotions met in me and quaked there. "What don't you like about him?"

"He's dead," she said, "there's that for a start."

"What about Daddy? He's dead too, and you've been loving him all this time."

My mother shook her head. "Agatha, it isn't the same thing. Think about what this boy told you tonight. He murdered his own father."

"I can't believe you'd use that against him. You heard what he said. He was just defending himself."

"But Agatha, it isn't what's said that is always the most telling. Don't you know that? Have I really raised you to be so gullible?"

"I am not gullible. I'm in love."

"I forbid it."

Certainly no three words, spoken by a parent, can do more to solidify love than these. It was no use arguing. What would be the point? She, this woman who had loved no one but a puddle for so long, could never understand what was going through my heart. Without more argument, I went to bed, though I slept fitfully, feeling torn from my life in every way, while my mother stayed up reading, I later surmised, from her book of myths. In the morning I found her sitting at the kitchen table, the great volume before her. She looked up at me with dark circled eyes, then, without salutation, began reading, her voice ominous.

"There are many kinds of ghosts. There are the ghosts that move things, slam doors and drawers, throw silverware about the house. There are the ghosts—usually of small children—that play in dark corners with spools of thread and frighten family pets. There are the weeping and wailing ghosts. There are the ghosts who know that they are dead, and those who do not. There are tree ghosts, those who spend their afterlife in a particular tree—a clue for such a resident might be bite marks on fallen fruit. There are ghosts trapped forever at the hour of their death (I saw one like this once, in an old movie theater bathroom, hanging from the ceiling). There are melting ghosts (we know about these, don't we?), usually victims of drowning. And there are breath-stealing ghosts. These, sometimes mistaken for the grosser vampire, sustain a sort of half-life by stealing breath from the living. They can be any age, but are usually teenagers and young adults, often at that selfish stage when they died. These ghosts greedily go about sucking the breath out of the living. This can be done by swallowing the lingered breath from unwashed cups, or, most effectively of all, through a kiss. Though these ghosts can often be quite seductively charming, they are some of the most dangerous. Each life has only a certain amount of breath within it and these ghosts are said to steal an infinite amount with each swallow. The effect is such that the ghost, while it never lives again, begins to do a fairly good imitation of life, while its victims—those whose breath it steals—edge ever closer to their own death."

My mother looked up at me triumphantly and I stormed out of the house, only to be confronted with the sea all around me, as desolate as my heart.

That night, when he came knocking on the door, she did not answer it and forbade me to do so.

"It doesn't matter," I taunted, "he's a ghost. He doesn't need doors."

"No, you're wrong," she said, "he's taken so much of your breath that he's not entirely spectral. He can't move through walls any longer.

He needs you, but he doesn't care about you at all, don't you get that, Agatha?"

"Agatha? Are you home? Agatha? Why don't you come? Agatha?" I couldn't bear it. I began to weep.

"I know this is hard," my mother said, "but it must be done. Listen, his voice is already growing faint. We just have to get through this night."

"What about the lamp?" I said.

"What?"

But she knew what I meant. Her expression betrayed her. "Don't you need to check on the lamp?"

"Agatha? Have I done something wrong?"

My mother stared at the door, and then turned to me, the dark circles under her eyes giving her the look of a beaten woman. "The lamp is fine."

I spun on my heels and went into my small room, slammed the door behind me. My mother, a smart woman, was not used to thinking like a warden. She had forgotten about my window. By the time I hoisted myself down from it, Ezekiel was standing on the rocky shore, surveying the dark ocean before him. He had already lost some of his lifelike luster, particularly below his knees, where I could almost see through him. "Ezekiel," I said. He turned and I gasped at the change in his visage, the cavernous look of his eyes, the skeletal stretch at his jaw. Seeing my shocked expression, he nodded and spread his arms open, as if to say, yes, this is what has become of me. I ran into those open arms and embraced him, though he creaked like something made of old wood. He bent down, pressing his cold lips against mine until they were no longer cold but burning like a fire.

We spent that night together and I did not mind the shattering wind with its salt bite on my skin, and I did not care when the lamp went out and the sea roiled beneath a black sky, and I did not worry about the dead weeping on the rocky shore, or the lightness I felt as though I were floating beside my lover, and when morning came, revealing the dead all around us, I followed him into the water, I followed him to the bottom of the sea, where he turned to me and said, "What have you done? Are you stupid? Don't you realize? You're no good to me dead!"

So, sadly, like many a daughter, I learned that my mother had been right after all, and when I returned to her, dripping with saltwater and seaweed, tiny fish corpses dropping from my hair, she embraced me. Seeing my state, weeping, she kissed me on the lips, our mouths open. I drank from her, sweet breath, until I was filled and she collapsed to the floor, my mother in her black dress, like a crushed funeral flower.

I had no time for mourning. The lamp had been out for hours. Ships had crashed and men had died. Outside, the sun sparkled on the sea. People would be coming soon to find out what had happened.

I took our small boat and rowed away from there. Many hours later, I docked in a seaside town and hitchhiked to another, until eventually I was as far from my home as I could be and still be near my ocean.

I had a difficult time of it for a while. People are generally suspicious of someone with no past and little future. I lived on the street and had to beg for jobs cleaning toilets and scrubbing floors, only through time and reputation working up to my current situation, finally getting my own little apartment, small and dark, so different from when I was the lighthouse keeper's daughter and the ocean was my yard.

One day, after having passed it for months without a thought, I went into the art supply store and bought a canvas, paint, and two paintbrushes. I paid for it with my tip money, counting it out for the clerk whose expression suggested I was placing turds in her palm instead of pennies. I went home and hammered a nail into the wall, hung the canvas on it, and began to paint. Like many a creative person I seem to have found some solace for the unfortunate happenings of my young life (and death) in art.

I live simply and virginally, never taking breath through a kiss. This is the vow I made, and I have kept it. Yes, some days I am weakened, and tempted to restore my vigor with such an easy solution, but instead I hold the empty cups to my face, I breathe in, I breathe everything, the breath of old men, breath of young, sweet breath, sour breath, breath of lipstick, breath of smoke. It is not, really, a way to live, but this is not, really, a life.

For several seconds after Alex finished reading the remarkable account, his gaze remained transfixed on the page. Finally, he looked up, blinked in the dim coffee shop light, and closed the black binder.

Several baristas stood behind the counter busily jostling around each other with porcelain cups, teapots, bags of beans. One of them, a short girl with red and green hair that spiked around her like some otherworld halo, stood by the sink, stacking dirty plates and cups. When she saw him watching, she smiled. It wasn't a true smile— not that it was mocking, but rather, the girl with the Christmas hair smiled like someone who had either forgotten happiness entirely or never known it at all. In response, Alex nodded at her, and to his surprise, she came over, carrying a dirty rag and a spray bottle.

"Did you read all of it?" she said as she squirted the table beside him and began to wipe it with the dingy towel.

Alex winced at the unpleasant odor of the cleaning fluid, nodded, and then, seeing that the girl wasn't really paying any attention, said, "Yes." He glanced at the wall where the paintings were hung.

"So what'd you think?"

The girl stood there, grinning that sad grin, right next to him now with her noxious bottle and dirty rag, one hip jutted out in a way he found oddly sexual. He opened his mouth to speak, gestured toward the paintings, and then at the book before him. "I, I have to meet her," he said, tapping the book. "This is remarkable."

"But what do you think about the paintings?"

Once more he glanced at the wall where they hung. He shook his head, "No," he said, "it's this," tapping the book again.

She smiled, a true smile, cocked her head, and put out her hand. "Agatha," she said.

Alex felt like his head was spinning. He shook the girl's hand. It was unexpectedly tiny, like that of a child's, and he gripped it too tightly at first. Glancing at the counter, she pulled out a chair and sat down in front of him.

"I can only talk for a little while. Marnie is the manager today and she's on the rag or something all the time, but she's downstairs right now, checking in an order."

"You"—he brushed the binder with the tip of his fingers, as if caressing something holy—"you wrote this?"

She nodded, bowed her head slightly, shrugged and, suddenly earnest, leaned across the table, elbowing his empty cup as she did. "Nobody bothers to read it. I've seen a few people pick it up but you're the first one to read the whole thing."

Alex leaned back, frowning.

She rolled her eyes, which, he noticed, were a lovely shade of lavender, lined darkly in black.

"See, I was trying to do something different. This is the whole point"—she jabbed at the book, and he felt immediately protective of it—"I was trying to put a story in a place where people don't usually expect one. Don't you think we've gotten awful complacent in our society about story? Like it all the time has to go a certain way and even be only in certain places. That's what this is all about. The paintings are a foil. But you get that, don't you? Do you know,"—she leaned so close to him, he could smell her breath, which he thought was strangely sweet—"someone actually offered to buy the fly painting?" Her mouth dropped open, she shook her head and rolled those lovely lavender eyes. "I mean, what the fuck? Doesn't he know it sucks?"

Alex wasn't sure what to do. She seemed to be leaning near to his cup. Leaning over it, Alex realized. He opened his mouth, not having any idea what to say.

Just then another barista, the one who wore scarves all the time and had an imperious air about her, as though she didn't really belong there but was doing research or something, walked past. Agatha glanced at her. "I gotta go." She stood up. "You finished with this?" she asked, touching his cup.

Though he hadn't yet had his free refill, Alex nodded.

"It was nice talking to you," she said. "Just goes to show, doesn't it?"

Alex had no idea what she was talking about. He nodded halfheartedly, hoping comprehension would follow, but when it didn't, he raised his eyebrows at her instead.

She laughed. "I mean you don't look anything like the kind of person who would understand my stuff."

"Well, you don't look much like Agatha," he said.

"But I am Agatha," she murmured as she turned away from him, picking up an empty cup and saucer from a nearby table.

Alex watched her walk to the tiny sink at the end of the counter. She set the cups and saucers down. She rinsed the saucers and placed them in the gray bucket they used for carrying dirty dishes to the back. She reached for a cup, and then looked at him.

He quickly looked down at the black binder, picked it up, pushed his chair in, and headed toward the front of the shop. He stopped to look at the paintings. They were fine, boring, but fine little paintings that had no connection to what he'd read. He didn't linger over them for long. He was almost to the door when she was beside him, saying, "I'll take that." He couldn't even fake innocence. He shrugged and handed her the binder.

"I'm flattered, really," she said. But she didn't try to continue the conversation. She set the book down on the table beneath the painting of the avocado. He watched her pick up an empty cup and bring it toward her face, breathing in the lingered breath that remained. She looked up suddenly, caught him watching, frowned, and turned away.

Alex understood. She wasn't what he'd been expecting either. But when love arrives it doesn't always appear as expected. He couldn't just ignore it. He couldn't pretend it hadn't happened. He walked out of the coffee shop into the afternoon sunshine.

Of course, there were problems, her not being alive for one. But Alex was not a man of prejudice.

He was patient besides. He stood in the art supply store for hours, pretending particular interest in the anatomical hinged figurines of sexless men and women in the front window, before she walked past, her hair glowing like a forest fire.

"Agatha," he called.

She turned, frowned, and continued walking. He had to take little running steps to catch up. "Hi," he said. He saw that she was biting her lower lip. "You just getting off work?"

She stopped walking right in front of the bank, which was closed by then, and squinted up at him.

"Alex," he said. "I was talking to you today at the coffee shop."

"I know who you are."

Her tone was angry. He couldn't understand it. Had he insulted her somehow?

"I don't have Alzheimer's. I remember you."

He nodded. This was harder than he had expected.

"What do you want?" she said.

Her tone was really downright hostile. He shrugged. "I just thought we could, you know, talk."

She shook her head. "Listen, I'm happy that you liked my story."

"I did," he said, nodding. "It was great."

"But what would we talk about? You and me?"

Alex shifted beneath her lavender gaze. He licked his lips. She wasn't even looking at him, but glancing around him and across the street. "I don't care if it does mean I'll die sooner," he said. "I want to give you a kiss."

Her mouth dropped open.

"Is something wrong?"

She turned and ran. She wore one red sneaker and one green. They matched her hair.

As Alex walked back to his car, parked in front of the coffee shop, he tried to talk himself into not feeling so bad about the way things went. He hadn't always been like this. He used to be able to talk to people. Even women. Okay, he had never been suave, he knew that, but he'd been a regular guy. Certainly no one had ever run away from him before. But after Tessie died, people changed. Of course, this made sense, initially. He was in mourning, even if he didn't cry (something the doctor told him not to worry about because one day, probably when he least expected it, the tears would fall). He was obviously in pain. People were very nice. They talked to him in hushed tones. Touched him, gently. Even men tapped him with their fingertips. All this gentle touching had been augmented by vigorous hugs. People either touched him as if he would break or hugged him as if he had already broken and only the vigor of the embrace kept him intact.

For the longest time there had been all this activity around him. People called, sent chatty e-mails, even handwritten letters, cards with flowers on them and prayers. People brought over casseroles, and bread, Jell-O with fruit in it. (Nobody brought chocolate chip cookies, which he might have actually eaten.)

To Alex's surprise, once Tessie had died, it felt as though a great weight had been lifted from him, but instead of appreciating the feeling, the freedom of being lightened of the burden of his wife's dying body, he felt in danger of floating away or disappearing. Could it be possible, he wondered, that Tessie's body, even when she was mostly bones and barely breath, was all that kept him real? Was it possible that he would have to live like this, held to life by some strange force but never a part of it again? These questions led Alex to the brief period where he'd experimented with becoming a Hare Krishna, shaved his head, dressed in orange robes, and took up dancing in the park. Alex wasn't sure but he thought that was when people started treating him as if he were strange, and even after he grew his hair out and started wearing regular clothes again, people continued to treat him strangely.

And, Alex had to admit, as he inserted his key into the lock of his car, he'd forgotten how to behave. How to be normal, he guessed.

You just don't go read something somebody wrote and decide you love her, he scolded himself as he eased into traffic. You don't just go falling in love with breath-stealing ghosts. People don't do that.

Alex did not go to the coffee shop the next day, or the day after that, but it was the only coffee shop in town, and had the best coffee in the state. They roasted the beans right there. Freshness like that can't be faked.

It was awkward for him to see her behind the counter, over by the dirty cups, of course. But when she looked up at him, he attempted a kind smile, then looked away.

He wasn't there to bother her. He ordered French Roast in a cup to go, even though he hated to drink out of paper, paid for it, dropped the change into the tip jar, and left without any further interaction with her.

He walked to the park, where he sat on a bench and watched a woman with two small boys feed white bread to the ducks. This was illegal because the ducks would eat all the bread offered to them, they had no sense of appetite, or being full, and they would eat until their stomachs exploded. Or something like that. Alex couldn't exactly remember. He was pretty sure it killed them. But Alex couldn't decide what to do. Should he go tell that lady and those two little boys that they were killing the ducks? How would that make them feel, especially as they were now triumphantly shaking out the empty bag, the ducks crowded around them, one of the boys squealing with delight? Maybe he should just tell her quietly. But she looked so happy. Maybe she'd been having a hard time of it. He saw those mothers on *Oprah*, saying what a hard job it was, and maybe she'd had that kind of morning, even screaming at the kids, and then she got this idea, to take them to the park and feed the ducks and now she felt good about what she'd done and maybe she was thinking that she wasn't such a bad mom after all, and if Alex told her she was killing the ducks, would it stop the ducks from dying or just stop her from feeling happiness? Alex sighed. He couldn't decide what to do. The ducks were happy, the lady was happy, and one of the boys was happy. The other one looked sort of terrified. She picked him up and they walked away together, she carrying the boy who waved the empty bag like a balloon, the other one skipping after them, a few ducks hobbling behind.

For three days Alex ordered his coffee to go and drank it in the park. On the fourth day, Agatha wasn't anywhere that he could see and he surmised that it was her day off so he sat at his favorite table in the back. But on the fifth day, even though he didn't see her again, and it made sense that she'd have two days off in a row, he ordered his coffee to go and took it to the park. He'd grown to like sitting on the bench watching strolling park visitors, the running children, the dangerously fat ducks.

He had no idea she would be there and he felt himself blush when he saw her coming down the path that passed right in front of him. He stared deeply into his cup and fought the compulsion to run. He couldn't help it, though. Just as the toes of her red and green sneakers came into view he looked up. I'm not going to hurt you, he thought, and then he smiled, that false smile he'd been practicing on her and, incredibly, she smiled back! Also, falsely, he assumed, but he couldn't blame her for that.

She looked down the path and he followed her gaze, seeing that, though the path around the duck pond was lined with benches every fifty feet or so, all of them were taken. She sighed. "Mind if I sit here?"

He scooted over and she sat down slowly. He glanced at her profile. She looked worn out, he decided. Her lavender eye flickered toward him, and he looked into his cup again. It made sense that she would be tired, he thought; if she'd been off work for two days, she'd also been going that long without stealing breath from cups. "Want some?" he said, offering his.

She looked startled, pleased, and then falsely unconcerned. She peered over the edge of his cup, shrugged, and said, "Okay, yeah, sure."

He handed it to her and politely watched the ducks so she could have some semblance of privacy with it. After a while she said thanks and handed it back to him. He nodded and stole a look at her profile again. It pleased him that her color already looked better. His breath had done that!

"Sorry about the other day," she said, "I was just. . . ."

They waited together but she didn't finish the sentence.

"It's okay," he said, "I know I'm weird."

"No, you're, well—" She smiled, glanced at him, shrugged. "It isn't that. I like weird people. I'm weird. But, I mean, I'm not dead, okay? You kind of freaked me out with that."

He nodded. "Would you like to go out with me sometime?" Inwardly, he groaned. He couldn't believe he just said that.

"Listen, Alex?"

He nodded. Stop nodding, he told himself. Stop acting like a bobblehead.

"Why don't you tell me a little about yourself?"

So he told her. How he'd been coming to the park lately, watching people overfeed the ducks, wondering if he should tell them what they were doing but they all looked so happy doing it, and the ducks looked happy too, and he wasn't sure anyway, what if he was wrong, what if he told everyone to stop feeding bread to the ducks and it turned out it did them no harm and how would he know? Would they explode like balloons, or would it be more like how it had been when his wife died, a slow, painful death, eating her away inside, and how he used to come here, when he was a monk, well, not really a monk, he'd never gotten ordained or anything, but he'd been trying the idea on for a while and how he used to sing and spin in circles and how it felt a lot like what he'd remembered of happiness but he could never be sure because a remembered emotion is like a remembered taste, it's never really there. And then, one day, a real monk came and watched him spinning in circles and singing nonsense, and he just stood and watched Alex, which made him self-conscious because he didn't really know what he was doing, and the monk started laughing, which made Alex stop, and the monk said, "Why'd you stop?" And Alex said, "I don't know what I'm doing." And the monk nodded, as if this was a very wise thing to say and this, just this monk with his round bald head and wire-rimmed spectacles, in his simple orange robe (not at all like the orange-dyed sheet Alex was wearing) nodding when Alex said, "I don't know what I'm doing," made Alex cry and he and the monk sat down under that tree, and the monk (whose name was Ron) told him about Kali, the goddess who is both womb and grave. Alex felt like it was the first thing anyone had said to him that made sense since Tessie died and after that he stopped coming to the park, until just recently, and let his hair grow out again and stopped wearing his robe. Before she'd died, he'd been one of the lucky ones, or so he'd thought, because he made a small fortune in a dot com, and actually got out of it before it all went belly up while so many people he knew lost everything but then Tessie came home from her doctor's appointment, not pregnant but with cancer, and he realized he wasn't lucky at all. They met in high school and were together until she died, at home, practically blind by that time, and she made him promise he wouldn't just give up on life. So he began living this sort of half-life, but he wasn't unhappy or depressed, he didn't want her to think that, he just wasn't sure. "I sort of lost confidence in life," he said. "It's like I don't believe in it anymore. Not like suicide, but I mean, like the whole thing, all of it isn't real somehow. Sometimes I feel like it's all a dream, or a long nightmare that I can never wake up from. It's made me odd, I guess."

She bit her lower lip, glanced longingly at his cup.

"Here," Alex said. "I'm done anyway."

She took it and lifted it toward her face, breathing in, he was sure of it, and only after she was finished, drinking the coffee. They sat like that in silence for a while and then they just started talking about everything, just as Alex had hoped they would. She told him how she had grown up living near the ocean, and her father had died young, and then her mother had too, and she had a boyfriend, her first love, who broke her heart, but the story she wrote was just a story, a story about her life, her dream life, the way she felt inside, like he did, as though somehow life was a dream. Even though everyone thought she was a painter (because he was the only one who read it, he was the only one who got it), she was a writer, not a painter, and stories seemed more real to her than life. At a certain point he offered to take the empty cup and throw it in the trash but she said she liked to peel off the wax, and then began doing so. Alex politely ignored the divergent ways she found to continue drinking his breath. He didn't want to embarrass her.

They finally stood up and stretched, walked through the park together and grew quiet, with the awkwardness of new friends. "You want a ride?" he said, pointing at his car.

She declined, which was a disappointment to Alex, but he determined not to let it ruin his good mood. He was willing to leave it at that, to accept what had happened between them that afternoon as a moment of grace to be treasured and expect nothing more from it, when she said, "What are you doing next Tuesday?" They made a date, well, not a date, Alex reminded himself, an arrangement, to meet the following Tuesday in the park, which they did, and there followed many wonderful Tuesdays. They did not kiss. They were friends. Of course Alex still loved her. He loved her more. But he didn't bother her with all that and it was in the spirit of friendship that he suggested (after weeks of Tuesdays in the park) that the following Tuesday she come for dinner, "nothing fancy," he promised when he saw the slight hesitation on her face.

But when she said yes, he couldn't help it; he started making big plans for the night.

Naturally, things were awkward when she arrived. He offered to take her sweater, a lumpy looking thing in wild shades of orange, lime green, and purple. He should have just let her throw it across the couch—that would have been the casual non-datelike thing to do—but she handed it to him and then, wiping her hand through her hair which, by candlelight looked like bloody grass, cased his place with those lavender eyes, deeply shadowed as though she hadn't slept for weeks.

He could see she was freaked out by the candles. He hadn't gone crazy or anything. They were just a couple of small candles, not even purchased from the store in the mall, but bought at the grocery store, unscented. "I like candles," he said, sounding defensive even to his own ears.

She smirked, as if she didn't believe him, and then spun away on the toes of her red sneaker and her green one, and plopped down on the couch. She looked absolutely exhausted. This was not a complete surprise to Alex. It had been a part of his plan, actually, but he felt bad for her just the same.

He kept dinner simple: lasagna, a green salad, chocolate cake for dessert. They didn't eat in the dining room. That would have been too formal. Instead they ate in the living room, she sitting on the couch, and he on the floor, their plates on the coffee table, watching a DVD of *I Love Lucy* episodes, a mutual like they had discovered. (Though her description of watching *I Love Lucy* reruns as a child did not gel with his picture of her in the crooked keeper's house, offering tea to melting ghosts, he didn't linger over the inconsistency.) Alex offered her plenty to drink but he wouldn't let her come into the kitchen or get anywhere near his cup. He felt bad about this, horrible, in fact, but he tried to stay focused on the bigger picture.

After picking at her cake for a while, Agatha set the plate down, leaned back into the gray throw pillows, and closed her eyes.

Alex watched her. He didn't think about anything, he just watched her. Then he got up very quietly so as not to disturb her and went into the kitchen where he carefully, quietly opened the drawer in which he had stored the supplies. Coming up from behind, eyeing her red and green hair, he moved quickly. She turned toward him, cursing loudly, her eyes wide and frightened, as he pressed her head to her knees, pulled her arms behind her back (to the accompaniment of a sickening crack, and her scream), pressed the wrists together and wrapped them with the rope. She struggled in spite of her weakened state, her legs flailing, kicking the coffee table. The plate with the chocolate cake flew off it and landed on the beige rug and her screams escalated into a horrible noise, unlike anything Alex had ever heard before. Luckily, Alex was prepared with the duct tape, which he slapped across her mouth. By that time he was rather exhausted himself. But she stood up and began to run, awkwardly, across the room. It broke his heart to see her this way. He grabbed her from behind. She kicked and squirmed but she was quite a small person and it was easy for him to get her legs tied.

"Is that too tight?" he asked.

She looked at him with wide eyes. As if he were the ghost.

"I don't want you to be uncomfortable."

She shook her head. Tried to speak, but only produced muffled sounds.

"I can take that off," he said, pointing at the duct tape. "But you have to promise me you won't scream. If you scream, I'll just put it on, and I won't take it off again. Though, you should know, ever since Tessie died I have these vivid dreams and nightmares, and I wake up screaming a lot. None of my neighbors has ever done anything about it. Nobody's called the police to report it, and nobody has even asked me if there's a problem. That's how it is among the living. Okay?"

She nodded.

He picked at the edge of the tape with his fingertips and when he got a good hold of it, he pulled fast. It made a loud ripping sound. She grunted and gasped, tears falling down her cheeks as she licked her lips.

"I'm really sorry about this," Alex said. "I just couldn't think of another way."

She began to curse, a string of expletives quickly swallowed by her weeping, until finally she managed to ask, "Alex, what are you doing?"

He sighed. "I know it's true, okay? I see the way you are, how tired you get and I know why. I know that you're a breath-stealer. I want you to understand that I know that about you, and I love you and you don't have to keep pretending with me, okay?"

She looked around the room, as if trying to find something to focus on. "Listen, Alex," she said, "listen to me. I get tired all the time 'cause I'm sick. I didn't want to tell you, after what you told me about your wife. I thought it would be too upsetting for you. That's it. That's why I get tired all the time."

"No," he said, softly, "you're a ghost."

"I am not dead," she said, shaking her head so hard that her tears splashed his face. "I am not dead," she said over and over again, louder and louder until Alex felt forced to tape her mouth shut once more.

"I know you're afraid. Love can be frightening. Do you think I'm not scared? Of course I'm scared. Look what happened with Tessie. I know you're scared too. You're worried I'll turn out to be like Ezekiel, but I'm not like him, okay? I'm not going to hurt you. And I even finally figured out that you're scared 'cause of what happened with your mom. Of course you are. But you have to understand. That's a risk I'm willing to take. Maybe we'll have one night together or only one hour, or a minute. I don't know. I have good genes though. My parents, both of them, are still alive, okay? Even my grandmother only died a few years ago. There's a good chance I have a lot, and I mean a lot, of breath in me. But if I don't, don't you see, I'd rather spend a short time with you than no time at all?"

He couldn't bear it, he couldn't bear the way she looked at him as if he were a monster when he carried her to the couch. "Are you cold?"

She just stared at him.

"Do you want to watch more *I Love Lucy*? Or a movie?"

She wouldn't respond. She could be so stubborn.

He decided on *Annie Hall*. "Do you like Woody Allen?" She just stared at him, her eyes filled with accusation. "It's a love story," he said, turning away from her to insert the DVD. He turned it on for her, then placed the remote control in her lap, which he realized was a stupid thing to do, since her hands were still tied behind her back, and he was fairly certain that, had her mouth not been taped shut, she'd be giving him that slack-jawed look of hers. She wasn't making any of this very easy. He picked the dish up off the floor, and the silverware, bringing them into the kitchen, where he washed them and the pots and pans, put aluminum foil on the leftover lasagna and put it into the refrigerator. After he finished sweeping the floor, he sat and watched the movie with her. He forgot about the sad ending. He always thought of it as a romantic comedy, never remembering the sad end. He turned off the TV and said, "I think it's late enough now. I think we'll be all right." She looked at him quizzically.

First Alex went out to his car and popped the trunk, then he went back inside where he found poor Agatha squirming across the floor. Trying to escape, apparently. He walked past her, got the throw blanket from the couch and laid it on the floor beside her, rolled her into it even as she squirmed and bucked. "Agatha, just try to relax," he said, but she didn't. Stubborn, stubborn, she could be so stubborn.

He threw her over his shoulder. He was not accustomed to carrying much weight and immediately felt the stress, all the way down his back to his knees. He shut the apartment door behind him and didn't worry about locking it. He lived in a safe neighborhood.

When they got to the car, he put her into the trunk, only then taking the blanket away from her beautiful face. "Don't worry, it won't be long," he said as he closed the hood.

He looked through his CDs, trying to choose something she would like, just in case the sound carried into the trunk, but he couldn't figure out what would be appropriate, so he finally decided just to drive in silence.

It took about twenty minutes to get to the beach; it was late, and there was little traffic. Still, the ride gave him an opportunity to reflect on what he was doing. By the time he pulled up next to the pier, he had reassured himself that it was the right thing to do, even though it looked like the wrong thing.

He'd made a good choice, deciding on this place. He and Tessie used to park here, and he was amazed that it had apparently remained undiscovered by others seeking dark escape.

When he got out of the car, he took a deep breath of the salt air and stood, for a moment, staring at the black waves, listening to their crash and murmur. Then he went around to the back and opened up the trunk. He looked over his shoulder, just to be sure. If someone were to discover him like this, his actions would be misinterpreted. The coast was clear, however. He wanted to carry Agatha in his arms, like a bride. Every time he had pictured it, he had seen it that way, but she was struggling again so he had to throw her over his shoulder where she continued to struggle. Well, she was stubborn, but he was too; that was part of the beauty of it, really. But it made it difficult to walk, and it was windier on the pier, also wet. All in all it was a precarious, unpleasant journey to the end.

He had prepared a little speech but she struggled against him so hard, like a hooked fish, that all he could manage to say was, "I love you," barely focusing on the wild expression in her face, the wild eyes, before he threw her in and she sank, and then bobbed up like a cork, only her head above the black waves, those eyes of hers, locked on his, and they remained that way as he turned away from the edge of the pier and walked down the long plank, feeling lighter, but not in a good way. He felt those eyes, watching him, in the car as he flipped restlessly from station to station, those eyes, watching him, when he returned home, and saw the clutter of their night together, the burned-down candles, the covers to the *I Love Lucy* and *Annie Hall* DVDs on the floor, her crazy sweater on the dining room table, those eyes, watching him, and suddenly Alex was cold, so cold his teeth were chattering and he was shivering but sweating besides. The black water rolled over those eyes and closed them and he ran to the bathroom and only just made it in time, throwing up everything he'd eaten, collapsing to the floor, weeping, *What have I done? What was I thinking?*

He would have stayed there like that, he determined, until they came for him and carted him away, but after a while he became aware of the foul taste in his mouth. He stood up, rinsed it out, brushed his teeth and tongue, changed out of his clothes, and went to bed, where, after a good deal more crying, and trying to figure out exactly what had happened to his mind, he was amazed to find himself falling into a deep darkness like the water, from which, he expected, he would never rise.

But then he was lying there, with his eyes closed, somewhere between sleep and waking, and he realized he'd been like this for some time. Though he was fairly certain he had fallen asleep, something had woken him. In this half state, he'd been listening to the sound he finally recognized as dripping water. He hated it when he didn't turn the faucet tight. He tried to ignore it, but the dripping persisted. So confused was he that he even thought he felt a splash on his hand and another on his forehead. He opened one eye, then the other.

She stood there, dripping wet, her hair plastered darkly around her face, her eyes smudged black. "I found a sharp rock at the bottom of the world," she said and she raised her arms. He thought she was going to strike him, but instead she showed him the cut rope dangling there.

He nodded. He could not speak.

She cocked her head, smiled, and said, "Okay, you were right. You were right about everything. Got any room in there?"

He nodded. She peeled off the wet T-shirt and let it drop to the floor, revealing her small breasts white as the moon, unbuttoned and unzipped her jeans, wiggling seductively out of the tight wet fabric, taking her panties off at the same time. He saw when she lifted her feet that the rope was no longer around them and she was already transparent below the knees. When she pulled back the covers, he smelled the odd odor of saltwater and mud, as if she were both fresh and loamy. He scooted over, but only far enough that when she eased in beside him, he could hold her, wrap her wet, cold skin in his arms, knowing that he was offering her everything, everything he had to give, and that she had come to take it.

"You took a big risk back there," she said.

He nodded.

She pressed her lips against his and he felt himself growing lighter, as if all his life he'd been weighed down by this extra breath, and her lips were cold but they grew warmer and warmer and the heat between them created a steam until she burned him and still, they kissed, all the while Alex thinking, I love you, I love you, I love you, until, finally, he could think it no more, his head was as light as his body, lying beside her, hot flesh to hot flesh, the cinder of his mind could no longer make sense of it, and he hoped, as he fell into a black place like no other he'd ever been in before, that this was really happening, that she was really here, and the suffering he'd felt for so long was finally over.

The Shipbuilder

His name was Quark. Yet the phone call that came late at night pulsated through his life, not in the pleasant manner of a star, but in the grievous one of a migraine. And why not? Why wouldn't he compare his entire life to the headache he experienced driving the familiar aorta back to Bellfairie?

"Missing? What do you mean he's missing?" Quark asked, pressing the phone close to his ear as if the late hour had affected his hearing. "Is this a joke?"

But of course it wasn't. The sheriff wasn't the joking sort.

"A confession?" Quark asked. "You mean, like an apology?"

He peered through the Ford's window into the gray dawn, but all he could remember—after the question—was the buzzing in his ear, as if, through some strange night magic, he heard the reverberation of his existence—that dark persistent screed.

It was true the Old Man could be cruel, once tying an apron to Quark's pants, knotting the yellow flowered fabric on the loop meant for a belt. Quark, in his innocence, didn't recognize the mockery. Enjoying the feel of material draped behind him, he began spinning; his arms raised toward the ceiling, fingers spread, head tilted back like someone nearly drowned who, just in the nick of time, broke surface.

"What are ya? Some kinda fag?" the Old Man asked.

Earlier, when he was awoken by the phone's chirp, Quark blinked like a confused time traveler before thinking maybe it was something wonderful: a mysterious portent, a secret admirer, a winning lottery ticket. He was showered, dressed, and on the road forty-five minutes later, peering through the dark until morning broke with a snakelike fissure of light, reminding him of the rain that violent night so long ago, lashing the windows until they were streaked with silver and the Old Man weaved through the small rooms as if trapped on a doomed ship. Quark remembered the oily smell, the waxy scent of crayons scattered across the table where he sat clutching the purple in his small fist. When the Old Man set down the plate, the fried fish lapped near the edge wept oil onto Quark's drawing.

Quark, the man, remembered the boy's hesitation; crayon held tight before it was dropped. How old was he? Six? Seven? Eight?

Maybe he was eight that night he sat at the small wooden table etched by knives. Time was lost between the first bite of catfish and the one Quark remembered next, bone drawn between teeth, placed carefully on his plate—not tossed, but assembled—when he became aware of the Old Man watching. Quark feared that to comment on the attention would destroy it; instead he sucked the last flakes of oily flesh, placing the translucent sliver neatly among the rest.

"What ya got there, boy?"

"Catfish," Quark said, proud of how he'd restored the bones, their silver reflecting the light.

"Thought it was a ship," the Old Man said, turning away.

"That's what it is." Quark reached across the dimming space to rearrange his bone sculpture. "These are waves, see?"

"Yah said 'catfish,' din' ya?"

"It's the name of my ship."

"Are ya a liar too?" The Old Man swept his hand across the table, spilling plated bones, sending papers aloft, crayons tumbling. His arm raised in violence turned Quark into an anemone; pummeled by the Old Man's rage until, at last, squeezed so hard he gasped for breath, Quark was released.

Quark gripped the steering wheel, reminding himself he was no longer that boy who woke early the next morning in pain, filled with the terrible realization of God's absence, who walked barefoot down the creaking stairs and across the wooden floor littered with papers and bones into the kitchen where he lit the oil lamp that awakened winged shadows. So small he had to stand on a chair to reach the sink, then drag chair to stove, where he stirred coffee grounds and water to boil, watching the stars outside the small, round window there. When Quark leaned across the stove to turn off the burner, the heat brushed against his stomach, reminding him of his pet cat gone missing a few months earlier. She used to lie on his belly and keep him warm.

He cracked an egg into a bowl, fished out the bits, beat it with a fork, measured it out with a teaspoon, unsure of the amount. He dragged the chair to fill two cups with hot water, then turned each cup over and watched the water spiral down the drain. When he poured the coffee through the filter he spilled some, which he mopped with a dish towel, creating a reddish brown stain he didn't like to look at; he thrust it into the trash beneath banana skins, eggshells, and newspapers.

The Old Man was sitting in his recliner, staring out the big front window when Quark approached with trembling cups, unsure how to proceed. "Take it," he said, surprised when the command worked.

Quark set his own cup on the small table in the clutter of maps and carving tools before returning to the kitchen for the chair he dragged (tearing papers and breaking bones) to position beside the Old Man. Together they stared out the window at the thatched lawn littered with rusty bicycle, deflated yellow ball, the abandoned garden, a small piece of silver fluttering in the sun and, in the distance—like a line drawn with Magic Marker across the bleak horizon—the bright blue sea.

Quark raised the cup to his lips, flinched against the heat, and sipped. It was his first taste of coffee. Bitter; he didn't like it, and that seemed right.

Even though Quark knew how the road banked around the bluff, distracting drivers with maintaining the curve, he was surprised by the initial appearance of sun-washed buildings nestled among boulders before the road began its descent. When Bellfairie reappeared, the enchanted palette of turquoise and white was replaced by murky water dotted with spinach-hued clots and houses so long in disrepair only a few chips of color remained: a streak of mustard yellow, a smear of red, half a wall painted pink, ruined by abandonment.

Quark sighed as he entered the narrow, labyrinthine streets. Several dismal houses sported dead plants in pots perched on sagging porches or cracked concrete stairs, as if awaiting revival.

Some might call that optimism, Quark thought, but it's actually denial.

Bellfairie was named after the doomed ship on which it was founded; crashed on the rocks, she sank with her cargo of bells that still rang from the depths. The survivors, washed to shore, decided to stay with their ghosts, using ship wood for lumber which, the Old Man said, made the sea angry. "She is unforgiving," he used to rant. "No one was meant to survive."

Perseverance, in almost any circumstance an attribute, fed off Bellfairie like a tumor, and if the bleak gardens weren't proof enough of that malignancy, surely the narrow figure, walking on the side of the road, was. Quark slowed to a stop, reached across the passenger seat to roll down his window.

Dressed all in black, Dean Yarly had taken this walk every morning Quark could remember; a devil worshipper, some said, who used the cove as chapel for sacrificing the missing pets of Bellfairie, the lost cats and dogs of Quark's childhood, though the Old Man spat when Quark once posited this theory.

"My ass. Devil worshipper, my ass. Don't you kids know nothing? Saying Dean Yarly is a devil worshipper's like calling your elbow a dick. You can tell your friends I said."

Dean didn't look to see who slowed beside him but raised his hand, ring and pinky finger half bent, thumb angled in, a cross between Boy Scout salute and benediction.

"Heya. How ya doin', Mr. Yarly?"

Quark checked the road ahead as he eased into neutral. When he turned back, Dean was grinning, affable as an egg.

"Quark? Is it Quark? Is it really you?"

Quark scratched the back of his neck.

"It's good you came," Dean said in an uncertain tone. "Don't you mind what no one says, okay, son? You ain't dead and Thayer ain't either; am I right?"

Confused, Quark nodded. Why he was bothering to behave falsely with Dean Yarly, he had no idea, though he recognized a trait that always seemed pronounced in Bellfairie, the need to guard against revelation.

"Where ya off to?"

"Nell's open?"

Dean shook his head. "Sold after her son got kilt in that wreck."

"Wayne?" Quark was surprised the name rose so easily to his lips.

"Head right off. Took several days to find it rolled down the bluff."

Wayne was one of the beautiful boys; hair made golden by the sun, broad shoulders and muscular arms from summers spent on his father's trawler.

"Didn't mean to shake you up, son. You two would be round the same age, am I right?"

Quark swatted the air, as if it didn't matter.

"After Nell left, it sat for a cuppa months and then some flatland-ers came and called it a watchamugger? A Sue she place? You can guess how that went. After they left, Dolly bought it. Don't worry about the sign. She just din't get around to a new one. Menu the same as Nell's, they tell me. I don't got much occasion to go there, myself."

Quark couldn't say if the sudden exhaustion he felt was brought on by the conversation, the long ride through the night, the terrible weight of not knowing where the Old Man was, or simply being back in Bellfairie with its overwhelming atmosphere of decay.

"Guess it's early," Quark said, as if this just occurred to him. "Think I'll grab a bite before I talk to the sheriff. You need a ride?"

Dean grimaced. Shook his head no.

Quark waved and continued down Seaside Lane, the air nipping the tired muscles of his face, the briny ocean scent filling his lungs. He remembered how he'd been before he left Bellfairie, during that brief period when he was old enough to imagine himself free of the Old Man's grasp, yet young enough to believe he had within him the potential to be golden too.

Thinking of Wayne, Quark almost missed the turn down Avalon, going too fast for the dip in the road. Over the years it had only grown deeper. Naturally, nothing was done about it. To the citizens of Bellfairie a pothole was a matter of terrain; not a problem with a simple remedy, but the inevitable erosion—impossible to combat— of life.

If Bellfairie had a main street, Avalon, where the buildings leaned away from the ocean's greedy maw, was it. Whenever Quark remembered it that way, he thought he must be exaggerating, but as he parked his truck he noted that the buildings clearly maintained a tilt. Even the American flag jutted from the post office at an angle; its red and white fringed edge pointed inland.

I should leave, he thought. *Why is this my problem?*

He turned off the ignition, reached to roll up the window, but stopped. Even with loose change right in the open, there was no need to worry about petty theft in Bellfairie, which was one of its few charms. His legs stiff from the long ride, Quark eased out of the cab and stood rattling keys like a gambler with dice, taking in the dismal remains: the post office with its crooked stairs, an empty storefront (once the dime store), a For Sale sign taped inside the dusty window, the Brass Lantern from which, he guessed, the last rum-soaked patron stumbled out about the time Quark was looking down on Bellfairie from that height where it seemed like a place someone might want to come home to.

The ground there had a magnetic quality, that's what folks said. It brought ships to the rocky shore, held fog close, and pulled the moon so near that on some nights the whole town appeared inhabited by ghosts. Quark thought if he wasn't careful, he'd get stuck, standing by his truck, rattling his keys. Hunched against the salty chill, he headed toward what used to be Nell's with its absurd sign, "SuShi Palace."

The bell when he opened the door might have been the same that announced his arrival all those years ago when he worked there as a dishwasher. The booths were still rust-colored, but the tables were covered with red tablecloths, which Quark guessed were leftover from SuShi Palace, as was the gold sea dragon hanging on the far wall where the fishnet had draped for so long. To his relief the old counter remained, a slab of teak said to have been used as a lifeboat by the shipwreck survivors, lined with bar stools and topped with silver napkin dispensers at reasonable intervals. People in Bellfairie liked their personal space.

Quark, being local-born, was aware of the abrupt stillness that settled on the place while he wiped his feet; the customers, in autumn flannel and cotton sweaters, nudging each other, jutting chins at his arrival. He shuffled through the diner with his head lowered as though still fighting the morning chill, a posture refined as soon as he was old enough to realize his size made folks uncomfortable. Frankenquark, that's what they used to call him. He reminded himself that, while he never had become golden, he was an adult and did not need to feel trapped by Bellfairie or his dismal store of memories.

Too late, he recognized the sheriff sitting there. Not that Quark had anything to hide, he just wasn't prepared for serious conversation. He nodded, but the sheriff had already returned to his coffee, draining his cup; raising his finger to signal for more. The waitress—Quark saw her nametag was "Dory," which would have made him laugh if he had been in the mood—— filled the sheriff's cup and, without waiting for instructions, Quark's too, peering at him, as if assessing.

"What ya havin' this mornin'?" she asked, her tone pleasant, her face placid. *Well, a person must get used to sailing smoothly along if she is named after a boat.* Quark chuckled, which caused Dory to glance at the sheriff.

Like she's glad he's here, Quark thought.

He looked down, happy to see Mr. Yarly was correct, the menu featured the classics. He tapped number five. Dory twisted her neck to see.

"Traditional or Belgium?" she asked.

Belgium? Belgium? Quark shook his head. "American."

"Belgium are the fat ones, kinda like cake. Traditional are thin and crisp."

Quark waved his hand. "Traditional," he said and Dory walked away, her gait plodding with a limp, which reminded him of someone, though he couldn't remember who.

"Good of you to come," the sheriff said.

Quark stirred so hard the coffee splattered over the rim of the cup. "You always were a slob," he heard the Old Man say, though this was obviously imagined.

"You know how he is. Stubborn." The sheriff shook his head. "Kept sayin' there was no reason to bother ya. Kept sayin' he was fine."

Quark pulled a reluctant napkin from the dispenser to wipe the spill.

"Just wanted to keep him from harming himself. Nick Rogers— can you believe that name—sounds like his folks were expecting him to be a comic book character, don't it? Anyhow it went to shit when Rogers got involved."

He pulled a dollar from his wallet and tucked it next to his plate, cleaned of any evidence of the meal that had been there, slapped his heavy hand on Quark's shoulder. "Didn't think you'd make it, but since you're here, you should probably go to the courthouse. Scheduled for nine. Don't expect nothing to come of it, but still might be a good idea for you to be there."

Quark nodded, but couldn't think of anything to say, and after a moment the sheriff walked away. Quark drank the coffee, which was bitter, slightly burnt, just the way he liked it, until Dory returned with his order. He hadn't had a number five in years. The Old Man loved it too, Quark recalled, stabbing through the sauce to the traditional waffle beneath, cutting harshly, eager to taste the oysters in sherried cream, surprised when tears came to his eyes, happy there was no one to notice.

You could leave, he thought.

By the next time Dory refilled his cup, Quark was feeling better. He glanced down the long counter, looking for the discarded newspapers usually littering the place, but all that remained of their once quintessential presence was something called *Bridal Bliss.*

"Ya don't recognize me, do ya?"

Quark willed his lips into what he hoped was a convivial smile before he saw it, the perpetually distressed countenance of—

"Doris. You knew me as Doris Lehart. Doris Kindal now."

Quark struggled through the equation of time, distance, forgotten names and faces, almost shouting when it came to him. "Tony? You married Tony?"

"That's right." She moved to give Quark a refill he blocked with his hand. "Thought I was seeing a ghost when you walked in," she said.

Quark shivered. *Cold in here,* he thought, remembering the unrelenting dampness of Bellfairie.

Dory looked at him with a strange, Mona Lisa smile, then left to pour for the other customers, returning later only long enough to slap his tab on the counter. He set two dollars beside his plate; double what he'd have left if he hadn't remembered her as Doris Lehart with that collection of dirty stuffed animals she pulled in the old red wagon with the loose lugnut or, later, as Whorey-Dory. My god, that's what they used to call her. He cut a sharp look and, all the way at the far end of the counter—in the midst of pouring—she turned to gaze at him as if she knew. Quark added another dollar, then worried it was obvious he was trying to assuage his guilt. He considered taking it back, thought better, and walked to the cash register where he waited to pay his bill.

A few words drifted from the gray-haired couple at the nearby table; the man intently drinking his coffee, the woman in her Bellfairie sweater leaning over the yolk-smeared plate. "Missing," she said and "probably dead" before the man clicked his tongue, which caused her to sit back so abruptly she knocked over the salt shaker. Right then the cash register rang and Quark turned to pay the girl who didn't look old enough to be out of school, but what did he know of such things?

"You on holiday?" he asked, handing her a ten.

She snorted, counting his change before answering. "That's right. It's all a holiday now. Fun times." When she closed the drawer, Quark saw she was pregnant which, for some reason, made him blush. To make matters worse, he tipped his imaginary hat at her and left SuShi's Palace with the girl's smirk embedded in his mind. She had dark hair, pale skin, and deeply red lips. Like Snow White.

Quark spent the short drive from the restaurant to his childhood home trying to remember the old fairy tale, but it had been a long time, and it kept getting mixed up in his mind, conflated with the pregnant girl, which created a disturbing montage, cartoonlike in its horror. *How did she die? She fell asleep, right? No, that doesn't make sense. She ate something first, didn't she? A pomegranate, right?*

The game of distraction served its purpose. Quark arrived at the old place as though magically transported, the memories lurking along the way undisturbed as the dead.

He stared at the house, its ungainly architecture squat in the middle of the stony yard. "They say you can't go home again."

He thought then of snow drifting from the metallic Bellfairie sky; white flakes slowly falling to the ground, covering the dirt, the cracks and peeled paint, the mismatched pots, all of Bellfairie smote by an icy benevolence, even the girl, lying in her open coffin, hands folded over her great belly, metamorphosed into a pleasant slope of white, a gentle hill of sleeping beauty.

With a sigh, Quark spun the steering wheel away from the house, driving fifty feet down the stone road before realizing he had a flat. He cursed, but did not kick the tire or hurl stones as the Old Man would have. Instead, Quark shoved his hands into his pockets and hunched his shoulders against the chill for the short walk into town.

He remembered how, when he was a boy, he loved the story the Old Man used to tell about how his mother had seaweed hair and left salt water in her wake. What was it he used to say? "Your mother left puddles, not footprints." Never said, exactly, that she was a selkie, or mermaid, or monster; only implied she wasn't entirely human, a notion Quark enjoyed until it made him uncomfortable.

He didn't even remember her, but when the judge mentioned the murder confession (with all the gravitas of noting a shopping list) and cited Starling as the supposed victim, Quark gasped as if sucker-punched, stunned until he realized, too late, everyone was standing. He rose, under the bailiff's pointed glare, for a moment afraid he would be indicted in the mess, but the judge turned away, disappearing through the door behind her desk.

It wasn't until after Rogers (surprisingly toothy and freckled) exited through the side door that the other attorney approached, her head tilted as if she needed to make such an adjustment in order to accommodate Quark's statue. Better at mimicry than innovation in any social interaction, he resisted the impulse to tilt his own head. When she extended her small hand, Quark concentrated to look in her eyes and not squeeze too hard.

"Glad you came. Did you see Rogers's face? Now all we have to do is find Thayer." She shook her head which, Quark noted, barely affected the neat helmet of straight hair.

"What's this business about my mother? Why didn't anyone tell me?"

She leaned back, her eyes widening.

Quark, used to the way strangers misread him, relaxed into a slump in an effort to appease. "Nobody said anything about murder."

"Only Rogers," she said. "I don't even think he really believes it, and you heard the judge; she was pissed, right? Quark? It's Quark, isn't it? I'm sure this is a lot to process, but you might want to check your attitude. Everyone knows Thayer. Did you even realize he was staying with the sheriff? Ever since the Alzheimer's—"

"Oh, I don't think—"

"Ah, shit. Sorry. I have to go. I have another appointment. I'm getting married. Here's my card."

"You're getting married today?"

"Cake tasting. Call if you think of anything, okay?" She sidled, crablike, between the rows of chairs. "You're staying, right? I hope you aren't planning to leave. I think he needs you."

Quark shook his head no, even as he said that, yes, he would stay "at the old homestead," grimacing at his choice of words.

"Quark?"

She stood beside the massive door carved with mermaids, anchors, whales, seagulls, and starfish (rumored to have once been the decorative panel of the ship captain's private chambers).

"Yes?"

"Everyone knows your mother committed suicide. People saw her jump, right? I remember Thayer, ever since I was a little girl, walking that bluff. I used to call him the crying man." She smiled before pushing open the door, momentarily flooding the room with that Bellfairie air; briny, sour, and fresh, like clams in a bed of sea salt and fennel.

Quark turned toward the dais recently abdicated by the judge. On Sunday someone would drape a cloth over the desk and replace gavel with chalice, the space transformed from courthouse to church. He thought of dropping to his knees but couldn't figure out what he'd do

next. Clearly the notion was reflective of his exhaustion. He flicked
the lights off on his way out the door which, in Bellfairie fashion,
was left unlocked. Though he found the idea of going back to the
house for a nap appealing, he walked in the opposite direction, already
adjusted to the sharp incline of the narrow sidewalks.

He hadn't forgotten; he'd only chosen not to think about her suicide. He used to wonder why she did it, imagining the wind in her
hair, the shipwreck bells tolling below, but all the pondering never
stopped her from jumping. He finally accepted he would never have
an answer; he would never know her story or reasons.

He thought of his work back home, the small bones awaiting
excavation, the delicate balance of preservation and decay, the quiet
room filled with shadows beyond the orb of light that guided knife
and needle. Far from Bellfairie with all its mysteries, Quark had built
a life for himself in taxidermy. He worked hard to find his own way
in the world, to escape his inheritance of loss, and he had never once,
in all those years, missed the Old Man he was now expected to search
for. Why? What was he supposed to do with him, once found?

"You haven't been around, son. I'm just sayin'. Nobody blames ya. But
what you need to understand is he's been sending letters like this for
quite a while. It's not like anybody believes him. Except Rogers, who's
too green to be taken seriously."

Quark shifted against the confines of the small chair. The room
was stifling, windows inexplicably closed.

"I'd like to see it." Quark felt he shouldn't have to explain. After
all, this was his own father they were talking about, this was his life.

Sheriff Healy sighed as he lifted his feet off the desk to thumb
through the pages there, then turned to rifle through the stacks of
paper on the shelf behind, mumbling about "this damn mess."

Quark couldn't fathom working in such disorder. *What else is lost
here,* he wondered, noting the newspapers, photographs, and file folders piled on all available surfaces including the computer with its dark
screen.

"You sure, now?"

He reached for the paper, heard the chair creak as the sheriff leaned back to watch. Apparently Sheriff Healy wouldn't neglect an opportunity for investigation any more than Quark could pass by a small animal without considering its skeletal structure. "Didn't get much sleep last night," Quark said to explain the trembling in his hand, not looking up to monitor the sheriff's response.

> *Not a whale, but a shark is what I want to come back as if there be any return or heaven for me it is the sea. I teethed on a shark's tooth my ma once said and I have shark eyes small like that though Quark got them bad. Those little dark eyes of his like roe. Where is that boy? I look everywhere for him but he never comes and I fully confess in sin against God and man that I killed him with my fists because he used to glow the way his mother did before I threw her off the bluff. The bells are ringing from below and I am a shipbuilder weak in the waterways and she stands on the road now to my house my Starling. I spread broken glass to keep away her ghost but where is Quark? What have I done what have these hands made?*
> *So ends this passage.*

Quark pretended he was still reading, sure his cheeks were red, the telltale giveaway of the flash of emotions he could not contain. *This explains a lot,* he thought. *It explains everything.* When he finally looked up it was into Sheriff Healy's gaze, direct as an old dog's; watching, waiting, patient and intense.

"How could anyone take this seriously? I'm not dead, am I?"

Sheriff Healy leaned forward, hand extended to take the paper Quark happily rescinded.

"Obviously, he's fallen off the deep end. He really did spread broken glass over the road. I got a flat."

"Well, Quark, you know that's a private road there. It's not municipal business."

"I'm not saying—" Quark caught himself. Took a deep breath. "I can't believe anyone took that seriously."

"Well, son, mostly I agree. Most everyone does. The judge agrees, which is a good thing all around. But now there is that issue, you know."

"What issue?"

Sheriff Healy frowned and leaned back, his eyes steady on Quark's face. "What do you remember about your mother, son?"

"Nothing." Quark thought of the stories the Old Man used to tell about the unnatural stillness before the storm that took his ship and all else on board.

"Quark? Are you listening?"

"Sorry, I—"

"You must have some memories."

"No. How could I? I was a baby when she died."

"You were eight, son."

"I was— What?"

"Have it right here." The sheriff tapped an open folder placed square on his desk.

Quark shook his head. "You've made a mistake."

The sheriff tapped the page once more. "Eight."

Quark felt his jaw drop.

"Everybody knows he was hard on you, son. Nobody blames you for staying away so long, but if there's anything you been too afraid to tell—"

"No." Quark shook his head, the way he used to as a kid. "No, no, no." He knew he was acting strangely but it took several beats before he could stop, and by then it was too late; Sheriff Healy was appraising him like someone reconsidering a purchase.

"No," Quark said. "What are you asking?"

Sheriff Healy cocked his finger at Quark. "Well, all right, then. Just keep in mind. If you recall anything, even a small thing, it might help find Thayer. You'd be surprised what I can do with a little clue."

"I will be sure to notify you if I think of anything."

"Well, you do that. In the meantime, try not to worry. Everyone's looking. Probably just sleeping off a bender somewhere."

He didn't know what to say to that. He didn't believe it was true, but wasn't sure if the sheriff did or not. Quark nodded and, once again, found himself tipping his imaginary hat as he made a hasty exit. It was a cool day, the sort of chill that went to the bones. In the distance, Quark could hear the metallic clang against mast that filled him with longing.

He decided to leave. It wouldn't be as if he were abandoning the Old Man, not really. No one was abandoned in Bellfairie, everyone minded one another's business too much; though no one had minded his. He shoved his hands into his jean pockets, awkwardly hunched into himself, thinking about the autumn sun, the sound of yearning, and the taste of salt water taffy when he got a whiff of sugar pouring out the air vents of a store featuring caramel apples. He was tired, his bones ached, and how was it possible he'd forgotten his own mother?

"You really are some kind of freak," the Old Man said, more than once.

A grown man can't cry in the middle of the street even in Bellfairie, unless at the scene of a terrible wreck, a suicide perhaps, or a car accident in which a loved one died. Quark knew this, even as tears rose to his eyes. The terrible thing wasn't forgetting his mother, or remembering the Old Man's taunts. The terrible thing was what the Old Man said next, only once, when he was drunk; but still.

"You really are some kind of freak, Quark, yet I love you."

He dipped his head beneath the gray sky, and turned down the nearest side street, immediately removed from the depressed shops and occasional baffled tourist (no one came to Bellfairie on purpose; it was always a wrong turn in someone's life). He walked with down-cast eyes all the way back to his truck, which remained parked on broken glass, lopsided with the deflated tire. He stood for a long time, looking at the house in the yard of stones. There was never any doubt, never any real doubt he would find the skeleton key beneath the rock, collapse on the old couch without even taking his shoes off, or that he would not say he was home, but that he was here, and he would not say he loved the Old Man, or that that the Old Man loved him, but that once he said he did. It wasn't much, Quark knew. Probably wasn't even enough. But it's what he had. Not all his memories were bad.

He dreamt the Old Man tapped him lightly on the shoulder and said, "I'm drowning." It was a dream, not a portent, and even if it were, what did it portend? In the language of dreams the Old Man taught everything could mean its opposite; a dream of a wedding meant a funeral, for instance, unless it didn't. Dreams could be predictions, omens, mysterious clues to the shipwreck of the mind, or utter nonsense. Yet, as he lay there, eyes closed, Quark's shoulder tingled. He wondered if the borders had been breached and if that was why he felt he was being watched. His heart beat wildly with the old fear as he opened his eyes, peered into the dark and jumped back—or what he could do while reclined—thrusting neck and shoulders into the old couch, gasping at the female figure standing in the corner before he recognized her for what she was: a dark-haired woman with bulging eyes carved from wood, a figurehead meant to protect vessel and crew at sea.

Though he wouldn't say he forgave the Old Man, the thought of him alone out there—in trouble—disturbed Quark. His work in taxidermy provided him a special knowledge of the fragility of bones and skin; he had no illusion about the danger he himself had been in. It was unacceptable to treat a child like a mortal enemy; there could be no excuse. Yet, Quark reasoned, what happened once did not need to be multiplied by every day of his life. He rubbed the back of his neck.

He was so tired when he collapsed on the couch he hadn't taken in his surroundings; the room still furnished with the Old Man's chair faced toward the picture window, the round table beside it, the planked wood table at the far end, near the kitchen. All the ordinary furnishings of a modest home anywhere, as far as Quark could tell; he had been in so few other houses.

He guessed he'd slept through the entire afternoon and night, evidence of an exhaustion not warranted by a single disrupted sleep, but Quark often suffered restless nights, something inherited from the Old Man. Strange that the first good rest he'd had in weeks happened in Bellfairie.

It occurred to him to sit in the Old Man's chair. Once gold, even the dim light could not hide the wear, aged into a piss yellow; nubby against Quark's hand when he rested his palm on the armrest.

How many mornings had the Old Man sat staring out the window as though his own eyes provided light to guide the shipwrecked home?

A small, unidentified movement drew Quark to look closely through the early morning fog. He abandoned the chair to walk nearer to the window. One can imagine so many things. She was only there for a moment, hovering, as the Old Man said, above the glass, a woman he might have remembered.

Or a Rorschach composed of mist and desire.

What did it matter? What did any of this matter?

She was gone.

So what if the Old Man's larder held a disturbing array of unpalatable items: the moldy bread, the unidentified frozen meat wrapped in brown paper? Quark was happy for the excuse to plan a return to SuShi Palace for a reprisal of the previous morning's excellent breakfast.

All he wanted was something to wear. What had he been thinking to come without a change of clothes? He stood at the threshold of the Old Man's room noting how it, too, was cast in tarnished gold; the narrow bed draped with faded yellow spread. The floorboards squeaked as he walked to the far side of the room where dingy drapes were pulled shut. He considered opening them to let in the light and backyard view, but what if the Old Man should suddenly return? Better, Quark reasoned, to step out of the forbidden space without leaving a trace of trespass beyond the reasonable endeavor of looking for something to wear. He searched through the Old Man's closet, as bare as a monk's; a few old shirts, jeans, a tie rack from which hung the Old Man's belts made of knotted rope.

At some point the sincere search turned into excavation. Coming upon the old leather-bound book in the dim light of the dusty room scented vaguely of camphor, buried in a drawer beneath socks and underwear, Quark felt only mildly curious, expecting lists of numbers and dates, accounts of weather; he gasped at the pen-and-ink drawings of ships, whales, and wrecks careening across the pages. He turned to the front of the book and read the inscription: "All the rivers run into the sea; yet the sea is not full."

Who was this man who quoted Ecclesiastes? Who was this man who drew so delicately? Who held Quark's hand when he was a small child walking to school? Who beat him savagely without apology but

confessed to murders never committed? Who was this man? Where
had he been and where had he gone? Who was he?

Quark found himself drawn to the witches' house, situated between
the small pond where children cheerfully sailed toy boats, and the
cemetery where headstones tilted against the bay beyond. Only one
woman from Bellfairie, Sarah Winter, had been convicted and, while
townsfolk assuaged their guilt by noting that she was sentenced elsewhere, the fact remained that not a single resident of the quaint community of decent folk came to her defense; just as no one helped
Quark when he was young. Why was that, he wondered. Why did
everyone feel responsible for Thayer and no one for him? Quark
thought he'd let go of all that bitterness but found it stored beside the
memories he had of the one person who treated him right.

Mrs. Winter, descendant of the convicted witch, used to substitute at the Our Lady of the Sea grade school, though she never followed lesson plans. Instead, she told "histories," as she called them,
about Bellfairie. Different from the ones the Old Man told; his were
riddled with superstitions and myths while her stories were sourced
in fact, like the one about the disastrous period when so many men
and boys were lost at sea that for one generation Bellfairie was mostly
populated by women and children. Quark remembered that story, in
particular, for the comfort it used to bring.

He didn't believe Mrs. Winter, ancient even when he was young,
would still be alive, but thought it possible the house had been passed
on to another family member. He knew things were different elsewhere but in Bellfairie people referred to family names rather than
street addresses, much to the dismay of UPS and FedEx drivers. For
as long as Quark could remember, the red clapboard house had been
called Wintercairn, and he dared to hope that Mrs. Winter, with her
propensity for stories, might have told some about him, or his mother,
or the Old Man.

He knocked on the wooden door, which opened without the
usual warning of locks being turned and chains undrawn that accompanied such events in the greater world. Quark was caught with his

hand raised in a fist, flabbergasted by the appearance of the attorney who stood before him, wearing a wedding dress.

He tried to smile. "I come in peace," he said.

She squinted, her head at a tilt. "Quark? What are you doing here? Wait. You're not obligated to tell me anything. Memory is unreliable."

"I didn't know you live here. I thought . . . I remember when Mrs. Winter was my substitute teacher. She knew the history of Bellfairie and I thought—"

"Oh, you came to see Aunt Phoebe?"

"I know she can't be alive but—"

"Don't let her hear you say that. Quick, come in. I don't want anyone to see us."

Once his eyes adjusted, Quark found the small room, furnished with books, flowered chairs, and a red loveseat, surprisingly pleasant. No bones or boiling cauldrons, no cobwebs or swooping bats, no children's fingers in glass jars, or generations of Bellfairie's missing pets, though a three-legged white cat sauntered across the hardwood floor, her narrow tail erect.

"Sorry. These old houses have low ceilings. How tall are you, anyway?"

"Six foot five. Last I looked." She did not seem to understand he made a joke and Quark forged on. "Is that your wedding dress?"

She glanced down at the drape of white lace pooled around her bare feet. Quark steadied himself against the sarcasm sure to follow. *Is that your wedding dress?* He hated small talk.

"I thought it would look better. Ever since I was little, my aunt said I could wear it, but now I'm not so sure."

The sleeves that belled over her wrists caused her to look amputated, the waistline landed at her hips, adding pounds, and the chest area puckered in a most unfortunate manner, making her appear deformed. Yet the lace reminded Quark of cherry blossoms and the neckline, which gaped widely as though she had been swallowed by the garment, revealed an attractive clavicle.

"I know a little about sewing," he said, "for my work. A few adjustments and it will look very nice."

"You think? Are you a tailor?"

"Taxidermist," Quark said, eyeing the three-legged feline, his professional assessment awakened.

She bent over and scooped up the cat, who glowered at Quark beneath lowered brow. "I'll see when she can talk to you. We're pinning the dress, but—"

"No, no, no." Quark shook his head as he began to back toward the door. "Don't bother, I'll—"

"Quark, stop. Wait. I'll just be a minute."

She turned with the white cat tucked under her arm switching its tail. In spite of all he knew to be true, Quark found himself thinking she looked like a good witch, even if ineffectual. He shook his head at himself. This was what happened in Bellfairie. He was being sucked into its crazy.

"Yes. I remember you. Still shaking your head against the world?"

"No, I . . ." Quark felt himself flush. *Stop shaking your head,* he thought and, after a few more beats, did.

"I don't recall you being so tall."

Quark didn't know what to say that wouldn't be rude.

"I suppose you're here about Thayer."

"Yes, I—"

"Heard he confessed to murdering half the town."

"Is this a bad time to talk?"

"Who said it was a bad time? Oh." She glanced over her shoulder. "They don't need me. They just include me to make me feel like I matter."

Quark wasn't sure how to proceed.

"This is where you say, 'don't be silly, of course you matter.'"

He felt his face flush.

"That's what I always liked about you: even as a boy you were unusually sincere." She shook her finger at him. "No bullshit. I like that. Come on then, why are you here?"

Quark nodded. That was the question, wasn't it? *Why am I here?* "I remembered how you knew all the history and I thought maybe you could tell me something. A clue. To find him."

"Thayer?"

"Or if you know anything about my mother. I don't remember much. In general."

"Oh, Starling."

Though Quark knew the obvious association, it was the first time his mother's name brought to mind a small bird and the sound wings make in that initial moment of flight. He felt, suddenly, sad. *Mother,* he thought.

"First, Thayer did not kill her. As I'm sure you, of all people, can attest. She was a darling child, the sweetest dimpled girl this rock ever knew. What's the old saying? She was the light in her father's eye. You understand. Those were different times; she roamed the town like no child these days is allowed. She used to stop by often for my ginger cake and cream. How that child loved cream! I used to call her Kitty! Oh, the darling girl." She dabbed the corner of her dry eye though there was no fraud in the sorrow, Quark was sure.

"Thayer was mostly at sea, you know, and Starling was largely raised by her mother until the tragedy."

"The tragedy?"

"So many tragedies in your family, Quark. People around here pride rationality but even the most stubborn Bellifarian thinks your family is cursed."

"Cursed?"

"Stop, Quark. I can't tolerate this new fashion of repeating single words as a parlay in conversation. It's an insult to my intelligence. Are you listening or not?"

"I haven't eaten breakfast yet and—"

"Of course I don't believe in curses. Don't look so surprised. I know what people say about the Winters. I may not believe in curses but I do believe in fools and Bellfairie has more than its fair share, Quark. I'm sorry to say, though I'm sure you're well aware, your grandfather is one of them."

"Oh, I don't know my grandfather."

"What? What's gotten into you? Why are you talking like an idiot?"

Quark mustered all the benevolence he could access. After all, Mrs. Winter was old.

"Did he hit you in the head once too often? Is that it?"

"Who? What . . . I don't even—"

"Your grandfather. Thayer!"

"Excuse me, Mrs. Winter, but Thayer is my father, not my grandfather."

"Quark. Come here. Come closer. Give me your hand. Now, look at me."

Although he towered over her, Quark felt like a boy again, looking down into Mrs. Winter's hazel eyes.

"You were my favorite student, Quark. Not like those other boys. Like I said. Sincere."

She squeezed his hand gently.

"Everyone knows he was changed by the tragedy. Broken. Made strange. Er. But I had no idea he never told you. Quark, listen to me. Thayer is your grandfather."

Quark didn't realize he was trying to pull his hand free until he felt the tightening of her clasp.

"Stop. Stop shaking your head. Listen. I'm sure he had his reasons for letting you believe otherwise all these years, but this isn't difficult to prove. There are records."

"But if he's not my father, who is?"

"Everyone loved Starling. She was popular with all the boys, but Thayer—"

"My grandfather?"

"Yes, Quark, try to keep up. I know you've had a shock, but this is important. And who knows? I might not be here next time you arrive with questions. I'm not immortal, you know. Now, where was I? Oh, yes. Thayer. He doted on her."

"On my mother?"

"Yes."

"Mrs. Winter are you saying that my . . . that he had an improper impulse toward—"

"No, Quark, that's not what I'm saying. I'm saying Thayer doted on his daughter, Starling, and there was nothing improper about it. Who would have guessed he would be such a good father? But he was."

Quark hated Bellfairie. That's why he left as soon as he could. The place was full of meanness, superstition, and God-fearing atheists, the sort who don't believe in heaven's rule but looked up at the sky to ask for help whenever there was trouble, the kind of people who'd make a kid feel special—cared for, even—while knowing secrets about that child's life, like how his father was really his grandfather and his mother . . . "What changed him?"

"Quark, maybe you should sit with your head between your knees."

"When did he stop being a good father?"

"Oh, as soon as you came along. Over time, he just got worse."

He had to leave. Was it too much to ask that he have the life he believed in? It felt a violence, it really did.

"Quark? Are you all right?"

"I'm adequate, Mrs. Winter."

"Adequate?"

"I need to go now."

"I know this is a shock. Maybe you should stay. I'll make strawberry tea. I remember you always liked tea."

"No. Thank you, Mrs. Winter, but no. I need to go."

He tipped his imaginary hat, turned on his heels and pulled at the heavy door, which did not give until she said, "Here, let me help," which filled him with the furious power of a man whose strength is challenged by an old lady. The door opened with a pop and he walked out into the Bellfairie air, leaving her to shut the door. He heard her say his name once, gently, but he just kept walking.

All in all it was a dispiriting morning. SuShi's had, inexplicably, "run out" of oysters, a situation Quark could not fathom.

"There's a whole ocean right there," he'd said, pointing his knife in the general direction. He had not meant it as a threat, though he was old enough to know one should not go waving knives about.

Dory had a day off, or was sick; at any rate she wasn't there. Nor was the sheriff, though he arrived fast enough, the squad car sirening through town getting everyone excited. By the time all was said and

done a small crowd had gathered outside the diner and, while Quark
was soon acquitted, the little mob stepped away from him with a
suspicious murmur when he walked past; a hungry orphan. Perhaps
a silly term for a grown man, he thought it nicely described a desola-
tion he'd felt all his life. There had never been, or at least he had no
memory of there ever having been, someone waiting at the door with
warm bread and jam, or candy in her pocket.

Or had there? For as soon as Quark mourned the lack, he pictured a dark-haired woman with a sad smile waiting in front of his
house, conjured, he assumed, like that morning's ghost, from longing.

The restaurant manager (a name Quark didn't recognize, someone new to Bellfairie, he guessed) followed him outside to apologize.
"Everyone's on edge," she said, "'cause of us not realizing there was a
serial killer in our midst."

She didn't know, of course, that Quark was the "killer's" kin. She
offered to serve him anything on the menu free of cost "for his trouble,"
at which point Quark once again requested the waffles with oyster sauce.

"We're out of oysters," she said, which brought them back to the
brink of trouble.

"Never mind." Quark tipped his imaginary hat, which caused her
to take two steps back, a false smile on her face. He thrust his hands
into the pocket of his father's/grandfather's pants. "Wyman's Market
still this way?" he asked.

Which is how Quark came to be carrying two brown paper bags
full of groceries up broken glass road, exhausted by their weight, and
just plain exhausted. Stunned to see the woman standing by the front
door, he felt a momentary surge, as though something in his chest had
taken flight, before he recognized the lawyer.

"Do you need help?"

"No, I'm fine," he lied. His right hand was particularly cramped.
He wasn't even sure he could make it up the steps without dropping
one or both bags.

"Really, you should let me—"

"What are you doing here? Where's your car?"

"I needed a walk. You know, after all that cake. Sheriff Healy
asked me to—"

"I haven't eaten yet," Quark said. The right-hand bag began to slip. He propped it up with his knees.

"Here, let me get the door," she reached across to open it.

He stepped inside, blinking against the change of light as he hurried to set one bag on the narrow kitchen counter and the other on the small table, then looked behind to discover she remained at the threshold, a silhouette against the bright sky beyond. Not sure what to do about her, he began unpacking the groceries: a loaf of sliced bread, a jar of peanut butter, a carton of eggs.

"Quark?"

He had almost forgotten about her, which made him feel unsettled. What was wrong with him? How could he forget everything so easily?

"I have some news about Thayer. That's why I'm here."

"I haven't had breakfast yet," Quark said as a fly buzzed narrowly past his face. "Come in. Shut the door and come in."

Butter, bacon, cream, a roasting chicken, carrots, onions, a small head of cauliflower, russet potatoes, and a package of toilet paper which he left in the bag rather than expose his bathroom needs; she looked uncomfortable enough, standing in the kitchen doorway.

"Good news. They found Thayer. Sheriff Healy's bringing him home."

"Here?"

She lifted a sneakered foot to frown at the sole. "Can I sit down a minute? I think I stepped on something."

Quark wasn't sure what was expected. After all, weren't the chairs obvious? He pulled one away from the table, and with a flourish, indicated she should sit, which she did, untying her shoe as she spoke.

"Turns out he was with Dean Yarly. You know he was a priest, right? Long time ago, but apparently thinks he still has to keep everyone's secrets. Anyway, Healy, oh, Jesus Christ, no wonder." She lifted her hand, thumb and pointer finger holding a sliver of glass. "I'm all right, Quark. You don't have to be . . . see, it didn't even break the skin. It was mostly in the shoe."

Uncomfortable with her naked foot, Quark quickly turned away. "Better check the other one," he said, laying six strips of bacon into the hot pan then adding a few more in case she was hungry too.

"I don't think that's necessary. I mean, what are the chances?"

"He spread broken glass all over the road."

"What?"

"'Cause of the ghost," Quark said. "She comes at night and stares at the house. My mother, I guess. He wants to keep her out."

"But that doesn't make . . ." She stopped in mid-sentence and unlaced the other shoe.

Quark offered a saucer, which she looked at quizzically until he said, "for the glass," and placed it on the floor beside her feet. Later, when he tossed out the evidence, Quark counted three shards, one spotted with blood.

After she left, Quark ate his eggs, toast, and bacon at the table. There was a brief period of consternation when he discovered neither salt nor pepper to be found but, once he accepted his fate, the break-fast was good enough. Afterward he made coffee, which he decided to take to the backyard, stepping out the kitchen door into a fairy tale of some kind. He blinked and shook his head, but it was not his imagi-nation. There was a ship in the backyard, or the bones of one at least.

He couldn't decide if he was impressed or dismayed. How long had this been going on, the Old Man building an ark? Surely this proved his mental capacity, didn't it? No one could build such a thing from the workings of a mind in chaos, could they?

He drank the first cup of coffee circling the ship, inspecting from all angles, finding it sure. The second he drank sitting on the same flat rock he used to pretend was a throne. He was often a prince back then, ruling an imaginary kingdom of eccentric residents, including a few talking animals, in the very space from which now rose the skeleton of ship woven through with sky. Quark decided not to try to make sense of it. Instead, he sat on the rock and drank his coffee while he waited for the Old Man's return.

In real life Quark spent long hours at the taxidermy table, absorbed in his work. He was not easily distracted or made restless. Who knows how long he sat before he heard the unmistakable sound of tires on gravel, car doors slammed, a curse?

He left the empty mug and hurried to the front of the house; felt an initial tug of fear at the sight of Thayer meandering toward the front door, unaware of Quark's presence or appraisal. Sheriff Healy, who stood by the side of the squad car, nodded at Quark, who nodded back before turning to greet the Old Man. Unsure what to call him, Quark said "hey" three times before Thayer looked up from beneath unruly brows. The blue cast of his gaze had been diluted by time but remained penetrating, giving him a slightly haunted look which, combined with the wild hair, mustache, and beard, made a crazed Santa or, as was appropriate, an old sea captain who "swallowed the anchor," as they say.

After fixing Quark with that long look, which filled him with guilt for the transgressions he'd made, going through the Old Man's closet, wearing his clothes, discovering the ship, Thayer opened his arms wide, as though to measure half a fathom, or so Quark thought before he realized it was a beckoning.

He stepped forward, arms at his side. The Old Man still possessed a surprising strength, though now Quark was so tall he could look over Thayer's head at Sheriff Healy, who remained leaning against the car, arms crossed over his chest, watching.

Finally released, Quark saluted the sheriff, who responded by stepping away from the car. Stone and glass crunched beneath his boots as he walked toward Quark while Thayer mumbled his way into the house.

"You're staying, right?" the sheriff asked. "He can't be left alone. I told him he could stay with me but he wants to be here. With you."

Quark nodded as this was all perfectly natural, though he felt strange. What was the feeling? *Something like happiness,* he thought, *to imagine the Old Man had chosen him.*

"I don't know how long," Quark said. "I have work."

"What is it you do again?"

"Taxidermy." And, when the sheriff frowned up at him, "I pre-serve animals so people and museums can keep them."

"Is that right?"

Quark nodded.

"You make a living at that?"

He shrugged.

"Well, I'll be damned. Do you do . . . pets?"

Quark hesitated. He considered lying but, after all, this was the sheriff whose dark eyes peered so closely at Quark he felt sure even the most innocent lie would be discerned. "Some."

"Yeah?" Sheriff Healy shook his head. "Well, it takes all kinds, don't it?"

Quark hated the way his own hand enveloped the sheriff's and the momentary surge of strength this incited. It was a man thing. The way they were all threatened by his size, though Quark never felt up to the competition; his own grip always gentle. The end of any handshake Quark ever shared was accompanied by a bemused look. It was to the sheriff's credit, Quark thought, that Healy's expression remained neutral.

"It's good you came, son," Healy said, already walking to his car.

Quark lingered to watch Healy maneuver a Y turn around the Ford, still parked where it had been abandoned. The squad car traveled slowly down the broken glass road, then stopped at the crossroad longer than necessary. Finally the left turn signal blinked, and Healy continued on his way.

Quark looked longingly at his truck. If he'd fixed that flat he'd be gone already. With a sigh, he turned to the house.

Thayer sat at the plank table, an open bottle of rum at his elbow. Quark sat across from him, pretending grave interest in the brown liquid. He raised his glass in response to Thayer's silent toast and gulped, in one horrible swallow, then set his glass on the table in unison with the Old Man. Quark hated the flavor. He did enjoy, however, the loosening that accompanied the rum. The Old Man scowled at Quark's inability to keep up, but after his own glass had been dispensed several times, Thayer began the old argument with himself. He was the luckiest man who ever crossed the sea or the unluckiest who ever lived. He had nine lives, or nine tragedies. He had been half drowned by a shark, swept overboard in a gale, lost his ship, terrorized by a ghost, ate bad mussels, kissed a witch, almost died from a tattoo, and nearly hit by lightning.

"You know what happens to a man when a bolt finds him, don't you, son?"

In Quark's pleasantly unknit state he felt tempted to ask the serious questions. But the lack of inhibition that considered the questions also depleted their urgency. *Time enough,* he told himself, and, *I'm not leaving until I know the truth.*

"Someone hit by lightning," he began, but the Old Man leaned across the table to deliver a rum-soaked response to his own query.

"A man hit by lightning can see the future. Read minds. Talk to ghosts."

"You are the only person," Quark said (as though he were intimate with many), "who thinks not being hit by lightning was an unfortunate event."

"Well, what do you know?" Thayer asked. "What do you know about fortune?"

Quark peered into his glass, inhaling the scent of vanilla, a hint of cinnamon and clove. It smelled like something he would enjoy. But what did he know? Really, what did he know about anything? He glanced at the Old Man, an unintimidating figure with trembling hands and unfocused gaze. An old man now, literally, babbling about ghosts, luck, and regret.

"The sea never did call your name, did it, boy?"

Quark lifted the glass and swallowed the burn. He learned early that he was not made for it, suffering nausea even on the pier if the day was windy enough. The Old Man, exiled from the ocean, paid others to take Quark out until everyone knew all it took were a few whitecaps for his skin to turn chalky, and no amount of orange slices could prevent the inevitable, apparently limitless, vomiting.

Quark became a joke, though even he knew it was not meant unkindly. People in Bellfairie often showed affection through humor. Unfortunately, Quark rode the teasing as well as the waves. Folks learned to leave him alone. They also learned not to take him out on their boats, which was fine by him. He hadn't thought about all this in years, but the woozy drunken feeling reminded him. He pushed the glass away with the back of his hand.

"What are you doing with that ship?"

Quark knew, from experience, that it was best to walk away from the kind of dead calm his question raised. Even so, he remained.

Thayer leaned forward, elbows on the table. "Did I ever tell you what happened out there?"

"Out where?"

"She went down—"

Quark sighed. How he hated this story of the Old Man's last ride.

"Eight of us when she went down. Eight. Only one survived. Me. I swam three days. I was young then. Like you." Thayer stopped, squinted at Quark. "Why'd you stay away so long?"

"I—"

"Did I tell you about the others? How I heard their screams?"

Quark looked down at his hands, and found them, in his inebriated state, shockingly large. *It's amazing,* he thought, *that I can do such delicate work with such monstrous hands.*

"First I recognized the screams, but after a while one man's screams start to sound like another's and then they sound inhuman. Like birds. Like your name; squawking seagulls."

"Why do you have to talk about this now? It was a long time ago. There was nothing—"

"And I swam away."

Yes, because of the sharks, Quark thought. He sat through recitations of this story so often that when he heard a seagull's mournful cry the first thing he thought was someone was dying.

"Why did you stay away so long?"

Quark rubbed his fingers across the gouge marks on the table. He had learned to whittle there. First thing he made was a canoe the size of his thumb. He wondered what ever happened to it.

"What are you going to do with that ship?"

The Old Man's eyes narrowed to chips of blue. Less Santa, much more the expression Quark remembered, sneering and cruel.

"What am I gonna do with that ship?" He mimicked Quark's plaintive tone. "What do you think I'm gonna do with her? I'm going back to sea, boy."

Quark turned to look out the big picture window, shocked at the bright blue sky cut by a lone seagull; a moment later Quark heard its mournful cry.

———

All life is, of course, a history of loss. A sturdy ship sails from home on a pleasant day, smoothly gliding across the sea until it slips over the horizon never to return. Mothers bear children, relinquished to a world that largely forgets how they were, truly one, a single body carrying two hearts, diminished by the strange mathematics of regeneration. Every life is composed of forgotten hours, the unremembered, the unknown and forever lost.

Quark was not a child, after all; though returning to his boyhood home had reacquainted him with the child he'd been in Bellfairie, awkward where it seemed he should have been most comfortable, lonely among his memories. All right, he had been odd boy out, Quark knew this. He had lived the consequences and accepted them.

What was this then? This terrible feeling that kept him awake, staring at the ceiling slanted over his bed, too close? Every time he drifted toward sleep he awoke with a start, his breathing labored. He wanted to push the ceiling away; how had he slept beneath it all those years like a boy in a casket propped open for viewing? What a thought! What a morbid idea! Yet, what was he to make of the great unmooring? His father was not his father. His mother was gone. She had always been gone. But, no, the sheriff said Quark had been eight years old before she left. Where was she? Somewhere in his mind, Quark felt certain, but how to find her?

Instead, he recalled his cat. Her name had been Cheryl. That made him smile, though it was quickly followed with the memory of Thayer's incredulity. "Cheryl?" he'd barked. "Where'd ya get a name like that?"

Quark sighed. What was the use? Why was he even trying to sleep? He rolled over, carefully planted his feet on the braided rug, shoulders hunched out of the old habit established when he went through the growth spurt that caused him to hit his head until he remembered he could no longer sit straight up in his own bed.

There was only a single small round window at the other end of the narrow room. Quark wondered what had become of the desk that used to stand beneath it, though it had never been anything special. In spite of his uncomfortable relationship with the sea, Quark used to pretend his room was the captain's quarters of a ship; the window a porthole which, that night, dispensed a milky light he initially mistook for dawn. Had he slept longer than he realized?

That's when he heard the tapping sound of . . . a hammer? Once he stepped off the small rug, he recoiled against the cold floor. *Summer is already over*, he thought, walking through the moonglow to peer out the window at the ship below, mysterious as a ghost vessel and, like all skeletons, strangely beautiful.

He leaned closer to the porthole to be sure. Yes, it was so; the Old Man balanced against the moon, hammering. Thayer had been drunk when Quark went to bed; he had to be drunk still. It wasn't safe for him to perch there, the hammered hand raised.

He could fall, Quark thought, *and this would all be over.*

He did not fall and, eventually, Quark turned away, walked past the bed, down the creaking stairs, past the plank table on which rested the empty bottle, the two glasses, through the kitchen lit by a stovetop light, out the back door and across the cold, stony yard.

"You'll never get her done in time," Quark hollered but the Old Man continued hammering. Quark kicked a stone with his bare foot. The hospital pants and t-shirt the Old Man wore couldn't possibly be warm enough. "You're gonna catch cold," he shouted. "You could get pneumonia."

Thayer stopped mid-swing, perched against the night sky, made incandescent by the moon, his hair like the wild fright of a cartoon character; ghostly, almost. "You think I'm going to get sick?" he bellowed.

"Come in. The neighbors—"

"The neighbors? What's got into you, Quark? Everyone's worried about my head and you're talking about neighbors? What neighbors? We ain't got neighbors and we never have."

"Sound carries. That's what I'm saying."

Thayer responded by resuming his work, hammering like a strange night woodpecker. Quark watched until he was sure that, in spite of reasonable expectations, the Old Man was stable, at least physically. Quark went back into the house, where he found his socks and shoes and a sweater draped across the couch. He couldn't believe himself, surprised to discover that beneath the anger, resentment, disappointment, and sheer bafflement there remained this desire.

When Quark returned, the Old Man's hammering changed tempo, but other than an occasional grunt of direction, they didn't speak as they worked. It was crazy, Quark knew; symptomatic, even. Though, after a while, he had to admit he enjoyed the deep silence of the night punctuated by the rhythmic sound of hammering, the distant whisper of waves, the moonglow. When Thayer pointed east and said, "She's bleeding. Time to go in now," Quark felt sorry to see the pink slit of morning. Together they climbed down the ship and walked back to the house. It felt good to fall into his boyhood bed, to sleep deeply into the dawn, untroubled by dreams or unanswered questions, his body sore. When, hours later, he was briefly awoken by the cry of a seagull, Quark wondered why he had never noticed before how much it sounded like his name, as if someone might want him.

Cold Fires

It was so cold that daggered ice hung from the eaves with dangerous points that broke off and speared the snow in the afternoon sun, only to be formed again the next morning. Snowmobile shops and ski rental stores, filled with brightly polished snowmobiles and helmets and skis and poles and wool knitted caps and mittens with stars stitched on them and down jackets and bright-colored boots, stood frozen at the point of expectation when that first great snow fell on Christmas night and everyone thought that all that was needed for a good winter season was a good winter snow, until the cold reality set in and the employees munched popcorn or played cards in the back room because it was so cold that no one even wanted to go shopping, much less ride a snowmobile. Cars didn't start but heaved and ticked and remained solidly immobile, stalagmites of ice holding them firm. Motorists called Triple A and Triple A's phone lines became so congested that calls were routed to a trucking company in Pennsylvania, where a woman with a very stressed voice answered the calls with the curt suggestion that the caller hang up and dial again.

It was so cold dogs barked to go outside, and immediately barked to come back in, and then barked to go back out again; frustrated dog owners leashed their pets and stood shivering in the snow as shivering dogs lifted icy paws, walking in a kind of Irish dance, spinning in that dog circle thing, trying to find the perfect spot to relieve themselves while dancing high paws to keep from freezing to the ground.

It was so cold birds fell from the sky like tossed rocks, frozen except for their tiny eyes, which focused on the sun as if trying to understand its betrayal.

That night the ice hung so heavy from the power lines that they could no longer maintain the electric arc and the whole state went black, followed within the hour by the breakdown of the phone lines. Many people would have a miserable night but the couple had a wood-burning stove. It crackled with flame that bit the dry and brittle birch and consumed the chill air where even in the house they had been wearing coats and scarves that they removed as the hot aura expanded. It was a good night for soup, heated on the cast-iron stove and scenting the whole house with rosemary and onion; a good night for wine, the bottle of red they bought on their honeymoon and had been saving for a special occasion; and it was a good night to sit by the stove on the floor, their backs resting against the couch pillows, watching the candles flicker in the waves of heat while the house cracked and heaved beneath its thick-iced roof. They decided to tell stories, the sort of stories that only the cold and the fire, the wind and the silent dark combined could make them tell.

"I grew up on an island," she said, "well, you know that. I've already told you about the smell of salt and how it still brings the sea to my breath, how the sound of bathwater can make me weep, how before the birds fell from the sky like thrown rocks, the dark arc of their wings, in certain light, turned white, and how certain tones of metal, a chain being dragged by a car, a heavy pan that clangs against its lid become the sound of ships and boats leaving the harbor. I've already told you all that, but I think you should know that my family is descended from pirates, we are not decent people, everything we own has been stolen, even who we are, my hair for instance, these blond curls can be traced not to any relatives for they are all dark and swarthy but to the young woman my Great-great-grandfather brought home to his wife, intended as a sort of help-mate but apparently quite worthless in the kitchen, though she displayed a certain fondness for anything to do with strawberries, you understand the same fruit I embrace for its short season; oh, how they taste of summer, and my youth!

"Now that I have told you this, I may as well tell you the rest. This blond maid of my Great-great-grandfather's house, who could not sew, or cook, or even garden well but who loved strawberries as if they gave her life, became quite adept at rejecting any slightly imperfect fruit. She picked through the bowls that Great-great-grandmother brought in from the garden and tossed those not perfectly swollen or those with seeds too coarse to the dogs, who ate them greedily then panted at her feet and became worthless hunters, so enamored were they with the sweet. Only perfect berries remained in the white bowl and these she ate with such a manner of tongue and lips that Great-great-grandfather who came upon her like that, once by chance and ever after by intention, sitting in the sun at the wooden kitchen table, the dogs slathering at her feet, sucking strawberries, ordered all the pirates to steal more of the red fruit, which he traded unreasonably for until he became quite the laughingstock and the whole family was in ruin.

"But even this was not enough to bring Great-great-grandfather to his senses and he did what just was not done in those days and certainly not by a pirate who could take whatever woman he desired— he divorced Great-great-grandmother and married the strawberry girl who, it is said, came to her wedding in a wreath of strawberry ivy, and carried a bouquet of strawberries from which she plucked, even in the midst of the sacred ceremony, red bulbs of fruit which she ate so greedily that when it came time to offer her assent, she could only nod and smile bright red lips the color of sin.

"The strawberry season is short and it is said she grew pale and weak in its waning. Great-great-grandfather took to the high seas and had many adventures, raiding boats where he passed the gold and coffers of jewels, glanced at the most beautiful woman and glanced away—so that later, after the excitement had passed, these same women looked into mirrors to see what beauty had been lost—and went instead, quite eagerly, to the kitchen where he raided the fruit. He became known as a bit of a kook.

"In the meantime, the villagers began to suspect that the strawberry girl was a witch. She did not appreciate the gravity of her situation but continued to visit Great-great-grandmother's house as if the other woman was her own mother and not the woman whose husband she had stolen. It is said that Great-great-grandmother sicced the dogs on her but they saw the blond curls and smelled her strawberry scent and licked her fingers and toes and came back to the house with her, tongues hanging out and grinning doggedly at Great-great-grandmother who, it is said, then turned her back on the girl who was either so naïve or so cunning that she spoke in a rush about her husband's long departures, the lonely house on the hill, the dread of coming winter, a perfect babble of noise and nonsense that was not affected by Great-great-grandmother's cold back until, the villagers said, the enchantment became perfect and she and Great-great-grandmother were seen walking the cragged hills to market days as happy as if they were mother and daughter or two old friends, and perhaps this is where it would have all ended, a confusion of rumor and memory, were it not for the strange appearance of the rounded bellies of both women and the shocking news that they both carried Great-great-grandfather's child, which some said was a strange coincidence and others said was some kind of trick.

"Great-great-grandfather's ship did not return when the others did and the other pirate wives did not offer this strawberry one any condolences. He was a famous seaman, and it was generally agreed that he had not drowned, or crashed his ship at the lure of sirens, but had simply abandoned his witchy wife.

"All that winter Great-great-grandfather's first and second wives grew suspiciously similar bellies, as if size were measured against size to keep an even girth. At long last the strawberry wife took some minor interest in hearth and home and learned to bake bread that Great-great-grandfather's first wife said would be more successfully called crackers, and soup that smelled a bit too ripe but which the dogs seemed to enjoy. During this time Great-great-grandmother grew curls, and her lips, which had always seemed a mastless ship anchored to the plane of her face, became strawberry shaped. By spring when the two were seen together, stomachs returned to corset size, and carrying between them a bald, blue-eyed baby, they were often mistaken for sisters. The villagers even became confused about which was the witch and which the bewitched.

"About this time, in the midst of a hushed ongoing debate among the villagers regarding when to best proceed with the witch burning—after the baby, whose lineage was uncertain, had been weaned, seemed the general consensus—Great-great-grandfather returned and brought with him a shipload of strawberries. The heavy scent drove the dogs wild. Great-great-grandfather drove the villagers mad with strawberries and then, when the absolute height of their passion had been aroused, stopped giving them away and charged gold for them, a plan that was whispered in his ears by the two wives while he held his baby, who sucked on strawberries the way other babies sucked on tits.

"In this way, Great-great-grandfather grew quite rich and built a castle shaped like a ship covered in strawberry vines and with a room at the back, away from the sea, which was made entirely of glass and housed strawberries all year. He lived there with the two wives and the baby daughter and nobody is certain who is whose mother in our family line.

"Of course the strawberry wife did not stay but left one night, too cruel and heartless to even offer an explanation. Great-great-grandfather shouted her name for hours as if she was simply lost until, at last, he collapsed in the strawberry room, crushing the fruit with his large body and rolling in the juice until he was quite red with it and as frightening as a wounded animal. His first wife found him there and steered him to a hot bath. They learned to live together again without the strawberry maid. Strangers who didn't know their story often commented on the love between them. The villagers insisted they were both bewitched, the lit candles in the window to guide her return given as evidence. Of course she never did come back."

Outside in the cold night, even the moon was frozen. It shed a white light of ice over their pale yard and cast a ghost glow into the living room that haunted her face. He studied her as if she were someone new in his life and not the woman he'd known for seven years. Something about that moonglow combined with the firelight made her look strange, like a statue at a revolt.

She smiled down at him and cocked her head. "I tell you this story," she said, "to explain if ever you should wake and find me gone, it is not an expression of lack of affection for you, but rather her witchy blood that is to be blamed."

"What became of her?"

"Oh, no one knows. Some say she had a lover, a pirate from a nearby cove, and they left together, sailing the seas for strawberries.

Some say she was an enchanted mermaid and returned to the sea. Some say she came to America and was burned at the stake."

"Which do you think is true?"

She leaned back and sighed, closing her eyes. "I think she's still alive," she whispered, "breaking men's hearts, because she is insatiable."

He studied her in repose, a toppled statue while everything burned.

"Now it's your turn," she said, not opening her eyes, and sounding strangely distant. Was that a tear at the corner of her eye? He turned away from her. He cleared his throat.

"All right then. For a while I had a job in Castor, near Rhome, in a small art museum there. I was not the most qualified for the work but apparently I was the most qualified who was willing to live in Castor, population 954, I kid you not. The museum had a nice little collection, actually. Most of the population of Castor had come through to view the paintings at least once but it was my experience they seemed just as interested in the carpeting, the light fixtures, and the quantity of fish in the river, as they were in the work of the old masters. Certainly the museum never saw the kind of popular attention the baseball field hosted, or the bowling lanes just outside of town.

"What had happened was this. In the 1930s Emile Castor, who had made his fortune on sweet cough drops, had decided to build a fishing lodge. He purchased a beautiful piece of forested property at the edge of what was then a small community, and built his 'cabin,' a six-bedroom, three-bath house with four stone-hearth fireplaces, and large windows that overlooked the river in the backyard. Even though Castor had blossomed to a population of nearly a thousand by the time I arrived, deer still came to drink from that river.

"When Emile Castor died in 1989, he stated in his will that the house be converted into a museum to display his private collection. He bequeathed all his estate to the support of this project. Of course, his relatives, a sister, a few old cousins, and several nieces and nephews, contested this for years, but Mr. Castor was a thorough man and the legalities were tight as a rock. What his family couldn't understand, other than, of course, what they believed was the sheer cruelty of his act, was where this love of art had come from. Mr. Castor, who fished and hunted and was known as something of a ladies' man, though he never married, smoked cigars—chased by lemon cough drops—and built his small fortune on his 'masculine attitude,' as his sister referred to it in an archived letter.

"The kitchen was subdivided. A wall was put up that cut an ugly line right down the middle of what had once been a large picture window that overlooked the river. Whoever made this decision and executed it so poorly was certainly no appreciator of architecture. It was ugly and distorted and an insult to the integrity of the place. What remained of the original room became the employee kitchen: a refrigerator, a stove, a large sink, marble countertops, and a tiled mosaic floor. A small, stained-glass window by Chagall was set beside the remaining slice of larger window. It remained, in spite of the assault it suffered, a beautiful room, and an elaborate employee kitchen for our small staff.

"The other half of the kitchen was now completely blocked off and inaccessible other than by walking through the employee kitchen. That, combined with the large window, which shed too much light to expose any works of art to, had caused this room to develop into a sort of oversized storage room. It was a real mess when I got there.

"The first thing I did was sort through all that junk, unearthing boxes of outdated pamphlets and old stationery, a box of old toilet paper, and several boxes of old Castor photographs, which I carried to my office to be catalogued and preserved. After a week or so of this I found the paintings, box after box of canvasses painted by an amateur hand, quite bad, almost at the level of a schoolchild, but without a child's whimsy, and all of the same woman. I asked Darlene, who acted as bookkeeper, ticket taker, and town gossip, what she thought of them.

"'That must be Mr. Castor's work,' she said.

"'I didn't know he painted.'

"'Well, he did, you can see for yourself. Folks said he was nuts about painting out here. Are they all like these?'

"'More or less.'

"'Should have stuck to cough drops,' she pronounced. (This from a woman who once confided in me her absolute glee at seeing a famous jigsaw puzzle, glued and framed, hanging in some restaurant in a nearby town.)

"When all was said and done we had fifteen boxes of those paintings and I decided to hang them in the room that was half of what had once been a magnificent kitchen. Few people would see them there, and that seemed right; they really were quite horrid. The sunlight could cause no more damage than their very presence already exuded.

"When they were at last all hung, I counted a thousand various shapes and sizes of the same dark-haired, gray-eyed lady painted in various styles, the deep velvet colors of Renaissance, the soft pastel hues of Baroque, some frightening bright green reminiscent of Matisse, and strokes that swirled wildly from imitation of van Gogh to the thick direct lines of a grade schooler. I stood in the waning evening light staring at this grotesquerie, this man's art, his poor art, and I must admit I was moved by it. Was his love any less than that of the artist who painted well? Some people have talent. Some don't. Some people have a love that can move them like this. One thousand faces, all imperfectly rendered, but attempted nonetheless. Some of us can only imagine such devotion.

"I had a lot of free time in Castor. I don't like to bowl. I don't care for greasy hamburgers. I have never been interested in stock car racing or farming. Let's just say I didn't really fit in. I spent my evenings cataloguing Emile Castor's photographs. Who doesn't like a mystery? I thought the photographic history of this man's life would yield some clues about the object of his affection. I was quite excited about it actually, until I became quite weary with it. You can't imagine what it's like to look through one man's life like that, family, friends, trips, beautiful women—though none were her. The more I looked at them, the more depressed I grew. It was clear Emile Castor had really lived his life and I, I felt, was wasting mine. Well, I am given to fits of melancholy, as you well know, and such a fit rooted inside me at this point. I could not forgive myself for being so ordinary. Night after night I stood in that room of the worst art ever assembled in one place and knew it was more than I had ever attempted, the ugliness of it all somehow more beautiful than anything I had ever done.

"I decided to take a break. I asked Darlene to come in, even though she usually took weekends off, to oversee our current high school girl, Eileen something or other, who seemed to be working through some kind of teenage hormonal thing, because every time I saw her, she appeared to have just finished a good cry. She was a good kid, I think, but at the time she depressed the hell out of me. 'She can't get over what happened between her and Randy,' Darlene told me. 'The abortion really shook her up. But don't say anything to her parents. They don't know.'

"'Darlene, I don't want to know.'

"Eventually it was settled. I was getting away from Castor and all things Castor related. I'd booked a room in a B & B in Sundale, on the shore. My duffel bag was packed with two novels, plenty of sunscreen, shorts and swimwear and flip-flops. I would sit in the sun. Walk along the shore. Swim. Read. Eat. I would not think about Emile Castor or the gray-eyed woman. Maybe I would meet somebody. Somebody real. Hey, anything was possible, now that I was getting away from Castor.

"Of course it rained. It started almost as soon as I left town and at times the rain became so heavy that I had to pull over on the side of the road. When I finally got to the small town on the shore, I was pretty wiped out. I drove in circles looking for the ironically named 'Sunshine Bed and Breakfast' until in frustration at the eccentricity of small towns, I decided that the pleasant-looking house with the simple sign 'B & B' must be it. I sat in the car for a moment hoping the rain would give me a break, and craned my neck at the distant looming steeple of a small chapel on the cliff above the roiling waters.

"It was clear the rain would continue its steady torrent, so I grabbed my duffel bag and slopped through the puddles in a sort of half trot, and entered a pleasant foyer of classical music, overstuffed chairs, a calico asleep in a basket on a table, and a large painting of, you probably already guessed, Emile Castor's gray-eyed beauty. Only in this rendition she really was. Beautiful. This artist had captured what Emile had not. It wasn't just a portrait, a photograph with paint if you will, no, this painting went beyond its subject's beauty into the realm of what is beautiful in art. I heard footsteps, deep breathing, a cough. I turned with reluctance and beheld the oldest man I'd ever seen. He was a lace of wrinkles and skin that sagged from his bones like an ill-fitting suit. He leaned on a walking stick and appraised me with gray eyes almost lost in the fold of wrinkles.

"'A beautiful piece of work,' I said.

"He nodded.

"I introduced myself and after a few confused minutes discovered that I was neither in Sundale nor at the Sunshine B & B. But I could not have been more pleased on any sunny day, in any location, than I was there, especially when I found out I could stay the night. When I asked about the painting and its subject, Ed, as he told me to call him, invited me to join him in the parlor for tea after I had 'settled in.'

"My room was pleasant, cozy, and clean without the creepy assortment of teddy bears too often assembled in B & Bs. From the window I had a view of the roiling sea, gray waves, the mournful swoop of seagulls, the cliff with the white chapel, its tall steeple tipped not with a cross but a ship, its great sails unfurled.

"When I found him in the parlor, Ed had a tray of tea and cookies set out on a low table before the fireplace which was nicely ablaze. The room was pleasant and inviting. The cold rain pounded the windows but inside it was warm and dry, the faint scent of lavender in the air.

"'Come, come join us.' Ed waved his hand, as arthritic as any I've ever seen, gnarled to almost a paw. I sat in the green wing chair across from him. An overstuffed rocking chair made a triangle of our seating arrangement but it was empty; not even the cat sat there.

"'Theresa!' he shouted, and he shouted again in a loud voice that reminded me of the young Marlon Brando calling for Stella.

"It occurred to me he might not be completely sane. But at the same moment I thought this, I heard a woman's voice and the sound of footsteps approaching from the other end of the house. I confess that for a moment I entertained the notion that it would be the gray-eyed woman, as if I had fallen into a Brigadoon of sorts, a magical place time could not reach, all time-ravaged evidence on Ed's face to the contrary.

"Just then that old face temporarily lost its wrinkled look and took on a divine expression. I followed the course of his gaze and saw the oldest woman in the world entering the room. I rose from my seat.

"'Theresa,' Ed said, 'Mr. Delano of Castor.'

"I strode across the room and offered my hand. She slid into it a small, soft glove of a hand and smiled at me with green eyes. She walked smoothly and with grace, but her steps were excruciatingly small and slow. To walk beside her was a lesson in patience, as we traversed the distance to Ed, who had taken to pouring the tea with hands that quivered so badly the china sounded like wind chimes. How had these two survived so long? In the distance, a cuckoo sang and I almost expected I would hear it again before we reached our destination.

"'Goodness,' she said, when I finally stood beside the rocking chair, 'I've never known a young man to walk so slowly.' She sat in the chair swiftly, and without any assistance on my part. I realized she'd been keeping her pace to mine as I thought I was keeping mine to hers. I turned to take my own seat and Ed grinned up at me, offering in his quivering hand a chiming teacup and saucer, which I quickly took.

"'Mr. Delano is interested in Elizabeth,' Ed said as he extended another jangling cup and saucer to her. She reached across and took it, leaning out of the chair in a manner I thought unwise.

"'What do you know about her?' she asked.

"'Mr. Emile Castor has made several, many, at least a thousand paintings of the same woman but nothing near to the quality of this one. That's all I know. I don't know what she was to him. I don't know anything.'

"Ed and Theresa both sipped their tea. A look passed between them. Theresa sighed. 'You tell him, Ed.'

"'It begins with Emile Castor arriving in town, a city man clear enough, with a mustache, and in his red roadster.'

"'But pleasant.'

"'He knew his manners.'

"'He was a sincerely pleasant man.'

"'He drove up to the chapel and like the idiot he mostly was, turns his back on it and sets up his easel and tries to paint the water down below.'

"'He wasn't an idiot. He was a decent man, and a good business-man. He just wasn't an artist.'

"'He couldn't paint water either.'

"'Well, water's difficult.'

"'Then it started to rain.'

"'You seem to get a lot.'

"'So finally he realizes there's a church right behind him and he packs up his puddle of paints and goes inside.'

"'That's when he sees her.'

"'Elizabeth?'

"'No. Our Lady. Oh, Mr. Delano, you really must see it.'

"'Maybe he shouldn't.'

"'Oh, Edward, why shouldn't he?'

"Edward shrugs. 'He was a rich man so he couldn't simply admire her without deciding that he must possess her as well. That's how the rich are.'

"'Edward, we don't know Mr. Delano's circumstances.'

"'He ain't rich.'

"'Well, we don't really—'

"'All you gotta do is look at his shoes. You ain't, are you?'

"'No.'

"'Can you imagine being so foolish you don't think nothing of trying to buy a miracle?'

"'A miracle? No.'

"'Well, that's how rich he was.'

"'He stayed on while he tried to convince the church to sell it to him.'

"'Idiot.'

"'They fell in love.'

"Ed grunted. 'They did. They both did.'

"'He offered a couple a barrels full of money.'

"'For the painting.'

"'I gotta say I do believe some on the church board wavered a bit but the women wouldn't hear of it.'

"'She is a miracle.'

"'Yep, that's what all the women folk said.'

"'Edward, you know it's true. More tea, Mr. Delano?'

"'Yes. Thank you. I'm not sure I'm following . . .'

"'You haven't seen it yet, have you?'

"'Theresa, he just arrived.'

"'We saw some of those other paintings he did of Elizabeth.'

"Ed snorts.

"'Well, he wasn't a quitter, you have to give him that.'

"Ed bites into a cookie and glares at the teapot.

"'What inspired him, well, what inspired him was Elizabeth, but what kept him at it was Our Lady.'

"'So are you saying, do you mean to imply that this painting, this Our Lady is magical?'

"'Not magic, a miracle.'

"'I'm not sure I understand.'

"'It's an icon, Mr. Delano, surely you've heard of them?'

"'Well, supposedly an icon is not just a painting, it is the holy manifested in the painting, basically.'

"'You must see it. Tomorrow. After the rain stops.'

"'Maybe he shouldn't.'

"'Why do you keep saying that, Edward? Of course he should see it.'

"Ed just shrugged.

"'Of course we didn't sell it to him and over time he stopped asking. They fell in love.'

"'He wanted her instead.'

"'Don't make it sound like that. He made her happy during what none of us knew were the last days of her life.'

"'After she died, he started the paintings.'

"'He wanted to keep her alive.'

"'He wanted to paint an icon.'

"'He never gave up until he succeeded. Finally, he painted our daughter Elizabeth.'

"'Are you saying Emile Castor painted that, in the foyer?'

"'It took years.'

"'He wanted to keep her alive somehow.'

"'But that painting, it's quite spectacular and his other work is so—'

"'Lousy.'

"'Anyone who enters this house wants to know about her.'

"'I don't mean to be rude but how did she—I'm sorry, please excuse me.'

"'Die?'

"'It doesn't matter.'

"'Of course it does. She fell from the church cliff. She'd gone up there to light a candle for Our Lady, a flame of gratitude. Emile had proposed and she had accepted. She went up there and it started raining while she was inside. She slipped and fell on her way home.'

"'How terrible.'

"'Oh, yes, but there are really so few pleasant ways to die.'

"Our own rain still lashed the windows. The fat calico came into the room and stopped to lick her paws. We just sat there, listening to the rain and the clink of china cup set neatly in saucer. The tea was good and hot. The fire smelled strangely of chocolate. I looked at their two old faces in profile, wrinkled as poorly folded maps. Then I proceeded to make a fool of myself by explaining to them my position as curator of the Castor museum. I described the collection, the beautiful house and location by a stream visited by deer, but I did not describe the dismal town, and ended with a description of Emile's horrible work, the room filled with poor paintings of their daughter, surely, I told them, Elizabeth belonged there, redeemed against the vast assortment of clowns, for the angel she was. When I was finished the silence was sharp. Neither spoke nor looked at me, but even so, as though possessed by some horrible tic, I continued. 'Of course we'd pay you handsomely.' Theresa bowed her head and I thought that perhaps this was the posture she took for important decisions until I realized she was crying.

"Ed turned slowly, his old head like a marionette's on an uncertain string. He fixed me with a look that told me what a fool I was and will always be.

"'Please accept my apology for being so . . .' I said, finding myself speaking and rising as though driven by the same puppeteer's hand. 'I can't tell you how . . . Thank you.' I turned abruptly and walked out of the room, angry at my clumsy social skills, in despair, actually, that I had made a mess of such a pleasant afternoon. I intended to hurry to my room and read my book until dinner, when I would skulk down the stairs and try to find a decent place to eat. That I could insult and hurt two such kind people was unforgivable. I was actually almost blind with self-loathing until I entered the foyer and saw her out of the corner of my eye.

"It is really quite impossible to describe that other thing that brings a painting beyond competent, even beyond beauty into the realm of great art. Of course she was a beautiful woman; of course the lighting, colors, composition, brushstroke, all of these elements could be separated and described, but this still did not account for that ethereal feeling, the sense one gets standing next to a masterpiece, the need to take a deep breath as if suddenly the air consumed by one is needed for two.

"Instead of going upstairs I went out the front door. If this other painting was anything like the one of Elizabeth, then I must see it.

"It was dark, the rain only a drizzle now, the town a slick black oil, maybe something by Dali with disappearing ink. I had, out of habit, pocketed my car keys. I had to circle the town a few times, make a few false starts, once finding myself in someone's driveway, before I selected the road that arched above the town to the white chapel, which even in the rain glowed as though lit from within. The road was winding but not treacherous. When I got to the top and stood on that cliff the wind whipped me, the town below was lost in a haze of fog that only a few yellow lights shone through. I had the sensation of looking down on the heavens from above. The waves crashed and I felt the salt on my face, tasted it on my lips. Up close the chapel was much larger than it looked from below, the steeple that narrowed to a needle point on which its ship balanced into the dark sky, quite imposing. As I walked up those stone steps I thought again of Edward saying he wasn't sure I should see it. I reached for the hammered iron handle and pulled. For a moment I thought it was locked, but it was just incredibly heavy. I pulled the door open and entered the darkness of the church. Behind me, the door heaved shut. I smelled a flowery, smoky scent, the oily odor of wood, and heard from somewhere a faint drip of water as though there was a leak. I was in the church foyer; there was another door before me, marked in the darkness by the thin line of light that shone beneath it. I walked gingerly, uncertain in the dark. It too was extremely heavy. I pulled it open."

He coughed and cleared his throat as though suddenly suffering a cold. She opened her eyes just a slit. The heat from the wood stove must have been the reason for the red in his cheeks; how strange he looked, as though in pain or fever! She let her eyes droop shut and it seemed a long time before he continued, his voice raspy.

"All I can say is, I never should have looked. I wish I'd never seen either of those paintings. It was there that I made myself the promise I would never settle for a love any less than spectacular, a love so great that it would take me past my limitations, the way Emile's love for Elizabeth had taken him past his, that somehow such a love would leave an imprint on the world, the way great art does, that all who saw it would be changed by it, as I was.

"So you see, when you find me sad and ask what's on my mind, or when I am quiet and cannot explain to you the reason, there it is. If I had never seen the paintings, maybe I would be a happy man. But always, now, I wonder."

She waited but he said no more. After a long time, she whispered his name. But he did not answer, and when she peeked at him from the squint of her eyes, he appeared to be asleep. Eventually, she fell asleep too.

All that night, as they told their stories, the flames burned heat onto that icy roof, which melted down the sides of the house and over the windows so that in the cold morning when they woke up, the fire gone to ash and cinder, the house was encased in a sort of skin of ice, which they tried to alleviate by burning another fire, not realizing they were only sealing themselves in more firmly. They spent the rest of that whole winter in their ice house. By burning all the wood and most of the furniture and eating canned food even if it was out of date, they survived, thinner and less certain of fate, into a spring morning thaw, though they never could forget those winter stories, not all that spring or summer and especially not that autumn, when the winds began to carry that chill in the leaves, that odd combination of sun and decay, about which they did not speak, but which they knew would exist between them forever.

The Corpse Painter's Masterpiece

The corpse painter lives in a modest Cape Cod at the end of a dirt road, once lined with pasture, cows, and corn. The farmland was sold off in the seventies for the new mall. Everyone said the corpse painter was quite foolish for refusing the developer's money, but what else can be expected of a corpse painter, after all? He remained in his little clapboard house with the pink rose bush growing around the mailbox. The old mailman, Baxter, used to put on a gardening glove to deliver the mail there, but the new one refuses; the corpse painter's mail is piled up at the post office in town, undeliverable because of thorns.

The mall entrance was not on the dirt road, yet for almost three decades, the corpse painter had to put up with the (mostly young) drivers who came out of the mall parking lot and made two wrong turns (or thought they were taking a shortcut) and ended up with their headlights glaring into the corpse painter's living room. The lights from the mall were bad enough. It hunkered like a strange massive spaceship obliterating the golden fields, the languid cows, the purple horizon. Those who found themselves at the end of the dirt road, facing the broken picket fence, the mailbox wrapped in roses with thorns like teeth, the corpse painter's sign dangling over the crooked porch, often realized where they were with a shock of combined pleasure and fear, like finding Santa Claus in a graveyard. Many had heard rumors of the corpse painter but dismissed them as childish myth. They took some pleasure in discovering the fact of him until the full implication took hold. The corpse painter needed neither dog nor keep-out sign; his occupation was enough. Only those entirely foreign to the area would linger, trying to determine if it would be a good idea to knock and ask for directions, though no one ever did. The lights of the mall glowed in the rearview mirror. Better to go back, it was thought. Visitors were quite rare anyway, it was not the sort of mall to attract outsiders, and by 2010, it was no longer a mall, but an empty building in an empty parking lot, though the lights still burned there, meant to keep away the kind of trouble abandoned buildings attract. The corpse painter often sat on the top step of his front porch, enjoying the effect of lights brightening against the dusk—anything can be beautiful if looked at long enough, even the ugly mall with its unnatural sunset, the white light an illumination, like bones.

The sheriff, who had been there before, knew that the corpse painter's stone driveway, which appeared to arc over a small hill to the barn-converted-to-garage below, had a tributary that veered narrowly to the back door of the house. The sheriff knocked on the aluminum door there, cataloguing, as he always did, the repairs needed to restore the place, which the corpse painter left unattended as though it was something meant to decompose.

When the corpse painter came to the door, he opened it wide. The sheriff wiped his shoes on the mat, remembering how he used to come with his own father as a boy. "Don't want to drag in mud and blood," the sheriff's father always said. Every time. The sheriff, who hated the saying, cannot get it out of his head. He wipes his shoes on the mat and hears his father's voice. The sheriff doesn't believe in ghosts, but he does believe in hauntings.

"Evening," the sheriff says, though why, he doesn't know. He takes off his cap. He was raised to be polite.

The corpse painter, who is a thin man, delicate in a way the sheriff finds disturbing, doesn't say anything, only stands there, watching. His eyes are large, gray-green. From what the sheriff can remember, the corpse painter takes after his mother, though she was a better housekeeper. She always greeted the sheriff, when he was a boy, with cumin bread, which she said kept restless spirits away.

The sheriff turns from the corpse painter's penetrating stare. "What's he like?" his wife asks. They have a modern marriage, not like his parents. "Now, you know not to say anything about this," his father always said after they visited the small house in the country, which, only in later years, filled the sheriff with shame as though he were the adulterer of his own mother.

"It's him," he says. Trying for mercy, he looks out the kitchen window at the junk-littered yard: a broken bicycle, a three-legged chair, unbound rope, something blackly snakelike, a deflated inner-tube, perhaps, all loosely scattered near the infamous fire pit.

The sheriff turns, hoping to catch the corpse painter unaware, to see something within those ferrety eyes that he could report; instead he sees what he always sees there. "He's all right," the sheriff tells his wife. "I just can't stand the way he looks at me."

"What's that mean?" his wife asks. "You have to be specific."

"Ok, let's look," the corpse painter says.

The sheriff puts his cap on and walks ahead of the corpse painter as they've been doing for years now. The sheriff knows that there are rumors about this; not everyone approves. He could lose his job over it, and imagines that one day he will. Over the years he has brought the corpse painter thieves, drug dealers, and murderers. Mostly murderers. Once, a long time ago now, there was a young woman no one claimed.

"She's already done," the corpse painter had said, shaking his head. "Don't bring me anyone beautiful."

The sheriff's boots crunch against the stones in the driveway. He inserts the key in the hatch and lifts it without ceremony, the air suddenly infused with the stink of death.

"Can't get 'em much uglier than this," the sheriff says, and immediately regrets it. He always was a smart aleck, which he has mostly tamed over the years, except in times of deep emotion. "Sorry," he mumbles. He meant to do this right. He meant to show compassion, but in a situation like this, it is hard to know how to do that.

But the corpse painter is already reaching in; nothing in the back of him betrays anything to the sheriff of the particular unusual nature of this situation. "Like he was going to stack a cord of wood," the sheriff later said to his wife, who, not satisfied, thought that maybe, just maybe after all these years, she might have to visit the corpse painter herself. She'd bring a pie, or banana bread, perhaps, though she knows from experience these sweets will most likely grow mold or

turn sour, thrown in the trash; who has an appetite near death? Maybe
it's different for the corpse painter, maybe it is a celebration, she has
no idea. She didn't mention the idea of bringing food, and the next
morning wondered how something so obviously bizarre by the light
of day could seem so normal in the dark.

"What time?" she asks when he leans over to kiss her good-bye.

"The usual."

"I'll be there."

"Was there ever any doubt?" the sheriff says, trying to be cheerful, though it comes out sounding smart-alecky. His wife, up to her
chin in blankets, looks embarrassed. "Good," he says, trying to make
it right, and she does look peaceful when he leaves the bedroom, her
eyes closed, her face like stone. The sheriff thought his wife would
grow out of it eventually, oh, not the sorrow, he never imagined that,
but he thought one day she would crawl out of bed, shower, maybe go
back to work, the way he had. In the beginning she'd be in bed when
he left in the morning, and still there when he came home after dark.
She was like that until, quite by accident, she discovered her love of
prison funerals. The sheriff backs his car out of the driveway. He's
careful about it. He's always been a careful driver, but children are so
small. At the bottom of the driveway he taps the horn, then proceeds
at a reasonable speed for the early morning traffic of schoolchildren;
he flicks on the radio, and listens for the weather, which is the only
thing he cares about on the news anymore. The sheriff thinks about
the corpse painter, who stayed up all night, painting, that's the hope.
The sheriff is concerned about what he might find when he goes
back there this morning. The corpse painter is a little nuts. Obviously.
Who can blame him?

The corpse painter's father was one of those men who became a
success in prison. He had a little business on the side, selling, of all
things, paper sculptures. Even now, the sheriff can't believe that the
other prisoners would have any interest in such nonsense, but sometimes a fad takes hold, especially during the holidays. Last Christmas,
the sheriff decided to test his theory that the success was based on
illusion, nothing that would matter in the rational world. He doesn't
know what became of the necklace he'd given his wife; he assumes the

chocolate-covered cherries were eaten, though he never saw her take a single bite; but the little paper house, with the paper picket fence, the paper shutters that opened and closed, the paper tree with blobs of something hanging from the paper branches, leaves he supposes, maybe bats, remains on the fireplace mantel where his wife put it on Christmas morning. He noticed, but did not comment on, the fact that she liked to decorate for the seasons. In the spring she set a saucer of wheat berries up there, watering them until they sprouted like grass, which she cut all summer long with the fingernail scissors that she used to use on the boy. Yesterday he'd noticed the small yard was littered with torn leaves, proving she'd gone out at least long enough to scoop a handful of the dead things up. This morning he'd seen the house, the tree, the yard all draped with black crepe paper. Did she do this for every funeral? Was it a bad sign or a sign of something good, or a sign of nothing, which is what the sheriff mostly believes in now. After all, he's seen things. He's seen bodies that look blasted, eyes open, the expression of horror locked there. For a while the sheriff thought if he only knew how to read those eyes, he'd find in them the reflection of the murderer. It was a crazy thought, of course. He never told anyone how his own son's eyes locked him inside their irises. Why had she let the boy out that morning? What child rides his tricycle in his pajamas? He never asked. They weren't reasonable questions and the answers wouldn't satisfy. Sometimes, after something horrible, a person goes crazy for a while. He screwed his head back on; he got on with his life. Not everyone does.

The corpse painter sits on his front step; too late to watch the sunrise, he watches the mall lights blink off, all of them at once, a sacred moment like seeing a shooting star, or a fish jump. He would like a cup of tea, but he's too exhausted to get up, too exhausted even to put the kettle on. When he inhales, deeply, he sees his breath. As a youngster, his mother told him it was his own soul he was seeing. The air smells sharply cold, the scent of dead leaves and the dirt turning hard; he also smells the oils he works with, rosemary and eucalyptus mostly, a little rose for the anus; his hands are a rainbow of pigment. He coughs. He should go inside. Put on something warm. Judging by this morning's temperature, this will be the last body of the year. There's no burying when the ground is frozen. His mother would have said the spirits made it happen the way it did. Another week, by the looks of it, maybe even another day, the body would not have been brought to him. The corpse painter made a rare trip to town for the sheriff's son's funeral, a strange affair with an open casket. The corpse painter felt revulsion when he saw the poor child made to look so unnatural, as though sleeping on the pink satin pillow. Certainly it was no comfort to the mother, how could it be, the child's lips reddened, the cheeks rosy as a clown's? Afterward, everyone was invited to the sheriff's house for some kind of party, but the corpse painter went home instead.

Yet, when the sheriff comes, pulling into the driveway, heading toward the garage, he doesn't appear to notice the corpse painter sitting there. He stands slowly, his muscles sore, as though he'd been out all night dancing. He walks around the back, crunching across the gravel. The sheriff doesn't jump, exactly, but he seems startled by the corpse painter, as though he's grown more comfortable in a world where a man's passage is marked by the unlocking of locks, the rattle of heavy keys.

"Mornin'," the sheriff says, tipping his head slightly. "All set?"

The sheriff has been bringing bodies to the corpse painter for twenty years now; he is the closest thing the corpse painter has to friend or family, and when has he ever not been ready? He has no idea how to respond to something so obvious; it would be like asking the sheriff if he misses his son. There is a lot the corpse painter doesn't understand about the way folks interact, but one thing he is certain of is that people want to be seen, not buried like that poor boy, beneath rouge and cream. Why else would there be death, after all, if not for revelation?

The corpse painter says none of this, of course. It, too, is obvious. Instead he merely waits until the sheriff turns away, they walk to the garage, their footsteps brittle across the stones; the corpse painter looks at the ground, a habit developed as a boy. He knows he's reached the garage when he sees the warped wood flaking chips of red. He pulls the door open with a rumble, like thunder.

The Sheriff hesitates before stepping inside, a handkerchief held to his nose. The corpse painter flicks on the light. He watches the Sheriff walk to the body, painted with pigmented oil, decomposing even as they stand there, the closest thing there is to living art, shimmering beneath the naked light, a harlequin, the illusion of movement created by the pore-size spots of color, gradated with white.

"You make him look—"the Sheriff starts, but catching himself, stops.

The corpse painter has had all night to look at the body, he can see it with his eyes closed, now he studies the Sheriff whose fleshy face, usually as constant as a mask, twitches and contorts, a small muscle beneath the eye, the flare of nostrils, a pulse at the neck, a protrusion beneath the cheek, certainly the tongue working there. "How?" the sheriff croaks.

The corpse painter knows the sheriff is not asking about technique. The corpse painter also knows how much courage it took for the sheriff to ask the question. But how? How to explain? He doesn't think he can say it any better than he already has, on the body.

"You're invited to the cemetery if you want. My wife will be there. She's been making them do it nice."

The corpse painter considers the offer. After all, this is not just any body, this is his father's body, the man who made the corpse painter's own body a harlequin of bruises, which is only a footnote to the horrible things done, and yet the corpse painter knows that creation never travels far from destruction.

"All right," the sheriff says, apparently mistaking the silence for an answer. He turns around, going back to the car for the box to carry the body in, knowing the corpse painter will follow.

The funeral goes the way they usually do. No one seems to care that the body, in spite of the cold, is beginning to leak through the poorly joined slats. The sheriff knows that a few people think his wife has gone nuts; he resents the way they humor her, even as he appreciates it. The prison chaplain does the blessing and a reading of the sheriff's wife's choosing, always strange and incongruent, though everyone pretends that excerpts from *The Velveteen Rabbit* and *Peter Pan* are perfectly normal funeral meditations.

The sheriff doesn't know what was read for the corpse painter's father, though later he wished he'd paid closer attention. He couldn't concentrate. He kept thinking of what lay inside that wooden box, a man who had done terrible things, made beautiful by one of his victims.

The sheriff's wife always invited the chaplain, the grave diggers, and the sheriff to the house after the funeral. Embarrassed, they always declined. The sheriff had no idea what strange emotion infected him that day, but he said yes, he'd come home for lunch, and then rested his heavy arm on the chaplain's shoulder, more or less dragging him along. The wife blinked in surprise at this. She whispered to the sheriff to drive home slowly, which he did, arriving at the house with the strange company of chaplain and grave diggers, just in time to see her scuttle inside with a bag from the Piggly Wiggly, which they all pretended not to notice.

She set out a tray of lunch meat and cheese slices, a basket of rolls, pickles and olives. When the sheriff saw what was lacking he went into the kitchen for the jars of mayonnaise and mustard, which his wife spooned into small bowls. They ate off paper plates perched on the edge of their knees, the scent of brewed coffee filling the house.

The conversation was stilted and strange, but afterward, when the visitors left, the sheriff's wife kissed him on the forehead before he returned to work. That night, she set the leftovers out for him, the bread slightly stale, the meat and cheese dry, but the sheriff made a big deal out of how he was hoping this was just what they'd have for dinner. She turned away, so he wasn't sure, but he thought she smiled.

That night the sheriff can't sleep. He lies in bed with his eyes wide open; how can she sleep, he wonders, with the light so bright? He finally gets up to look out the window, but there is not, as he'd supposed, a new streetlight there, and the old has not been repositioned to shine directly on him. The sheriff, when he thinks about all this later, decides that he must have been half asleep, which would explain his strange behavior. He'd padded on his bare feet, cold across the floor to the kitchen, opening the refrigerator, certain that it was the source of light, and there was, in fact, a light there, burning whitely, but how did it remain when the door was closed? He has no idea how many times he opened and closed the refrigerator door, trying to work it out before his wife found him there and brought him back to bed. He tried to tell her about the light but she told him there was no light anywhere, to close his eyes, go to sleep, which apparently he did.

But the next night it happens again, and the night after that as well, until the sheriff is so tired he can't think straight. He doesn't even try to go to bed but lies in his lounge chair, and when the light arrives, follows it out the door to the end of the block in his pajamas, before he comes to his senses and goes back for the car.

He follows the light through the quiet streets, until he thinks he knows where he's going, and it turns out he is right. He parks his car at the cemetery. The light emanates from there, brighter than anywhere else. The sheriff shakes his head against the impossibility of what his mind has imagined; he is a rational man, this isn't happening, but still he must follow, he must, he walks slowly over the hill, past the headstones decorated with pumpkins and turkeys to the grave he knew he'd arrive at, the headstone carved with a small lamb, a little pot of yellow flowers beneath it: his son.

The sheriff begins pawing at the ground, scraping his cold fingers against the hard earth; he will get in there if he has to use his teeth. He isn't even embarrassed when Sam, the graveyard's neighbor and unofficial guard, finds him and tries to get him to stop. The sheriff refuses to answer and after a bit, Sam leaves. When he returns, the sheriff's fingers are bloody. Sam, whose own son was born the same year as the sheriff's, has a pickax, a hoe, a shovel, a large thermos of hot water, and chains. The morning sun is bleeding the sky pink by the time they hoist the tiny casket.

Sam doesn't ask why. Not then, or ever. He doesn't want to know. He hopes never to understand this particular kind of madness.

They carry the casket to the car. The sheriff turns back to repair the damage left in the cemetery but Sam tells him to go.

"Get out of here with that," he says.

Which the sheriff does, driving carefully because of the bright light burning in his car, almost blinding him. It's a good thing he knows these roads so well.

The corpse painter tends to sleep in during the winter, catching up on his rest after all those nights of painting the dead; he sleeps a lot, sometimes he doesn't change out of his pajamas for a week. Once the frost arrives, he prunes the roses back, his mail is delivered again, he spends his days catching up on bills, paging through thick catalogues of art supplies and magazines with photographs of perfect little teapots, expensively framed paintings, artists with tousled hair and knowing smiles, which he finds deeply disturbing. The corpse painter drinks coffee and watches *Oprah*. He falls asleep wherever sleep finds him—the couch, the lounge chair, the kitchen, sitting at the table—he dreams about the dead, working with the flesh coarsening beneath his fingers, waking with the terrible knowledge that when he dies, there will be no one to do the same for him, which seems a terrible waste.

He is in the midst of such a terror, waking in the chair where he'd fallen asleep, when he sees the sheriff's car turn into the driveway, disappearing around the side of the house, the way he does when he brings a body. The corpse painter wipes his hand across his chin, feeling the stubble of whiskers. He is confused. Why is the sheriff here at this time of year? Was winter's approach only a dream? Is it still summer, the roses embracing the mailbox, the grass green, everything in the house, the stacks of mail, the catalogues, the mugs with moldy coffee a symptom of spring? Has the corpse painter slept all winter? He shuffles in his slippers to the back door, where the sheriff stands, knocking on the aluminum frame.

The corpse painter opens the door for the sheriff, who shakes his head, turns, walks down the steps toward his car. The corpse painter, not sure what else to do, follows, though it is cold out here in pajamas, and his feet hurt in the soft-soled slippers, walking across stones.

The sheriff inserts the key in the latch and raises it, ignoring the corpse painter's protest. He is struck silent anyway by the small casket there, once white, now muddied. He knows who it is. He wipes his eyes while he tries to work out what to say.

"I know, I know," says the sheriff. "It's really bright, but you get used to it after a while. Like the sun."

The corpse painter shakes his head.

"Hey, I got a pair of sunglasses in the glove compartment. You can have them." The sheriff walks to the front of the car. The corpse painter watches a clod of dirt slide down the casket. The sheriff returns and hands the sunglasses to the corpse painter, who can't think what else to do with them, so he puts them on.

"Hey," the sheriff says, "you look good with those." He scratches his chin. That's when the corpse painter notices that the sheriff's hands are scraped and bloody, that he, too, is wearing pajamas.

"Come inside," the corpse painter says. "I'll make coffee."

The sheriff frowns. "I don't know. Don't you think he'll—"

"He's fine," the corpse painter says.

The sheriff tilts his head, then, with a slight nod, closes the hatch and follows the corpse painter into the house, which is a real mess, but warm. The sheriff has never sat at the corpse painter's kitchen table, not when he was a boy and came with his father and not in all the years since he's been bringing bodies here. They sit together in the dim light, though the sheriff can still see the glow emanating from the car beyond the window. They drink coffee and talk. The corpse painter delicately addresses the limitations of bones but the sheriff says he's not worried. "I've seen what you can do," he says. "I know you'll get it right." The corpse painter is not beyond being flattered. He nods as though it's no problem when the sheriff says he wants it in time for Christmas. "A gift for the wife," he says. "Anyway, I should get back. I don't want her to guess what I'm up to. I want it to be a surprise." The corpse painter walks with the sheriff to the car. One of them could do it alone, but they carry the casket together, into the house, set it on the kitchen table, surrounded by all the mail. Suddenly self-conscious, not used to the newly established camaraderie, they say an awkward good-bye.

———

Sometimes in the weeks that follow, when the sheriff wakes in the middle of the night, he wonders if he imagined everything: the boy's death, the horror, the guilt, the long hours, the emptiness, the wife's sorrow, the corpse painter, the darkness, and the light. In the dark, the sheriff thinks, chuckling softly to himself, it is so easy to think that the light was only a dream. He lies there, with his hands behind his head, watching the shadows on the ceiling, and considers how much of life is filled with the shock of all those certain things. Every year it happens like this. The frost is shocking, as is the snow, the first flakes drifting past the window and sticking to nothing at all, very shocking. Sometimes, when he looks at his wife, expecting to see the woman he married but finding instead this person whose face has morphed into something resembling a marshmallow, a not unpleasant face, but old, he is shocked, and he is shocked by the mirror as well. They were all shocked by the boy's death, though that of course was the only thing certain once he was born. The sheriff's wife snores softly. She's been better lately. He thinks. And that is not shocking at all; it is almost ordinary, though not ordinary, of course, because if it were ordinary, he would not be lying in his bed thinking about the ordinariness of it. The sheriff has never been very philosophical, but what person doesn't stop on occasion to take account?

Lately, they've been sleeping with the curtains open. His wife objected at first, but told him after a few nights that she'd grown to like it. Sometimes, they lie together and look out the window at the moon, or watch the snow drift past the streetlamp. He thought, on just such an occasion, to tell her about the light that had woken him, shining from their son's grave, but didn't want to ruin the surprise.

So, on Christmas Eve, when he drives to the corpse painter's house, the sky gray with clouds, the sheriff is pleased with himself for keeping such a big secret. *This is going to be good,* he thinks.

The corpse painter had never worked like this. He had not used these tools, and he had not worked with bone before. He had not worked in the winter, with its poor lighting and the cold that rendered his fingers stiff. For the first time since he has been running the place, he ordered a cord of wood for the wood-burning stove. The corpse painter worked by fire day into night, listening to boys' choirs on the classical station, their voices filling the corpse painter with beauty as though beauty was something that could become a part of being human, not something seen, but something known, like breath. He carved, and etched, filed and sanded. A child has two hundred and eight bones, but of course many were broken, shards of sharp points, strange shapes he couldn't identify. Some he set aside. He couldn't possibly get them all done; he concentrated on the largest. He sent for wax in bricks he melted on the stove. He forgot to eat, only remembering when his hands were shaking; he ate nuts and cheese while he sang along with the boys, remembering the boy he had been, as he worked on the bones, and in this way he worked until Christmas Eve, and the corpse painter showed the sheriff, and the sheriff said it was good, and invited the corpse painter for Christmas dinner. The corpse painter surprised them both by saying maybe he would. The sheriff carried the box; it was a large box lined with paper so the bones wouldn't rattle. The corpse painter told the sheriff about the rest, the tiny pieces, the broken shards, the bits he hadn't used. The sheriff just shook his head. *No, no* he said, *you keep them. Never mind.*

By the time the sheriff left, it was almost dark, the snow had stopped, there had been just enough to make the children happy, to create a winter wonderland like the one his wife had fashioned on the mantel with bits of cotton around the paper house. They hadn't had a tree since the accident, but this year she'd hung a wreath on the front door, and she'd bought some new decorations in strange colors, a pink feathery thing, a silver ball, even a reindeer, though it was a strange shade of green, not like Christmas at all, more the color of a bruise. The sheriff understood. It was a way of starting over. Not from the beginning, which, shockingly (he chuckled) was gone forever, but from where they were now.

They ate supper at the table. She'd made mashed potatoes, and boiled chicken, then panicked when she realized how white it looked on the plate. "What are you talking about," he said. "It's perfect," and it did taste very good. There were the usual phone calls, then they watched TV—he sat in his chair, and she on the couch—flipping past the Christmas movies, settling finally for the weather station, until it broadcasted Santa's passage across the sky; she turned it off, and said, "He would have been seven this year." This too was shocking. He tried to imagine it, but could not. They went to bed. They lay side by side, watching the dark sky out their window, and the streetlights glow. The longer he lay there, the more certain the sheriff was that this was the time to give her the present, obviously, why hadn't he thought of it before? It was a gift for the dark, after all.

"Are you awake?" he asks.

"I was just thinking."

"I forgot to tell you. I invited him for dinner tomorrow."

"Who?"

"I'm not sure he'll even come. We have extra, right? There's always so much food for Christmas."

"I haven't cooked like that in years."

"We could have sandwiches."

The sheriff's wife is almost amused. How could he do this? What was he thinking? By the streetlamp glow, she looks at her husband. She hasn't looked at him in years, only recently realizing that something's not right about him, which she finds reassuring. How could anything ever be right again? For a while, she'd thought he'd moved on somehow, back to normal. "We're not having sandwiches. I bought a turkey breast and a box of stuffing."

"The corpse painter," he says.

"He's coming here? To our house?"

"Probably not. Hey," the sheriff says, as though he only just thought of it. "I got you a present." He jumps out of bed and trots out into the hallway while she lies there thinking about the strangeness of life. When he returns, carrying the large package, he is grinning broadly, like one of those crazy jack-o'-lanterns. She scoots back to sit up against the pillows. He places the large, surprisingly heavy package in her lap, kisses her on the forehead.

———

After the sheriff left with the gift for his wife, the corpse painter considered the remaining bones. He thought of making jewelry, or delicate carvings, intricate knots, or infinitesimal vases, but in the end he dumped them in the fire pit. This is what they'd always done on Christmas Eve, only later learning that the bones his father brought home were never his to burn. He said they were from the butcher, roadkill, something dead in the forest. The corpse painter never imagined his father was a good man, he doesn't know how his mother ever did, but neither of them had guessed at the cost of those bones.

He waits until the dark is settled like something permanent, the sky everywhere deeply black, starless, and the clouds black too in the deep ink of night. He pulls on his socks, his boots, remembering in these simple gestures the small fingers shivering at the buckles, daring to believe in the magic of a night he did not know was haunted. He opens the door and almost turns back. It is so cold he can see his soul. He loves the sound he makes walking across the snow-dusted stones, then just the snow. No one shouts for him to hurry, there is no uncertainty of how the night will end, like a tumor, though he does have to remind himself that his father is dead, painted and buried. He throws sticks in with the bones, that's the way to start a fire. He watches it burn until it is good and set, then feeds it until the flames shoot up to the sky, and he is warm, remembering the things he wants to forget, wishing he could cast them into the fire as well.

The sheriff's wife turns the strange things in her hand. "These are bones," she says, not certain until she says it and he doesn't disagree. "Turn on the light so I can see better," she says.

But the sheriff has a different idea. He takes one from the box and sets it on the dresser, amidst the junk of receipts, spare change, lint, and socks. He shoves all that away to set the thing there, and then, he lights it; she sees the carving like lace, light spills across the room in flakes, like snow, light flutters to the ceiling like angels.

"Where did you—"

He sets more on the small wooden chair, shoving the papers off to do so (*what are those papers anyway*, she wonders, *I must be going crazy*),

The Christmas Witch

The children of Stone collect bones, following cats through twisted, narrow streets, chasing them away from tiny birds, dead gray mice (with sweet round ears, pink inside like seashells), and fish washed on the rocky shore. The children show each other their bone collections, tiny white femurs, infinitesimal wings, jawbones with small teeth intact. Occasionally, parents find these things; they scold the little hoarder, or encourage the practice by setting up a science table. It's a stage children go through, they assume, this fascination with structure, this cold approach to death. The parents do not discuss it with each other, except in passing. ("Oh yes, the skeleton stage.") The parents do not know, they do not guess that once the found bones are tossed out or put on display, the children begin to collect again. They collect in earnest.

Rachel Boyle has begun collecting bones, though her father doesn't know about it, of course. Her mother, being dead, might know. Rachel can't figure that part out. Her mother is not a ghost, the Grandma told her, but a spirit. The Grandma lives far away, in Milwaukee. Rachel didn't even remember her when she came for the funeral. "You remember me, honey, don't you?" she asked and Rachel's father said, "Of course she remembers you." Rachel went in the backyard where she tore flowers while her father and the Grandma sat at the kitchen table and cried. After the Grandma left, Rachel and her father moved to Stone.

Rachel doesn't get off the school bus at her house, because her father is still at work. She gets off at Peter Williamson's house. The first time she found Peter with his bone collection spread out before him on the bedroom floor she thought it was gross. But the second time she sat across from him and asked him what they were for.

Peter shrugged. "You know," he said.

Rachel shook her head.

"Didn't they teach you anything in Boston? They're for Wilmot Redd, the witch. You know. A long time ago. An old lady. She lived right here in Stone. They hung her. There's a sign about her on Old Burial Hill but she's not buried there. No one knows where she ended up."

That's when Rachel began collecting bones. She stored them in her sock drawer, she stored them under her bed, she had several in her jewelry box, and two chicken legs buried in the flowerpot from her mother's funeral. The flowers were dead, but it didn't matter; she wouldn't let her father throw them out.

For Halloween, Rachel wants to be dead but her father says she can't be. "How about a witch?" he says. "Or a princess?"

"Peter's going to be dead," she says. "He'll have a knife going right through the top of his head, and blood dripping down his face."

"How about a cat? You can have a long tail and whiskers."

"Mariel is going to be a pilgrim."

"You can be a pilgrim."

"Pilgrims are dead! Jeez, Dad, didn't they teach you anything in Boston?"

"Don't talk to me like that."

Rachel sighs. "Okay, I'll be a witch."

"Fine, we'll paint your face green and you can wear a wig."

"Not that kind of witch."

Her father turns out the light and kisses her on the forehead before he leaves her alone in the dark. All of a sudden Rachel is scared. She thinks of calling her father. Instead, she counts to fifty before she pulls back the covers and sneaks around in the dark of her room, gathering the bones, which she pieces together into a sort of puzzle shape of a funny little creature, right on top of her bed. She uses a skull, and a long bone that might be from a fish, the small shape of a mouse paw, and a couple of chicken legs. She sucks her thumb while she waits for it to do the silly dance again.

———

On Tuesday, Mrs. Williamson has a doctor's appointment. Rachel still gets off the bus with Peter. They still go to his house. There, the baby-sitter waits for them. Her name is Melinda. She has long blond hair, a pierced navel, pierced tongue, ears pierced all the way around the edge, and rings on every finger. She wraps her arms around Peter and wrestles him to the floor. He screams but he is smiling. After a while she lets go and turns to Rachel.

Rachel wishes Melinda would wrap her arms around her, but she doesn't. "My name's Melinda," she says. Rachel nods. Her father already told her. He wouldn't let her be watched by a stranger. "Who wants popcorn?" Melinda says and races Peter into the kitchen. Rachel follows, even though she doesn't really like popcorn.

Peter tells Melinda about his plans for Halloween. He tells her about the knife through his head while the oil heats up in the pan. Melinda tosses in a kernel. Peter runs out of the room.

"What are you going to be?" Melinda asks, but before Rachel can answer, Peter is back in the kitchen, the knife in his head, blood dripping around the eyes. Melinda says, "Oh, gross, that's so great, it looks really gross." The kernel pops. Melinda pours more kernels into the pan and then slaps the lid on. "Hey, dead man," she says, "how about getting the butter?"

Peter gets a stick of butter out of the refrigerator. He places it on the cutting board. He takes a sharp knife out of the silverware drawer. Popcorn steam fills the kitchen. Rachel feels sleepy, sitting at the island. She leans her head into her hand; her eyes droop. Peter makes a weird sound and drops the knife on the counter. Blood trickles from his finger and over the butter. Melinda sets the pan on a cold burner, turns off the stove, and wraps Peter's finger in paper towel. Rachel isn't positive but she thinks Peter is crying beneath his mask.

"It's okay," Melinda says. "It's just a little cut." She steers Peter through the kitchen toward the bathroom. Rachel looks at the blood on the butter; one long red drop drips down the side. She stares at the kitchen window, foggy with steam. For a second she thinks some-one is standing out there, watching, but no one is. Peter and Melinda come back into the kitchen. Peter no longer has the knife through his head. His hair is stuck up funny, his face pink, and he has a Band-Aid on his finger. He sits at the island beside Rachel but doesn't look at her. Melinda slices the bloody end of butter and tosses it into the trash. She cuts a chunk off, places it in a glass bowl and sticks it in the microwave. "So, what are you going to be for Halloween?"

"Wilmot Redd," Rachel says.

"You can't," says Melinda.

"Don't you know anything?" Peter asks.

"Be nice, Peter." Melinda pours the popcorn into a big purple bowl and drips melted butter over it. "You can't be Wilmot Redd."

"Why not?"

Melinda puts ice in three glasses and fills them with Dr Pepper. She sits down at the island, across from Peter and Rachel. "If I tell you, you can't tell your dad."

Rachel has heard about secrets like this. When a grownup tells you not to tell your parents something, it is a bad secret. Rachel is thrilled to be told one. "I won't," she says.

"Okay, I know you think witches wear pointy black hats and act like the bad witch in *The Wizard of Oz* but they don't. Witches are just regular people and they look and dress like everyone else. Stone is full of witches. I can't tell you who all is a witch, but you would be surprised. Who knows? Maybe you'll grow up to be a witch yourself. All that stuff about witches is a lie. People have been lying about witches for a very long time. And that's what happened to Wilmot Redd. Maybe she wasn't even a witch at all, but one thing for sure, she wasn't an evil witch. That's the part that's made up about witches and that's what they made up about her, and that's how come she wound up dead. You can't dress up as Wilmot Redd. We just don't make fun of her in Stone. Even though it happened a long time ago, most people here still feel really bad about it. Most people think she was just an old woman who was into herbs and shit—don't tell your dad I said 'shit' either, all right? Making fun of Wilmot Redd is like saying you think witches should be hung. You don't think that, do you? All right then, so don't dress up as Wilmot Redd. You can go as a made-up witch, but leave poor Wilmot Redd out of it. No one even knows what happened to her, I mean after she died. That's how much she didn't matter. They threw her body off a cliff somewhere. No one even knows where her bones ended up. They could be anywhere."

"Do you collect bones?" Rachel asks and Peter kicks her.

"Why would I do that?" Melinda says. "You have some weird ideas, kid."

Witches everywhere. Teacher witches, mommy and daddy witches, policeman witches too, boy witches and girl witches, smiling witches, laughing witches, bus driver witches. Who is not a witch in Stone? Rachel isn't, she knows that for sure.

Rachel makes special requests for chicken "with the bones," she says, and she eats too much, giving herself a stomachache.

"How many bones do you need?" her father asks, because Rachel has told him she needs them for a school project.

"I don't know," she says. "Jack just keeps saying I need more."

"Jack sounds kind of bossy," her father says.

Rachel nods. "Yeah, but he's funny too."

Finally, Halloween arrives. Rachel goes to school dressed as a made-up witch. She notices that there are several of them on the bus and the playground. They start the morning with doughnuts and apple cider and then they do math with questions like two pumpkins plus one pumpkin equals how many pumpkins.

Rachel raises her hand and the lady at the front of the room who says she is Miss Engstrom, their teacher, but who doesn't look anything like her, says, "Yes, Rachel?"

"How many bones does it take to make a body?"

"That's a very good question," the lady says. She's wearing a long purple robe and she has black hair that keeps sliding around funny on her head. "I'll look that up for you, Rachel, but in the meantime, can you answer my question? You have two pumpkins and then your mother goes to the store and comes home with one more pumpkin. How many pumpkins do you have?"

"Her mother is dead," a skeleton in the back of the room says.

"I don't care," says Rachel.

"I mean your father," the lady says. "I meant to say your father goes to the store."

But Rachel just sits there and the lady calls on someone else.

They get an extra long recess. Cindi Becker tears her princess dress on the swing and cries way louder than Peter cried when he cut his finger. Somebody dressed all in black, with a black hood, won't speak to anyone but walks slowly through the playground, stopping occasionally to point a black-gloved finger at one of the children. When one of the kindergartners gets pointed at, he runs, screaming, back to his teacher, who is dressed up as a pirate.

Rachel finds Peter with the knife in his head and says, "Don't tell, but I'm still going to be Wilmot Redd tonight." The boy turns to her, but doesn't say anything at all, just walks away. After a while, Rachel realizes that there are three boys on the playground with knives in their heads, and she isn't sure if the one she spoke to was Peter.

They don't have the party until late in the afternoon. The lady who says she is Miss Engstrom turns off the lights and closes the drapes.

Rachel raises her hand. The lady nods at her.

"When my mom went to the store a bad man shot her—"

The lady waves her arms, as if trying to put out a fire, the purple sleeves dangling from her wrists. "Rachel, Rachel," she says. "I'm so sorry about your mother. I should have said your father went to the store. I'm really sorry. Maybe I should tell a story about witches."

"My mother is not a witch," Rachel says.

"No, no, of course she's not a witch. Let's play charades!"

Rachel sits at her desk. She is a good girl for the most part. But she has learned that even without her face painted, she can pretend to be listening when she isn't. Nobody notices that she isn't playing their stupid game. Later, when she is going to the bus, the figure all dressed in black points at her. She feels the way the kindergartner must have felt. She feels like crying. But she doesn't cry.

She gets off the bus at Peter Williamson's house with Peter, who acts crazy, screaming for no reason, letting the door slam right in her face. I hate you, Peter, she thinks, and is surprised to discover that nothing bad happens to her for having this thought. But when she opens the door, Melinda is standing there, next to Peter, who still has the knife in his head. "Don't you understand? You can't dress up as Wilmot Redd."

"Where's Mrs. Williamson?" Rachel asks.

"She had to go to the doctor's. Did you hear me?"

"I'm not," Rachel says, walking past Melinda. "Can't you see I'm just a made-up witch?"

"Is that what you're wearing tonight?"

Rachel nods.

"Who wants popcorn?" Melinda says. Rachel sticks her tongue out at Peter. He just stands there, with the knife in his head.

"Hey, aren't you guys hungry?" Melinda calls from the kitchen.

Peter runs, screaming, past Rachel. She walks in the other direction, to Peter's room. She knows where he keeps his collection, in his bottom drawer. Peter hasn't said anything about it, maybe he hasn't noticed, but Rachel has been stealing bones from him for some time now. Today she takes a handful. She doesn't have any pockets so she drops the bones into her Halloween treat bag from school. She is careful not to set the bag down. She is still carrying it when her father comes to get her.

They walk home together, through the crooked streets of Stone. The sky is turning gray. Ghosts and witches dangle from porches and crooked trees behind picket fences. Pumpkins grin blackly at her.

Rachel's father says that after dinner Melinda is coming over.

"She just wants to see what kind of witch I am," Rachel says.

Her father smiles. "Yes, I'm sure you're right. Also, I asked her if she could stay and pass out treats while I go with you. That way no one will play a trick on us."

"Melinda might," Rachel says, but her father just laughs, as if she were being funny.

When they get home, Rachel goes into her bedroom while her father makes dinner. He's making macaroni and cheese, her favorite, though tonight the thought of it makes her strangely queasy. Rachel begins to gather the bones from all the various hiding places, the box under her bed, the sock drawer. She puts them in a pillowcase. When her father calls her for dinner, she shoves the pillowcase under her bed.

In the kitchen, a man stands next to the stove with a knife in his head. Rachel screams, and her father tears off the mask. He tells her he's sorry. "See." He lifts the mask up by the knife. "It's just something I bought at the drugstore. I thought it would be funny."

Rachel tries to eat but she doesn't have much of an appetite. She picks at the yellow noodles until the doorbell rings. Her father answers it and comes back with Melinda, who smiles and says, "How's the little witch?"

"Not dead," Rachel answers.

Rachel's father looks at her as if she has a knife in her head.

They go from house to house begging for candy. The witches of Stone drop M&M's, peanut butter cups, and popcorn balls into Rachel's plastic pumpkin. Once, a ghost answers the door, and once, when she reaches into a bowl for a small Hershey's bar, a green hand pops up through the candy and tries to grab her. Little monsters, giant spiders, made-up witches, and bats weave gaily around Rachel and her father. The pumpkins, lit from within, grin at her. Rachel thinks of Wilmot Redd standing on Old Burial Hill watching all of them, waiting for her to bring the bones.

But when Rachel gets home, the bones are gone. The pillowcase, filled with most of her collection and shoved under her bed, is missing. Rachel runs into the living room, just in time to see Melinda leaving with a white bundle under her arm. Rachel stands there in her fake witch costume and thinks, *I wish you were dead.* She has a lot of trouble getting to sleep that night. She cries and cries and her father asks her over and over again if it's because of her mother. Rachel doesn't tell him about the bones. She doesn't know why. She just doesn't.

Two days later, Melinda is killed in a car accident. Rachel's father wipes tears from his eyes when he tells her. Mrs. Williamson cries when she thinks Peter and Rachel aren't watching. But Peter and Rachel don't cry.

"She stole my bones," Rachel says.

"Mine too," says Peter. "She stole a bunch of them."

Melinda's school picture is on the front page of the newspaper, beside a photograph of the fiery wreck.

"That's what she gets," Rachel says, "for stealing."

Peter frowns at Rachel.

"Wanna trade?" she asks.

He nods. Rachel trades a marshmallow pumpkin for a small bone shaped like a toe.

That night, after her father kisses her on the forehead and turns off the light, she takes her small collection of bones and tries to make them dance, but the shape is all wrong. It just lies there and doesn't do anything at all.

The day of Melinda's funeral, Rachel's father doesn't go to work. He's a lawyer in Boston and it isn't easy, the way it is for some parents, to stay home on a workday, but he does. He picks Rachel up at school just after lunch.

The funeral is in a church in the new section of Stone, far from the harbor and Old Burial Hill. On the way there, they pass a group of people carrying signs.

"Close your eyes," her father says.

Rachel closes her eyes. "What are they doing?"

"They're protesting. They're against abortion."

"What's abortion?"

"Okay, you can open them. Abortion is when a woman is pregnant and decides she doesn't want to be pregnant."

"You mean like magic?"

"No, it's not magic. She has a procedure. The procedure is called having an abortion. When that's over, she's not pregnant anymore."

Rachel looks out the car window at the pumpkins with collapsed faces, the falling ghosts, a giant spiderweb dangling in a tree. "Dad?"

"Mmhm?"

"Can we move back to Boston?"

Her father glances down at her. "Don't you feel safer here? And you already have so many friends. Mrs. Williamson says you and Peter get along great. And there's your friend Jack. Maybe we can have him over some Saturday."

"Melinda said there are a lot of witches in Stone."

Her father whistles, one long, low sound. "Well, she was probably just trying to be funny. Here we are." They are parked next to a church. "This is where Melinda's funeral is."

"Okay," says Rachel but neither of them moves to get out of the car.

"Let's say a prayer for Melinda," her father says.

"Here?"

He closes his eyes and bows his head while Rachel watches a group of teenage girls in cheerleading uniforms hugging on the church steps.

"Now, do you wanna get ice cream?"

Rachel can't believe she's heard right. She knows about funerals and they don't have anything to do with ice cream, but she nods, and he turns the car around, right in the middle of the street, just as the church bells ring. Rachel's father drives all the way back to the old section of Stone, where they stop for ice cream. Rachel has peppermint stick and her father has vanilla. They walk on the sidewalk next to the water and watch the seagulls. Rachel tries not to think about Wilmot Redd, who stands on Old Burial Hill, waiting.

Her father looks at his watch. "We have to get going," he says. "It's almost time for Peter to get off the bus."

"Peter?"

"His mother has to go to the doctor's. I told her he could come to our house."

Rachel's father goes out to meet Peter when he gets off the bus and they walk in together, talking about the Red Sox. They walk right past Rachel. "Dad?" she says, but he doesn't answer. She follows them into the kitchen. Her father is spreading cream cheese on a bagel for Peter. Later, when she is playing in her bedroom with him, Rachel says, "I wish your mom had an abortion," which makes Peter cry. When her father comes into the room, he makes her tell him what she did and she tells him she didn't do anything, but Peter tells on her and her father says she is grounded.

Miss Engstrom tells them that they are very lucky to live in Stone, so near to Danvers and Salem and the history of witches. Rachel says that she knows there are a lot of witches in Stone and Miss Engstrom laughs and then all the children laugh too. Later, on the playground, Stella Miner and Leanne Green hold hands and stick out their tongues at Rachel, and Minnity Dover throws pebbles at her. Miss Engstrom catches Minnity and makes her sit on the bench for the rest of recess. Rachel swings so high that she can imagine she is flying. When the bell rings, she comes back to Earth, where Bret and Steve Keeter, the twins, and Peter Williamson wait for her. "We wish your mom had an abortion," Peter says. The twins nod their golden heads.

"You don't even know what that means," says Rachel and runs past them, toward Miss Engstrom, who stands beside the open door, frowning.

"Rachel," she says, "you're late." But she doesn't say anything to the boys, who come in behind Rachel, whispering.

"Shut up!" Rachel shouts.

Miss Engstrom sends Rachel to the office. The principal says he is going to call her father. Rachel sits in the office until it's almost time to go home, and then she goes back to the classroom for her books and lunchbox.

"Wanna know what we did while you were gone?" Clara Vanmeer whispers when they line up for the bus.

Rachel ignores her. She knows what they did. They are witches, all of them, and they put some kind of spell on her. *I wish you were all dead*, Rachel thinks, and she really means it. It worked with Melinda, didn't it? But not her mom. She never wished her mom would die. Never never never. Who did? Who wished that for her mother who used to call her Rae-Rae and made chocolate chip pancakes and was beautiful? Rachel hugs her backpack and stares out the window at the witches of Stone, picking their kids up from school. The bus drives past rotten pumpkins and fallen graveyards. Rachel's head hurts. She hopes Mrs. Williamson will let her take a nap but when they get there, the house is locked. Peter rings the doorbell five hundred times, and pulls on the door, but Rachel just sits on the step. Nobody is home, why can't he just get that through his head? Finally, Peter starts to cry. "Shut up," Rachel says. She has to say it twice before he does.

"Where's my mother?" Peter asks, wiping his nose with the sleeve of his jacket.

"How should I know?" Rachel watches a small black cat with a tiny silver bell around its neck emerge from the bush at the neighbor's house. Unfortunately, it is not carrying a dead bird or mouse.

Peter starts crying again. Loudly. Rachel's head hurts. "Shut up!" she says, but he just keeps crying. She stands up and readjusts her backpack.

Rachel is already walking down the tiny sidewalk when Peter calls for her to wait. They walk to Rachel's house, but of course that is locked as well. Peter starts crying again. Rachel takes off the backpack and sets it on the step. The afternoon sun is low, the sky gray and fuzzy like a sweater. Her head hurts and she's hungry. Also, Peter is really annoying her, "I want my mother," he says.

"Well, I want my mother too," Rachel says. "But that doesn't help. She's dead, okay? She's dead."

"My mom's dead?" Peter screams, so loud that Rachel has to cover her ears with her hands. That's when Mrs. Williamson comes running up the sidewalk. Peter doesn't even see her at first because he's so hysterical. Mrs. Williamson runs to Peter. She sits down beside him, says his name, and touches him on the shoulder. He looks up and shouts, "Mom!" He wraps his arms around her, saying over and over again, "You're not dead." Rachel resists the temptation to look down the sidewalk to see if her own mother is coming. She knows she is not.

They walk back to the Williamsons' house together. Rachel, trying not to drag her backpack, follows. "I'm sorry," she hears Mrs. Williamson say. "I had a doctor's appointment and I got caught in traffic. I tried to call the school, but I was too late, and then I tried to find someone to come to the house, but no one was home."

Peter says something to Mrs. Williamson. She can't hear him and she leans over so he can whisper in her ear. Rachel stands behind them, watching. Mrs. Williamson turns and stares at Rachel. "Did you tell him I was dead?" she asks.

Rachel shakes her head no, but she can tell Mrs. Williamson doesn't believe her.

"When the Pilgrims came to America they wanted to live in a place where they could practice their religion. They were trying to be good people. So when they saw someone doing something they thought was bad, they wanted to stop it. Bad meant the devil to them. They didn't want to be around the devil. They wanted to be around God." Miss Engstrom stands at the front of the room dressed as a Puritan. She puts the Puritan dress on every day for social studies. Her cheeks are pink and her hair is sticking to her face. She is trying to help them understand what happened, she says, but Cindi Becker has said, more than once, that her mom doesn't want Miss Engstrom teaching them religion. "It's not religion," Miss Engstrom says, "it's history."

Every day Miss Engstrom puts on the Pilgrim dress and pretends she's a Puritan. The children are supposed to pretend they are witches. "Act natural," she tells them. "Just be yourselves." But when they do, they get in trouble; they have to stand in the stockade or go to the jail in the back of the room. The stockade is made out of cardboard, and the jail is just chairs in a circle. Rachel hates to be put in either place. By the fourth lesson, she has figured out how to sit at her desk with her hands neatly folded. When Miss Engstrom asks Rachel what she is doing, she says, "Praying," and Miss Engstrom tells her what a good Puritan she is. By the sixth lesson the class is filled with good Puritans, sitting with neatly folded hands. Only Charlie Dexter is stuck in the stockade and Cindi Becker is in the jail in the back of the room. Miss Engstrom says that they are probably witches. Rachel decides that social studies is her favorite subject. She looks forward to the next lesson. What will happen to the witches when they go on trial? But the next day they have a substitute and the day after that, another. They have so many substitutes Rachel can't remember their names. One day, one of the substitutes tells the class that she is their new teacher.

"What happened to Miss Engstrom?" Rachel asks.

"My mother had her fired," says Cindi Becker.

"She's not coming back," the teacher says. "Now, let's talk about Thanksgiving."

Rachel is so excited about Thanksgiving she can't stand it. A whole turkey! Think of the bones! Each night Rachel rearranges her bone collection. It is a difficult time of year for it. Cats still wander the crooked streets of Stone but they are either eating everything they kill, or killing less, because there are few bones to be found. Rachel arranges and rearranges, trying to form the shape that will dance for her. Damn that Melinda, Rachel thinks. What would happen if Rachel had bones like that in her collection? Human bones?

Rachel has a fit when her father tells her they are going to the Williamsons' house for Thanksgiving. "This will be better," he says. "You can play with Peter and his cousins. Don't you think it would be lonely with just you and me at our house?"

"The bones!" Rachel cries. "I want the bones!"

"What are you talking about?" her father asks.

Rachel sniffs. "I want the turkey bones."

Rachel's father stares at her. He is cutting an apple and he stands, holding the knife, staring at her.

"You know, for my project."

"Are you still doing that, now that Miss Engstrom is gone?"

Rachel nods. Her father says, "Well, we can make a turkey. But not on Thursday. On Thursday we're going to the Williamsons'."

The night before Thanksgiving, though, her father gets a phone call. He says, "Oh, I am so sorry." And, "No, no please don't even worry about us." He nods his head a lot. "Please know you are in our prayers. Let us know if we can do anything." After he hangs up the phone, he sits in his chair and stares at the TV screen. Finally, he says, "It looks like you got your wish."

He looks at his watch, and then, all in a hurry, they drive to the grocery store, where he buys a turkey, bags of stuffing, and pumpkin pie. He throws the food into the cart. Rachel can tell that he is angry but she doesn't ask him what's wrong. She'd rather not know. Besides, she has other stuff to worry about. Like is there a bad man in this store? Will he shoot them the way he shot her mother?

When they get home, her father says, "Mrs. Williamson lost the baby."

"What baby?" Rachel asks.

"She was pregnant. But she lost it."

Rachel remembers, once, when Mrs. Williamson got angry at Peter when he came home from school without his sweater. "You can't be so careless all the time," Rachel remembers her saying.

"Well, she shouldn't be so careless," Rachel says.

"Rachel, you have to start learning to think about other people's feelings once in a while."

Rachel thinks about the lost baby, out in the dark somewhere. "Mrs. Williamson is stupid," she says.

Rachel's father, holding a can of cranberry sauce with one hand, points toward her room with the other. "You go to your room," he says. "And think about what you're saying."

Rachel runs to her room. She slams the door shut. She throws herself on her bed and cries herself to sleep. When she wakes up there is no light shining under the door. She doesn't know what time it is, but she thinks it is very late. She gets up and begins collecting bones from all the hiding places; bones in her socks, bones in her underwear drawer, bones in a box under the bed, bones in her jewelry box, and bones in her stuffed animals, cut open with the scissors she's not supposed to use. She hums as she assembles and reassembles the bones until at last they quiver and shake. She thinks they are going to dance for her but instead, they stab her with their sharp little points.

"Stop it," Rachel says. She takes them apart again, stores them in separate places and goes to sleep, crying for her mother.

The next morning, Rachel watches the parade on TV while her father makes stuffing and cleans the turkey. When the phone rings, he brings it to Rachel, and turns the TV sound off. The Grandma asks her how school is going and how she likes living in Stone, and finally, how is she? Rachel answers each question, "Fine," while watching a silent band march across the TV. The Grandma asks to speak to her father again and Rachel goes to the kitchen. Her father reaches for the phone and says, "My God, Rachel, what happened to your arms?" Rachel looks down at her arms. There are small red spots and tiny bruises all over them.

"She has bruises all over her arms," her father says.

Rachel grabs a stick of celery and walks toward the living room. Her father follows, still holding the phone. "Rachel, what happened to your arms?"

Rachel turns and smiles at him. Ever since her mom died, her dad has been trying hard. Rachel knows this, and she knows that he doesn't know she knows this. But there are certain things he isn't very good at. Rachel is positive that if her mom were still alive, she wouldn't even have to ask what had happened, she'd know. Rachel feels sorry for her dad but she doesn't want to tell him about the bones. Look what happened when she barely even mentioned them to Melinda. So Rachel makes something up instead. "Miss Engstrom," she says.

"What are you talking about? Miss Engstrom? She isn't even your teacher anymore."

Rachel only smiles sweetly at her father. He repeats what she told him into the phone. Rachel walks into the living room. She wraps herself in the red throw and sits in front of the TV, watching the balloon man fill up the screen as she munches on celery. How many bones does it take, anyway? Miss Engstrom never did answer her question.

Later, when the doorbell rings, her father shouts, "I'll get it," which is sort of strange because she is never allowed to answer the door. She hears voices and then her father comes into the room with a policeman and a policewoman. Rachel thinks they've come to arrest her. She's a liar, a thief, and a murderer, so it had to happen. Still, she feels like crying now that it has.

Her father has been talking to her, she realizes, but she has no idea what he's said. He turns the sound off the TV and he and the policeman walk out of the room together. The policewoman stays with Rachel. She sits right next to Rachel on the couch. For a while they watch the silent parade, until the policewoman says, "Can you tell me what happened to your arms, Rachel?"

"I already told my dad," Rachel says.

The policewoman nods. "The thing is, I just want to make sure he didn't leave anything out."

"I don't want to get in trouble."

"You're not in trouble. We are here to help. Okay, honey? Can I see your arms?"

Rachel shakes her head no.

The policewoman nods. "Who hurt you, Rachel?"

Rachel turns to look at her. She has blond hair and brown eyes with yellow flecks in them. She looks at Rachel very closely. As if she knows the truth about her.

"You can tell me," she says.

"The bones," Rachel whispers.

"What about the bones?"

"But you can't tell anyone."

"I might have to tell someone," the policewoman says.

So Rachel refuses to speak further. She shows the lady her arms, but only because she figures it will make her go away, and it does. After she looks at Rachel's arms the policewoman goes out in the kitchen with her dad and the policeman. Rachel turns up the volume. Jessica Simpson, dressed in white fur, like a kitten without the whiskers, is singing. Her voice fills up the room, but Rachel can still hear the murmuring sound of the grownups talking in the kitchen. Then the door opens and closes and she hears her father saying good-bye. Rachel's father comes and stands in the room, watching her. He doesn't say anything and Rachel doesn't either but later, when they are eating turkey together, he says, "You might still be just a little girl but you can get grownups in a lot of trouble by telling lies."

Rachel nods. She knows this. Miss Engstrom taught them all about the history of witches. Rachel chews the turkey leg clean. It was huge and she is quite full, but now she has a turkey leg, almost as big as a human bone, to add to her collection. She sets it on her napkin next to her plate. As if he can read, her mind her father says, "Rachel, no more bones."

"What?"

"Your bone collection. It's done. Over. Find something else to collect. Seashells. Buttons. Barbie dolls. No more bones."

Rachel knows better than to argue. Instead, she asks to be excused. Her father doesn't even look at her; he just nods. Rachel goes to her bedroom and searches through the mess of clothes in the wicker chair until she finds her Halloween costume. When her father comes to tell her it's time for bed, he says, "You can wear that one last time but then we're putting it away until next year."

"Can I sleep in it?" Rachel asks.

Her father shrugs. "Sure, why not?" He smiles, but it is a pretend smile. Rachel smiles a pretend smile back. She crawls into bed, dressed like a pretend witch. Her father kisses her on the forehead and turns out the light. Rachel lies there until she counts to a hundred and then she sits up. She gathers the bones, whispering in the dark.

A few days later, the witch costume has been packed away, the first dusting of snow has sprinkled the crooked streets and picket fences of Stone, and Rachel has forgotten all about how angry she was at her father. Since Mrs. Williamson lost the baby, she no longer watches Rachel. Rachel thinks this is a good idea because she doesn't feel safe with Mrs. Williamson, but she hates being in school all day. All the other children have been picked up from the after-school program and it's just Rachel and Miss Carrie, who keep looking out the school window, saying, "Boy, your dad sure is late."

Rachel sits at the play table, making a design with the purple, blue, green, and yellow plastic shapes. She is good at putting things together and Miss Carrie compliments her work. Rachel remembers putting the spell on her father and she regrets it. She pretends the shapes are bones; she puts them together and then she takes them apart, she whispers, trying to say the words backward, but it is hard to do and Miss Carrie, who isn't a real grownup at all, but a high school girl like Melinda, says, "Uh, you're starting to creep me out."

Miss Carrie calls her mother, using the purple cell phone she carries in the special cell phone pocket of her jeans. "I don't know what to do," she says. "Rachel is still here. Her dad is really late. Hey, Rache, what's your last name again?" Rachel tells Carrie and Carrie tells her mom. Just then, Mrs. Williamson arrives. She is wearing a raincoat, even though it isn't raining, and her hair is a mess. She tells Carrie that she is taking Rachel home. Rachel doesn't want to go with Mrs. Williamson, the baby loser, but Carrie says, "Oh, great," to Mrs. Williamson and then says into the phone, "Never mind, someone finally came to pick her up." She is still talking to her mother when Rachel leaves with Mrs. Williamson, who doesn't say anything until they are in the car.

"Peter told me what you said, Rachel, about how I should have had an abortion, and I want you to know, that sort of talk is not allowed in our house. I really don't even want you playing with Peter anymore. Not one word about abortion or dead mothers or anything else you have up your sleeve, do you understand?"

Rachel nods. She is looking out the window at a house decorated with tiny white icicle lights hanging over the windows. "Where's my dad?" she asks.

Mrs. Williamson sighs. "He's been delayed."

Rachel is afraid to ask what that means. When they get to the Williamsons' house, Mrs. Williamson pretends to be nice. She asks Rachel if her book bag is too heavy and offers to carry it. Rachel shakes her head. She is afraid to say anything for fear that it will be the wrong thing. There is a big wreath on the back door of the Williamsons' house and it has a bell on it that rings when they go inside. Mr. Williamson and Peter are eating at the kitchen table. The house is deliciously warm but it smells strange.

Mrs. Williamson takes off her raincoat and hangs it from a peg in the wall. Rachel drops her book bag below the coats, and stands there until Mrs. Williamson tells her to hang up her coat and sit at the table.

When Rachel sits down, Mr. Williamson points a chicken leg at her and says, "Now listen here, young lady—" but Mrs. Williamson interrupts him.

"I already talked to her," she says.

Rachel is mashing her peas into her potatoes when her father arrives. He thanks Mr. and Mrs. Williamson and he says, "How you doing?" to Peter, though Peter doesn't answer. Mrs. Williamson invites him to stay for dinner but he says thank you, he can't. Rachel leaves her plate on the table and no one tells her to clear it. She puts on her coat. Her father picks up her backpack. He thanks the Williamsons again and then taps Rachel's shoulder. Hard.

"Thank you," Rachel says.

They walk out to the car together, their shoes squeaking on the snow. The Williamsons' house is decorated with white lights; the neighbors have colored lights and two big plastic snowmen with frozen grins and strange eyes on their front porch.

"What did you say to that policewoman?" Rachel's father asks.

He isn't looking at Rachel. He is staring out the window, the way he does when he is driving in Boston.

"Miss Engstrom didn't do it," she says.

"They seem to think I hurt you, do you understand—" He doesn't finish what he is saying. He pulls into their driveway, but instead of getting out of the car to open the garage door, he sits there. "Just tell the truth, Rachel, okay? Just tell the truth. You know what that is, don't you?"

"I did," Rachel says. She feels like crying and also, she thinks she might throw up.

"Who did that to you, then? Who did that to your arms?"

"The bones."

"The bones?"

Rachel nods.

"What bones?"

"You know."

Her father makes a strange noise. He is bent over, and his eyes are shut. Praying, Rachel thinks. The car is still running. Rachel looks out the window. She cranes her neck so she can see the Sheekles' yard. They have it decorated with six reindeer made out of white lights. The car door slams. Rachel watches her father open the garage door. She watches him walk back to the car, lit by the headlights, his neck bent as if he is looking for something very important that he has lost.

"Dad?" Rachel says when he gets back in the car. "Are you mad?"

He shakes his head. He eases the car into the garage, turns off the ignition. They walk to the house together. When they get inside, he says, "Okay, I want all of them."

"All of what?" Rachel says, though she thinks she knows.

"That bone collection of yours. I want it."

"No, Dad."

He shakes his head. He stands there in his best winter coat, his gloves still on, shaking his head. "Rachel, why would you want to keep them, if they are hurting you?"

It's a good question. Rachel has to think for a moment before she answers. "Not all the time," she says. "Mostly they don't. They used to be my friend."

"The bones?"

Rachel nods.

"The bones used to be your friend?"

"Jack," she says.

He doesn't look at her. He *is* angry! He lied when he said he wasn't.

"Rachel," he says, softly, "honey? Let's get the bones. Okay? Let's put them away . . . where they can't . . . bones aren't . . . Jesus Christ." He slams his fist on the kitchen table. Rachel jumps. He covers his face with his hands. "Jesus Christ, Marla," he says.

Marla is Rachel's mother's name.

Rachel isn't sure what to do. She takes off her hat and coat. Then she walks into her bedroom and begins gathering the bones. After a while she realizes her father is standing in the doorway, watching.

Rachel hands her father all the bones. "Be careful," she says. "They killed Melinda." He doesn't say anything. That night he forgets to tell Rachel when to go to sleep. She changes into her pajamas, crawls into bed, and waits but he forgets to kiss her. He sits in the living room, making phone calls. The words drift into Rachel's room, "bones, mother murdered, lies, problems in school." Rachel thinks about Christmas. What will she get this year? Will she get a new Barbie? Will she get anything? Or has she been a bad girl? Will someone kill her father? Will Mrs. Williamson come to take care of her, and then lose her the way she lost the baby? Will Santa Claus save her? Will God? Will anyone? Will they get white lights for their tree or colored? Every year they switch but Rachel can't remember what they had last year. Rachel hopes it's a colored light year, because she likes the colored lights best. The last thing she hears before she falls asleep is her father's distant voice. "Bones," he says. "Yes that's right, bones."

The next morning, Rachel's father tells her she isn't going to school. She's going with him to Boston. "I made an appointment for you, okay, honey? I think you need a woman to talk to. So I made an appointment with Dr. Trentwerth."

Rachel is happy not to go to school with the nasty children of Stone. She is happy not to have to sit in the classroom and listen to Mrs. Fizzure, who never dresses like a Puritan and doesn't put anyone in the stockade or jail. Rachel is happy to go to Boston. They listen to Christmas music the whole way there. Rachel's appointment isn't until ten o'clock, so she has to sit in her dad's office and be very quiet while he does his work. He gives her paper and pens and she draws pictures of Christmas trees and ghosts while she waits. When it's time to go to her appointment, her father looks at her pictures and says, "These are very nice, Rachel." Rachel actually thinks they are sort of scary, though she didn't draw the ghosts the way a kindergartner would, all squiggly lines and black spot eyes. She made them the way they really are, a lady smiling next to a Christmas tree, a baby asleep on a floor, a cat grinning.

Dr. Trentwerth has a long gray braid that snakes down the side of her neck. She's wearing an orange sweater and black pants. Her earrings are triangles of tiny gold bells. She says hello to Rachel's father but she doesn't shake his hand. She shakes Rachel's hand, as if she might be someone important. They leave her father sitting on the couch looking at a magazine.

Rachel is disappointed by the doctor's office. There are little kid toys everywhere. A stuffed giraffe, a dollhouse, blocks, trucks, and baby dolls with pink baby bottles. Rachel doesn't know what she's supposed to do. "Be polite," she remembers her father telling her.

"You have a nice room," Rachel says.

"Would you like some tea?" the doctor asks. "Or hot cocoa?"

Rachel walks past all the baby toys and sits in the chair by the window. "Cocoa please," she says.

Dr. Trentwerth turns the electric teakettle on. "Your father tells me you've been having some trouble with your bone collection," she says.

"He doesn't believe me."

"He said the bones hurt you."

Rachel nods. Shrugs. "But not all the time. Like I said. Just once."

The doctor tears open a packet of hot cocoa, which she empties into a plain white mug. She pours the water into it. "Let's just let that sit for a while," she says. "It's very hot. Whose bones hurt you, Rachel?"

Rachel sighs. "Cat bones, mice bones, chicken bones, you know."

Dr. Trentwerth nods. "Your father says you moved to Stone after your mother died. What was that like?"

"We were both really sad, me and Dad. Everyone was. We got a lot of flowers."

Dr. Trentwerth hands the mug to Rachel. "Careful, it's still hot."

Dr. Trentwerth is right. It is hot. Rachel brings it toward her mouth but it is too hot. She sets it, carefully, on the table next to the chair.

"Tell me about where you live," the doctor says as she sits down across from Rachel.

"Well, everyone is a witch," Rachel says. "Okay, not everyone, but almost everyone, and one time, a long time ago, there was a woman there named Wilmot Redd and some people came and took her away 'cause they said all witches had to die. They hung her and no one did anything about it. Miss Engstrom, she was my teacher, got taken away too, and Melinda, my babysitter, died, but that's because she stole the bones and now my father has them and I don't want him to die but he probably will. Mrs. Williamson is this lady who sometimes takes care of me and she looks real nice but she loses babies and she lost one and no one even is looking for it. If my mom was still alive she would rescue me."

"And the bones?"

"They used to keep me company at night."

"Where would you be when the bones kept you company, Rachel?"

"In my room."

"In your bedroom?"

"Mmhhm."

"I see."

"But then they stopped being nice and started hurting me."

"Whose bones, Rachel?"

"My dad has them now."

"Where did your dad's bones hurt you?"

"They were still mine then."

"Where did the bones hurt you, Rachel?"

"On my body."

"Where on your body?"

Suddenly, Rachel has a bad feeling. How does she know Dr. Trentwerth isn't one of them too? Rachel reaches for her mug and sips the hot cocoa. Dr. Trentwerth sits there, watching.

———

The moon is not a bone. Rachel knows this, but when the moon stares down at her, like an eye socket, Rachel wonders if she is just a small insect rattling around inside a giant skull. She knows this isn't true. She's not a baby, after all. She knows this isn't how reality works, but she can't help herself. Sometimes she imagines flying up to the moon, and climbing right through that hole to find everyone she's ever lost on the other side. She doesn't care about Melinda but she cares a lot about her mom and dad.

Rachel no longer lives in Stone and she no longer lives with her father. A lady and two policemen came to school one day and took Rachel away. She was cutting paper snowflakes at the time, and little bits of paper fluttered from her clothes as they walked to the car. Now Rachel lives with the Freemans. Big plastic candy canes line the walk up to the Freemans' front porch, which is decorated with blinking colored lights. A wreath with tiny gift-wrapped packages glued to it hangs on the front door. (But there are no gifts inside; Rachel checked.) The house smells sweet with the scent of holiday candles. Mrs. Freeman tells Rachel to be careful around the candles and not to bother Mr. Freeman when he is watching TV, which is most of the time.

Rachel's bedroom is in the back of the house. It has green itchy carpet and two twin beds and a dresser that is mostly blue, with some patches of yellow and lime green, as though someone started to paint it and then gave up on the project. The curtains on Rachel's window are faded tiny blue flowers with yellow centers and they are Rachel's favorite things in the room. Lying in her bed, Rachel can look out the window at the moon and imagine crawling right out of her world into a better one.

On the first night, Mrs. Freeman came into the bedroom and held Rachel while she cried and told her things would get better. In the morning, Mr. Freeman drove Rachel to school. He walked with a limp and he burped a lot, but before he left her in the school office he told her she was a brave girl and everything was going to be better soon.

"The Freemans are nice," the lady who took Rachel away from Stone told her. "Mrs. Freeman was once in the same situation you are in. She understands just what you're going through. And Mr. Freeman is a retired police officer. He got shot a few years ago. You're lucky to go there."

But Rachel didn't feel like a lucky girl, even when the Freemans took her to the Christmas tree lot and let her choose their tree, or when Mrs. Freeman put lotion on Rachel's chapped hands, or when they took her to an attorney's office, a very important woman who acted as if everything Rachel said mattered.

Rachel doesn't feel lucky until the day Mr. Freeman says, "Rachel, the lawyers think you should go back and live with your father." Mrs. Freeman cries and says, "Tomorrow's Christmas Eve, how can they do this?" But Rachel is so happy she almost pees in her pants. When the lady comes to pick Rachel up, Mrs. Freeman says, "I have half a mind not to let you take her." But Mr. Freeman says, "Rachel, get your suitcase." Mrs. Freeman hugs Rachel so tightly that for a second she is afraid she really isn't going to let her go, but then she does. The lady who waits for Rachel says, "This isn't my fault. This is hard for all of us." "It's hardest for her," Mrs. Freeman says and after that, Rachel doesn't hear the rest. Down the street the Mauley kids are building a snowman. "I hate you, George Mauley," Rachel screams at the top of her lungs. "What did you do that for?" the lady asks. "Get in the car." But Rachel has no idea why she did it. As they drive past the Mauley children, Rachel turns her face toward the window, so her back is to the lady. She sticks her tongue out at George Mauley, but he is busy putting stones in the snowman's eyes and doesn't notice. "I want you to know, you are not alone," the woman says. "Maybe things didn't work out this time, but we are watching. You just keep telling the truth, Rachel, and I promise you things will get better."

It starts snowing. Not a lot, just tiny flakes fluttering down the white sky. Rachel remembers the snowflake she had been cutting when the lady took her away from Stone. What happened to her snowflake?

"Here we are then," the lady says. "Don't forget your suitcase." They walk into a big restaurant with orange booths along the wall and tiny Christmas trees on the tables. The waitresses wear brown dresses with white aprons and little half-circle hats that look like miniature spaceships crashed into all their heads. A woman is standing in one of the booths, waving and calling Rachel's name. The lady walks toward her. Rachel follows.

The woman wraps her arms around Rachel. She smells like soap. When she lets go of Rachel, she doesn't stand up but stays at Rachel's level, staring at her. Pink lipstick is smeared above her lips so she looks a little bit like she has three lips. Her eyebrows are drawn high on her forehead, beneath curls that are a strange shade of pink and orange, and she wears poinsettia earrings. "You remember me, don't you, honey?" she says. Then she looks up at the lady and frowns. "You can go now." She pulls Rachel close; together they pivot away from the lady. "Here, let me take that." She leans over and takes Rachel's suitcase. Rachel looks over her shoulder at the lady who is already walking away. "You don't remember me, do you? It's me. Grandma."

"Where's Dad?"

The Grandma sighs. "Are you hungry?" She guides Rachel into the booth and then slides in across from her. "This has all been expensive, you know. The lawyers and everything. He's at work. But he'll be home by the time we get there. Do you want a hamburger? A chocolate shake? What did you say to those people? Okay, I promised I wouldn't talk about it. Don't touch the little tree, Rachel, can't you just sit still for five minutes? It's just for looking."

Rachel's stomach feels funny. "Can I have an egg?"

"An egg? What kind of egg? Don't you want a hamburger?"

Rachel shakes her head. She starts to cry.

"Don't cry," the Grandma says. "It's over, all right? If you want an egg, you can have an egg. Were the people mean to you, Rachel? Did anyone hurt you?"

"Fried, please," Rachel says. "And can I have toast?"

"You can tell me, you know," the Grandma says. "Did anything happen to you while you were gone? Did anyone touch you in a bad way?"

Rachel is tired of the questions about bad touch. She is tired of grownups. Also she is cold. She just looks at the Grandma and after a while the Grandma says, "We decorated the tree last night. Your father hadn't even bought one yet. But don't worry; I set him straight about that. After everything you've been through! Well, he just wasn't thinking clearly. He's been through a lot too. Blue spruce. It looks real nice."

The waitress comes and the Grandma orders a fried egg and toast for Rachel and the fish platter for herself. The waitress says, "Rachel?"

Miss Engstrom! Dressed as a waitress!

"Do you know each other?" the Grandma says.

"I used to be Rachel's teacher," Miss Engstrom says.

"In Boston?" asks the Grandma.

Miss Engstrom shakes her head, "No, in Stone. How are you, Rachel? Are you having a good holiday? Do you like your new teacher?"

"Wait, I know who you are. I know all about you."

"I wish you would come back," Rachel says.

"I forbid you to speak to my granddaughter, do you hear me? Where's the manager?"

Miss Engstrom's face does something strange, it sort of collapses, like an old jack-o'-lantern, but she shakes her head and everything goes back to normal. She smiles a fake smile at Rachel and walks away. The Grandma says, "She's the one who hurt you, isn't she? Where's that social worker when you need her? Why didn't you tell them about her, Rachel? Could you just tell me that?"

"Miss Engstrom never hurt me," Rachel says. "She was nice."

"Nice? She left bruises on your arms, Rachel."

Rachel sighs. She is *sooo* tired of stupid grownups and their stupid questions. "I told everyone," she says, "it wasn't her. It wasn't my dad, okay? It was the bones that did it."

"What bones? What are you talking about?"

But Rachel doesn't answer. She's learned a thing or two about answering adults' questions. Instead, she picks up the salt shaker and salts the table. The Grandmother grabs the shaker. "Just sit and wait for your egg," she says. "Maybe you could use this time to think about what you've done."

Rachel folds her hands neatly in front of her, just as she learned to do in Miss Engstrom's class. She is still sitting like that when Miss Engstrom returns with their order.

"You can eat now, Rachel," the Grandmother says. Rachel unfolds her hands and cuts her egg. The yellow yolk breaks open and smears

across her plate. She can feel both Miss Engstrom and the Grandmother watching, but she pretends not to notice. The music is "Frosty
the Snowman." Rachel eats her egg and hums along.

"Stop humming," says the Grandma; then, to Miss Engstrom,
"You can go. We don't want anything else."

Miss Engstrom touches Rachel's head softly. Rachel looks up at
Miss Engstrom and sees that she is crying. Miss Engstrom nods at
Rachel, one quick nod, as if they have agreed on something, then she
sets the bill down on the table and walks away.

"Your father will be happy to see you," the Grandmother says.
"Eat your egg. We've still got a long drive ahead of us."

Rachel's father does act happy to see her. He says, "I am so happy you
are home," but he hugs her as if she is covered in mud and he doesn't
want to get his clothes dirty.

The Christmas tree is already decorated. Rachel stares at it and
the Grandma says, "Do you like it? We did it last night to surprise
you." It is lit with tiny white lights, and oddly decorated with gold
and white balls.

"Where are our ornaments?" Rachel asks.

"We decided to do something different this year," the Grandma
says. "Don't you just love white and gold?"

Rachel doesn't know what to say. Clearly she is not expected to
tell the truth. "Why don't you go unpack," the Grandma says, nodding at the suitcase. "Make yourself at home." She laughs.

Rachel is surprised, when she enters her bedroom, to discover that
her bed is gone, replaced by two twin beds, just like at the Freemans'.
One bed is covered with Rachel's old stuffed animals; they stare at her
with their black eyes. She assumes this is her bed. Rachel inspects the
animals and discovers that the ones she had cut open and stuffed with
bones have been sewn shut, all except her white bear, and he is missing. The other bed is covered with a pink lacy spread and several fat
pillows. Next to it is a small table with a lamp, a glass of water, a few
wadded tissues, and a stack of books.

"Surprise!" the Grandma says. "We're roomies now. Isn't this fun?"

Rachel nods. Apparently this is the right thing to do. The Grandma lifts the suitcase onto Rachel's bed. "Now, let's unpack your things and we can just forget about your little adventure and get on with our lives." The Grandma begins unpacking Rachel's suitcase, refolding the clothes before she puts them in the dresser. "Didn't anyone there help you with your clothes?" she says, frowning.

Rachel shrugs.

The Grandma closes the suitcase, clasps it shut, and puts it in the closet, right next to a set of plaid luggage. "Do you want a cookie? How about a gingerbread man? I've been baking up a storm, let me tell you."

Rachel follows the Grandma into the kitchen. Baking up a storm? she thinks. Maybe the Grandma is a witch; that would explain a lot. Her father is in the kitchen, talking on the phone, but when he sees her, he stops. He smiles at her, with the new smile of his, and then he says, "She just walked into the kitchen. Can I call you back?" The Grandma is talking at the same time, something about chocolate chip eyes. Rachel's father says, "I love you too," softly into the phone but Rachel stares at him in shock. Is he talking to her mother? Rachel knows that doesn't make sense. She's not a baby, after all, but who is he talking to?

"Here," the Grandma says, "choose."

Rachel looks down into the cookie tin the Grandma has thrust before her. Gingerbread men lie there with chocolate chip eyes and wrinkled red mouths. ("Dried cranberry," the Grandma says.) Rachel chooses the one at the top and immediately begins eating his face. Her father sits across from her and shakes his head when the Grandma thrusts the tin toward him. "I missed you," he says.

The gingerbread man is spicy but the eyes and nose are sweet. Rachel doesn't care for the mouth but that part is gone fast enough.

"Your grandmother has been nice enough to come here to live with us."

The Grandmother sets a glass of milk down in front of Rachel. "Oh, I was ready for a change. Who needs Milwaukee?"

Rachel doesn't know what to say about any of it. She chews her gingerbread man and drinks her milk. Her father and the Grandma

seem to have run out of ideas as well. They simply watch her eat.
When she's finished, she yawns and the Grandmother says, "Time
for bed."

Rachel looks at her father, expecting him to do something. Just
because she yawned doesn't mean she's ready for bed! But her father
isn't any help.

"Say good night," the Grandma says.

"Good night," says Rachel. She gets up, pushes the chair in, and
rinses her glass. The Grandma follows her into the bedroom. She
stays there the whole time Rachel is getting undressed. Rachel feels
embarrassed but she doesn't know what else to do, so she pretends she
doesn't mind the Grandma sitting on her bed talking about how much
fun it's going to be to share the room. "Every night just like a slumber
party," she says. After Rachel goes to the bathroom, brushes her teeth,
and washes her face and hands, the Grandma tells her to kneel by her
bed. The Grandma, complaining the whole time about how difficult
it is, kneels down beside her.

"Lord," she says. "Please help Rachel understand right from
wrong, reality from imagination, truth from lies and all that. Thank
you for sending her home. Do you have anything to add? Rachel?"

Rachel can't think of anything to say. She shakes her head. The
Grandma makes a lot of noise as she stands up again.

Rachel crawls into bed and the Grandma tucks the covers tight, so
tight that Rachel feels like she can't breathe. Then the Grandma kisses
Rachel's forehead and turns out the light. Rachel waits, for a long time,
for her father to come in to kiss her good night but he never does.

It is very dark when Rachel wakes up. The room is dark and there
is no light shining under the door. It takes a moment for Rachel to
realize why she's woken up. A soft rustling sound is coming from the
closet.

"Grandma?" Rachel whispers, and then, louder, "Grandma?"

The Grandma wakes up, sputtering, "Marla? Is that you?"

"No. It's me, Rachel. Do you hear that noise?"

They listen for a while. It seems, to Rachel, a very long time and
she is just starting to worry that the Grandma will think she is lying
when the rustling starts again.

"We've got a mouse," the Grandma says. "Don't worry, I have a feeling Santa Claus might bring you a cat this year."

Very soon the Grandma is snoring in her bed. The rustling sound stops and then, just as Rachel is falling asleep, starts again. Rachel stares into the dark with burning eyes. It doesn't matter what the grownups do, she realizes, she's not safe anywhere.

Carefully, Rachel feels around in the dark for her bunny slippers. She picks up a shoe by mistake, and is startled by how large it is until she realizes it must belong to the Grandmother. She sets it down and picks up first one slipper, and then the other.

Her bunny slippers on, Rachel tiptoes out of the bedroom into the hallway, which is softly lit by the white glow of the Sheekles' Christmas-light reindeer. Rachel isn't sleepwalking, she is completely awake, but she feels strange, as though somehow she is both entirely awake and asleep at the same time. Rachel feels like she hears a voice calling from a great distance. But she isn't hearing it with her ears; it's more like a feeling inside, a feeling inside and outside of herself too. This doesn't make sense, Rachel knows, but this is what is happening. Maybe the grownups aren't right about anything, about what is real, or what is possible.

When she walks outside, the bitter cold hits Rachel hard. But she does not go back to her warm bed; instead she walks in the deadly dark of Stone, lit by occasional Christmas lights, and the few cars from which she hides, all the way to Old Burial Hill, where the graves stand in the oddly blue snow, marking the dead who once lived there.

Rachel isn't afraid. She lies down. It is cold. Well, of course it is. She shivers, staring up at the stars, which, come to think of it, look like chips of bones. Maybe the skull she's been trapped in has been smashed open by some giant child who is, even now, searching through the pieces, hoping to find her. She closes her eyes.

"No, no. Not your bones. You've misunderstood everything."

Rachel opens her eyes. Standing before her is the old woman.

"Get up. Stamp your feet."

Rachel just lies there so the woman pulls her up.

"Are you a witch?" Rachel asks.

"Clap your hands and stamp your feet."

"Are you real?"

But the old woman is gone and Rachel's father is running toward her. "What are you doing here?" he says. "Rachel, what is happening to you?"

He wraps her tight in his arms and picks her up. One of her bunny slippers falls from her foot and lands softly on the snow-covered grave but he doesn't notice. He is running down the hill. Rachel, bouncing in his arms, watches the bunny slipper get smaller and smaller. She holds her father tight.

The Grandma is waiting for them in the kitchen where she is heating milk on the stove. She has on a flowered robe; her pinky-red hair, sparkling in the light, circles her face like a clown.

"She was in the graveyard," Rachel's father says.

The Grandma touches Rachel's bare arm with her own icy fingers. "Get a blanket. She's chilled to the bone."

Rachel's father sets her on the kitchen chair. He gently pries her fingers from around his neck. "I'll be right back," he says. "You have to let me go."

Rachel watches the doorway until he returns, carrying the white comforter from his bed. He wraps Rachel in it ("like a sausage," he used to say in happier times) then sits down with her on his lap.

Rachel's father kisses her head. She starts to feel warm. "Rachel," her father says, "never do that again. We'll visit your mother's grave in Boston more often, if that's what you want, but don't just leave in the middle of the night. Don't scare us like that."

Rachel nods. The Grandmother hands her a Santa Claus–face mug of hot chocolate, and sets another on the table in front of Rachel's father.

Rachel sips her hot chocolate, gives the Grandma a close look.

"Good, isn't it?" the Grandma says.

Rachel nods.

"Milk. That's the secret ingredient. None of that watery stuff."

The Grandmother sets the tin of gingerbread men on the table and Rachel reaches for one, teetering on her father's lap. He hands her a gingerbread man and takes one for himself.

"Well, it's a good thing you didn't fall asleep out there," the Grandma says.

Rachel swallows the gingerbread foot. "I started to but someone woke me up. I think it was that witch, Wilmot Redd. She found me and she made me stand up. She told me she didn't want my bones."

Rachel's father and the Grandmother look at each other. Rachel stops chewing and stares straight ahead, waiting to see if her father will make her get off his lap or if the Grandma will call the lady to come and take her away again.

"Rachel, Wilmot Redd was just some old lady. A fisherman's wife," Rachel's father says gently.

The Grandma sits down at the kitchen table. She looks at Rachel so hard that Rachel finally has to look back at her. The Grandma's face is extraordinarily white and Rachel thinks it looks just a little bit like a paper snowflake.

"I think I know who it might have been," she says. "Have you ever heard of La Befana? She's an old woman. Much older than me. And scary looking. Ugly. She carries around a big old sack filled with gifts that she gives to children. A long time ago the three wise men stopped by her house to get directions to Bethlehem, to see the Christ Child, you know. And after she gave them directions they invited her along but she didn't go with them 'cause she had too much housework to do. Of course she immediately regretted being so stupid and she's been trying to catch up ever since, so she goes around giving gifts to all the children just in case one of them is the Savior she neglected to visit, all those years ago, just 'cause she had dirty laundry to take care of. I bet that's who helped you tonight. Old La Befana herself." The Grandmother turns to look at Rachel's father. "It's about time this family had some luck, right? And what could be luckier than to be part of a real live Christmas miracle?"

Rachel's father hugs her and says, "Well, this little miracle better go to bed. Tomorrow is Christmas Eve, you don't want to sleep through it, do you?"

The Grandmother takes the mug of hot chocolate and the half-eaten gingerbread man from Rachel. Her father carries her to bed, tucks her in, and kisses her forehead. Rachel is falling asleep, listening to the faint murmuring voices of her father and the Grandmother, when she hears the noise. She goes to the closet, opens it, and sees right away, the Halloween treat bag in the corner, rustling as though the mouse is trapped inside. She is just about to shut the door when the small hand reaches out of the bag, grasps the paper edge, and another hand appears, and then, a tiny bone head.

"Is that you?" Rachel whispers.

The bones don't answer. They just come walking toward her, their sharp points squeaking.

Rachel slams the closet door shut. She runs out of her room. The Grandma and her father are sitting next to the tree. When they turn to her, their faces are flicked with yellow, blue, and green, they grin the wide skeletal grin of skulls. "Honey, is something the matter?" her father asks. Rachel shakes her head. "Are you sure? You look like you've seen—"

The Grandma interrupts, "Is it the mouse? Did you see the mouse?"

Rachel nods.

"Don't worry about it," the Grandma says. "Maybe Santa Claus will bring you a kitty this year."

Rachel refuses to go back to bed until her father and the Grandmother walk with her. They tuck her in, and again her father kisses her forehead, and the Grandma does the same, and then they leave her alone in the dark. After a while she hears the bones squeaking across the floor. Rachel feels around in the dark until she finds the Grandmother's big shoe. Rachel waits until she hears the squeaking start once more. When it does, she pounds where the sound comes from, and the first two times, she hits only the floor but the next five or six, she hears the breaking of bones, the small cries and curses. Her father and Grandmother run into the room and turn on the light. "Well, you killed it," the Grandma says, looking at her strangely. "I'll go get the broom and dustpan."

Rachel's father doesn't say anything. They just stand there, looking at the mess on the floor, and then at the mess on the bottom of the Grandmother's shoe.

Later, after it's all cleaned up, Rachel crawls back into bed. She pulls the blankets to her chin and rolls to her side. Her father and the Grandmother stand there for a while before they walk out of the room. For a long time Rachel listens in the dark but all she hears is her own breathing, and she falls asleep to the comforting sound.

When she wakes again it is Christmas Eve and snowing outside, glistening white flakes that tumble down the sky from the snow queen's garden, the Grandma says.

Because it is a special day the Grandma lets Rachel have gingerbread cookies and hot chocolate for breakfast on the couch while her father sleeps late. "He's worn out after everything you've been through," the Grandma says. Occasionally Rachel thinks she hears mewing from her father's room but the Grandma says, "Anyone can sound like a cat. It's probably just a sound he makes in his sleep. You, for instance, last night you were singing in your sleep."

"I was?" Rachel asks.

"Didn't anyone ever tell you that before? You sing in your sleep."

"I do?"

The Grandma nods. "You're a very strange little girl, you know," she says.

Rachel chews the gingerbread face and sighs.

"Now what do you suppose this is all about?"

The Grandma stands next to the Christmas tree, looking out the window. Rachel gets off the couch and squeezes between the Grandma and the tree. A gray cat meanders down the crooked sidewalk in front of the house. In its mouth it holds a limp mouse. Walking behind the cat is a straggling line of children in half-buttoned winter coats and loosely tied scarves, tiptoeing in boots and wet sneakers, not talking to each other or catching snowflakes on their tongues, only intently watching the cat with their bright eyes.

"Like the Pied Piper," the Grandma says.

Rachel shrugs and goes back to the couch. "It's just a bunch of the little kids," she says. "Who's the Pied Piper?"

The Grandma sighs. "Don't they teach you anything important these days?"

Rachel shakes her head.

"Well, it looks like I'll have to," the Grandma says.

And she does.

Holiday

She says her name is Holiday, but I know she's lying. I remember her face. It was all over the news for weeks, years even, but of course she doesn't know that. I briefly consider telling her, saying something like, "Hey, did you know you're a star?" But that would necessitate bringing up the subject of her death, and I'm not clear if she knows that she's a ghost, or that almost everyone thinks her parents killed her. That doesn't seem like the kind of thing any kid should have to hear, so instead I say, "Holiday? That's a pretty name."

Her body starts jerking in a strange way as she moves across my bedroom floor, her arms held out, her hands moving to some secret rhythm, and I think she's re-enacting her death, the way some ghosts do, until I realize that she's tap-dancing, her blond curls bouncing, that little-miss smile plastered across her face, bright red like she just finished eating a cherry Popsicle. I figured she came to tell me who offed her, but instead she came to dance and tell me lies.

"Why don't you come here." I pat beside me on the bed. Just like that she's gone. Like I'm a pervert or something. Poor dumb kid.

That's all there is until about a week later. This time I'm asleep on the couch and she wakes me up, singing a country western song. She's wearing a black cowboy hat with a big gold star on the front, a little black-and-red-fringed skirt, a denim shirt with silver buttons, and red tasseled cowboy boots that come about halfway up her calves. She looks pretty cute. She's singing in the dulcet tone of someone twice her age, and right away I understand the confusion people felt about her, the strange aura of sexuality that comes off her and shouldn't.

When she sees me watching, she waves, her little fingers slightly bent, but she doesn't miss a beat, even when she winks.

This is so freaking weird I don't know what to do, so I wait until she's finished and then I applaud.

She curtsies, holding out the skirt with the tips of her tiny fingers; her perfect blond curls undisturbed by her dance and song.

"So," I say, "Holiday, right?"

She nods, her red lips smirked.

"You hungry?" I pick up the half-full bag of Doritos on the coffee table in front of the couch and extend it toward her. She shakes her head. "Wanna watch a movie?" I ask. She just stands there, staring at me, squinting slightly, looking like she just might start crying, as though I have awoken her from some dream about Barbie dolls and Christmas and a perfect life, into this reality of being murdered and stuck, for all eternity, at age six, tap-dancing forever. I look through my DVD collection, *Kill Bill* (1, 2, and 3) *Seven Samurais, The Shining, Howard Stern's Private Parts* (severely underrated and underappreciated, by the way), *City of Women, My Architect, Wild Weather Caught on Tape* (a gift from an old girlfriend), and *The Wet Women of California*, which, swear to God, I had forgotten all about. None of it exactly seems like the sort of thing to watch with a six-year-old murdered kid, so instead I turn on the TV and settle on the cooking channel, but I guess it wasn't the right choice because next thing I know, I'm sitting alone watching this chick with a giant smile pouring liquid over hamburger meat. "Hey," I say to the air, "come back, we don't have to watch this." But of course no one answers and no one appears. I pick up one of the DVDs, and put it in, just to get rid of the headache I feel coming on. In two seconds, I'm watching naked big-breasted women dive into the ocean, roll in the sand, and frolic with the waves and each other. I drink my warm beer and start to play with myself until I get the creepy feeling that maybe she's still in the room. I take my hand out of my pants, flick off the DVD, and turn over, my face pressed against the couch.

The next day I go to the library. There's a whole shelf devoted just to her. I page through the books and look at all the pictures. Yep, it's her, all right. I don't check out the books, just in case she comes back. I don't want her to see them and get scared or anything. I don't know why she's coming to see me, but I want her to come back. When I read about how her father found her, wrapped in a blanket, as though someone was worried she would be cold, but with that rope around her neck, and all the rest, I feel like something inside me wakes up, and it's not a completely disturbing feeling. I spend the whole day at the library and when I leave I'm tired, and hungry, but before I do anything else, I go to Wal-mart and buy the boxed collection of Shirley Temple DVDs. They were her favorite. Next time she comes, I'm going to be prepared. Sarah Vehler, who was in my brother's class in high school, is the checkout girl. She's gained about five hundred pounds since then and I barely recognize her, but she recognizes me just fine. "I didn't know you have kids," she says. What am I supposed to do, tell her I've got a ghost? Instead, I just shrug. Maybe that was a mistake. I don't know. This was all new territory for me. I tried to do what was right.

When Terry, my agent, calls to see how the book is coming along, I tell him it's just fine. "But hey," I say, "I'm thinking of going in another direction, sort of."

"Shoot," Terry says.

I stumble around a bit and even though he's thousands of miles away, I know he's chewing his nicotine gum faster and faster until finally he says, "Listen, just give it to me in a sentence, all right?"

"I wanna write about—" and I say her name.

"Who?"

For a long time she was everyone's little girl. The whole country followed her story and wanted vengeance for what was done to her, but now, hardly anyone even remembers her name.

"Oh, wait, the little Miss America kid, right? What's she got to do with anything? Did your parents know her parents or something?"

"Well, not exactly, but—"

"Don't blow this, okay? Memoir writing isn't what it used to be, all right? Just stick to the facts, make sure it's all documented."

"But I—"

"Stick to your own story. You got enough there to keep you busy, right?"

"But Terry," I say, "when I think about her, I mean, don't you think what happened to her was a real travesty?"

"Travesty? Right. Of course it was. But what happened to you was a real travesty too, wasn't it? Your whole family torn apart by false accusations, your father dying in prison for something he didn't do. That's the travesty you know. That's the one you can write about."

"I just think—"

"Okay, I know what's happening here. Something in your mind, in your subconscious is trying to distract you from writing this, am I right? Huh?"

"I guess," I say, glancing at my computer.

"Tell you what, why don't you just take a couple of days? Give yourself a break. Watch movies. Take walks in the park. Get laid. Take some time off, is what I'm saying, not weeks or anything but you know, take a few days, then you can come back to this all refreshed, Okay?"

"Okay," I say.

"Who cares if you're a few days late, right?"

"Right."

"Just forget about the kid," he says. "She's not your story."

We say good-bye and I walk over to the computer and click on the file. I stare at the blank screen, certain that if I could just come up with the title, I could probably sail through the whole thing. But the title is elusive. Instead I take Terry's advice and watch a movie, several in fact. Shirley Temple in black and white, highly, highly underrated. I don't even know when she appears. But suddenly we are sitting on the couch, laughing. It feels so good to laugh like that I decide not to say anything. I don't want to scare her off. I don't know when she left. I fell asleep and when I woke up, she was gone.

The next day I sit staring at the screen on my computer for two hours. I know it sounds like an exaggeration, but I timed it. I try several titles. *My Father's Rules. I Am Not His Son. Rising Above the Prison He Resides In. Last Chance.* You get the picture, right? Crap. I click off the computer and take Terry's advice. I go to the park.

They are so young. So perfect, with their perfect skin and little teeth and they are dirty, and bratty, and crying, and laughing and completely absorbed by the sand in the sandbox, or the need to traverse the bars, dangling above the dangerous ground, holding tight, and it's obvious it hurts, but they are determined, stubborn, wild, beautiful. I could watch them for hours, but instead I just watch for a little while; I know too well what the grownups will think about someone like me, a young man, all alone, watching children play. I turn away, hunched against the sudden cold, walking slowly, soon no longer able to hear the laughter and the sound of their voices, shouting names, or shouting nonsense.

God, how I envy them.

When I get home my brother is standing on my porch, hunched into his jacket, his hands in his pockets. "Hey," he says.

"Hey," I say. "What's up?"

He shrugs, glances at my door and then gives me that pretend smile of his.

"I don't have any," I say.

"What? Oh, that hurts, bro," he says. "I'm sincerely hurt. I just thought, you know, I'd stop by."

I nod, but I do it with a smirk so that he knows I know the truth, even if we are going to play this game. I take the key out of my pocket and let us into the house.

"Christ," he says.

"What?"

"Don't you ever clean up after yourself? Mom would shit if she saw this."

"Well, she's not going to see it, all right? We both know that. What do you want?"

He shrugs, but he's casing the joint. I'm a writer. I notice these things. "Man, I'm just so hurt, bro," he says. "What, you think I only come when—"

"Yeah," I say. "Yeah, I do."

We stand there, staring at each other, then he shrugs and walks into my living room, sits on the couch, I'm only half paying attention. He picks up the remote control. "Wait," I say, but it's too late, Shirley Temple is dancing across the screen, all dimples and innocence.

I don't know what to do so I just stand there.

He's laughing so hard, he's bent over at the waist, and I start laughing too, and that's when he jumps up and grabs me by the collar and pushes me against the wall.

"I should fucking kill you," he says.

"It's not like that. I'm doing some research."

"Fucking pervert."

"I'm not the one," I say, only 'cause I'm desperate, only 'cause he's got this look in his eyes like he might really kill me.

He pushes me harder into the wall. He leans against me. "What did you say?"

"I'm not the one he liked most," I say and he lets go as if I'm on fire. For a moment we are just standing there, breathing heavy and staring at each other. I try to make it right. I reach over to touch his shoulder but he jerks away.

He wipes his hand through his hair, licks his lips, and then wipes them with the back of his hand, and his eyes stay cold.

"Come on," I try again.

He leans toward me, like he would kill me if he could stand to touch me. He speaks, real slow, breathing onion into my face, "But you're the one who's grown up to be just like him."

"It's fucking research," I shout. He nods, like, sure, he doesn't believe me. He walks out of my house, my fucking addict brother, thinking he's got it all together and that I'm the one falling apart. I lock the door behind him, and when I turn, she's there, tap-dancing across the kitchen in the outfit that caused all the controversy, the one with the feathers, and the black net stockings. "Oh, hi," I say. "Did you catch any of that?"

She pirouettes in a furious twirl, a great flurry of tapping feet, and another twirl; I am sincerely amazed and clap until my hands feel raw. She smiles and smiles and then waves her arm, like a magician's assistant, and that's when I see the other little girl. She's taller, her skin is black, her hair in two ponytails high on her head; she's dressed just like a regular kid, a t-shirt, shorts, and flip-flops. "Hi," I say. "What's your name?"

She smiles, but it is a shy smile, her lips closed.

"Her name is Holiday too."

I nod, puzzling this out.

"And today is her birthday."

I turn to the girl, who looks up at me with her beautiful black eyes.

"Your birthday?"

Both girls nod solemnly.

"Well, I don't, let me see what I can find. I wasn't expecting . . ." I rummage through the kitchen drawers and cabinets, making excuses all the while. "I wish I had known, I'm just so unprepared. A birthday? If I had known, I would have, I mean, balloons and cake . . ." The girls look up at me, bright-eyed. "But I'm sorry, I don't, this is the best I can. Happy birthday," I say, and set a plate on the table. In the middle of the plate is a jelly sandwich, and in the center of the sandwich is the stub of a lit candle left over from when I was still trying to impress dates. The whole thing looks pretty lame but the girl claps all the same. She tries valiantly to blow the candle out, and then they both try, and after a while they just look up at me, and I do it for them.

I'm not sure what to do next so I ask them if they want to watch Shirley Temple movies. We go into the living room and sit on the couch and I think they had a good time, though in the morning I discover the jelly sandwich untouched on the plate. It's stale but I eat it just the same, sitting in front of the computer, searching the Internet sites of missing and murdered children, looking for the birthday girl, but I never do find her.

Suddenly it's like I'm running some kind of day care center for dead kids. She keeps bringing them to me, I don't know why. We watch Shirley Temple movies, though she's the one who likes them best, and, I have to admit, she can be pretty bratty about it at times. Actually, they all can be pretty bratty. They're little kids, what can I say? They fight over which movie to watch, they run up and down the stairs, they jump off the kitchen table and the back of the couch. I recognize some of them. Without asking, I know some of their names. I mean, come on, some of these kids are famous. Others, like the little

black girl, I never do figure out. When they're all around, I sometimes
think I'm going to lose it, but when no one comes, when it's just me,
all alone, staring at the computer again, still trying to find the perfect
title, the perfect little phrase to describe what happened to my family,
I miss their smelly mouths, their waxy ears, their noise, their demands,
their little bodies twisted in odd positions of sleep and play, and I
miss their laughter, the gorgeous sound of their laughter. Her dancing. I miss her dancing. And I miss her, most of all.

But she says it's getting boring at my house. She says it's too noisy.
She says she might not come around any more and when I ask her to
dance she just shakes her head, no; she doesn't feel like it. That's when
I say, without thinking about it or anything, why don't we have a party,
and she says, "You mean like a jelly sandwich with a candle stuck in
it?" (I told you, she can be bratty.) But I say, no, I mean like a big
party, with balloons and party hats and paper maché streamers, would
you like that? "And a Christmas tree?" she asks. Well, I wasn't really
thinking of that but I can tell she wants one so I say sure. She smiles,
"And big red Valentine's hearts?" I say, all right. "And Easter baskets?
And chocolate eggs?" And I say sure, of course, it'll be a holiday party,
an every holiday party, and I don't say this part, but you know, for all
the ones they've missed. She gives me a big hug then, her little arms
tight around my neck, and she kisses me right on the mouth.

I buy red, green, orange, and black streamers, balloons that have
"Happy Birthday" printed on them, a paper tablecloth with turkeys
and pilgrims on it. I get a seventy-five percent discount on the scare-
crow, the ceramic pumpkin, and a clown costume, but I have to pay
a ridiculous price for the fake Christmas tree already decorated with
lights and ornaments. I buy cupcakes, even though I'm not sure any
of the dead kids eat, and I buy two kinds of paper plates, one with
Barbie on them, and the other with dinosaurs. I get several different
kid DVDs (I have to admit even I'm getting a little sick of Shirley
Temple) and a CD of Christmas classics.

Sarah Vehler is working again. She is standing there, chewing on
a hangnail, and not checking anyone out, but I stand in line behind
a woman with two little kids, a boy and a girl. The boy is furiously
sucking his thumb, and the girl is begging for candy. The woman, their

mother, I assume, is ignoring them, paging through a *People* magazine. I smile at the little girl, and for just a second she stops asking for candy and stares at me. Her eyes remind me of beach glass. Sarah Vehler calls my name and when I look up, she waves me over. "Don't you have nothing better to do than stand in line all day?" she says. "Wow, looks like you're planning a full year of parties. How many kids you got anyway?" I shrug, and to change the subject tell her I like her earrings. I have long since learned that the real way to gain a woman's trust is to tell her you like her earrings but Sarah Vehler just looks at me like I said something crazy and of course that's when I realize she isn't wearing earrings. I laugh. "I mean last time," I say. "I remember the ones you had on last time, and I meant to tell you they were real nice." Then, things only get more ridiculous when she tells me she never wears earrings. "I'm sorry," I say, grabbing the bags and the box of cupcakes. "I thought it was you, but it must have been someone else." She just looks at me like she is thinking real hard, and then she says, "I saw your brother the other day and he says you don't have any kids at all."

I smile, to be polite, and then tilt my chin, like, you got another customer. She turns, and sees the guy who has a disturbingly blank expression on his face, but when she looks at me again, I shrug, as if to say, too bad we can't talk.

When I get home, I have to clean the place. I've let it go and my mother would shit if she saw it, but she never tries to visit, and doesn't even call. She's got her own life now, and doesn't like to be reminded of the old one, I guess, the one me and my brother are stuck in forever. I pick up beer cans and paper plates and realize this hasn't exactly been the best environment for children. I freaking hate to clean, but after a while I sort of get into it, I put one of the new DVDs in, I don't know what it was called but it was bright and noisy and cheerful, it kept me company. I even washed the windows. Then I hung up the streamers, twisting them from the ceiling in the kitchen and the living room, and I set up the tree, and the tablecloth, and the plates, and then I put the clown costume on, and I looked at myself in the mirror. I was wearing a bright red, yellow, blue, and green polka-dotted jumpsuit, giant red shoes that flopped six inches from my toes, a bright red wig, and a red nose. I looked at myself for awhile, trying to figure out who I reminded myself of, and then I flashed back to a birthday party—was it for me or my brother?—my father dressed up like a clown. I grab my phone and call. The answering machine picks up.

"The thing is," I say, "I mean, come on. Don't give up on me so fast, okay? It was just a movie. It's research, all right? Fuck. I mean really, fuck. Look, I didn't give up on you even with all the drugs and the stealing and shit, right? Right?" It seems like I should say something else, something perfect, but I can't think what that would be so I hang up and call Terry.

"The thing is," I say, "I haven't been completely honest."

There's a moments' pause. A long moment before he says, "Shoot."

"The thing is," I say, "what I want to write about isn't an innocent man." I wait, but he doesn't say anything. "The children . . ." She is standing there, in the middle of the living room, staring at the Christmas tree with the strangest expression on her face. She is dressed just like a regular little girl, in little girl pajamas and a bathrobe. I wave at her and point to the phone, signaling that I'll be winding the call up soon, but her expression doesn't change; she looks at me with confusion and sorrow.

"What about the kids? What's your point? Can you just give it to me in a sentence?"

"The children were telling the truth, my father was not an innocent man."

Terry whistles, long and low. "Fuck," he says.

"You're the first person I ever told."

"Well, this puts us in the crapper without any shit, that's for sure."

"What?" She is reaching for the tree, touching it lightly with her fingertips, as though afraid it will disappear.

"Listen, if that's the case, what we got is just another story about a fucking pedophile. Those are a dime a dozen. The market is saturated with them. It's not a special story any more, it's just . . . now wait a second, that kid, you're not saying he had anything to do with that kid's murder are you, 'cause if you were saying that, well, then we'd have a story."

"No." She is petting the tree, and this part really gets to me: she leans in to smell it; even though it is fake, she presses her face real close to the branches and then she realizes I am watching and she looks at me again, but in a new way, like she has something she wants to say, like she needs me. "I gotta go," I say.

"I mean even if you think he could have possibly had something to do with it, that we might be able to sell. It gets tricky, 'cause you know all of a sudden everyone's fact checking the hell out of memoirs, but we might be able to work that angle, you know, not that you really believe he killed her, 'cause everyone knows her parents did it, right, but like you could tie her into your story and the idea that your father was someone like her father, you might have something there, ok? We might be able to sell that."

She has big eyes, and they are sad, and she wants to tell me something important, maybe she's going to tell me who did kill her. "Listen, I gotta go," I say. Terry keeps talking; he's getting excited now, just the way, all those years ago, everyone got excited about her murder. I click the phone off.

"What is it?" I say, "You can tell me."

"I wet myself," she says, in the softest little girl voice.

Sure enough, there's a wet stain down the front of her pajamas, and a puddle on the rug beneath the Christmas tree. "That's okay," I say, even as the dank odor reaches me. "Sometimes that happens. Why don't you go in the bathroom and take off your clothes. Do you have a way, I mean, I don't know how this works, do you have some clean clothes with you?"

She shakes her head.

I nod, like, okay, no problem. The phone rings and she looks relieved when I don't make any move to answer it. Instead I search through the piles of clothes on my bedroom floor until I find a dingy white T-shirt and a brand new pair of boxer shorts, which of course will be huge on her, so I also give her a tie. She looks up at me with confusion when I hand her the stuff. "It'll be like a costume, for the party. Kind of different from the kind you usually wear, I know. Go in the bathroom, okay, and wash yourself off and take off your wet pajamas and put on the t-shirt, and these shorts, and tie these with this, see, like a belt."

"Will you wipe me?" she says.

I shouldn't be surprised by this; I've read all about how she still asked people to wipe her, even though she was dressed up like a movie star. "No. You have to do it yourself, okay?"

She shakes her head and starts to cry.

One thing I can't stand is a crying kid. "Okay," I say, "Okay, just don't cry, all right?"

We walk into the bathroom and I help her out of her pajamas. Her skin is white, pure as fresh soap, and she is completely unembarrassed of her nakedness. She smiles when I wipe her, first with toilet paper, and then with a towel dampened with warm water and I just try not to think about anything, about how tiny she is, or how perfect. I help her put the clean t-shirt on and the boxer shorts, which I cinch around her little waist with the tie, and by then she is laughing and I am too and we stand before the mirror to look at ourselves but all I see is me, in the ridiculous clown costume. Where does she keep disappearing to? I call her name, searching through all the rooms, thinking she's playing some kind of game, but I can't find her anywhere. The doorbell rings and I run to answer it, laughing because it's very funny the way she's hidden outside, but when I open the door, my brother is standing there.

"Oh, fuck," he says.

"It's not the way it looks."

He looks behind me, at the streamers, the table set with Barbie and dinosaur plates, the cupcakes, the Christmas tree. "Fuck," he says.

"No, wait," I holler, and when he doesn't stop I follow him, flopping down the stairs, "Wait," I say, running after him, though it is difficult in the too-big red shoes, the red wig bouncing down my forehead, "it's not how it looks."

He turns, and I smile at him, knowing he'll understand—after all, we share the same childhood—but instead he looks at me with a horrified expression, as if I am a terrifying ghost, and then he turns his back on me and runs. I don't try to follow him; instead I walk back to my house. Someone in a passing car shouts something and throws a paper cup of soda at me, but misses. I am surprised by this, it seems to me clowns deserve a little respect; after all, they only exist to make people laugh.

When I get back inside, I shut the door and sit on the couch in front of the TV and watch the cartoon people, who are shaped like balloons. There are no dead children and there are no secrets in a world where everyone is brightly colored and devoid of the vulnerabilities of flesh. In balloon world all the problems explode or float away. Even though it's been cold and cloudy for weeks, the sun comes out and fills the room with an explosion of light until I can no longer see the picture on the TV screen. One of the streamers comes loose and dangles over my head, twirling, and I can't help but think that in spite of what Terry said, there is plenty of shit for the crapper, but it doesn't matter, because in the distance, I hear the soft hum of a little girl singing. And just like that my mood improves, because I am waiting for the children, and just thinking about them makes me smile.

The Chambered Fruit

Stones. Roots. Chips like bones. The moldering scent of dry leaves and dirt, the odd aroma of mint. What grew here before it fell to neglect and misuse? I remember this past spring's tulips and daffodils, sprouted among the weeds, picked and discarded without discrimination. I was so distracted by my dead daughter that I rarely noticed the living. I take a deep breath. Mint thyme. It should have survived the neglect, perhaps did, but now has fallen victim to my passionate weeding, as so much of more significance has fallen victim before it. I pick up a small, brown bulb and set it, point up, in the hole, cover it with dirt. Geese fly overhead. I shade my eyes to watch them pass, and then cannot avoid surveying the property.

Near the old barn are piles of wood and brick meant to further its renovation. Leaves and broken branches litter the stacks. The wood looks slightly warped, weathered by the seasons it's gone untended. The yard is bristly with dried weeds and leaves. The house has suffered the worst. Surely, instead of planting bulbs I should be calling a contractor. It can't be good, the way it looks like it's begun to sink into the earth or how the roof litters shingles that spear into the ground around it. But who should I call? How far do I have to search to find someone who doesn't know our story?

I think of it like the nursery rhyme. Inside the old farmhouse with the sagging porch, through the large, sunny kitchen, past the living room with the wood-burning stove, up the creaking stairs and down the hall lined with braided rugs, past the bathroom with the round window and claw-footed tub, past the yellow-and-white bedroom we called the guest room, past her room (where the door is shut) to our bedroom—my bedroom now—there is, on the bedside table, a picture of the three of us. It's from her last birthday. Twelve candles on the cake. She is bent to blow them out, her face in pretty profile. Her dark hair brushes against the smooth skin of her puffed cheek; her eye, bright with happiness, dark-lashed beneath its perfectly arched brow. Jack and I stand behind her. Both of us are blurry, the result of Jack having set up the camera for automatic timer, his running to be in the shot, me moving to make room for him. He looks like her, only handsome, and I look like, well, someone passing by who got in the picture by mistake, a blur of long, untidy hair, an oversize shirt, baggy slacks. The camera captures and holds their smiles forever, locked in innocence and joy, and my smile, strained, my focus somewhere past the borders of the picture, as if I see, in the shadows, what is coming.

When I think of everything that happened, from the beginning, I look for clues. In a way, there are so many it baffles strangers that we couldn't see them. But to understand this, and really, I'm beyond expecting anyone else to understand this, but for my own understanding, I have to remember that to be human is a dangerous state. That said, Jack's nature is not profoundly careless, and I am not, really, in spite of everything you might have read or concluded, criminally naïve. Though of course I accept, even as I rebel against its horrible truth, that a great deal of the fault was ours. Sometimes I think more ours than his. When I look for clues to the dangerous parents we'd become I have to accept the combustible combination that occurred, just once, when Jack was careless and I was naïve and that's all it took. We lost her.

You may be familiar with my old work. Folk scenes, sort of like Grandma Moses except, frankly, hers are better. Maybe the difference is that hers were created from real memories and mine were made from longing. No one I know has ever ridden in a horse-drawn sleigh, with or without bells. We did not hang Christmas wreaths on all the doors and from the street lamps lit with candles. We did not send the children to skate at the neighborhood pond (which didn't exist, the closest thing being the town dump) or burn leaves and grow pumpkins (well, the Hadleys grew pumpkins, but their farmhouse was an old trailer, so it didn't really fit the picture). We did garden, but our gardens did not all blossom into perfect flower at the same moment on the same day, the women standing in aprons, talking over the fence. The sun shone but it didn't shine the way I painted it, a great ball of light with spears of brightness around it.

These are the paintings I made. Little folk scenes that were actually quite popular, not in town, of course, but in other places where people imagined the world I painted existed. I made a decent living at it. Even now, when all I paint are dark and frightening scenes of abduction and despair that I show no one (who would come anyway; even old friends keep their distance now), I live off the royalties. My paintings are on calendars, Christmas cards, coasters, t-shirts. In the first days of horror, when the news coverage was so heavy, I thought someone would certainly point out that I (the neglectful mother of the dead girl) was also the painter C. R. Rite, but as far as I know the connection was never made and my income has not suffered for my neglect.

Jack still represents my work, which also makes it strange that no one ever made the connection. Maybe people assumed we were actually farmers, though the locals certainly knew that wasn't true. Maybe the media was just too busy telling the grisly details of our story to focus any attention on the boring issue of our finances. Certainly that matter isn't very titillating. What people seemed to want to hear was how our daughter died, an endless nightmare from which I can't ever wake, that strangers actually watch and read as some form of entertainment.

I accept my fault in this, and I know it's huge. I live every day with the Greek proportions of our story. In the classic nature I had a fault, a small area, like Achilles's heel, that left me vulnerable.

But not evil. As Jack likes to point out, we didn't do that to her and we would have stopped it from happening if we knew how.

The unforgivable thing, everyone agrees, is that we didn't see it. How evil do you have to be? We did not keep our daughter safe and she's dead because of that. Isn't that evil enough?

———

When we moved here, Steff was eight. She didn't know that we were
really country people, having lived her whole life in the city. At first
she spent all her time in her room with her books and her dolls but
eventually, during that giddy first hot summer when I walked about
in my slip (when the construction crew wasn't working on the barn)
eating raspberries off the bushes and planting sunflower seeds and
hollyhocks (though it was too late and they wouldn't bloom), she
joined me, staying close, afraid of all the space, the strangeness of sky.
Eventually, she came to love it too and brought blankets into the yard
for picnics, both real and imagined, and paper to color, which, in true
Buddha-child fashion she left to blow about the yard when she was
finished. When one of these pictures blew across my path, a scene of
a girl picking flowers, a shimmering angel behind her, I memorized it
and then let it blow away, thinking it would be a gift for somebody
unlucky enough not to have a child who drew pictures of that other
world which children are so close to.

In the city, Steffie had attended a small private school with a philosophy that sheltered children from the things in our world that
make them grow up so fast. The influence of media was discour-
aged and, contrary to national trend, computer use was considered
neither necessary nor particularly beneficial to children. At eight,
Steffie still played with dolls, and believed in, if not magic, at least
a magicalness to the world; a condition that caused strangers to
look at her askance and try to measure her IQ but for which I took
great pride. In her school they learned the mythic stories, needle-
work, and dance. Friends of mine with children in public or other
private schools talked of the homework stress and the busyness of
their lives, transporting kids from practice to practice. When I visited these friends, their children did not play the piano or happily
kick soccer balls in the yard. In spite of all those lessons, or, I sus-
pected, because of them, these children sat listless and bleary-eyed
in front of the television or wandered about the house, restless and
bored, often resorting to eating, while Steffie played with dolls or
spoons, whatever was available. I feel that our society has forgotten

the importance of play, the simple beginnings of a creative mind. The value of that. Not that anyone is interested in parental guidance from me now.

At any rate, Steffie got off the bus, that first day, in tears. Several of the children would not sit with her because, they said, we were a bunch of hippies who ran around the yard in our underthings. When Steffie told me this, I cried right along with her. I'd made a life out of forgetting the world. I found its reminders sharp and disturbing.

Eventually, she adjusted and I did too. I wore clothes in the yard, though I was baffled how anyone knew I'd ever done differently. Steff put away her dolls and proudly carried her heavy backpack filled with books and maps and serious questions about the real world, completely neglecting anything about the spiritual. Incredibly (to me) she liked it. A lot. She loved the candy they were rewarded with, the movies they watched. "I like it because it's normal," she said, and I realized that she knew we were not.

The years passed. I had the barn converted to an art studio and planned to further the renovation so that I could turn it into a sort of community art center for teenagers. I imagined Saturday mornings teaching painting, others teaching things like weaving, or, when Steffie began to take an interest in it, even dance. I think part of the motivation for this plan was the idea of filling the place with teenagers and helping Steffie's social life, which still seemed, though she never complained, strangely quiet for a child her age.

So, when Jack bought the computer, I thought it was a good idea. He said he needed it for the business and Steffie had been complaining for some time that she "needed" one too. He brought home the computer and I didn't argue. After all, he and Steff were the ones dealing with the notorious "real" world and I was the one who got to spend all morning painting happy pictures and the rest of the day gardening, or baking cookies, or reading a good book. Who in the world lived a life like mine?

When the computer was set up and ready to use in his office, Jack called me to come look. I looked into the brightly colored screen and felt numbed by it. Steff, however, was thrilled. Soon the two of them were talking a strange language I didn't understand. I drifted off into private thoughts, mentally working on paintings, scenes from a time before the world was enchanted by screens.

About three months before (oh, God, I still cannot write these words without trembling) her last birthday, Jack began campaigning that we get Steff her own computer. I didn't like the idea but I couldn't say why, though I held my ground until one Saturday when I drove into town to the post office and saw a group of girls who looked to be Steffie's age, and who I thought I recognized from classroom functions, sitting at the picnic table outside the ice cream place. A few of the girls caught me staring, and they began whispering behind open hands. I turned away. Had I done this to her? Was it my strangeness that made her unpopular? I went home and told Jack to go ahead and buy the thing. We gave it to her for her twelfth birthday, that's when we took the picture, the one I still have on the bedside table.

Steff was thrilled. She hugged us both and gave us kisses and thanked us so much that I began to believe we had done the right thing. I was baffled how this silent box was going to make her life better but after seeing those girls together, I was ready to try anything.

They set up the computer in her room. At night, after dinner, they each went off for hours, clicking and staring at their separate screens. I lit candles and sat, with the cat in my lap, reading. I guess I had some vague ideas about homework, and I'd heard that there were ways to view great paintings from distant museums on the computer. I assumed she was doing things like that. I thought she should be doing more interacting with the world. I thought this as I sat reading, with the cat on my lap, and tried to believe that one solitude is the same as any other.

As though she'd been given the magic elixir for a social life, she began talking about various friends. Eventually one name came up more and more frequently. Celia read the same books Steffie did and liked to draw and dance. When Celia asked Steff to sleep over I was thrilled until I found out Stephanie had never actually met the girl but only "talked" to her on the computer.

Of course, I said this would not happen. She could be anyone; why, Celia might not even be a girl, I said. No, she could not sleep over at this stranger's house, who, coincidentally, lived only twenty-four miles away.

Steff burst into tears at the dinner table, threw her napkin on the plate. "You don't want me to be normal," she said. "You want me to be just like you and I'm not!" Then she ran out of the kitchen, up the stairs to her bedroom, where she actually slammed the door, all of this perhaps not unusual behavior for an almost teenager but completely new for Steff.

Jack looked at me accusingly.

"You can't expect me to let her go off to some stranger's house. We don't even know the family."

"Whose family do we know?"

I understood his point. I had sheltered us, all of us, with my sheltered ways.

"When it comes down to it, if she went anywhere in town, we wouldn't know those people either."

"It's not the same thing. People have reputations." As soon as I saw the look on Jack's face, I realized that our reputation was probably more extensive than I knew. If not for me, they would be having a normal life. I was the odd one. It was all my fault.

"What if I speak to the girl's parents, would that make you more comfortable?"

For a moment, I considered that we invite the girl's family over, we could have a barbecue, but the thought of having to spend a whole evening entertaining anyone horrified me. When it comes right down to it, my daughter died because of my reluctance to entertain. How ridiculous and horrifying. Instead, I agreed that she could go if Jack talked to Celia's parents first.

We went up to her room together. We knocked and entered. I expected to find her lying across the bed, my posture of teenage despair, but instead, she was sitting at the desk, staring into the computer.

"We've decided you can go, but we want to speak to her parents first."

She turned and grinned, bathed in computer glow, all the color gone from her pretty face and replaced with green.

"Is that Celia now?" Jack asked.

She nodded.

"Ask her for her number."

She began typing. I turned and walked away. What was I so creeped out about? This was the new world. My daughter and my husband were a part of it, as was I, even if with reluctance.

Jack spoke to Celia's father that night. It turned out they had a lot in common too. He was an insurance salesman. His wife, however, was very different from me, a lawyer out of town until Friday night. Jack covered the mouthpiece. "He wants to pick Steff up around four-thirty on Friday. He's going to be passing through town. They'll pick Celia up at her dance class, and Sarah will get home from D.C. about five-thirty. He's spoken to her and she's happy to have Stephanie over. What do you think?"

"How does he sound?"

"He sounds a lot like me."

Steff was standing in the kitchen doorway watching. I wasn't used to her squinty-eyed appraisal, as if suddenly there was something suspicious about me.

"Okay," I said.

Steff grinned. Jack took his hands off the mouthpiece. "That'll work out fine," he said in a boisterous voice. They really both looked so thrilled. Had I done this to them? Kept them so sheltered that Stephanie's sleepover at a friend's house on a Friday night, an absolutely normal occurrence for any girl her age, was such an enormous event?

Was this all my fault?

He was right on time. It was a beautiful spring day, unseasonably warm. I found him immediately affable, friendly, grinning dimples. I thought he looked younger than Jack or me, though in reality he was a year older. I guess people without consciences don't wrinkle like the rest of us. I opened the door and we shook hands. He had a firm handshake, a bit sweaty, but it was a warm day. Jack came out and the two of them got to talking immediately. I slipped away to get Steff. I went to her bedroom. Her backpack was packed, the sleeping bag rolled next to it, but she was not in the room. I walked over to the window and saw her in the garden, picking flowers. I opened the window. She looked up and waved, the flowers in her hand arcing the sky. I waved, pointed to his car. She nodded and ran toward the house. I brought the ridiculously heavy backpack and sleeping bag downstairs. When I got to the kitchen, she was standing there, her cheeks flushed, holding the bouquet of daffodils and tulips while Jack and Celia's father talked. I helped her wrap the stems in a wet paper towel and aluminum foil. "This is a very nice idea," I whispered to her at the sink.

She smiled and shrugged. "Celia said her mom likes flowers too."

What was it about that that set off a little warning buzzer in my head? All these coincidences. I shook it back; after all, isn't that how friendships are made, by common interests? We turned and the fathers stopped talking. Celia's father grinned at Steff. Once more the alarm sounded but he bent down, picked up the pack, and said something like, What do kids put in these things, Celia's is always so heavy too. They walked to the door. I wanted to hug Stephanie but it seemed silly and probably would be embarrassing to her, and, after all, hadn't I already embarrassed her enough? The screen door banged shut. I stood in the kitchen and listened to the cheerful voices, the car doors slam, the engine, the sound of the gravel as they drove away. Too late, I ran out to wave good-bye. I have no idea if Steffie saw me or not.

Jack wrapped his arms around my waist, nuzzled my neck. "The garden? Kitchen? Name your place, baby."

"I should have told her to call when she gets there."

"Honey, she'll be back tomorrow."

"Let's call her, just to make sure she's comfortable."

"Chloe—"

"After we call her, the garden."

———

There was a sudden change in the weather. The temperature dropped thirty degrees. We closed windows and doors and put on sweaters and jeans. It began to rain about 5:30 and it just kept raining. We called at six, seven, eight. No one answered. It began to hail.

"Something's wrong," I said.

"They probably just went to a movie."

We called at nine. It rang and rang.

"I'm going there."

"What? Are you kidding? Do you have any idea how embarrassing that would be for her?"

"Well, where are they, Jack?"

"They went to a movie, or the mall, or out for pizza. Not everyone lives like us."

Ten. Still no answer.

I put on my coat.

"Where are you going?"

"Give me the directions."

"You can't be serious."

"Where are the directions?"

"Nothing's wrong."

"Jack!"

"I don't have any directions."

"What do you mean? How are we supposed to pick her up?"

"Turns out he's coming back this way tomorrow. He's going to drop her off."

Lightning split the sky and thunder shook the house. "Do you even have an address?"

"I'm sure everything's all right," he said, but he said it softly and I could hear the fear in his voice.

We called at 10:20, 10:30, 10:41, 10:50, 10:54. At last, at 10:59, a man's voice.

"Hello, this is Steffie's mother, is this—" I don't even know his name. "—Is this Celia's father?"

"I just picked up the phone, lady, ain't no one here."

"What do you mean? Who are you? Where is everyone?"

"This is just a phone booth, okay?"

I drop the phone. I run to the bathroom. In the distance I hear Jack's voice, he says the number and then he says, "Oh, my God," and I don't hear the rest, over the sound of my retching.

Police sirens blood red. Blue uniforms and serious faces. Lights blaze. Pencils scratch across white pads. Jack wipes his hand through his hair, over and over again. Dry taste in my mouth. The smell of vomit. The questions. The descriptions. Fingerprint powder. I take them to her bedroom. Strange hands paw her things. Her diary. Someone turns her computer on. "Do you know her password?" I shake my head. "Well," says the man reading her diary, "it appears she really believed there was a Celia." What? Of course she did, can I see that? "Sorry, ma'am, it's evidence." Downstairs. More uniforms and rain-coats. Police banter about the weather. Blazing lights. The telephone rings. Sudden silence. I run to answer it. "Hello." It's Mrs. Bialo, my neighbor; she says, is everything all right? No, it's not. I hang up the phone. The activity resumes. Suddenly I see a light like the tiny flicker of a hundred fireflies hovering close to me and I hear her voice. *Mom?* I fall to my knees sobbing. Jack rushes over and holds me like I'm break-able. There is a temporary and slight change in the activity around us but then it continues as before and goes on like this for hours. In early morning there is a freak snowfall. We start getting calls from news-papers and magazines. A TV truck parks at the end of our drive. My neighbor, Mrs. Bialo, shows up with banana bread and starts making coffee. I stand on the porch and watch the snow salting down. The red tulips droop wounded against the icy white. The daffodils bow their silent bells. I listen to the sound of falling snow. I haven't told anyone what I know. What would be the point? Who would believe me? But I know. She's dead. She's dead. She's gone.

Let's go quickly over the details. The body. Oh, her body. Found. The tests confirm. Raped and strangled. My little darling.

———

Then, incredibly, he is found too. Trying to do the same thing again but this time to a more savvy family. He even used the name Celia. The sergeant tells me this with glee. "They always think they're so clever, but they're not. They make mistakes." How excited everybody is. They found him. He can't do it again. This is good. But I don't feel happiness, which disappoints everyone.

Jack agrees to go on a talk show. They convince him he will be helping other families and other little girls, but really, he's there so everyone can feel superior. One lady stands up. She is wearing a sensible dress and shoes. She is a sensible mother, anyone can see that, and she says, "I just don't understand, in this day and age, how you could let your daughter go off with a stranger like that?" She says it like she really cares, but she beams when the audience claps because really, she just wants to make her point.

Jack tries to say the stuff about how really everyone takes chances when they send their children off to other homes. I mean, we're all really strangers, he says. But they aren't buying it, this clever audience. The sensible lady stands up again and says, "I'm really sorry about what happened to your daughter but you gotta accept that it's at least partly your fault." There is scattered applause. The host tries to take it back. "I'm sure no one here means to imply this is your fault," he says. "We only want to learn from your mistakes." The audience applauds at that as well. Everyone gets applause except Jack.

After the taping he calls me in tears. I'm not much help as I am also feeling superior, since I would never be so stupid as to fall for the "You're helping others" line the talk show people keep trying. He says it was terrible, but on the day it airs, he insists we watch. It is terrible.

We move through the house and our lives. I think I will never eat again and then, one day, I do. I think we well never make love again and then, one night, something like that happens but it is so different, there is such a cold desperation to it, that I think it will never happen again, and it doesn't.

Six months later there is a trial. We are both witnesses for the prosecution so we can't attend. The defense attorney does a mean job on us but the prosecutor says, "He's just trying to distract the jury. It's not going to work. In fact, it'll probably backfire, generating more sympathy."

Fuck their sympathy, I say.

Jack looks as if I've just confirmed the worst rumors he's heard about me. The attorney maintains his placid expression, but his tone of voice is mildly scolding when he says, "The jury is your best hope now."

I think of her picking flowers in the garden that afternoon, the way she waved them in an arc across the sky.

When the verdict is read I stare at the back of his head. I think how, surely, if I had really studied him that day, instead of being so distracted by self-doubt, I never would have let him take her. The shape of his ears at the wrong height, the tilt of his head, something about his shoulders, all of it adds up. It's so obvious now.

"Guilty," the foreman says.

The courtroom is strangely quiet. Somehow, it is not enough.

When Jack and I get home he goes into his office. I wander about, until finally I settle on a plan. I take the fireside poker and walk up the stairs to her room, where I smash the computer. When I'm done Jack is standing there, watching. "That's a very expensive machine," he says.

"Fuck you," I say.

It doesn't get any better. At the end of the month, he moves out.

Fat, white flakes fall all day. The pine trees are supplicant with snow. I sit in my rocking chair like an old woman, the blue throw across my lap. I thought about starting a fire with the well-seasoned wood left over from last winter, but when I opened the stove and saw those ashes I didn't have the energy to clean them out. I rock and watch the snow fall. The house creaks with emptiness. The phone rings. I don't answer it. I fall asleep in the chair and when I wake it's dark. I walk to the kitchen, turn on the outside light. It's still snowing. I turn off the light and go to bed, not bothering to change out of my sweats and turtleneck. The phone rings and I grumble into the blankets but I don't answer it. I sleep what has become my usual restless sleep. In the morning it's still snowing.

Day after day it snows. Finally, the power goes out. The phone lines are down. I don't mind this at all. Oddly, I am invigorated by it. I shovel the wood-burning stove's ashes into an old paint can, find the wood carrier, and bring in stacks of wood and kindling. I build a fire and once I'm sure it's really started good, go upstairs and get my book, some blankets and pillows. I find the flashlights in the kitchen, both with working batteries, search through the linen closet and then the kitchen cupboards until I remember and find the portable radio on the top shelf in the basement. I stoke the fire, wrap myself in a blanket. How efficient we were, how well organized, how prepared for this sort of emergency, how completely useless, even culpable, when she needed us most. I turn on the radio. It will snow and snow, they say. We are having a blizzard. There are widespread reports of power outages. The Red Cross is setting up in the high school, which, actually, is also currently out of power so residents are advised to stay home for now. I click off the radio.

The phone is ringing.

"Hello?"

"Mom, where are you?"

"Steff? Steff?"

But there is no response. I stand there, holding the phone while the kitchen shadows lengthen around me. Still I stand there. I say her name over and over again. I don't know how long I stand there before I hang up, but when I do, I'm a changed woman. If I can't keep her alive, and it's been all too obvious that I can't, I'll take her dead. Yes, I want this ghost.

The person you most love has died and is now trying to contact you. You are happy.

You do whatever you can to help. You go out in the middle of the worst blizzard on record since there has been a record and drive to town. A trip that usually takes ten minutes today takes an hour and a half and you are happy. You go to the local drugstore and walk right past the aisles stripped of batteries and Sterno cans and candles to the toy section, where you select a Ouija board and tarot cards and you don't care when the clerk looks at you funny because you already have a strange reputation and who even cares about reputation when your dead daughter is trying to talk to you. You are not scared. You are excited. You know you probably should change your expression and look bored or disinterested as the clerk tallies up your purchases on a notepad because the cash register doesn't work due to the power outage and you probably should say something about buying this for your teenage niece but instead you stand there grinning with excitement. You sense the clerk, who looks to be a teenager herself, only a few years older than your dead daughter, watching you leave the store and walk through the storm to your truck, the only vehicle in the parking lot.

It takes even longer to get home and by the time you do, the fire has gone out and the house is cold. You are too excited to stop everything to build another fire. Instead you set up the Ouija board on the kitchen table. The cat comes over to smell it. You light a candle. The cat rubs against your leg. You sit at the table. You rest your fingers lightly on the pointer. You remember this from when you were young. "Steff," you say, and the sound of it is both silly and wonderful in the silent house. As if, maybe, she's just in another room or something. "Steff, are you here?" You wait for the pointer to move. It does not. "Steff?" Suddenly the house is wild with light and sound. The kitchen blazes brightly, the refrigerator hums, the heater turns on. The phone rings. You push back the chair, stand, and bang your thigh against the table. The phone rings and rings. "Hello?"

"Mom?"

"Steff, Steff, is that you?"

The dial tone buzzes.

You slam the phone down. The cat races out of the room with her tail puffed up.

You turn to the Ouija board. The pointer rests over the word. Yes. You try to remember if you left it there but you don't think you did or maybe it got knocked there when you hit your leg, but why are you trying to explain it when there is only one explanation for your dead daughter's voice on the phone? Slowly you turn and look at the silent phone. You pick up the receiver and listen to the dial tone.

You don't know whether to laugh or cry and suddenly your body is convulsing in some new emotion that seems to be a combination of both. You sink to the kitchen floor. The cat comes back into the room and lies down beside you. The dead can't make phone calls but the living can lose their minds. You decide you won't do that. You get up.

You try to believe it didn't happen.

But just in case, every time the phone rings, I answer it. I speak to an endless assortment of telemarketers wanting to sell me newspapers, a different phone service, offering me exciting opportunities to win trips to Florida or the Bahamas. Jack calls about once a week and we generally have the same conversation. (I'm fine. He can't come back. I haven't forgiven him. I haven't forgiven myself. I don't expect to. Ever.) Once there is a call where no one speaks at all and I'm terrified to hang up the phone so I stand there saying hello, hello, and finally I say, Steff? and there's a click and then the dial tone. Once, an old friend of mine from the city calls and I tell her all lies. How I've begun painting scenes of idyllic life again, how I've begun the healing process. I tell her the things people want me to say and by the end of the conversation she's happy she called and for a few minutes I feel happy too, as though everything I said was true.

I start receiving Christmas cards in the mail, strange greetings of Peace on Earth with scrawled condolences or blessings about this first Christmas without her. Jack calls in tears and tells me how much he misses her and us. I know, I know, I say gently, but you still can't come back. There is a long silence, then he hangs up.

I go into town only for groceries. I lose track of the days so completely that I end up in the supermarket on Christmas Eve. Happy shoppers load carts with turkeys and gift wrap and bottles of wine, bags of shrimp, crackers and cheese. I pick through the limp lettuce, the winter tomatoes. While I'm choosing apples I feel someone watching me and turn to see a teenage girl of maybe sixteen or seventeen standing by the bananas. There is something strange about the girl's penetrating stare beneath her homemade knit cap, though it is not unusual to catch people staring at me; after all, I'm the mother of a dead girl. I grab a bag of apples. I wonder if she knew Steff. I turn to look over by the bananas but she's not there.

"I don't know if you remember me or not."

The girl stands at my elbow. The brown knit cap is pulled low over her brow with wisps of brown hair sticking out. She has dark brown eyes, lashed with black. She might be pretty.

"I waited on you during the first storm at Walker's drugstore."

I nod, at a loss at what to say to this strange, staring girl.

She leans close to me. I smell bubblegum, peppermint, and something faintly sour. "I can help," she whispers.

"Excuse me?"

She looks around, in a dramatic way, as if we are sharing state secrets, licks her chapped lips and leans close again. "I know how to talk to dead people. You know, like in that movie. I'm like that kid." She leans back and looks at me with those dark, sad eyes and then scans the room as if frightened of the living. "My name is Maggie Dwinder. I'm in the book." She nods abruptly and walks away. I watch her in her old wool coat, a brown knit scarf trailing down her back like a snake.

"Oh, how are you doing, dear?"

This face sends me back to that day. Snow on tulips. My daughter's death. "Mrs. Bialo, I never thanked you for coming over that morning."

She pats my arm. One of her fingernails is black, the others are lined with dirt. "Don't mention it, dear. I should of made a effort long before. I wouldn't bother you now, except I noticed you was talking to the Dwinder girl."

I nod.

"There's something wrong with that child, her parents are all so upset about it, her father being a reverend and all. Anyhow, I hope she didn't upset you none."

"Oh no," I lie, "we were just talking about apple pie."

My neighbor studies me closely and I can imagine her reporting her findings to the ladies at the checkout, how I am so strange. I'm glad I lied to the old snoop, and feel unreasonably proud that in this

small way I may have protected the girl. It doesn't take a Jungian ana-
lyst to figure it out. It felt good to protect the girl.

It's the coldest, snowiest winter on record and Christmas morning is
no different. The wind chill factor is ten below and it's snowing. I stack
wood into the carrier, the icy snow stinging my face. My wood supply
is rapidly dwindling but I dread trying to buy more wood now, during
the coldest winter anyone can remember. I can just imagine the banter-
ing: "Lady, you want wood? Seasoned wood?" Or the pity: "Is this, are
you, I'm so sorry, we're out of wood to sell but wait, we'll bring you
ours." Or the insult: "What? You want me to bring it where? Not after
what you did to that girl, they should have put you in jail for child
neglect, letting her leave like that with a stranger." Head bent against
the bitter chill, both real and imagined, I carry the wood inside.

There is nothing like that feeling of coming into a warm house
from the cold. I turn on the classical music station, make a fire, fill
the teakettle, and put it on the kitchen stove. The radio is playing
Handel's *Messiah*, the teakettle rattles softly on the burner, the cat curls
up on the braided rug. I wrap my arms around myself and watch the
snow swirl outside the window. Inexplicably, it stops as suddenly as
if turned off by a switch. The sun comes out, the yard sparkles, and
I realize I'm happy. The teakettle whistles. I turn to take it off the
burner, search through the cupboard for the box of green tea. I wrap
the teabag string around the teapot handle, pour the hot water. If we
never got that stupid computer, if we never (stupidly) let her go with
him, how different this morning would be, scented by pine and punctuated with laughter, the tear of wrapping paper and litter of ribbons
and bows. I turn, teapot in hand, to the kitchen table and see that the
storm has returned to its full vigor, the crystallized scene obliterated.
As it should be. In my grief this stormy winter has been perfect.

I find my strange Christmas perfect too. I make a vegetable soup
and leave it to simmer on the stove. The radio station plays beautiful music. All day the weather volleys between winter wonderland
and wild storm. I bring out the old photo albums and page through
the imperfect memories, her smile but not her laughter, her face but

not her breath, her skin but not her touch. I rock and weep. Outside, the storm rages. This is how I spend the first Christmas without her, crying, napping, in fits of peace and rage.

I go to bed early and, for the first time since she died, sleep through the night. In the morning, a bright winter sun is reflected a thousand times in the thick ice that coats the branches outside my bedroom window and hangs from the eaves like daggers. The phone rings.

"Hello?"

"Mom?"

"Steff, talk to me, what do you want?"

"Maggie Dwinder."

"What?"

But there is no answer, only a dial tone.

I tear up half the house looking for the local phone book, searching through drawers and cupboards, until at last I find it in Jack's old office on the middle of the otherwise empty desk. Jack used to sit here in a chaos of papers and folders, a pencil tucked behind his ear, the computer screen undulating with a swirl of colored tubes that broke apart and reassembled over and over again. I bring the phone book to the kitchen where I page through to the Ds and find Dwinder, Reverend John, and Nancy. My hand is shaking when I dial.

"Hello," a cheerful voice answers on the first ring.

"Hello, is Maggie there?"

"Speaking."

"Maggie, I spoke to you on Christmas Eve, at the grocery store."

"Uh-huh?"

"You said you could help me."

"I'm not sure I, oh." The voice drops to a serious tone. "I've been expecting you to call. She really has something important to tell you." While I absorb this, she adds, "I'm really sorry about what happened." Her voice changes to a cheerful tone, "Really? All of it? That's great!"

"I'm sorry I—"

"No way! Everything?"

"Maggie, are you afraid of being overheard?"

"That's the truth."

"Maybe you should come over here."

"Okay, when?"

"Can you come now?"

"Yeah, I have to do the dishes and then I can come over."

"Do you know where I live?"

"Doesn't everybody?"

"Can you get here or should I . . ."

"No. I'll be over as soon as I can."

She took so long to arrive that I started watching for her at the window. In the midst of more bad weather, I saw the dark figure walking up the road. At first, even though I knew she was coming, I had the ridiculous notion that it was Steffie's ghost, but as she got closer, I recognized the old wool coat, the brown knit hat and scarf crusted with snow. She walked carefully, her head bent with the wind, her hands thrust in her pockets, her narrow shoulders hunched against the chill, her snow-crusted jeans tucked into old boots, the kind with buckles. I asked myself how this rag doll was going to help me, then opened the door for her. For a moment she stood there, as if considering turning back, then she nodded and stepped inside.

"You must be freezing. Please, take off your coat."

She whipped off the knit hat and revealed straight brown hair that fell to her shoulders as she unwrapped the long, wet scarf, unbuttoned her coat (still wearing her gloves, one blue, the other black). She sat to unbuckle her boots, while I hung her things in the hall closet. When I returned, she sat at the kitchen table, hunched over in a white sweatshirt. It occurred to me that she might fit into one of Steffie's baggier sweaters but I offered her one of mine instead. She shook her head and said (as she shivered), "No thanks, I'm warm enough."

"Do you want some tea?" She shrugged, then shook her head. "Hot chocolate?"

She looked up and smiled. "Yes, please." I opened the refrigerator, took out the milk. "I like your house. It's not at all like I heard."

I pour the milk into the pan. "What did you hear?"

"Oh, different stuff."

I set the pan on the burner and start opening cupboards, looking for the chocolate bars from last winter.

"Some people say you're a witch."

This is a new one and I'm so startled by it that I bang my head on the shelf. I touch the sore spot and turn to look at her.

"Of course I don't believe it," she says. "I think of you more as a Mother Nature type."

I find the bars and, after only a short search, the sharp knife we used for cutting the dark chocolate, which I drop in with the milk, and stir.

"I never saw anyone make it like this before. We always just add water."

"We used to make real whipped cream for it too."

"Of course I wouldn't care if you was, 'cause, you know, I sort of am."

"Excuse me?"

"Well, you know, like, I told you, dead people talk to me."

I'm glad I have an excuse not to look at her as I stir and stir, waiting for the chocolate to melt. When it has, I pour in the rest of the milk, whisking it to just below a boil, then pour two mugs full. There is a temporary break in the weather. Sun streams across the kitchen table. I hand the little witch her mug. She holds it with both hands, sniffs it, and smiles.

"You don't look like a witch."

She shrugs. "Well, who knows?"

I sit across from her with my own mug of hot chocolate. Yes. Who knows? All I know is that Steffie told me she wanted Maggie Dwinder. So here she is, sipping hot chocolate in my kitchen, and I'm not sure what I'm supposed to do with her.

As if sensing my inquiry, she stops sipping and looks at me over the rim of the cup. "She wants to come back."

"Come back?"

"She misses you, and she misses it here." She slowly lowers the cup, sets it on the table. "But there's a problem. A couple problems, actually. She can't stay, of course. She can only be here for a little while and then she has to go back."

"No, she doesn't."

"She's been gone a long time."

"You don't have to tell me that."

She bites her chapped lips.

"I'm sorry. This isn't easy for me."

"Yeah. Anyway, she can't stay. I'm sorry too, but that's the way it is. Those are the rules and, also . . ."

"Yes?"

"I don't think you're going to like this part."

"Please tell me."

She looks up at me and then down at the table. "The thing is, she doesn't want to stay here anyway, she sort of likes it where she is."

"Being dead?"

Maggie shrugs and attempts a feeble smile. "Well, you could say that's her life now."

I push back from the table, my chair scraping across the floor. "Is that supposed to be funny?" Maggie shrinks at my voice. "Why?"

"I don't know," she says, softly. "Maybe she figures she sort of belongs there now."

"When?"

"What?"

"When does she want to come?"

"That's why she talked to me. 'Cause she said you've been really upset and all, but she wonders if you can wait until spring?"

"Spring?"

"Yeah. She wants to come in the spring. If it's okay with you." Maggie watches me closely as I consider this imperfect offer, my daughter returned but only borrowed from the dead. What rational response can there be? Life is composed of large faiths, in the series of beliefs that sustain us, we little humans whose very existence is a borrowing from the dead. I look into Maggie's brown eyes, I fall into them and feel as if I'm being pulled into the earth. All this, as we sit at the kitchen table, a world done and undone, a life given and taken.

"Yes," I say. "Tell her spring will be fine."

We are like one of my paintings. Small, in a vast landscape. The snow glistens outside. We are not cold, or hungry, or anything but this, two figures through a lit window, waiting.

Maggie and I became friends of sorts. She liked to sit in the kitchen and chat over hot chocolate about her school day. (Most of her classmates and all her teachers were "boring.") The cat liked to sit in her lap.

There were no more phone calls from Stephanie. "Don't worry about that," Maggie reassured me, "she'll be here soon enough and you can really talk."

It was the worst winter on record. Maggie said that the students were really "pissed" because they would have to make up days in June.

I grew to look forward to her visits. Eventually we got to talking about painting and she showed me some of her sketches, the ones assigned by the art teacher—boxes, shoes, books—and the ones she drew from her imagination: vampires and shadowed, winged figures, pictures that might have warned me were I not spending my days painting girls picking flowers, with dark figures descending on them. I thought Maggie was wise. She understood and accepted the way the world is, full of death and sorrow. This did not seem to affect her happiness. On the contrary, she seemed to be blossoming, losing the tired, haggard look she had when I first met her. I mentioned this to her one day over hot chocolate and she opened her mouth, then bit her lip and nodded.

"What were you going to say?"

"I don't know if I should."

"No, go ahead."

"It was your daughter."

"What was my daughter?"

"She was wearing me out. I know she wasn't meaning to, but it's like she was haunting me ever since she, I mean, she wouldn't leave me alone."

"That doesn't sound like Steffie."

"Yeah, well, I guess people change when they're, you know, dead."

I nod.

"Anyway, it stopped once I talked to you. I guess she just wanted to make sure you got the message."

I remember that time as being almost joyful. What a relief it was to think of our separation as temporary, that she would return to me as she had been before she left, carrying flowers, her cheeks flushed, her eyes bright with happiness.

I got the phone call on a Tuesday afternoon. I remember this so clearly because I marked it with a big, black X on the calendar, and also, that day, though it was already April, there was another storm, so sudden that six motorists were killed in a four-car pileup, one of them a teenage boy. But that was later, after Maggie's parents left.

Maggie's mother calls in the morning, introduces herself, and says that she and her husband want to talk to me, could they stop by for a visit.

How can I refuse them? They are Maggie's parents and I'm sure concerned and curious about this adult she is spending so much time with. Nancy, Maggie's mother, sounds nice enough on the phone. When they arrive an hour later, I think I could like her and, to my surprise, the reverend too.

She has a wide, pleasant face, lightly freckled, red hair the color of certain autumn leaves, and hazel eyes that measure me with a cool but kind mother-to-mother look. She wears a long, dark wool skirt, boots, and a red sweater.

Her husband has a firm handshake and kind brown eyes. His hair is dark and curly, a little long about the ears. He has a neatly trimmed beard and mustache. I am immediately disturbed and surprised to find myself somewhat attracted to him. He wears blue jeans and a green sweater that looks homemade and often worn.

They sit side by side on the couch. I sit in the rocker. A pot of tea cools on the table between us, three cups and saucers on the tray beside it. "Would you like some tea?"

Nancy glances at her husband and he nods. "Thank you," he says, "allow me." He reaches over and pours tea for the three of us. I find this simple gesture comforting. How long it has been since anyone has done anything for me.

"I have to thank you," I say. "You've been so kind about allowing Maggie to visit and her company has been much appreciated."

They nod in unison. Then both begin to speak. With a nod from his wife, the reverend continues.

"I feel I owe you an apology. I should have visited you much sooner and then, perhaps, none of this would have happened." He laughs one of those rueful laughs I was always reading about. "What I mean to say is, I should have offered you my services when you were suffering but I thought that you probably had more spiritual assistance than you knew what to do with." He looks at me hopefully.

But I cannot offer him that redemption. Oddly, there had been no one. Oh, many letters offering prayers, and accusations, and a couple Bibles mailed to the house, but no one stood and held my hand, so to speak, spiritually. There was something distasteful about my involvement in Steffie's horrible death; no one wanted any part of it.

He looks into his teacup and sighs.

"We're sorry," Nancy says in a clear, steady voice. "We've been involved with our own problems and because of that it seems we haven't always made the right choices. It's affected our judgment."

"Please, don't worry about it. You're kind to come now."

The reverend sets his cup on the table. "We're here about Maggie."

"She's a lovely girl."

Nancy sets her cup and saucer on the table, licks her lips. I smile at the gesture, so reminiscent of her daughter. "We thought, well, we want you to understand, we hope you understand, that we thought you, being an artist, and Maggie, being so creative. . . ."

The reverend continues. "We prayed and pondered, and thought maybe you two would be good for each other."

"We made the choice to let her be with you for both your sakes."

"Certainly we had no idea."

"Oh, no idea at all."

Suddenly I feel so cold. I sit in the rocking chair and look at the two of them with their earnest faces. I want them to leave. I don't understand yet what they've come to say, but I know I don't want to hear it.

The reverend looks at me with those beautiful eyes and shakes his head. "We're sorry."

Nancy leans forward and reaches as though to pat me on the knee but the reach is short and she brushes air instead. "It's not her fault. It's just the way she is. We only hope you can find it in your heart to forgive her."

The reverend nods. "We know what we're asking here, a woman like you, who has so much to forgive already."

My hands are shaking when I set my teacup down. "I don't know what you're talking about."

The reverend just looks at me with sorrowful eyes. Nancy nods, bites her lower lip, and says, "We know what she's been telling you," she says. "We found her diary."

I open my mouth. She raises her hand. "I know, I would have thought the same thing. It's horrible to read your child's diary, but I did, and I don't regret it." She glances at her husband, who does not return the look. "How else can a mother know? They're so secretive at this age. And I was right. After all, look what she's been doing."

I look from her to the reverend. "We know, we can guess how tempting it's been for you to believe her," he says.

"She's ill, really ill."

"We knew this even before—"

"I read her diary."

"But we never thought she—"

"How could we? We hope you understand, she's mentally ill. She didn't mean to cause you pain."

The cold moves through me. Why are they here with their petty family squabbles? So she read her daughter's diary, while I, imperfect mother, never even looked for Steffie's, or had any idea what her e-mail address was. Why are they here apologizing for their living daughter? Why do I care? "I'm not sure I—"

"There's also a scrapbook. If I would have known, if we would have known—"

"A scrapbook?"

The reverend clears his throat. "She was obsessed with your daughter's death. I try to understand it, but God help me, I don't. She saved every article—"

"Every picture."

I imagine Maggie cutting up newspapers, gluing the stories into a red scrapbook, the kind I had as a girl. "It's all right," I say, though I'm not sure that it is. "A lot of people were fascinated by it." I imagine myself on an iceberg, drifting into the deep, cold blue.

The reverend opens his mouth but Nancy speaks, like a shout from the unwanted shore. "You don't understand. We know what she's been telling you, about your daughter coming back, and of course, we hope you realize it's all made up."

There. The words spoken. I close my eyes. The ice in my blood crashes like glass. The reverend's voice whispers from the distance. "We're sorry. It must have been tempting to believe her—"

"She called me. I spoke to her."

He shakes his head. "It was Maggie."

"A mother knows her daughter's voice."

"But you were so upset, right? And she never said much, did she? And in your state—"

"Nancy," the reverend says gently.

The room is filled with sad silence. I can't look at either of them. How stupid I have been, how unbearably stupid. I see the reverend's legs, and then his wife's, unbending.

The world is ending, I think, all darkness and ice, like the poem.

"We should leave," says the reverend.

I watch the legs cross the room. Listen to the closet door, the rattle of hangers. Whispering. "We're sorry," says Nancy. Footsteps in the kitchen. Door opened. "Snow!" Closed.

All darkness and despair. The greatest loneliness. A shattering. Ice. Who knows how long until at last I throw the cups across the room, the teapot, still full. Brown tea bleeds down the wall. I scream and weep into darkness. Now I know what waits at world's end. Rage is what fills the emptiness. Rage, and it is cold.

How we suffer, we humans. Pain and joy but always pain again. How do we do this? Why? Some small part of me still waits for spring. Just to be sure. I know it is absurd, but the rational knowing does not change the irrational hope.

I figured Maggie's parents had told her that they talked to me. I couldn't imagine she would want to face my wrath, though she couldn't know that I didn't even have the energy for anger anymore. Instead I felt a tired sorrow, a weariness with life. She did come, in the midst of a downpour, knocking on my door after school, wearing a yellow slicker. I finally opened the door just a crack and peered out at her, drenched like a stray dog, her hair hanging dark in her face, her lashes beaded with water.

"Go home, Maggie."

"Please. You have to talk to me."

She is crying and snot drips from her nose toward her mouth. She wipes it with the back of her hand, sniffing loudly.

I simply do not know what to say. I close the door.

"You were the only one who ever believed me!" she shouts.

Later, when I look out the window, she is gone, as if I imagined her, made her up out of all my pain.

I decide to sell the house though I don't do anything about it. I sleep day and night. One day I realize I haven't seen the cat for a long while. I walk around whistling and calling her name but she doesn't appear. I sit at the kitchen table and stare out the window until gradually I realize I'm looking at spring. Green grass, leaves, tulip and daffodil blooms thrust through the wreck of the garden. Spring. I open windows and doors. Birds twitter in branches. Squirrels scurry across the lawn. Almost a year since we lost her. Gone. My little darling.

Then I see someone, is it, no, in the garden, picking daffodils, her long, dark hair tied with a weedy-looking thing, wearing the dress she had on last year, tattered and torn, my daughter, my ghost.

"Stephanie!" I call.

She turns and looks at me. Yes. It is her face but changed, with a sharpness to it I had not foreseen. She smiles, raises her arm and sweeps the sky with flowers and I am running down the steps and she is running through the garden calling, "Mom, Mom, Mom!" I think when I touch her she will disappear but she doesn't, though she flinches and squirms from the hug. "You can't hold me so close anymore," she says.

So I hold her gently, like the fragile thing she is, and I'm weeping and she's laughing and somehow, with nimble fingers, she braids the bouquet into a crown, which she sets on my head. She covers my face with kisses, so soft I'm sure I'm imagining all of it but I don't care anyway. I never want to wake up or snap out of it. I want to be with her always. "Steffie, Steffie, Steffie, I've missed you so much."

She has bags under her eyes and her skin is pale and cold. She stares at me, unsmiling, then reaches up, takes the crown from my head and places it on her own. "You've changed a lot." She turns and looks at the yard. "Everything has."

"It's been a hard year," I say to her narrow back and bony elbows. She looks like such a little orphan, so motherless standing there in that dirty dress. I'll make her something new, something pretty. She turns and looks at me with an expression like none I'd ever seen on her in her lifetime, a hate-filled face, angry and sharp. "Steff, honey, what is it?"

"Don't. Tell. Me. How hard. This year. Has been."

"Oh sweetie." I reach for her but she pulls back.

"I told you. Don't touch me."

"At all?"

"I'm the queen," she says. "Don't touch me unless I touch you first."

I don't argue or disagree. The queen, my daughter, even in death maintains that imagination I so highly prize. When I ask her if she is hungry she says, "I only ate one thing the whole time I was gone." I feel this surge of anger. What kind of place is this death? She doesn't want to come inside while I make the sandwiches and I'm afraid she'll be gone when I come out with the tray, but she isn't. We have a picnic under the apple tree, which is in white bloom and buzzing with flies, then she falls asleep on the blanket beside me and, to my surprise, I fall asleep too.

I wake, cold and shivering, already mourning the passing dream. I reach to wrap the picnic blanket around me and my hand touches her. Real. Here. My daughter, sleeping.

"I told you not to touch me."

"I'm sorry. Honey, are you cold?"

She rolls over and looks up at me. "You do realize I'm dead?"

"Yes."

She sets the wilted crown back on her head and surveys the yard. "You really let everything go to shit around here, didn't you?"

"Stephanie!"

"What?"

Really, what? How to be the mother of a dead girl? We sit on the blanket and stare at each other. What she is thinking, I don't know. I'm surprised, in the midst of this momentous happiness, to feel a sadness, a certain grief for the girl I knew who, I guess, was lost somewhere at the border of death. Then she sighs, a great old sigh.

"Mom?" she says, in her little girl voice.

"Yes, honey?"

"It's good to be back."

"It's good to have you here."

"But I can't stay."

"How long?"

She shrugs.

"Is it horrible there?"

She looks at me, her face going through some imperceptible change that brings more harshness to it. "Don't ask the dead."

"What?"

"Don't ask questions you don't want the answer to."

"Just stay. Don't go back."

She stands up. "It doesn't work like that."

"We could—"

"No, don't act like you know anything about it. You don't."

I roll up the blanket, pick up the tray. We walk to the house together beneath the purple-tinged sky. When we get to the door she hesitates. "What's wrong?" She looks at me with wide, frightened eyes. "Steff, what is it?" Wordlessly, she steps inside. I flick on the kitchen light. "Are you hungry?"

She nods.

The refrigerator is nearly empty so I rummage through cupboards and find some spaghetti and a jar of sauce. I fill a pan with water and set it on the stove.

"Is Dad coming back?"

"Would you like to see him?"

She shakes her head vigorously no.

"Steff, don't be mad at him, he didn't know—"

"Well, he really fucked up."

I bite my lip, check the water. Where is my little girl? I turn and look at her. She is walking around the kitchen, lightly brushing her hand against the wall, a strange, unlovely creature, her hair still knotted with a weed, crowned with wilted daffodils.

"Do you want to talk about it, what happened to you?"

She stops, the tips of her fingers light against the wall, then continues walking around the room, humming softly.

I take this to be a no. I make spaghetti for six and she eats all of it, my ravenous ghost child. What is this feeling? Here is my dead daughter, cold and unkind and difficult and so different from the girl she used to be that only now do I finally accept that Stephanie is gone forever, even as she sits before me, slurping spaghetti, the red sauce blooding her lips.

The dead move in secrets, more wingless than the living, bound by some weight; the memory of life, the impossible things? Dead bones grow and hair and fingernails too. Everything grows but it grows with death. The dead laugh and cry and plant flowers that they pick too soon. The dead do not care about keeping gardens in blossom.

Dead daughters don't wear socks or shoes and they won't go into old bedrooms unless you beg and coax and then you see immediately how they were right all along. Dead daughters have little in common with the living ones. They are more like sisters than the same girl and you realize, just as you miss the daughter you've lost, so does the dead girl miss, really miss, the one she was.

The dead pick up paintbrushes and suddenly their hands move like rag dolls and they splatter paint, not like Jackson Pollock, or even a kindergartner. All the paint turns brown on the paintbrush and drips across the canvas or floor or wall, until they, helpless, throw it to the ground.

All the dead can do is wander. You walk for hours with your dead daughter pacing the yard she will not (cannot?) leave. She picks all the flowers and drops them in her step. She sleeps suddenly for hours, and then does not sleep for days. She exhausts you. The days and nights whirl. The last time you felt like this was when she was an infant.

One day, as you sit at the kitchen table, watching her tearing flowers from the garden in the new dress you made that already hangs raglike and dirty around her, you think of Maggie Dwinder and you realize you miss her. You put your face in your hands. What have you done?

"What's wrong with you?"

You would like to believe that she asks because she cares but you don't think that's true. Something vital in her was lost forever. Was this what happened at death or was it because of how she died? You accept you'll never know. She refuses to talk about it, and really, what would be the point? You look at her, weedy, dirty, wearing that brittle crown. "Maggie Dwinder," you say.

"As good as dead."

"What?"

She rolls her eyes.

"Don't you roll your eyes at me, young lady."

"Mother, you don't know anything about it."

"She's your friend, and mine. She told me you would come. She suffered for it."

"Oh, big deal, mommy and daddy watch her very closely. She has to go see the psychiatrist. She doesn't have any friends. Big fucking deal. What a hard life!"

"Steff."

"Don't tell me about suffering. I know about suffering."

"Steff, honey—"

"Everyone said it was a mistake for me to come back here. They said you wouldn't like me anymore."

"Honey, that's not true. I love you."

"You love who I used to be, not who I am now."

"Well, you're dead."

"Like it's my fault."

The dead are jealous, jealous, jealous and they will do anything to keep you from the living, the lucky living. They will argue with you, and distract you, and if that doesn't work, they will even let you hug them, and dance for you, and kiss you, and laugh, anything to keep you. The dead are selfish. Jealous. Lonely. Desperate. Hungry.

It isn't until she brings you a flower, dead for weeks, and hands it to you with that poor smile, that you again remember the living. "I have to call Maggie."

"Forget about her."

"No, I have to tell her."

"Look at me, Mommy."

"Sweetheart."

"Look what you did."

"It wasn't me."

She walks away.

"It wasn't."

She keeps walking.

You follow. Of course, you follow.

The phone rings. Such a startling noise. I roll into my blankets. Simultaneously I realize the night was cool enough for blankets and that the phone didn't ring all summer. I reach for it, fumbling across the bedside table, and knock off the photograph from Steff's last birthday.

"Hello?"

"See you next spring."

"Steff? Where are you?"

There is only a dial tone. I hang up the phone. Throw off the covers. "Steff!" I call. "Steff!" I look in her bedroom but she's not there. I run down the stairs and through the house, calling her name. The blue throw is bunched up on the couch, as if she'd sat there for a while, wrapped up in it, but she's not there now. I run outside, the grass cold against my feet. "Steff! Steff!" She is not in the garden, or the studio. She is not in the yard. A bird cries and I look up through the apple tree branches. One misshapen apple drops while I stand there, shivering in my nightgown. Everything is tinged with brown, except the leaves of the old oak, which are a brilliant red.

A squirrel scurries past. There is a gentle breeze and one red leaf falls. I wrap my arms around myself and walk into the house, fill the teakettle, set it on the burner to boil. I sit at the kitchen table and stare at the garden. I should plant some bulbs. Order firewood. Arrange to have the driveway plowed when it snows. The teakettle whistles. I walk across the cool floor, pour the water into the pot. I leave it to steep and go to the living room, where she left the blue throw all balled up. I pick it up and wrap it around myself. It smells like her, musty, sour.

It smells like Maggie too, last Christmas Eve when she spoke to me in the supermarket. What a risk that was for her. Who knows, I might have been like Mrs. Bialo, or her parents; I might have laughed at her. Instead, I became her friend and then cast her aside at the first sign of trouble.

How many chances do we get? With love? How many times do we wreck it before it's gone?

I don't even drink the tea but dress in a rush. All my clothes are too big on me and I see in the mirror how tired I look, how much new gray is in my hair. Yet, there's something else, a sort of glow, a happiness. I miss her, the one who died, and her ghost is my responsibility, a relationship based on who we lost, while Maggie is a friend, a relationship based on what we found.

All summer I only left for groceries. Stephanie would stand at the top of the driveway, watching me with those cold, narrow eyes as if suspicious I wouldn't come back. Out of habit I look in the rearview mirror, but all I see is a patch of brown grass, the edge of the house.

It's easy to find the Dwinder residence. They live right next to the church in a brick house with red geraniums dropping teardrop-shaped petals onto the porch. I ring the bell. Nancy answers, in a pink terry cloth robe.

"I'm sorry, I forgot how early it is."

She brushes a hand through her red hair. "That's all right. We were getting ready for church."

"There's something I have to tell Maggie. Is she home?"

"I don't know if that's such a good idea."

"Honey, who is it?" The reverend comes to the door in plaid flannel pants and a t-shirt, his dark hair tousled, his face wrinkled with sleep. "Oh. Chloe, how are you?"

"I'm sorry to disturb you, it's just—"

"She wants to talk to Maggie."

"I'll tell her you're here." The reverend turns back into the house.

Nancy continues to stare at me, then, just as I hear Maggie saying, What does she want? she blurts, "She's been better since she's stopped seeing you." I'm not sure if this is meant as an accusation or an apology and before I can find out, Maggie comes to the door dressed in torn jeans and a violet t-shirt, her hair in braids. She meets my gaze with those dark eyes.

"Coffee's ready!" the reverend calls and Nancy turns away, her pink-robed figure receding slowly down the hall.

"Yeah?"

"I was hoping, if you can forgive me, I was hoping we could be friends again."

"I can't be her replacement, you know."

"I know."

"You hurt me a lot."

"I know. I'm sorry. Can you ever forgive me?"

She frowns, squints, then tilts her head slightly, and looks up at me. "I guess."

"Please. Stop by. Any time. Like you used to."

She nods and shuts the door gently in my face.

On a sunny but cold day, as the last crimson leaves flutter to earth, and apples turn to cider on the ground, I shovel last winter's ash onto the garden. A flock of geese flies overhead. I shade my eyes to watch them pass and when I look down again, she is standing there in baggy jeans and an old blue peacoat, unbuttoned in the sun.

It's as though I've been living in one of those glass domes and it's been shaking for a long time, but in this moment has stopped, and after all that flurry and unsettling, there is a kind of peace. "Maggie."

For a moment we only look at each other, then she puts her hand on her hip, rolls her eyes, and says, "You wouldn't believe what they're making us do in gym, square dancing!"

All life is death. You don't fool yourself about this anymore. You slash at the perfect canvas with strokes of paint and replace the perfect picture of your imagination with the reality of what you are capable of. From death, and sorrow, and compromise, you create. This is what it means, you finally realize, to be alive.

You try to explain this to Maggie. You hear yourself talking about bitter seeds, and sweet fruit. She nods and doesn't interrupt but you know you have not successfully communicated it. This is all right. The grief is so large you're not sure you want her, or anyone, to understand it, though you wish you could describe this other emotion.

You stand in the ash of your garden. All this time you didn't realize what you'd been deciding. Now you are crying, because with the realization of the question comes the answer. It is snowing and white flakes fall onto the garden, sticking to the brown stems and broken flowers, melting into the ash. You look up to the sunless white sky. Cold snow tips your face and neck. You close your eyes, and think, yes. Oh, life. Yes.

Anyway

"What if you could save the world? What if all you had to do was sacrifice your son's life, Tony's for instance, and there would be no more war, would you do it?"

"Robbie's the name of my son," I say. "Remember, Mom? Tony is your son. You remember Tony, don't you?"

I reach into the cabinet where I've stored the photograph album. I page through it until I find the picture I want, Tony and me by his VW just before he left on the Kerouac-inspired road trip from which he never returned. We stand, leaning into each other, his long hair pulled into a ponytail, and mine finally grown out of the pixie cut I'd had throughout my single-digit years. He has on bell-bottom jeans and a tie-dyed t-shirt. I have on cut-offs and a simple cotton short-sleeved button-down blouse and, hard to see but I know they are there, a string of tiny wooden beads, which Tony had, only seconds before, given to me. I am looking up at him with absolute adoration and love.

"See, Mom." I point to Tony's face. She looks at the picture and then at me. She smiles.

"Well, hello," she says, "when did you get here?"

I close the book, slide it into the cabinet, kiss her forehead, pick up my purse, and walk out of the room. I learned some time ago that there is no need for explanation. She sits there in the old recliner we brought from her house, staring vacantly at nothing, as if I have never been there, not today, or ever.

I stop at the nurse's station, hoping to find my favorite nurse, Anna Vinn. I don't even remember the name of the nurse who looks up at me and smiles. I glance at her nametag.

"Charlotte?"

"Yes?"

"My mother asked me the strangest question today."

Charlotte nods.

"Do the patients ever, you know, snap out of it? Have you ever heard of that happening?"

Charlotte rests her face in her hand, two fingers under the rim of her glasses, rubbing her temple. She sighs and appraises me with a kind look. "Sometimes, but you know, they . . ."

"Snap right back again?"

"Would you like to talk to the social worker?"

I shake my head, tap the counter with my fingertips before I wave, breezy, unconcerned.

Once outside, I look at my watch. I still have to get the groceries for tomorrow's dinner. It's my father's birthday and he wants, of all things, pot roast. Luckily, my son, Robbie, has agreed to cook it. All I have to do is buy it. I've been a vegetarian for eighteen years and now I have to go buy a pot roast.

What if you could save the world? I remember my mother asking the question, so clearly, as if she were really present—in her skin and in her mind—in a way she hasn't been for years.

"Mom," I say, as I unlock the car door, "I can't even save this cow."

That's when I realize that a man I've seen inside the home, but whom I don't know by name, stands between my car and his (I assume). He stares at me for a moment and then, with a polite smile, turns away.

I start to speak, to offer some explanation for what he's overheard, but he is walking away from me, toward the nursing home, his shoulders hunched as if under a weight, or walking against a wind, though it is early autumn and the weather is mild.

On Sunday, my dad and Robbie sit in the kitchen drinking beer while the pot roast cooks, talking about war. I have pleaded with my father for years not to talk to Robbie this way, but he has always dismissed my concerns. "This is men talk," he'd say, elbowing Robbie in the ribs, tousling his hair while Robbie, gap-toothed and freckled and so obviously not a man, grinned up at me. But now Robbie is nineteen. He drinks a beer and rubs his long fingers over the stubble of his chin. "Don't get me wrong," my dad says, "it's a terrible thing, okay? There's mud and snakes and bugs, and we didn't take a shower for three months." He glances at me and nods. I know that this is meant as a gesture on his part, a sort of offering to me and my peacenik ways.

The smell of pot roast drives me from the kitchen to the backyard. It's cooler today than yesterday, and the sky has a grayish cast. Most of the leaves have fallen, the yard littered with the muted red, gold, and green. I sit on the back step. "Didn't take a shower for three months," my father says again, loudly. I hear him through the kitchen windows that I had cracked open, trying to alleviate the odor of cooked meat.

I listen to the murmur of Robbie's voice.

"Oh, but it was a beautiful thing," my dad says. "It was the right thing to do. Nobody questioned it back then. We were saving the world."

For dessert we have birthday cake, naturally. My dad's favorite, chocolate with banana filling and chocolate-chip-studded chocolate frosting. I feel quite queasy by this point, the leftover pot roast congealing in the roaster on top of the stove, Robbie's and my father's plates gleaming with a light gray coating—it was all I could do to eat my salad. "Why don't we have our cake in the living room?" I say.

"Aw, no," my father says. "You don't have to get all fancy for me."

But Robbie sees something in my face that causes him to stand up quickly. "Come on, Pops," he says, and, as my father begins to rise, "you and Mom go in the living room and talk. I'll bring out the cake."

I try not to notice the despair that flits over my father's face. I take him by the elbow and steer him into the living room, helping him into the recliner I bought (though he does not know this) for him.

"I saw Mom today," I say.

He nods, scratches the inside of his ear, glances longingly at the kitchen.

I steel myself against the resentment. I'm happy about the relationship he's developed with Robbie. But some small part of me, some little girl who, in spite of my forty-five years, resides in me and will not go away, longs for my father's attention and, yes, even after all these years, approval.

"She asked me the strangest question."

My father grunts. Raises his eyebrows. It is obvious that he thinks there is nothing particularly fascinating about my mother asking a strange question.

"One time," he says, "she asked me where her dogs were. I said, 'Meldy, you know you never had any dogs.' So she starts arguing with me about how of course she's always had dogs, what kind of woman do I think she is? So, later that day I'm getting ice out of the freezer, and what do you think I find in there but her underwear, and I say, 'Meldy, what the hell is your underwear doing in the freezer?' So she grabs them from me and says, 'My dogs!'"

"*Ha-a-appy birrrrrthday to youuuu.*" Robbie comes in, carrying the cake blazing with candles. I join in the singing. My father sits through it with an odd expression on his face. I wonder if he's enjoying any of this.

Later, when I drive him home while Robbie does the dishes, I say, "Dad, listen, today Mom, for just a few seconds, she was like her old self again. Something you said tonight, to Robbie, reminded me of it. Remember how you said that during the war it was like you were saving the world?" I glance at him. He sits, staring straight ahead, his profile composed of sharp shadows. "Anyway, Mom looked right at me, you know, the way she used to have that look, right, and she said, 'What if you could save the world? What if all you had to do was sacrifice one life and there would be no more war, would you do it?'"

My father shakes his head and mumbles something.

"What is it, Dad?"

"Well, that was the beginning, you know."

"The beginning?"

"Yeah, the beginning of the Alzheimer's. 'Course, I didn't know it then. I thought she was just going a little bit nuts." He shrugs. "It happened. Lots of women used to go crazy back then."

"Dad, what are you talking about?"

"All that business with Tony." His voice cracks on the name. After all these years he still cannot say my brother's name without breaking under the grief.

"Forget it, Dad. Never mind."

"She almost drove me nuts, asking it all the time."

"Okay, let's just forget about it."

"All those fights we had about the draft and Vietnam, and then he went and got killed anyway. You were just a girl then, so you probably don't remember it almost tore us apart."

"We don't have to talk about this, Dad."

I turn into the driveway. My father stares straight ahead. I wait a few seconds and then open my car door; he leans to open his. When I walk beside him to guide him by the elbow, he steps away from me. "I'm not an invalid," he says. He reaches in his pocket and pulls out his keys. Together we walk to the door, which he unlocks with shaking hands. I step inside and flick on the light switch. It is the living room of a lonely old man, the ancient plaid couch and recliner, family photographs gathering dust, fake ivy.

"Satisfied?" he says, turning toward me.

I shake my head, shrug. I'm not sure what he's talking about.

"No boogeymen are here stealing all your inheritance, all right?"

"Dad, I—"

"The jewels are safe."

He laughs at that. I smile weakly. "Happy birthday, Dad," I say.

But he has already turned and headed into the bedroom. "Wait, let me check on the jewels."

My father, the smart aleck.

"Okay, Dad," I say, loudly, so he can hear me over the sound of drawers being opened and closed. "I get the point. I'm leaving."

"No, no. The jewels."

Suddenly I am struck by my fear, so sharp I gasp. He's got it too, I think, and he's going to come out with his socks or underwear and he's going to call them jewels and—

"Ah, here they are. I honest to God almost thought I lost them."

I sit down on the threadbare couch I have offered to replace a dozen times. He comes into the living room, grinning like an elf, carrying something. I can't bear to look.

"What's the matter with you?" he asks, and thrusts a shoebox onto my lap.

"Oh, my God."

"These are yours now."

I take a deep breath. I can handle this, I think. I've handled a lot already; my brother's murder, my husband's abandonment, my mother's Alzheimer's. I lift the lid. The box is filled with stones, green with spots of red on them. I pick one up. "Dad, where did you get these? Is that blood?"

He sits in the recliner. "They were in the bedroom. They're your responsibility now."

"Are these—"

"Bloodstone, it's called. At least that's what your mother said, but you know, like I told you, she was already getting the Alzheimer's back then."

"Bloodstone? Where did she—"

"I already told you." He looks at me, squinty-eyed, and I almost laugh when I realize he is trying to decide if I have Alzheimer's now. "She wouldn't stop. She almost drove me crazy with her nonsense. She kept saying it, all the time, 'Why'd he have to die anyway?' You get that? 'Anyway,' that's what she said, 'Why'd he have to die anyway,' like there was a choice or something. Finally one day I just lost it and I guess I hollered at her real bad and she goes, 'What if you could save the world? What if all you had to do was sacrifice one life, not your own, but, oh, let's say, Tony's, and there would be no more war, would you do it?' I reminded her that our Tony—" His voice cracks. He reaches for the remote control and turns the TV on but leaves the sound off. "She says, 'I know he's dead anyway, but I mean before he died, what would you have done?'"

"And I told her, 'The world can go to hell.'" He looks at me, the colors from the TV screen flickering across his face. "The whole world can just go to hell if I could have him back for even one more day, one more goddamned hour." For a moment I think he might cry, but he moves his mouth as if he's sucking on something sour and continues. "And she says, 'That's what I decided. But then he died anyway.'"

I look at the red spots on the stones. My father makes an odd noise, a sort of rasping gasp. I look up to the shock of his teary eyes.

"So she tells me that these stones were given to her by her mother. You remember Grandma Helen, don't you?"

"No, she died before—"

"Well, she went nuts too. So you see, it runs in the women of the family. You should probably watch out for that. Anyway, your mother tells me that her mother gave her these stones when she got married. There's one for every generation of Mackeys, that was your mother's name before she married me. There's a stone for her mother and her mother's mother, and so on, and so on, since before time began, I guess. They weren't all Mackeys, naturally, and anyhow, every daughter gets them."

"But why?"

"Well, see, this is the part that just shows how nuts she was. She tells me, she says, that all the women in her family got to decide. If they send their son to war and, you know, agree to the sacrifice, they are supposed to bury the stones in the garden. Under a full moon or some nonsense like that. Then the boy will die in the war but that would be it, okay? There would never be another war again in the whole world."

"What a fantastic story."

"But if they didn't agree to this sacrifice, the mother just kept the stones, you know, and the son went to war and didn't die there, he was like protected from dying in the war but, you know, the wars just kept happening. Other people's sons would die instead."

"Are you saying that Mom thought she could have saved the world if Tony had died in Vietnam?"

"Yep."

"But Dad, that's just—"

"I know. Alzheimer's. We didn't know it back then, of course. She really believed this nonsense too, let me tell you. She told me if she had just let Tony die in Vietnam at least she could have saved everyone else's sons. There weren't girl soldiers then, like there are now, you know. 'Course he just died anyway."

"Tony didn't want to go to Vietnam."

"Well, she was sure she could have convinced him." He waves his hand as though brushing away a fly. "She was nuts, what can I say? Take those things out of here. Take the box of them. I never want to see them again."

When I get home the kitchen is, well, not gleaming, but devoid of pot roast. Robbie left a note scrawled in black marker on the magnetic board on the refrigerator. *Out. Back later.* I stare at it while I convince myself that he is fine. He will be back, unlike Tony who died or Robbie's father who left me when I was six months pregnant because, he said, he realized he had to pursue his first love, figure skating.

I light the birch candle to help get rid of the cooked meat smell, which still lingers in the air, sweep the floor, wipe the counters and the table. Then I make myself a cup of decaf tea. While it steeps, I change into my pajamas. Finally, I sit on the couch in front of the TV, the shoebox of stones on the coffee table in front of me. I sip my tea and watch the news, right from the start so I see all the gruesome stuff, the latest suicide bombing, people with grief-ravaged faces carrying bloody bodies, a weeping mother in robes, and then, a special report, an interview with the mother of a suicide bomber clutching the picture of her dead son and saying, "He is saving the world."

I turn off the TV, put the cup of tea down, and pick up the shoebox of stones. They rattle in there, like bones, I think, remembering the box that held Tony's ashes after he was cremated. I tuck the shoebox under my arm, blow out the candle in the kitchen, check that the doors are locked, and go to bed. But it is the oddest thing: the whole time I am doing these tasks, I am thinking about taking one of those stones and putting it into my mouth, sucking it like a lozenge. It makes no sense, a strange impulse, I think, a weird synapse in my brain, a reaction to today's stress. I shove the shoebox under my bed, lick my lips and move my mouth as though sucking on something sour. Then, just as my head hits the pillow, I sit straight up, remembering.

It was after Tony's memorial, after everyone had left our house. There was an odd smell in the air, the scent of strange perfumes and flowers (I remember a bouquet of white flowers already dropping petals in the heat) mingled with the odor of unusual foods, casseroles and cakes, which had begun arriving within hours after we learned of Tony's death. There was also a new silence, a different kind of silence than any I had ever experienced before in my eleven years. It was a heavy silence and, oddly, it had an odor all its own, sweaty and sour. I felt achingly alone as I walked through the rooms, looking for my parents, wondering if they, too, had died. Finally, I found my father sitting on the front porch, weeping. It was too terrible to watch. Following the faint noises I heard coming from there, I next went to the kitchen. And that's when I saw my mother sitting at the table, picking stones out of a shoebox and shoving them into her mouth. My brother was dead. My father was weeping on the porch and my mother was sitting in the kitchen, sucking on stones. I couldn't think of what to do about any of it. Without saying anything, I turned around and went to bed.

It is so strange, what we remember, what we forget. I try to remember everything I can about Tony. It is not very much, and some of it is suspect. For instance, I think I remember us standing next to the Volkswagen while my dad took that photograph, but I'm not even sure that I really remember it because when I picture it in my mind, I see us the way we are in the photograph, as though I am looking at us through a lens, and that is not the way I would have experienced it. Then I try to remember Robbie's father, and I find very little. Scraps of memory, almost like the sensation when you can hear a song in your head but can't get it to the part of your brain where you can actually sing it. I decide it isn't fair to try this with Robbie's father because I had worked so hard to forget everything about him.

I wonder if all my mother has really lost is the ability to fake it anymore. To pretend, the way we all do, to be living a memory-rich life. Then I decide that as a sort of homage to her, I will try to remember her, not as she is now, in the nursing home, curled in her bed into the shape of a comma, but how she used to be. I remember her making me a soft-boiled egg, which I colored with a face before she dropped it into the water, and I remember her sitting at the sewing machine with pins in her mouth, and once, in the park, while Tony and I play in the sandbox, she sits on a bench, wearing her blue coat and her Sunday hat, the one with the feathers, her gloved hands in her lap, talking to some man and laughing, and I remember her sitting at the kitchen table sucking on stones. And that's it. That's all I can remember, over and over again, as though my mind is a flipbook and the pages have gotten stuck. It seems there should be more, but as hard as I look, I can't find any. Finally, I fall asleep.

Two weeks after my father's birthday, Robbie tells me that he has enlisted in the Marines. Basically, I completely freak out, and thus discover that a person can be completely freaked out while appearing only slightly so.

"Don't be upset, Mom," Robbie says after his announcement.

"It doesn't work like that. You can't do this and then tell me not to be upset. I'm upset."

"It's just, I don't know, I've always felt like I wanted to be a soldier, ever since I was a little kid. You know, like when people say they 'got a calling'? I always felt like I had a calling to be a soldier. You know, like Dad with figure skating."

"Hmm."

"Don't just sit there, Mom, say something, okay?"

"When are you leaving?"

He pulls out the contract he signed, and the brochures and the list of supplies he needs to buy. I read everything and nod and ask questions, and I am completely freaked out. That's when I begin to wonder if I have been fooling myself about this for my whole adult life, even longer. Now that I think about it, I think maybe I've been completely freaked out ever since my mother came into my room and said that Tony's body had been found in a Dumpster in Berkeley.

I start to get suspicious of everyone: the newscaster, with her wide, placid face reading the reports of the suicide bombings and the number killed since the war began; my friend Shelly, who's a doctor, smiling as she nurses her baby (the very vulnerability of which she knows so intimately); even strangers in the mall, in the grocery store, not exactly smiling or looking peaceful, generally, but also not freaking out, and I think, oh, but they are. Everybody is freaking out and just pretending that they aren't.

I take up smoking again. Even though I quit twenty years ago, I find it amazingly easy to pick right back up. But it doesn't take away the strange hunger I've developed, and so far resisted, for the bloodstones safely stored in the shoebox under my bed.

When I visit my mother it is with an invigorated sense of dread. Though I grill her several times, I cannot get her to say anything that makes sense. This leaves me with only my dad.

"Now, let me get this right, Mom believed that if she buried the bloodstones—are you supposed to bury just one, or all of them?—then that meant Tony would die, right, and there would never be another war?"

"He had to die over there, see? In Vietnam. He had to be a soldier. It didn't matter when he died in California; that didn't have anything to do with it, see?"

"But why not?"

"How should I know?" He taps the side of his head with a crooked finger. "She was nuts already way back then. Want my opinion, it was his dying that did it to her, like the walnut tree."

"What's a walnut tree have to do with—"

"You remember that tree in front of our house. That was one magnificent tree. But then the blight came, and you know what caused it? Just this little invisible fungus, but it killed that giant. You see what I'm talking about?"

"No, Dad, I really don't."

"It's like what happened with . . . It was bad, all right? But when you look at a whole entire life, day after day and hour after hour, minute after minute, we were having a good life, me and your mom and you kids. Then this one thing happened and, bam, there goes the walnut tree."

That night I dream that my mother is a tree or at least I am talking to a tree in the backyard and calling it Mom. Bombs are exploding all around me. Tony goes by on a bicycle. Robbie walks past, dressed like a soldier but wearing ice skates. I wake up, my heart beating wildly. The first thing I think is, What if it's true? I lean over the side of the bed and pull out the shoebox, which rattles with stones. I lick my lips. What if I could save the world?

I open the lid, reach in, and pick up a stone, turning it in my fingers and thumb, enjoying the sensation of smooth. Then I let it drop back into the box, put the lid on, shove it under the bed, and turn on the bedside lamp. For the first time in my entire life, I smoke in bed, using a water glass as an ashtray. Smoking in bed is extremely unwise, but, I reason, at least it's not nuts. At least I'm not sitting here sucking on stones. That would be nuts.

While I smoke, I consider the options, in theory. Send my son to war and bury the stones? Did my father say under a full moon? I make a mental note to check that and then, after a few more puffs, get out of bed and start rummaging in my purse until I find my checkbook, with the pen tucked inside. I tear off a check and write on the back of it, *Find out if stones have to be buried under full moon or not.* Satisfied, I crawl back into bed, being very careful with my lit cigarette.

There's a knock on my bedroom door. "Mom? Are you all right?"

"Just couldn't sleep."

"Can I come in?"

"Sure, honey."

Robbie opens the door and stands there, his brown curls in a shock of confusion on his forehead, the way they get after he's been wearing a hat. He still has his jacket on and exudes cool air. "Are you smoking?"

I don't find this something necessary to respond to. I take a puff. I mean, obviously I am. I squint at him. "You know, people are dying over there."

"Mom."

"I'm just saying. I want to make sure you know what you're getting into. I mean, it's not like you're home in the evenings watching the news. I just want to make sure you know what's going on."

"I don't think you should smoke in bed. Jesus, Mom, it really stinks in here. I'm not going to die over there, okay?"

"How do you know?"

"I just do."

"Don't be ridiculous. Nobody knows something like that."

"I have to go to bed, Mom. Don't fall asleep with that cigarette, okay?"

"I'm not a child. Robbie?"

"Yeah?"

"Would it be worth it to you?"

"What?"

"Well, your life? I mean, are you willing to give it up for this?"

I bring the cigarette to my lips. I am just about to inhale when I realize I can hear him breathing. I hold my own breath so I can listen to the faint but beautiful sound of my son breathing. He sighs. "Yeah, Mom."

"All right then. Good night, Robbie."

"Good night, Mom." He shuts the door, gently, not like a boy at all, but like a man trying not to disturb the dreams of a child.

The next day's news is particularly grim: six soldiers are killed and a school is bombed. It's a mistake, of course, and everyone is upset about it.

Without even having to look at the note I wrote to myself on the back of the check, I call my father and ask him if the stones are supposed to be buried when there's a full moon. I also make sure he's certain of the correlations, bury stones, son dies but all wars end, don't bury stones and son lives but the wars continue.

My father has a little fit about answering my questions but eventually he tells me, yes, the stones have to be buried under a full moon (and he isn't sure if it's one stone or all of them), and yes, I have the correlations right.

"Is there something about sucking them?"

"What's that?"

"Did Mom ever say anything about sucking the stones?"

"This thing with Robbie has really knocked the squirrel out of your tree, hasn't it?"

I tell him that it is perfectly rational that I be upset about my son going off to fight in a war.

He says, "Well, the nut sure doesn't fall far from the tree."

"The fruit," I say.

"What's that?"

"That expression. It isn't the nut doesn't fall far from the tree, it's the fruit."

The day before Robbie is to leave, I visit my mother at the nursing home. I bring the shoebox of stones with me.

"Listen, Mom," I hiss into the soft shell of her ear. "I really need you to do everything you can to give me some signal. Robbie's joined the Marines. Robbie, my son. He's going to go to war. I need to know what I should do."

She stares straight ahead. Actually, staring isn't quite the right description. The aides tell me that she is not blind, but the expression in her eyes is that of a blind woman. Exasperated, I begin to rearrange the untouched things on her dresser: a little vase with a dried flower in it; some photographs of her and Dad, me and Robbie; a hairbrush. Without giving it much thought, I pick up the shoebox. "Remember these?" I say, lifting the lid. I shake the box under her face. I pick up one of the stones. "Remember?"

I pry open her mouth. She resists, for some reason, but I pry her lips and teeth apart and shove the stone in, banging it against the plate of her false teeth. She stares straight ahead but makes a funny noise. I keep her mouth open and, practically sitting now, almost on the arm of the chair, grab a handful of stones and begin shoving them into her mouth. Her arms flap up, she jerks her head. "Come on," I say, "you remember, don't you?"

Wildly, her eyes roll, until finally they lock on mine, a faint flicker of recognition, and I am tackled from behind, pulled away from her. There's a flurry of white pant cuffs near my face, and one white shoe comes dangerously close to stepping on me.

"Jesus Christ, they're stones. They're stones."

"Well, get them out."

"Those are my stones," I say, pushing against the floor. A hand presses my back, holding me down.

"Just stay there," says a voice I recognize as belonging to my favorite nurse, Anna Vinn.

Later, in her office, Anna says, "We're not going to press charges. But you need to stay away for a while. And you should consider some kind of counseling."

She hands me the shoebox.

"I'm sure I was trying to get the stones out of her mouth."

She shakes her head. "Are you going to be okay? Driving home?"

"Of course," I say, unintentionally shaking the shoebox. "I'm fine."

When I get outside, I take a deep breath of the fresh air. It is a cold, gray day, but I am immediately struck by the beauty of it, the beauty of the gray clouds, the beauty of the blackbirds arcing across the sky, the beauty of the air on my face and neck. I think: *I cannot save him.* Then I see a familiar-looking man. "Excuse me?" I say. He continues, head bent, shoulders hunched, toward the nursing home. "Excuse me?"

He stops and turns, slightly distracted, perhaps skeptical, as if worried I might ask for spare change.

"Don't we know each other?"

He glances at the nursing home, longingly, I think, but that can't possibly be correct. Nobody longs to go in there. He shakes his head.

"Are you sure? Anyway, I have a question. Let's say you could save the world by sacrificing your son's life, would you do it?"

"I don't have a son. Or a daughter. I don't have any children."

"But hypothetically?"

"Is this, are you . . ." He thrusts his hands into his pockets. "Is this some kind of religious thing? 'Cause I'm not looking to convert."

"Are you sure we don't know each other?"

"I've seen you before." He glances over his shoulder. For a moment I'm sure he's going to say something important, but instead he turns away and hurries to the nursing home.

I walk to the car with my box of stones. I have to decide. Robbie leaves in the morning. It's time to stop fooling around.

This, I think, is like a Zen koan. What is the sound of one hand clapping? The secret for these things is not to be too clever. The fact that I am aware of this puts me at risk of being too clever. Okay, focus, I think as I carefully stop at a green light, realize what I've done, and accelerate as the light changes to yellow. It's really very simple. Do I bury the stones? Or not? Glancing at the box, I lick my lips.

When I get home, Robbie is there with several of his friends. They are in his room, laughing and cursing. I knock on his door and ask him if he'll be home for dinner. He opens it and says, "Mom, are you all right?"

"I was just trying to get the stones out of her mouth."

He shakes his head. "What are you talking about?" His eyes are the same color as the stones, without the red spots, of course. "You remember about the party, right?"

"The party?"

"Remember? Len? He's having a party for me? Tonight?"

I remember none of this, but I nod. It's apparently the right thing to do. There's some rustling going on behind him and a sharp bang against the wall, punctuated by masculine giggles. Robbie turns around. "Guys, be quiet for a minute." He turns back to me and smiles, bravely I think. "Hey, I don't have to go."

"It's your party. Go. I want you to."

He's relieved, I can tell. I carry the shoebox of stones into my bedroom, where I crawl into bed and fall asleep. When I wake up, feeling sweaty and stinky, creased by the seams of my clothing, it is like waking from a fever. The full moon sheds a cool glow into the room and throughout the house as I walk through it aimlessly. In the kitchen I see that Robbie amended the note on the magnetic board on the refrigerator. *Gone. Back later. Love.*

I go to the bedroom to get the box of stones. I drop them onto the kitchen table. They make a lovely noise, like playing with marbles or checkers when I was young and Tony was young too, and alive. I pick up a stone, pop it into my mouth, and see, almost like a memory but clearer (and certainly this is not my life), the life of a young man, a Roman, I think. I don't know how long this process takes, because there is a strange, circular feeling to it, as though I have experienced this person's entire life, not in the elongated way we live hours and days and years but rather as something spherical. I see him as a young boy, playing in a stream, and I see him with his parents, eating at some sort of feast, I see him kiss a girl, and I see him go to battle. The battle scenes are very gruesome but I don't spit out the stone because I have to know how it turns out. I see him return home, I see his old mother's tearful face but not his father's, because his father was killed in the war, but then there are many happy scenes, a wedding, children; he lives a good life and dies in a field one day, all alone under a bright sun, clutching wet blades of grass with one hand, his heart with the other. I pick up another stone and see the life of another boy, and another, and another. Each stone carries the whole life of a son. Now, without stopping to spit them out, I shove stones into my mouth, swirling through centuries of births and wars and dying until at last I find Tony's, from the blossomed pains of his birth, through his death in Berkeley, stabbed by a boy not much older than he was, the last thing he saw, this horrified boy saying, "Oh, shit." I shove stones into my mouth, dizzy with the lives and deaths and the ever-repeating endless cycle of war. When my mouth is too full, I spit them out and start again. At last I find Robbie's, watching every moment of his birth and growing years while the cacophony of other lives continues around me, until I see him in a bedroom, the noise of loud music, laughter, and voices coming through the crack under the door. He is naked and in bed with a blond girl. I spit out the stones. Then, carefully, I pick up the wet stones one at a time until I again find Robbie's and Tony's. These I put next to the little Buddha in the hallway. The rest I put into the box, which I shove under my bed.

The next day I drive Robbie to the bus depot.

"I don't want you worrying about me. I'm going to be fine," he says.

I smile, not falsely. The bus is late, of course. While we wait we meet two other families whose children are making the same trip as Robbie is. Steve, a blue-eyed boy with the good looks of a model, and Sondra, whose skin is smooth and brown, lustrous like stone. I shake their hands and try to say the right things, but I do not look into those young, bright faces for long. I cannot bear to. When their parents try to make small talk, I can only murmur my replies. Nobody seems to blame me. It is expected that I act this way, upset and confused. Certainly nobody suspects the truth about me, that I am a murderer, that I have bargained their children's lives for my son's.

When it comes time to say good-bye, I kiss him on the cheek. Oh, the wonderful warmth of his skin! The wonderful certainty that he will survive!

I stand and wave as the bus pulls away. I wave and wave even though I can't see his face, and I have no idea if he can see mine, I

The Mothers of Voorhisville

The things you have heard are true; we are the mothers of monsters. We would, however, like to clarify a few points. For instance, by the time we realized what Jeffrey had been up to, he was gone. At first we thought maybe the paper mill was to blame; it closed down in 1969, but perhaps it had taken that long for the poisonous chemicals to seep into our drinking water. We hid it from one another, of course, the strange shape of our newborns and the identity of the father. Each of us thought we were his secret lover. That was much of the seduction. Though he was also beautiful, with those blue eyes and that intense way of his.

It is true that he arrived in that big black car with the curtains across the back windows, as has been reported. But though Voorhisville is a small town, we are not ignorant, toothless, or the spawn of generations of incest. We *did* recognize the car as a hearse. However, we did not immediately assume the worst of the man who drove it. Perhaps we in Voorhisville are not as sheltered from death as people elsewhere. We, the mothers of Voorhisville, did not look at Jeffrey and immediately think of death. Instead, we looked into those blue eyes of his and thought of sex. You might have to have met him yourself to understand. There is a small but growing contingent of us that believes we were put under a type of spell. *Not* in regard to our later actions, which we take responsibility for, but in regard to him.

What mother wouldn't kill to save her babies? The only thing unusual about our story is that our children can fly. (Sometimes, even now, we think we hear wings brushing the air beside us.) We mothers take the blame because we understand, someone has to suffer. So we do. Gladly.

We would gladly do it all again to have one more day with our
darlings. Even knowing the damage, we would gladly agree. This is not
the apology you might have expected. Think of it more as a manifesto.
A map, in case any of them seek to return to us, though our hope of
that happening is faint. Why would anyone *choose* this ruined world?

Elli

The mothers have asked me to write what I know about what happened, most specifically what happened to me. I am suspicious of
their motives. They insist this story must be told to "set the record
straight." What I think is that they are annoyed that I, Elli Ratcher,
with my red hair and freckles and barely sixteen years old, shared a
lover with them. The mothers like to believe they were driven to the
horrible things they did by mother-love. I can tell you, though; they
have always been capable of cruelty.

The mothers, who have a way of *hovering* over me, citing my recent
suicide attempt, say I should start at the beginning. That is an easy thing
to *say*. It's the kind of thing I probably would have said to Timmy, had
he not fallen through my arms and crashed to the ground at my feet.

The mothers say if this is too hard, I should give the pen to someone else. "We all have stuff to tell," Maddy Melvern says. Maddy is,
as everyone knows, jealous. She was just seventeen when she did it
with Jeffrey and would be getting all the special attention if not for
me. The mothers say they really mean it—if I can't start at the beginning, someone else will. So, all right.

It's my fifteenth birthday, and Grandma Joyce, who taught high
school English for forty-six years, gives me one of her watercolor cards
with a poem and five dollars. I know she's trying to tell me something
important with the poem, but the most I can figure out about what it
means is that she doesn't want me to grow up. That's okay. She's my
grandma. I give her a kiss. She touches my hair. "Where did this come
from?" she says, which annoys my mom. I don't know why. When she
says it in front of my dad, he says, "Let it rest, Ma."

Right now my dad is out in the barn showing Uncle Bobby the
beams. The barn beams have been a subject of much concern for my

father, and endless conversations—at dinner, or church, or in parent-teacher conferences, the grocery store, or the post office—have been reduced to "the beams."

I stand on the porch and feel the sun on my skin. I can hear my mom and aunt in the kitchen and the cartoon voices from *Shrek 2*, which my cousins are watching. When I look at the barn I think I hear my dad saying "beams." I look out over the front yard to the road that goes by our house. Right then, a long black car comes over the hill, real slow, like the driver is lost. I shade my eyes to watch it pass the cornfield. I wonder if it is some kind of birthday present for me. A ride in a limousine! It slows down even more in front of our house. That's when I realize it's a hearse.

Then my dad and Uncle Bobby come out of the barn. When my dad sees me, he says, "Hey! You can't be fifteen, not my little stink-bottom," which he's been saying all day, "stinkbottom" being what he used to call me when I was in diapers. I have to use all my will and power not to roll my eyes, because he hates it when I roll my eyes. I am trying not to make anyone mad, because today is my birthday.

As far as I can figure out, that is the beginning. But is it? Is it the beginning? There are so many of us, and maybe there are just as many beginnings. What does "beginning" mean, anyway? What does anything mean? What is meaning? What *is*? Is Timmy? Or is he not? Once, I held him in my arms and he smiled and I thought I loved him. But maybe I didn't. Maybe everything was already me throwing babies out the window; maybe everything was already tiny homemade caskets with flies buzzing around them; maybe everything has always been this place, this time, this sorrowful house and the weeping of the mothers.

The Mothers

We have decided Elli should take a little time to compose herself. Tamara Singh, who, up until Ravi's birth, worked at the library on Tuesdays and Thursdays and every other Saturday, has graciously volunteered. In the course of persuading us that she is, in fact, per-fect for the position of chronicler, Tamara—perhaps overcome with

enthusiasm—cited the fantastic aspects of her several unpublished
novels. This delayed our assent considerably. Tamara said she would
not be writing about "elves and unicorns." She explained that the
word *fantasy* comes from the Latin *phantasia*, which means "an idea,
notion, image, or a making visible."

"Essentially, it's making an idea visible. Everyone knows what we
did. I thought we were trying to make them see why," she said.

The mothers have decided to let Tamara tell what she can. We
agree that what we have experienced, and heretofore have not ade-
quately explained (or why would we still be here?)—might be best
served by "a making visible."

We can hope, at least. Many of us, though surprised to discover
it, still have hope.

Tamara

There is, on late summer days, a certain perfume to Voorhisville. It's
the coppery smell of water, the sweet scent of grass with a touch of
corn and lawn mower gas, lemon slices in ice-tea glasses, and citro-
nella. Sometimes, if the wind blows just right, it carries the perfume
of the angel roses in Sylvia Lansmorth's garden, a scent so seductive
that everyone, from toddlers playing in the sandbox at Fletcher's Park
to senior citizens in rocking chairs at the Celia Wathmore Nursing
Home, is made just a little bit drunk.

On just such a morning, Sylvia Lansmorth (whose beauty was not
diminished by the recent arrival of gray in her long hair), sat in her
garden, in the chair her husband had made for her during that strange
year after the cancer diagnosis.

She sat weeping among her roses, taking deep gulps of the sweet
air, like a woman just surfaced from a near-drowning. In truth, Sylvia,
who had experienced much despair in the past year, was now feeling
an entirely different emotion.

"I want you to get on with things," he'd told her. "I don't want you
mourning forever. Promise me."

So she made the sort of unreasonable promise one makes to a
dying man, while he looked at her with those bulging eyes, which

had taken on a light she once thought characteristic of saints and psychopaths.

She'd come, as she had so many times before, to sit in her garden, and for some reason, who knows why, was overcome by this *emotion* she never thought she would feel again—this absolute love of life. As soon as she recognized it, she began to weep. Still, it was an improvement, anyone would say, this weeping and gulping of air; a great improvement over weeping and muffling her face against a pillow.

Of all the sweet-smelling places in Voorhisville that morning, the yoga studio was the sweetest. The music was from India, or so they thought. Only Tamara guessed it wasn't Indian music, but music meant to sound as though it was; just as the teacher, Shreve, despite her unusual name, wasn't Indian but from somewhere in New Jersey. If you listened carefully, you could hear it in her voice.

Right in the middle of the opening chant there was a ruckus at the back of the room. Somebody was late, and not being particularly quiet about it. Several women peeked, right in the middle of *om.* Others resisted until Shreve instructed them to stand, at which point they reached for a water bottle, or a towel, or just forgot about subterfuge entirely and simply looked. By the time the class was in its first downward dog, there was not a person there who hadn't spied on the noisy latecomer. He had the bluest eyes any of them had ever seen, and a halo of light around his body, which most everyone assumed was an optical illusion. It would be a long time before any of them thought that it hadn't been a glow at all, but a burning.

Shreve noticed, when she walked past him as he lay in corpse position, the strong scent of jasmine, and thought that, in the mysterious ways of the world, a holy man, a yogi, had come into her class.

Shreve, like Sylvia, was a widow. Sort of. There was no word for what she was, actually. She felt betrayed by language, among other things. Her fiancé had been murdered. Even the nature of his death had robbed her of something primary, as if *how* he died was more important than that he had. She'd given up trying to explain it. Nobody in Voorhisville knew. She'd moved here with her new yoga teacher certificate after the second anniversary of the event and opened up this studio with the savings she'd set aside for the wedding. His parents paid for the funeral, so she still had quite a bit left, which was good, because though the studio was a success by Voorhisville's standards, she was running out of money. It was enough to make her cranky sometimes. She tried to forgive herself for it. Shreve wasn't sure she had enough love to forgive the world, but she thought—maybe—she could forgive herself.

With her hands in prayer position, Shreve closed her eyes and sang "shanti" three times. It meant "peace," and on that morning Shreve felt like peace had finally arrived.

Later, when the stranger showed up for the writers' workshop at Jan Morris's house, she could not determine how he'd found out about the elitist group, known to have rejected at least one local writer on the basis of the fact she wrote fantasy. Jan asked him how he'd found them, but Sylvia interrupted before he could answer. Certainly it never occurred to her to think he was up to anything diabolical. Also, it became clear that Sylvia knew him from a yoga class she attended. By the time he had passed out the twelve copies of his poem—his presence made them a group of thirteen, but they were intellectuals, not a superstitious bunch—well, it just didn't matter how he found them.

Afterward, as the writers left, Jan stood at the door with the stranger beside her, waving good-bye until she observed two things: first, that the last car remaining in the driveway was a hearse, and second, that the stranger smelled, quite pleasantly, of lemons.

Jan preferred to call him "the stranger." Never mind Camus; it had a nice ring to it all on its own. Eventually, when the mothers pieced things together, it seemed the most accurate moniker. They didn't know him at all. None of them did. Not really.

One night in early June, after events began to unfold as they did, Jan looked for her copy of the stranger's poem, which she remembered folding inside a book, like a pressed flower. But though she tore apart the bookshelf, making so much noise she woke the baby, she never found it. She called the others and asked each of them, trying to sound casual ("Remember that poet, who came to the workshop just that once? And that poem he wrote?"), but none of them could locate their copy either.

Sylvia remembered that night well; waving good-bye to Jan and Jeffrey, who were standing in the doorway together, haloed by the light of all those overwhelming lemon-scented candles. Jeffrey was a good deal taller than Jan. Sylvia realized she could look right into his blue eyes without even seeing the top of the other woman's head.

When Jan called in June, Sylvia pretended to have only a minor memory of Jeffrey and the poem, but as soon as she hung up she began searching for it, moving ponderously, weighed down by her pregnancy and the heat. How could she have misplaced it? She had intended to give it to the child some day, a way to say, "Here, you have a father and he is a genius." But also, Sylvia felt, it was proof that what she had done had been the only reasonable response. The poem revealed not just his intelligence, but also his heart, which was good. Sylvia had to believe this, though he left her. Her husband had left her, too . . . and yes, all right, he had died, but Jeffrey made no promises. He'd come and gone, which Sylvia considered fortunate. She didn't need, or want, the complication of his presence. But she did want that poem.

That night, when Sylvia's water broke, she was surprised at how it felt: "As though there had been an iceberg inside of me, which suddenly melted," she told Holly.

Holly, the midwife and a keeper of many secrets, had a house in Ridgehaven, but that May, she rented a small room from the Melverns, who were thrilled to have her in such close proximity to their pregnant seventeen-year-old daughter. Holly had told no one what she had seen: all those pregnant women in Voorhisville who didn't appear to have a man in their lives. While this was certainly not scandalous, she did find the number significant. When the babies began arriving that last week in May, it became clear to Holly that something had happened to the women of Voorhisville. *Something indescribable.*

For Jeffrey's appeal—though he was a good-looking man— went beyond description. Though there weren't *many*, there *were* other attractive men in Voorhisville who the women had not fucked; receiving nothing in exchange but a single night, or afternoon, or morning (after yoga class, in the studio, the air sweet with jasmine). When the women tried to define just what was so compelling about the stranger, they could not come to a consensus.

Lara Bravemeen, for instance, remembered his hands, with their long-narrow fingers and their slender wrists. She said he had the hands of a painter.

Cathy Vecker remembered the way he moved. "Like a man who never hurried . . . but not lazy, you see. Self-contained, that's what I mean."

Tamara mentioned his eyes, which everyone else thought so obvious there was no need to comment.

Elli Ratcher stopped chewing on a hangnail long enough to say, "When he held me, I felt like I was being held by an angel. I felt like I would always be safe. I felt holy."

At which point the women sighed and looked down at their shoes, or into their laps. Because to look at Elli was to remember she had been just fifteen. Though no one could be sure about Jeffrey's age, he was certainly a man. What he'd done to all of them was wrong, but what he'd done to Elli—and Maddy, they hastened to add—went beyond wrong into the territory of evil.

Maddy

My name is Maddy Melvern—well, Matilda, which just goes to show how grownups like to make up the world they live in; my parents naming me like I was living in a fairy tale instead of Voorhisville. Let's just set the record straight, I don't remember no sweet-smelling day here or none of that shit. Voorhisville is a dump. The houses, almost all of them, except the Veckers', are all peeling paint and crooked porches. Voorhisville is the kind of town where if a window gets broke it's gonna stay broke, but someone will try to cover it up with cardboard or duct tape. Duct tape holds Voorhisville together. Roddy Tyler's got his shoes duct-taped, and there's duct tape in the post office holding the American flag up, and there's duct tape on the back of the third pew in St. Andrew's balcony. I don't know why. There just is. I was born here and I ain't old enough to do nothing about it. I can't explain why anyone else would stay. I know the mothers like to say there are sweet-smelling days in Voorhisville, but there ain't.

I agree with Elli. Jeffrey was a angel. And just to be clear, my baby was a angel too. All our babies were. No matter what anyone says. I don't care if he stayed. What was he going to do? Work at the canning factory? Maybe you can picture him doing that and then coming home to, like, have barbecues and shit, but I sure can't. He didn't fall for it, you know, that way of doing things *right*. What I say is that if everybody in Voorhisville's so concerned with doing things right, then just as soon as we get out of here I'm going to live my life doing things *wrong*.

It was the first day of school and me, Leanne, Sasha, and some of the guys was walking to Sasha's house when we see this hearse parked in front of St. Andrew's. Mark dares me to go into the church. I'm like, what's the big shit about that? So when the door shuts behind me they all take off, laughing like a bunch of retards.

I kind of liked it. It was peaceful, all right? And it did smell good in there. And everything was clean. So I'm looking at this big statue they got of Jesus on the cross? He's got the crown with the thorns on his head, and he's bleeding, and I don't know why, but whenever I see statues and pictures of Jesus and shit like that, I sort of hate him. I know that's insulting to many people, but he annoys me, with that crown piercing his skull and those nails in his feet and hands and shit. I never understand why he didn't do nothing about it, if he was so powerful and all? "You belong in Voorhisville," is what I thought, and I guess I said it out loud 'cause that's when a voice behind me goes, "Excuse me?"

So, I turned and there he was. At first I thought he was the priest, but he set me straight. We talked for a long time and then after a while he said we had to go somewhere safe. I kind of laughed, because ain't churches supposed to be super safe, but he took my hand, and we went up to the balcony. I don't know why, we just did, okay? That's where it happened. I know me and Elli ain't been getting along so much here, but she's right: it ain't bad, what we did. I know, doing it in the church makes it seem bad, but it was good, okay? Like how they said it would be, not like . . . not . . . Okay, I've been with boys my own age, and I've had *bad*, and this was not like that. And I ain't just talking about his *dick*. I'm talking about the feeling. What'd she call it? Holy.

But that don't mean that Voorhisville ain't all stinky and shit. We don't gotta lie about that. We should tell it right because what this shows everyone is that something like this could happen anywhere. If it happened in Voorhisville, it could happen in any town, and I don't see that as being a bad thing.

Tamara

The third anniversary of Shreve's fiancé's death fell on a Saturday when yoga class was scheduled, but she decided to teach anyway, and was glad she did. She started class with a short meditation. She didn't tell the women what to think or feel. They just sat there, breathing in and out. Shreve thought about her plans. After class, she would go home and change into something comfortable (but not her pajamas, as she'd done for years one and two), make herself a nice pot of tea, light a candle, and look at photographs.

By the time she opened her eyes, those hard minutes had passed. On that day, though not everyone remembers, Voorhisville smelled like chocolate. Emily Carr woke up at 4:30 and began baking. By 6:30, when Stecker's opened, she was waiting there with a long list of ingredients. She baked chocolate bread, and a chocolate cake layered with a raspberry filling, a chocolate torte, and good old-fashioned— why mess with perfection?—chocolate chip cookies. Though the day was warm, she also mixed up some Mexican hot chocolate, which she poured into a large thermos. She made a batch of chocolate muffins and six dozen dark chocolate cherry cookies. Then Emily filled several baskets with cookies, muffins, and slices of cake, torte, and bread, and began delivering her treats to the neighbors.

"But why?" they asked, to which she just shrugged. Until, when she got to Shreve's house, she said, "Let me know what you think. I'm going to open a bakery and I'm trying to find out what people like."

At that point, Emily began to cry. Shreve invited her inside. Wiping her eyes as she stepped into the warm living room, Emily said, "I'm happy. That's why I'm crying. I'm so happy." Then she noticed the photographs spread across the floor, the wedding dress on the couch, the stricken look on Shreve's face.

"My fiancé died," Shreve said, "three years ago today."

Emily, who had forgotten the date entirely until Bobby Stewart said, "What is this? Some kind of September eleventh thing?" resisted the impulse to ask Shreve if he'd been one of the thousands. Instead, she said, "There's a thermos of hot chocolate."

Shreve looked from the basket to the photographs, the wedding dress, the box of tiny bells. "I don't know what to do."

"We could go to the park."

That's what they did. On that mild September evening the women sat beneath the oak tree in Fletcher's Park, ate too much chocolate, and became friends.

The following Saturday, after Emily's first yoga class, the women went garage sale-ing together. Both women appreciated a bargain, and both women had appreciated Jeffrey, though they wouldn't know this until October, when they confided their fears to each other and—like high school girls, giggling, nervous, and unsure—went to the drugstore for pregnancy tests, which, oddly, were all sold out. They drove all the way to Centerville to purchase them, during which time they told their stories of the stranger with blue eyes and thus discovered that they had shared a lover.

"Did you notice how he smelled?" Shreve asked.

"Chocolate," Emily said. "Do you ever get mad at him? The way he just left?"

"Actually, I sort of prefer it this way. I'm not looking for anything else. You?"

Emily shook her head. "It's the weirdest thing, because normally I would. I mean, I think so, at least. I've never done anything like that with a stranger. But for some reason, I'm not angry."

Were the women of Voorhisville enchanted? Bewitched? Had a great evil befallen them? It was hard to imagine that anything bad happened that autumn, when everyone glowed.

Later, they had to agree it was more than strange that they all got pregnant, even those using birth control, and none of them suffered morning sickness. It was also odd that, given the obvious promiscuity involved, no one got an STD. But that fall, all anyone cared about was that the women of Voorhisville were beautiful.

Lara no longer stood at the small window in the upstairs hallway spying on her neighbor. Yes, Sylvia was beautiful. She had always *been* beautiful, even at her husband's funeral, her face wracked with grief. But there were many beautiful women in Voorhisville. Why hadn't Lara noticed before?

One morning, shortly after September eleventh (she later recalled the date because she'd eaten Emily's chocolate cake for breakfast), Lara stood naked in front of the bedroom mirror. Why had she spent all that time studying Sylvia? Lara turned, twisting her neck to get a sideways look.

She decided to begin painting again. She would paint her own strong legs, the sag of flesh at her stomach, her tired eyes. She had to paint all this to try to express the feeling she had, of no longer being a sum of parts. Her parts would be there, but that's not what the painting would be about. It would be a self-portrait, Lara decided, and it would be huge.

When Lara realized she was late, she phoned the pharmacy. "I'm not coming in today," she said. She didn't offer an explanation. Even as she said it, she wasn't sure she would ever return to work. She knew how this would sit with Ed. He wouldn't like it, but it wasn't as though she expected him to support her; she had her own savings.

As Lara dressed, she thought about Jeffrey. She'd taken a huge risk; he could have been a psycho. He could have stalked her. Or told Ed! Instead, he disappeared. For weeks, Lara looked for the hearse, but she never saw it again. He was gone as mysteriously as he'd arrived. She'd been lucky, Lara thought—guilty, yes, but lucky.

It didn't even occur to her she might be pregnant.

Theresa Ratcher knew she was. She would say, later, that she knew immediately.

When Lara drove past the Ratcher farm on her way to Centerville for art supplies, Theresa Ratcher was standing in the driveway, shading her eyes, as though expecting a visitor. The women waved at each other. Lara sighed. Even Theresa Ratcher was beautiful in her old housewifey dress, her clunky shoes, her corn-colored hair in a messy ponytail.

Theresa watched the car arc over the hill with one hand on her tummy, which had not been flat since Elli was born fifteen years ago. Pete would never suspect a thing. Why would he? Why would anyone? She closed her eyes and tilted her face toward the sun. "What are you doing?" Pete said. Theresa opened her eyes, wide, as though caught. Her husband's face had hardened with time, and he smelled of manure, but she loved him. She placed her hand on his crotch. After a moment, she turned and walked away. He followed, surprised when she didn't go into the house but walked behind the barn, where she lay down on the grass and lifted up her dress, revealing her freckled thighs, the white crotch of her panties. This was very much like how it had happened, when, still teenagers, they'd made Elli.

Here's your dad, Theresa thought.

What all (or most) of the women of Voorhisville would have said was that beautiful was everywhere that fall: it was in the light and shadows and the muted green leaves that eventually burned into a blaze of color, it was in the duct-taped houses, in the bats that flew out of St. Andrew's belfry each night, and the logey bees buzzing among the pumpkins and squash.

Beautiful was in the women, the way they talked, walked, the things they did: the stretch of limbs in yoga, the scent of chocolate from Emily's kitchen. Jan Morris had never written so proficiently— or, she felt—and the writers in the workshop agreed—more beautifully. Lara Bravemeen began painting again, which caused an argument with her husband, a fight Lara could only think of as beautiful in its passion.

Strange things were happening to the women of Voorhisville. Anyone could see that.

"Like bones, and skin, and blood," Elli Ratcher later said. "What could be more beautiful than that? What could be more strange?"

The Mothers

We, the mothers, understand the enormity of the task involved in relaying the events that preceded the seminal one. We appreciate the impossibility of incorporating each personal account into this narrative, and, after much discussion and several votes, made the decision to tell this story through the voices of a representative few. It is an imperfect solution, we know, but then again, we are in an imperfect situation. However, we would like to stress that we reject the penis-glorifying tone that's been taken, as though we, the women of Voorhisville, were only completed through penetration. We would like to make it clear that we believe the women of Voorhisville were always beautiful, always interesting, always evolving, always capable of greatness.

Tamara

The Veckers own the big white house on the hill. They *pay* people to do their gardening, mow the lawn, trim the bushes. Several Voorhisville residents think it's unjust that the Veckers win the Gardeners' Association's blue ribbon each year, as well as the grand prize for their Christmas decorations; that big house outlined with thousands of little white lights, all those windows and doors bordered too, so that it looks like some strip mall.

Nobody is exactly sure how the Veckers got to be so rich. Even Cathy Vecker, twenty-five years old and recently returned from Los Angeles, looking a good deal older than her age, has no idea where the family money came from. The topic never held much interest for her. Cathy *knew* everyone was not as fortunate as she was; but what could she do about it? Whenever she thought about all the poor people—Roddy Tyler with his duct-taped shoes, for instance—it just made her weary.

Because what *could* they do? The Veckers were rich, but they weren't *that* rich; they were no Bill *Gates*, that's for sure. Even Cathy, who had never been good at math, knew the numbers didn't work out. The world had more people than dollars in the various Vecker accounts. If the Veckers gave away every cent they owned, nobody would be rich, and the Veckers would join the masses of those without enough. For a while, Cathy had worried that she was becoming a socialist, but once she worked through the logic, she was relieved to discover that she was just a regular rich American.

Being a rich American meant Cathy could follow her dreams. She moved to Los Angeles to pursue modeling and acting. Cathy Vecker *was* pretty. She was not as beautiful as Sylvia Lansmorth, but everyone knew that Sylvia was exceptional—though overly attached to her roses. Sylvia's husband was gorgeous too, or had been, before he died. He was a carpenter. Cathy's mother and grandmother, hired him from time to time for special projects.

Cathy had never been happier for the Vecker money than she was upon returning from Los Angeles. She was thrilled she didn't have to come up with an immediate solution to the challenging question of what she would do with her life. It wasn't that she meant to shrug the question off—she had every intention of addressing it eventually—but it was a relief not to have to rush to a conclusion, get a job *waitressing* or something.

Los Angeles had been an experiment, and she'd failed miserably. All the women in Los Angeles were gorgeous. It was kind of weird, actually. Also, Cathy discovered, she couldn't really act. It wasn't until she saw a recording of her audition that she recognized that. Why hadn't anyone told her? Why hadn't someone just *said* it?

By the end of August, Cathy had narrowed her choices to going to college—though she hadn't applied, she felt certain her family connections could get her into St. Mary's or the university—or opening a small business. She was bogged down in the details. What would she major in? What kind of business would she start?

Then she became distracted. She *thought* she was falling in love, or at least that explained the powerful attraction, the *chemistry*, the reason she *did it* in the back of a *hearse*, like somebody who couldn't afford a room somewhere. Later, Cathy had to admit there was something about it that felt dangerous and exciting. She thought she'd gotten that sort of thing out of her system in Los Angeles, but apparently not.

He didn't ask for her phone number, but she didn't worry. She was a Vecker. Everyone knew how to get in touch with the Veckers. By September, she realized he wasn't going to call. By the end of that month, despite the Pill—which Cathy had been taking since she was fifteen, when she had her first affair with Stephen Lang, who (she didn't know it was a cliché at the time) cleaned their pool—Cathy guessed she was pregnant. A quick trip to the drugstore and a home pregnancy test confirmed it. Cathy knew she should be upset, but honestly, she wasn't. She placed her hand on her flat stomach and said, "I'll do this."

She decided she'd start a community theatre, right there in Voorhisville. A Christmas play in December, maybe a musical; possibly *Our Town* in the spring; something modern in between. It wouldn't have to make money. The Veckers could *do* this. They couldn't support the world, or America, but they could do this. Cathy could run it, even while she raised her child, and she could live off one of the Vecker accounts, and she could do *something* good for Voorhisville.

The senior Mrs. Vecker received the news—first of the pregnancy, then of the community theatre—with the traditional Vecker attitude. Cathy was worried her grandmother would be upset, but it turned out there had not been an exact alignment between Grandma Vecker's own wedding and Cathy Vecker's mother's birth; a matter covered up, at the time, by an extended European honeymoon. "Didn't you *know* that?" Mrs. Vecker asked.

Whereas Grandma Vecker said, "It's quite clever of you to start without the man hanging around. Everything you need from him, you've already got."

After her husband died, Sylvia Lansmorth found herself in the unusual position of being rich. Well, not *rich*, exactly, not like the Veckers, but she no longer had to work at the canning factory, a job she'd held since she was fifteen. Who would have guessed that Rick Lansmorth—who was, after all, just a carpenter—had the foresight to take out sizable life insurance policies for both of them? But he had.

All these months later, Sylvia was still finding the wooden figurines Rick had been working on during his chemo; tiny creatures that fit in the palm of her hand: a swan tucked in his toolbox (she'd been looking for the hammer); what appeared to be the beginnings of a wolf (the shape formed, a few lines cut for fur but no eyes or mouth) on the kitchen windowsill; a tiny mouse with a broken tail in the garden. Rick used to sit outside wrapped in blankets, even when the sun was hot, and Sylvia guessed he'd thrown it in frustration. Not the sort of thing he would normally do, but dying had been hard.

Sylvia was not living the life she'd imagined when she was a high school girl who thought her job at the canning factory was temporary. She used to look at the women working there and wonder why they stayed. Now, Sylvia knew. It just happened.

She and Rick had planned to leave Voorhisville. First, he tried building up a clientele in Centerville, but he was just another guy with a toolbox there. People in Voorhisville knew and trusted him, and while there wasn't much work, what work there was, he got. Then he moved to Alaska. The plan was that he would get established before Sylvia joined him. They missed each other, of course, but it was a sacrifice they were willing to make. They thought they had time. Instead, he came back to Voorhisville with cancer and stories of moose.

After Sylvia quit her job, she spent a great deal of time in the garden; so much so that, as fall approached, she realized that her main occupation had been dying, and she didn't have anything to replace it with. She would have denied that she had wished for it, or expected it; she would have resisted calling it a miracle; but just when the garden started to look barren, she discovered she was pregnant, the result of one single sexual encounter with a stranger she had no desire to see again. Sylvia had gotten quite good at crying over the past year. Why couldn't it be Rick's child? Why couldn't he still be alive? What could possibly come of conception in a *hearse*? How Freudian was that?

Sylvia considered an abortion. Then she got in her car, drove to Centerville, and went to the Barnes & Noble, where she spent a good deal of money on pregnancy and parenting books.

"Wow, we've really had a run on these lately," the clerk said.

Sylvia liked having a secret. It wasn't that she was ashamed. She just liked having this private relationship with her baby. Once her neighbor, Lara Bravemeen (whose upstairs windows brooded over Sylvia's garden), asked why she'd stopped going to yoga, and she just shrugged. Sylvia had recently discovered that most people accepted a shrug for an answer.

In January, Sylvia learned that Lara Bravemeen was pregnant too. Their children could play together. That is, if the Bravemeens stayed married and continued to live next door. Lately, there'd been a lot of shouting over there.

Never having been pregnant before, Sylvia had nothing to compare it to except TV shows, but she thought it was perfect. She felt wonderful the whole time. Holly, the midwife, said, "Sometimes it's almost harder if you have an easy pregnancy. It makes the birth just that much more of a shock."

Sylvia, who had been feeling very much like a madonna—not the rock star, but the perfectly peaceful mother type—just smiled.

The pain was monumental. Right from the start. Ed called the doctor and she said, "How far apart?" and Ed asked Lara, "How far apart?" and Lara screamed, "What?" So Ed repeated the question. "There's no time between, you moron," Lara hollered. Ed relayed this to the doctor, (editing out the "moron," of course), who said, "When did the contractions start?" and Ed said, "Five minutes ago." That's when the doctor said, "Bring her in now." Ed said, "Right now?" and the doctor said, "Wait. You're in Voorhisville, right?" and he said, "Yes," and she said, "Call the ambulance," and Ed said, "Is there a problem?" and Lara screamed and the doctor said, "Call them." So Ed called the ambulance and they came right away. It was Brian Holandeigler and Francis Kennedy (no relation to any of the famous ones), who tried to make jokes to calm Ed and Lara down, but between screams of agony, Lara was vicious. "She's not usually like this," Ed said. "Fuck you!" Lara shouted. "You're going to be all right," Francis said. "Fuck you!" Lara screamed. "Try to breathe," Ed said. "Remember the breathing?" "Fuck, fuck, fuck," Lara screamed.

Something was wrong. Something was terribly wrong. She knew it. And here she was, surrounded by these idiot men ("Idiots!" she shouted) who thought she was hysterical.

"I'm dying!" she screamed.

"You're not dying," Ed said.

It felt like she was being scraped raw inside by talons. It felt like her guts were being carved out. Or like teeth! It felt like small, sharp teeth were chewing her up inside.

"Do something!" she shouted.

"Well, we really can't do much," Brian said.

"What?" Ed and Lara said.

"I could take a look," Brian said.

"But we're not supposed to transport women in labor," Francis said. "We're supposed to stay here. Unless there's a problem."

"There's a fucking problem!" Lara shouted.

"Do you mind if I look?" Brian said as he slipped his hands around the waistband of Lara's pants. Ed found the image disturbing, and turned away. Lara saw him turn away. She managed, through her pain, to form the words again: "Fuck you." Brian sat up. "Hold your legs together," he said. "What?" Lara said. "Is it coming?" Ed said. "Of course it's—" Lara interrupted herself to scream. "Close your legs!" Brian shouted. "Are we taking her?" Francis said. "Yes. Yes. Oh, God, yes," Brian said. "Close your legs!" he yelled at Lara. "Oh, God; oh Jesus," Brian said. Lara screamed. Ed leaned down and held her hand. "Please," he said, "close your legs." "I want it out!" Lara shouted. "Please," Ed said, "do what they say." "Excuse me," Francis said, and shoved Ed away.

Brian and Francis set the stretcher on the floor beside the couch. "I'm dying!" Lara screamed. Brian and Ed lifted her to the stretcher. "Close your legs," Brian said. Lara closed her legs. "Don't drop her," Ed said as he opened the door. "Can I come with you?" "Two steps," Francis said to Brian, who was backing out. Ed shut the door. He looked at Sylvia's dark house. *Death could come to anyone, anywhere,* he thought. "Are you coming?" Francis said. Ed jumped into the ambulance. The siren screamed, but it was nothing compared to Lara's screams. "Let me see where you're at," Francis said. He spread a sheet over Lara's lap and bent under to have a look. When his head came out of the sheet, his eyes were wide, his skin white. "Oh, Jesus," Francis said. "Hold your legs together."

Lara tried to hold her legs together, but it felt like she was being sliced by knives. "Ed," she shouted. "Ed?"

"I'm here, baby, I'm right here." He squeezed her hand.

She screamed. She screamed the whole ride from Voorhisville to the hospital in Becksworth. When they got there, the doctor was waiting for them.

"How about an epidural?" she said. "You better take a look," Brian said. She lifted the sheet and looked. "Take her to the OR," the doctor said. "What's happening?" Ed said. "You stay here," a nurse said. "What's happening?" Ed said to Brian and Francis. They both stared at him, then Francis said, "There might be some complications." Ed sat down. Brian and Francis left. The hospital was so quiet Ed thought he could still hear Lara's screams. But it couldn't have been her, because Lara had gone to the right, and the screams were coming from the left.

Jan Morris lay screaming in her hospital bed, but no one was paying much attention. Someone had checked her when she came in, and pointed out that she wasn't even dilated yet. Jan insisted they contact her doctor. "She wants to know," she said. But Jan's doctor was busy with some other emergency, so Dr. Fascular took the call instead. The nurse checked Jan again, decided that she was making a big fuss over nothing, and administered an epidural. The mother was in her forties, and they were often the biggest pains. They wanted everything a certain way. But Jan kept screaming until it finally occurred to someone that there might be a problem.

The nurse who looked at Jan later said, over coffee and eggs with her twelve-year-old son, that it was the most shocking thing she'd ever seen. The woman hadn't even been *dilated* ten minutes ago—or, okay, it might have been closer to twenty minutes, but then suddenly there was . . . she thought there might be an arm, a leg, something like that. Anyway, after she saw the strange *thing* protruding from Jan Morris's vagina, she ran to call Dr. Fascular again.

"What thing?" the nurse's son asked.

"I don't know how to describe it. It was just sticking out, and it was like a, like the tip of a triangle, and it was sharp."

"You touched it?"

"Look," she said, and showed him the small cut on her finger.

"What happened next?" the boy asked.

She remembered touching that bloody tip with her finger; she remembered the sear of pain and running to call the doctor. The next thing she knew, several hours had passed and she was punching her time card to go home. Even though she was tired and her feet were sore and she certainly wanted to be there when her son woke up, she went to the nursery where she found the baby, a sweet-as-they-all-are prune-shaped thing, wrapped tightly in a blanket, sleeping. She read the chart and saw that there was nothing unusual noted.

Maddy

Yeah, well, that nurse didn't see nothing wrote down about it because they could hold them inside like the way you put your fingers in a fist, or maybe more like the way you close a eye. That's what the babies did. They pulled them in real tight and it just looked like, I don't know, kind of extra wrinkled and stuff. Who pays attention to a baby's back, anyways? Not most people. Most people wanna look at a baby's face or fingers and toes. There is a weird fascination with grownups looking at a baby's fingers or toes. Also, baby's shit. My mom could go on and on about JoJo's shit. Was it greenish? Was it runny? She'd get mad at me when I rolled my eyes. "You can tell things about your baby's health, Maddy," she'd say.

My mom liked to behave all superior about babies with me 'cause she had two, and she figured that made her a expert. Also, I really think she liked the fact I was a teenage mother 'cause it proved her theory that I was a fuckup all along. Weird as it is, though, I sometimes wish I had my mom here with me like Elli has hers. But how fucked is that? Both of them doing it with the same guy? It makes me shiver every time I think about it.

JoJo was born at home, even though we didn't plan it that way. Just 'cause we had a midwife renting Billy's old room in the basement don't mean we was going to use her. Holly was really busy. Once she came upstairs and asked me to turn the music down, but she asked like she knew it was a big pain for me to do, and so I turned it down. And one night we sat on the front steps and talked. I thought she was nice.

But it's not like I got to choose much about JoJo. My mom liked to act like everything was up to me. "He's your baby," she'd say. "He's your responsibility"—she said this about diaper changing and when he was crying. But other times she'd say, "Just 'cause you had a baby don't mean you're all grown up now."

My mom said I had to go to a hospital. "It's just ridiculous that in this day in age, with all the best modern medicine has to offer, a woman would choose to give birth at home like they was living in Afghanistan or something." My mom loved to mention Afghanistan whenever she could. My brother Billy got killed there, and after that she blamed Afghanistan for anything wrong in the world.

After I talked to Holly that night on the porch, I wanted her to help when the baby came. It's not like she tried to convince me, or nothing like that. We barely talked about it. Mostly we talked about other stuff. But I liked her, and I didn't like Dr. Fascular. He has cold hands and is always grumpy and shit.

My mom was all like, "No way," and said it had to be at the hospital. But there wasn't much she could do when it happened the way it did, all of a sudden, with me alone in the house. I didn't expect it to hurt like it did. It hurt a lot. I didn't scream, even though I really wanted to. I just went down to Billy's old room and laid down on Billy's old bed, which was now Holly's, and waited for her to get home. It hurt so bad I took the bedspread and rolled it up at the end and stuck it in my mouth. Every time I felt like screaming, which was pretty much all the time, I bit down.

I don't know how long it was before Holly came home. She said, "Maddy?"

I just screamed. I let the bedspread fall out of my mouth and I screamed loud enough to bring my mom and dad down the stairs, and then there was this whole part where they got mad at Holly, and even though I was screaming and shit, I had to explain to them that she didn't have nothing to do with it, and then my dad said he was going to get the car, and Holly was looking at my vagina and saying, "I don't think so."

I heard it hurt a lot to have a baby, but nothing nobody said told me how much. I don't even want to think about it.

So Mom starts arguing with Holly, and then all of a sudden Holly says, "This baby is halfway here. If you want to take her all the way to Becksworth, you go ahead. But I sure hope you are prepared to deliver it." Which, ha ha, got my mom to shut up.

Okay, so like it hurt more than anything I ever imagined. It hurt more than when Billy got killed, and I didn't think there would ever be nothing that hurt worse than that. Later, Holly told me it was not a usual birth. Still, I don't think I'll ever do it again. Like I could! Ha, stuck here with all these women.

I was exhausted. I just wanted to go to sleep. Holly said, "What are you going to name him?" And I said, "JoJo." And my mom said, "I knew it. I knew it was Joey Marin." My mom was obsessed with trying to figure out who JoJo's dad was. "It ain't Joey Marin," I said, but she just looked all superior. Holly cleaned him up and she said he was beautiful. And that's coming from someone who delivered hundreds of babies, so that should tell you something. Then she gave him to me, wrapped up like a bratwurst in a bun. Everybody stood there, even my dad. Like I was going to breastfeed in front of him! I guess Holly figured that out, 'cause she said she had some things to talk to them about in private. When Mom and Dad were both out the door, I told Holly I was sorry I got her in trouble. "That's all right," she said. "I thought this room could use a birth." I saw what she meant. Except for Holly's clothes and a little glass jar on the dresser filled with some wildflowers, the room was just the way it was when Billy left to get killed in the war.

So I took off my t-shirt and put JoJo up by my boob, and he started sucking.

The next day, after I moved back upstairs and my mom cleaned all of Holly's sheets and even baked her a tube of chocolate chip cookies to thank her for everything she did, I was undressing JoJo, and the next thing I knew, my finger was bleeding and JoJo was crying and my mom was standing there going, "What are you doing to him?"

"I ain't doing nothing to him," I said. "I pricked my finger."

"This is no longer all about you," she said, and, "You better make sure you keep one hand on him when he's on the changing table, or it won't be long before he'll just roll off." About as soon as JoJo was born, my mom started imagining all the horrible ways he could die.

I looked at JoJo laying there with his face all scrunched up and all I could think was that I had a huge problem. I didn't love him, all right? For the first time in my entire life I wondered if this is what was wrong with me and my mom, that she just didn't love me and couldn't do nothing about it. I felt real bad, and angry too. I decided that wasn't going to happen with me and JoJo.

I picked him up and took him with me to the bed, and that's when I saw them sticking out. They were *tiny*, like his fingers and toes were tiny. They were tiny like that.

"Holy shit, JoJo," I said. "You've got wings."

Tamara

When Tamara met Raj and found out he was Hindu, she didn't think much about it. It wasn't until she was already falling in love that she discovered how much his faith mattered to him. She told him she wasn't sure she could convert, but he said she didn't need to. It might have been easier if she could fool herself into believing that her infidelity had been Raj's fault, but Tamara could not believe that. She had cheated on him for the worst reason of all: because she felt like it.

There was justice in her pregnancy. It was a Catholic thought, she knew, but no matter how many years had passed since she'd gone to church, she could not escape the idea that God did things like this to Catholics. He punished them for being bad.

Tamara knew it was not uncommon for pregnant woman to have horrible dreams, but she was sure hers were the worst. Several times, Raj died. Once, she drowned the baby. (How could she even *dream* that?) She had many dreams that featured birth defects. When she woke up crying, Raj held her, soothed her, made her tea, told her jokes. He was the perfect husband, which just made everything worse.

Tamara thought of confessing. Being raised Catholic, how could she *not* think of that? But she couldn't decide. Was she confessing to help their marriage, or just to relieve her guilt? What was the *right* thing to do? She no longer trusted her judgment. How could she, after she'd displayed such a colossal lack of any? After it all came out and everything fell apart the way it did, she would decide she must have been put under some sort of spell, though the other women say things like, "Sure, if that's what you wanna call it, honey."

Tamara had passed the bar exam, so she was technically a lawyer, but hardly anyone knew that. She never practiced. She hated law school, but didn't dare quit after her parents had put so much money into it. She hadn't really mentioned, in any of her phone calls or e-mails to her parents, that she wasn't doing anything with her degree, but instead was working part-time at the Voorhisville library while writing another novel. She'd never told them about the four previous novels she'd written (but not published) so it was difficult to tell them about the fifth. They wouldn't approve. Her father used to make fun of her art major friends. He called them "the future poor of America."

She and Raj moved to Voorhisville because they had fantasies about small town life. Raj, who worked as a litigation attorney in Becksworth, and therefore wasn't really in Voorhisville much, still believed it was a quaint community, a perfect place for children. Tamara wasn't so sure. She'd *seen* things: the way Michael Baile (whose cousin was on the school board) got all the contracts for the school maintenance jobs, even though there were consistent complaints about the quality of his work. The way almost everyone talked about Maddy Malvern's spiral into sexual promiscuity, but did nothing about it. The way Roddy Tyler flopped around in those duct-taped shoes even in the winter, despite the fact that he worked for the richest people in town. Tamara did not think Voorhisville was quaint, though it did have the annual Halloween parade with all the children dressed in costumes walking down Main Street. *That* was quaint. And Fourth of July in Fletcher's Park, with Girl Scouts selling baked goods, Boy Scouts selling popcorn, and Mr. Muller twisting balloons into animal shapes while the senior citizen band played God knows what . . . well, *that* was quaint too. But Tamara saw the looks Raj, with his dark skin, got. "Doesn't it bother you?" she asked, but he just laughed. That's just the way Raj was. He didn't care. It had been harder for Tamara. She wasn't used to being a victim of prejudice.

"It would be like this in almost any small town in America," Raj said. "You can't let it upset you."

But it did. It upset Tamara very much. It confused her, too. She could never be sure. Had the man at the post office been rude because

he knew she was married to someone with dark skin, or had he just
been a rude man? What about the checkout girl at the supermarket, and the lady who cut her off at the corner of Henry Street and
Wildwood?

The novel Tamara was working on was called *Underskin*, about a
nomadic tribe of tree dwellers and the consumers who ate them. It
was a love story, a dark fantasy, a brutal indictment of prejudice, and
her best work. But after her strange encounter with the blue-eyed man,
it was contaminated. Also, Tamara would later note, wryly, she had to
resist the urge to put in a band of avenging angels. They weren't part
of her plan for the book, and yet they kept appearing. She kept crossing them out.

Essentially, the work that had been going so well before she
cheated on her husband started going very badly. This, Tamara knew,
was God's way of getting her. This and her pregnancy; that's how she
thought of it. She thought God had made her pregnant just to prove
a point—which, she reasoned, was unnecessary, because she already
knew she shouldn't have cheated, so why'd God have to make her pregnant as well?

After Tamara took two home pregnancy tests, she called Planned
Parenthood and made an appointment she never kept. Much later,
when the bad things happened and she was stuck with all the other
women chronicling their stories, she wondered if this decision had
been a matter of enchantment.

When she told Raj they were expecting, he kissed her all over.
(Raj, thankfully, mistook her tears for joy.) They talked about names
and the dreams they had for the child. "I just want her to be happy,"
Tamara said, and Raj laughed and said, "That's a big dream."

Over the next several months, Tamara found herself praying. She
prayed to God, and she prayed to Krishna too. She prayed to everyone she could think of, like the Virgin Mary, and her great-uncle Cal,
who would probably be embarrassed by all this, but was the only
dead person Tamara had been close to. *Hi, Uncle Cal,* she'd think. *This
is Tamara. I'm married now. And I made a mistake. Please, please make sure that
this baby is Raj's and not, well . . . I'm sorry. I shouldn't have done it. I know
that. Thank you, Uncle Cal.* She prayed to Kali, with her four arms and

that mysterious smile of hers. She even prayed to that elephant—she could never remember his name, but Raj had a small statue of him in the living room, and she prayed to him because he looked nonjudgmental. For eight months, Tamara suffered in fear and anguish while her body blossomed, effortlessly. "I don't know why women complain about being pregnant," she told Holly.

"Sometimes it's more difficult to have an easy pregnancy," Holly said, "because then you're not really prepared for the birth."

At this, Tamara smiled.

But when the pain arrived it was the worst feeling Tamara could ever imagine. One second she was sitting at her desk crossing out angels, and the next she was on the floor, screaming. She was in so much pain she couldn't even *move*. It hurt to *breathe*. It was torture to get up or slide across the floor, which is how she tried to reach the phone, because Raj had gone into work even though her due date was approaching. ("I'll just call if anything happens," she said. "We'll have plenty of time. All the books say so.") Tamara screamed and writhed on the floor for hours before Raj found her there. During those hours, Tamara accepted that she was being punished. She also accepted that she was going to die. She even reached the point where she *wanted* to die.

"I'll call Holly," Raj said.

"I'm dying," she said.

"You're not dying," he said. Then she opened her mouth and screamed, and his eyes got round, and he called Holly.

Later, Holly said it was not an ordinary birth. "I think something's happening here," she said mysteriously. Tamara was studying her baby, trying to decide who the father was. After several minutes of intense scrutiny, she asked, "Who do you think he looks like?"

Holly looked down at the baby, then at Tamara.

She knows, Tamara thought. *How could she?*

But Holly did not reach into her bag of birthing supplies to bring out a large scarlet letter. Instead, she left without addressing the question.

He *did* have blue eyes, but lots of babies do. His hair was dark, his skin was pink, and his body was an amazing, intricate, perfect blessing. After all those horrible dreams, and the months of guilt, and most especially the horrible pain of birth, Tamara felt blessed. In the end it didn't matter who the father was. Well, it *mattered*, of course, but also, it didn't. The only thing that *really* mattered was the baby.

Tamara thought she knew how she'd feel about her first child: protective, loving, proud. She had not been prepared to feel the way she did. In fact, she would say she had underestimated the power of the love she would feel for this little boy as much as she'd underestimated the pain of his birth.

It was three days later, after Raj had gone to the Becksworth airport to pick up her parents, when Tamara discovered the tiny sharp wings protruding from her baby's back. By then she already loved him more than she had ever loved anyone or anything else. Her love was monstrous. When she saw the wings, she turned him over and stared into those deep eyes of his and said, "Nobody is ever going to know, little one."

When Raj came home with her parents and their frightening amount of luggage, he kissed her on the cheek and said, "Everything okay?" She nodded. Later, when she had time to consider the disturbing events that followed, she pinned her ruin to that moment. The "thing she'd done with the stranger," as she'd come to think of it, had been wrong, but she could no longer wish it away without wishing away her child.

No, what had sealed her fate was that moment when she decided to lie to her husband about the baby's wings. It was no longer the three of them against the world, but mother and child against everyone else.

So many women were pregnant Shreve started a prenatal yoga class. "Something in the water," they'd say, or "Who's *your* milkman?"

Emily and Shreve thought they shared the biggest joke of all. Emily liked to say that they were "fuck-related," though Shreve found this crude. They could not agree on what had happened to them. Emily thought Jeffrey was a jerk, while Shreve thought he was some sort of holy man.

"I can't believe you think that," Emily said. "Saints don't have sex."

"Not a saint," Shreve said. "A yogi. And they do."

"Oh, come on! He was just a man. He was just like other men."

Shreve sighed, apparently remembering something wonderful beyond words.

This, of course, stressed Emily out. Did Shreve have better sex with him than Emily did? Was he gentler? *Rougher?* Had something profound happened between those two? Was he more *attracted* to Shreve? Was Shreve better at sex than Emily was?

She suggested that, in the interest of peace, they stop talking about it, and Shreve agreed.

Agreeing to disagree on the nature of what occurred with Jeffrey had been the first big test of their friendship. The next big test happened later.

Emily discovered her baby's small, sharp, featherless wings on June fifth, while changing Gabriel into one of his cute little baseball outfits (Red Sox, of course). She watched in amazement as the tiny wings unfolded and folded shut again, drawn into his back. She touched the spot, certain she'd imagined the wings, a weird hallucination. Maybe she'd just never gotten to that point in the pregnancy books. She almost convinced herself that was what had happened, when, with a burp, the wings appeared once more. Emily reached to touch one. The next thing she knew, she was walking down the street with Gabriel secured in his Snugli against her chest. She patted the baby's back, but didn't feel anything unusual.

At that exact moment, Shreve was saying to her baby, Michael, "You're going to meet your half brother today." She believed Jeffrey had been some kind of an angel sent to her by her dead fiancé. She wasn't sure *why* her dead fiancé had sent the angel to Emily also, except that it gave her son a brother . . . and that was a very good reason, the more she thought about it.

Michael had blue eyes, a remarkable head of dark curls, and two dimples. His pink flesh was already filling out, losing that newborn look. He had a round face and a round body, round hands, almost round feet, and a little tiny round penis. When Shreve turned him over to admire the beautiful symmetry of his little round butt, she watched, in amazement, as two wings blossomed from his back.

"I *knew* it," she said.

She wanted to investigate the wings, but Emily would be there any minute, so Shreve hurriedly dressed Michael in a pink romper (she didn't believe in the certain-colors-for-certain-genders thing) and wrapped him in the yellow blanket Emily had given her. It was rather warm in the house for a blanket, but Shreve thought it the best protection against any revelation of his wings.

Right then, the doorbell rang. "Hellooo," Emily called, in a soft singsong voice. "Is there a mommy home?"

"Come in," Shreve singsonged back, walking to the door with Michael in her arms.

"He's beautiful," Emily said. "He looks a lot like his brother."

"Oh, let me see."

"He just fell asleep. I don't want to wake him."

"Okay," Shreve said, realizing that she had no idea what kind of mother Emily would be. "Well, come in. I'll make some tea."

The first time Emily had seen Shreve's tiny kitchen—which was painted blue, yellow, and red—she thought it quite strange, but she had grown to like the cozy space. She sat at the small wooden table while Shreve prepared the teakettle and teapot, all while holding Michael.

"You look completely comfortable," Emily said. "You probably gave birth like it was nothing."

Shreve couldn't even smile the memory away. She turned to her friend with an expression of horror. "No. It was terrible."

"Me too," Emily said.

"I mean, I expected pain, but it was—"

"I know, I know," Emily said, so loud she woke up Gabriel. She didn't move toward unstrapping the Snugli, but remained seated, jiggling her knees while the baby cried harder.

Shreve did not like to judge, but the thought occurred to her that Emily might not be very good at this mothering thing. "We could go in the living room," Shreve said. "Lay them down on the blanket and introduce them to each other."

"Sometimes he cries like this," Emily heard herself saying, stupidly.

Shreve thought that even the way Emily tried to soothe her baby, like a police officer patting down a suspect, proved that not all women are natural mothers.

The teakettle whistled and Michael joined in the crying. Shreve, laughing, turned to take the kettle off the burner.

"Okay," Emily said over her baby's wailing. "Let's go in the living room."

It was warm enough that Shreve had opened the windows. The chakra wind chimes hanging outside were silent in the still air. Shreve realized she wouldn't be able to justify laying Michael down wrapped in a blanket. Instead, she got the little carrier seat one of her yoga students had given her.

At the time, Shreve had not expected to ever use the thing. She intended to raise her child without ever making his body conform to the unnatural rigidity of plastic. Now Shreve placed the carrier at the edge of the blanket on the floor. She set Michael—who had already stopped crying—into it, and adjusted the straps. Emily could see his beautiful face and perfect little body, but there was no danger of exposing his wings.

"Oh," Emily said. "I thought we were going to lay them down together."

"I'll get the tea. If he gets fussy, just leave him there, okay?"

Emily unfastened the Snugli and took Gabriel out. He looked at her with those intense blue eyes of his. She patted his back, and he started to make small noises. "Shhh, it's okay," she cooed. "Mommy's just checking." Satisfied, she laid him on the blanket in the sun, facing Michael.

Immediately the two babies grinned at each other.

"Shreve," Emily called, "come quick. You have to see this!"

Shreve ran into the room. "I told you not to touch him," she said, stopping short when she saw that Michael remained in the carrier.

Emily decided to forgive Shreve's odd behavior. She pointed at the brothers. "Look," she said, "it's like they recognize each other."

"I can't believe he can do that already," Shreve said.

"What?"

"Lift his head up like that."

"Oh, yeah." Emily shrugged. "He's really strong."

"Look at them," Shreve said.

"It's like they're old friends."

Shreve walked back to the kitchen and returned with the tray, which she set on the table next to the futon. She poured a cup for each of them. Emily sipped her tea, still focused on her baby's back. That's when she remembered that there had been a paper mill in Voorhisville, years ago. She'd heard about it once, she couldn't remember where. Maybe there were chemicals in Voorhisville, in the soil, or perhaps in the water. "Have you ever heard anything bad about the city water?" she asked.

"Oh, I use bottled water," Shreve said. "He's beautiful. Have you thought of a name yet?"

"Gabriel."

"Like the angel?"

"I guess it's old-fashioned."

"I like it," Shreve said, but was thinking, *Does she know something? Is she trying to trick me?* "Why'd you choose it?"

Emily shrugged.

The two women sat sipping their tea and staring glumly at their beautiful children, Michael and Gabriel, who continued to coo and gurgle, occasionally even thrusting little fists in the other's direction, as though waving.

"Emily?" Shreve asked.

"Uh-huh?"

"Do you believe in miracles?"

"Now I do," Emily said. "You know, I've been thinking. Let's say that we found out there was some kind of chemical, oh, in the soil, or something—you know, from the paper mill, for instance. Let's say it was doing something to the people in Voorhisville. Would we call it a miracle? You know, if it was a chemical reaction or something? I mean even if what happened was, well, miraculous? Or would we call it a disaster?"

"What are you talking about?" Shreve asked.

"Crazy thoughts, you know. I guess from the hormones."

Shreve nodded. "Well, you know what they say."

"What?"

"God works in mysterious ways."

"Oh," Emily said. "That. Yeah. I guess."

The two mothers sat on the futon, sipping green tea and watching their babies. The sun poured into the room, refracted by the chakra wind chimes. The babies cooed and gurgled and waved at each other. Shreve took a deep breath. "Do you smell that?"

Emily nodded. "Sylvia's roses," she said. "They're brilliant this year. Hey, did you know she's pregnant?"

"Maybe there *is* something in the soil."

"I think maybe so," Emily agreed.

On that day, it was the closest they came to telling each other the truth.

Theresa Ratcher had joined the library book club with her daughter Elli right after her fifteenth birthday. They left the house at 5:20 p.m. with the car windows rolled down, because the Chevy didn't have air-conditioning. Elli sat in the front seat, leaning against the door, which Theresa had told her a million times not to do, in case it popped open. Theresa drove with one elbow sticking out the window, the hot air blowing strands of hair out of her ponytail. Elli had been humming the same melody all week. Theresa reached to turn on the radio, but thought better of it and pretended to wipe a smudge off the dashboard instead. She knew they would just have an argument about what station to listen to. The news was depressing these days.

"Maybe you could think of something else to hum?"

Elli turned, her mouth hanging open, a pink oval.

"You've been on that same song for a while."

"Sorry," Elli said, her tone indicating otherwise.

"I like to hear you hum," Theresa lied. "It's just, a change of tune would be nice."

Elli reached over and snapped on the radio. Immediately the car was filled with static and noise, until she finally settled on something loud and talky.

Theresa glanced at her daughter. Did she really *like* this sort of "music"? This fuck-you and booty-this and booty-that groove-thing stuff? It was hard to tell. Elli sat slumped against the car door, staring blankly ahead.

Theresa glanced at her pretty daughter leaning both arms on the open window's ledge, as though trying to get as far away from her mother as possible. She resisted the urge to tell Elli to make sure her head and arms weren't too far outside the car; this was the sort of stuff that deepened the wedge between them. Still, Theresa argued with herself, she *had* heard that story about the two young men driving home after a night of drinking, the passenger, his head hanging out the window, hollering drunken nonsense one minute and the next— whoosh, decapitated by a guide wire. "Stick your head back in the car this instant."

Elli gave her one of those you're-ruining-my-life looks that Theresa hated.

"I just don't want you getting your head chopped off."

"This isn't Iraq," Elli said.

"What?"

"Nothing. I was making a joke."

"It's not funny. That's not funny at all." Theresa glanced at her daughter, hunched against the door, arm crooked, elbow hanging out the window. "Billy Melvern died over there. The Baylors' daughter is leaving in a week."

"It was Afghanistan."

"What?"

"Billy Melvern didn't die in Iraq. It was Afghanistan."

"Still," Theresa said.

Elli sighed.

Theresa snapped off the radio. Elli snickered loudly. They drove the rest of the way to Voorhisville in silence.

What was it about him? Later, Theresa would spend many hours trying to name the thing that made Jeffrey so attractive. He arrived late, and, with a nod toward the moderator, sat down. That was it. He sat there, nodding, occasionally recrossing his legs as they talked about Faulkner, Hemingway, Shakespeare, and Woolf.

Theresa felt like she was in way over her head. She thought this would be like Oprah's Book Club. Well, before Oprah started doing classics. To Theresa's amazement, Elli was talking about one of Shakespeare's plays. That's the first time the stranger spoke. He said, "We are such stuff as dreams are made on," and Elli smiled.

It was just a *smile.* There was nothing extraordinary about it. Well, other than that Elli had smiled. Theresa didn't give it another thought after that. Certainly she hadn't thought it *meant* anything.

Afterward, when they were trying to decide if they would all go out for coffee, Mickey Freedman showed up and invited Elli to spend the night. "Are you *sure* it's okay with your mother?" Theresa was perpetually suspicious of Mickey Freedman who, though only Elli's age, always acted so *confident.*

"Yeah, it's no problem," Mickey said. "You wanna call her?"

Theresa considered the small purple phone the girl dug out of her backpack. The truth was, Theresa had no idea how to use these portable devices. She turned to Elli, who was chewing gum as though it was a competitive event. "Well, have a good time," Theresa said, trying to sound breezy, fun.

The girls didn't wait a second. They were gone, leaving the scent of gum, as well as something Theresa only noticed after the fact: a worrisomely smoky scent, wafting in the air behind them.

At that point, Theresa discovered everyone had left without her. There were only two places in Voorhisville where a book group could meet for coffee and conversation: The Fry Shack, out on the highway, or Lucy's, which was a coffee shop in the pre-Starbucks sense of the word—a diner, really; though Lucy was fairly accommodating of the new fashion for only ordering coffee, as long as it was during off hours. Theresa walked out of the library and took a deep breath.

"Smells nice, doesn't it?" the stranger said.

He was standing by the side of the building. Almost as though he'd been waiting.

Theresa nodded.

"Mind if I join you?"

What could she do? She couldn't be rude, could she? He seemed perfectly nice, it was still light out, and it was *Voorhisville*, for God's sake. What bad thing could possibly happen here?

"I'm not going to Lucy's," Theresa said, turning away from him.

"Neither am I," he said, and fell in step beside her.

What had it been; what had it meant? Over and over again as the leaves fell to the dry flameless burn of that season, Theresa Ratcher asked herself these questions, as though if she asked enough, or in the right mental tone, the answer would appear. What had it been; what had it meant? As leaves fell in golden spiral swirls, on autumn days that smelled like apples. What had it been; what had it meant? As ghosts and vampires and dead cheerleaders carried treat bags and plastic jack-o'-lanterns through town—Theresa had forgotten what day it was—she returned home to find her husband in the living room watching *The Godfather* again, and she stood in the kitchen and stared out at the lonely, unbroken dark.

What had it been; what had it meant? When she said, "I'm pregnant," and her husband looked at her and said, "Are you kidding?" and she said, "No," and he said, "This is going to be expensive," and then, "Wait, I'm sorry, it's just . . . are you happy?" and she had shrugged and gone to the kitchen and looked out the window at the lonely, dark fields of broken corn.

What had it been; what had it meant? Standing in the frozen yard, snowflakes falling, swirling around her and then suddenly gone, leaving a cold ray of sun and the feeling in her body as though tortured by her bones.

What had it been; what had it meant? Opening the door to Elli's bedroom, and seeing her standing there, naked, and realizing that she had not merely been gaining weight. "I'm your mother. Why didn't you tell me?" Theresa asked. "I hate you," Elli screamed, trying to cover her distended belly with a towel.

Elli

We are running out of the library, giggling because we are free! I see the guy from the library, not the old one with the tie, but the cute one with the eyes like Eminem. He smiles at me and I smile at him and Mickey goes all nuts and says, "Who is that?" and I just shrug. We are walking down the street and Mickey says, "The graveyard," and I go, "What?" and she says, "Old Batface'll tell my folks if we have a party or anything, but I know where my dad hides his peppermint schnapps. Let's go home and make hot chocolate with peppermint schnapps and go to the graveyard. You're not scared, are you?"

"I'm not afraid of ghosts," I say. "It's real people that freak me out. What if Batface sees us leave?"

"She watches *Seinfeld* all night long. We'll go out the back door."

So we walk down the street to Mickey's house and that line keeps going through my head: "We are such stuff as dreams are made on." I feel like I am in a dream, like I have a body but I don't feel inside it, like we are surrounded by fireflies, even though it's light out, like the sky is filled with twinkling; and I feel free. Free from my mom with all her fears and rules and that depressed way of hers, and free from Dad with his stupid jokes, and free from the farm with its shitty smell and the silence except for all the birds and bugs.

Mickey says, "Who should we invite?"

"Where's your brother?" I ask. "Isn't he supposed to be watching you?"

"Vin's got one goal between today and Sunday night, when my parents get back, and that's to get into Jessica's pants. He doesn't care what I do, as long as I don't get in his way."

Sure enough, when we open the door, we see a purse and two wineglasses. Upstairs, there is the sound of pounding, and Mickey looks at me and says, "Do you know what that is?" I shake my head. (*We are such stuff as dreams are made on.*) "He's doing her," she says and we giggle until we are bent over. Then Mickey opens cupboards and says, "Here, make the hot chocolate. I'll be right back."

I fill the teakettle with water and put it on the burner and think, *What are we doing, why are we doing this?* Then Mickey is back, talking on the phone, saying, "Yeah, all right." Through the window I can see right into Mrs. Wexel's living room where she's sitting in a chair in front of the TV, and in the TV is tiny Jerry Seinfeld saying something to tiny Elaine, and even from all this distance I think how big their teeth are. Mickey puts the teakettle on and says, "They're going to meet us there."

We are such stuff as dreams are made on.

I pour hot water into the thermos and the light begins to fade and we leave out the back door, cutting across driveways and yards until we are on the road walking past the crooked house with the roses that smell so sweet, going up the hill to the graveyard, which is glowing. Mickey says, "You're sure you're not afraid?"

I say, "We are such stuff as dreams are made on."

"Did you make that up?"

Before I can answer, Larry is standing there and Mickey says, "Where's Ryan? Where are the guys?" Larry says, "He couldn't come. Nobody could come." He looks at me and nods and we trudge up the hill, weaving through the graves, past the angel, back past where all the dead babies are buried. We spread out the blanket and drink hot chocolate with peppermint schnapps. I feel like one of those body diagrams in science class. I picture a red line spreading to my lungs and my heart and into my stomach as the hot liquid goes down, and I think, *We are such stuff as dreams are made on.* The fireflies are blinking around the tombstones and in the sky, which is sort of purple, and that is when I realize Mickey and Larry are totally making out, and just then she opens her eyes and says, "Elli, would you mind?" So I get up and walk away, weaving through the headstones and the baby toys, the stuffed animals on the graves. I head up the hill to where the angel is, and that's when I see him sitting there, and he smiles at me, just like he did at the library, and I am thinking, *We are such stuff as dreams are made on,* and I must have said it out loud because he goes, "Yes."

I thought I saw a light shining out of him, like a halo, but let's face it, I was wasted and everything was sort of glowing—even the graves were glowing. He didn't try to talk to me and he didn't ask me to come over, I just did. He didn't ask me to sit down beside him, but I did, and he told me I had beautiful bones: "Slender, but not sharp." I never saw wings, but I thought I felt them, deep inside me. He smelled like apples, and when I started crying, he whispered over and over again, *We are such stuff as dreams are made on.* At least, I think he did.

I passed out, until Mickey was standing over me going, "Jesus Christ, Elli, I thought you were dead or something. Why didn't you answer me?"

"Did you do it?" I asked.

"He didn't bring any condoms."

"But you still did it, right?"

"What are you, nuts? I don't wanna get AIDS or something."

"Larry isn't going to give you AIDS."

"Come on, I feel sick. Let's go home. You all right?"

"I had the strangest dream."

She was already walking down the hill, the blanket trailing from her arms, dragging on the ground. I looked up at the angel and said, "Hello? Are you here?"

"Shut up, Elli. Someone's going to call the cops."

I felt like a ghost walking out of the graveyard. "Hey, Mickey," I said, "it's like we're ghosts coming back to life."

"Just shut up," Mickey said.

Dogs barked and lights came on the whole way back to her house, where the two wineglasses were still there but the purse was gone. Mickey dropped the blanket on the floor and said, "I am so wasted."

I said, "Nobody even knows we are here."

Mickey rested her hand on my shoulder and said, "Maybe you shouldn't drink so much."

I followed her up the stairs into her room where we went to bed without changing our clothes. It wasn't long before Mickey was snoring and I just lay there blinking in the dark, and it kept repeating in my head, over and over again: *We are such stuff as dreams are made on.* I fell asleep thinking it and I woke up thinking it and I'm still thinking it and I just keep wondering, *Is any of this real?*

Tamara

June in Voorhisville. The sun rises over the houses, the library, Lucy's Diner, the yoga studio, the drugstore, the fields of future corn and wheat, the tiny buds of roses, the silent streets. Pink crab apple petals part for honeybees; tulips gasp their last, red throats to the sun; butterflies flit over dandelions; and the grass is lit upon by tiny white moths, destined to burn their wings against streetlamps.

The mothers greet the day with tired eyes. So soon? It isn't possible. The babies are crying. Again. The mothers are filled with great love, and also something else. Who knew someone so small could eat so much!

Cathy Vecker complains to her mother and grandmother, who encourage her to consider bottle feeding. "Then we can hire a summer girl," her mother says.

Jan Morris calls the real estate office where she works and breaks down in tears to the young receptionist there, who calls her own mother, who shows up at Jan's an hour later with two Styrofoam cups of bitter tea, bagels from Lucy's, and a pamphlet entitled "Birthing Darkness: What Every Woman Should Know about Post-Partum Depression" as well as—inexplicably—Dr. Phil's weight loss book.

Sylvia takes her son into the garden, where she sits in the twig chair and thinks how tired her husband was before he died, and how she feels tired like that now, except alive. She cries onto her son's shoulders.

Lara dresses her baby in a yellow onesie, checking his back several times, convincing herself that the strange thing she saw had been a hallucination. She is very tired. She can't believe how much she has to arrange just to walk down the street to her studio. She feels like she's packing for a week: diapers, socks, change of clothes, nursing blankets, an extra bra, a clean shirt. All while the baby lies there, watching.

The mothers of Voorhisville are being watched. Rumors have begun to circulate about strange births and malformed babies, though the gossip seems unfounded. Sure, the mothers look exhausted, but there's nothing unusual about that. Yes, they describe the pains of birth as severe, but women have always said so. The only strange thing about the babies, despite what Brian and Francis think they saw, despite the rumors that nurse spreads all the way in Becksworth, is that they are all boys, and they are all beautiful.

Far from the rumors of town, out past the canning factory, over the hill behind the site of the old paper mill, Theresa Ratcher stands in her pantry, staring at glass jars filled with jelly. She means to be assessing what remains from the winter; instead, she is mesmerized by the colors. She stands, resting her hands on her great belly, as though beholding something sacred; certainly something more spectacular than strawberry, jalapeño, or yellow-tomato jelly. Her husband is in the field. She has no idea where Elli is. Theresa doesn't like to think about Elli, and she doesn't like to think about why she doesn't like to think about her. For a moment, Elli, with her long limbs and protruding belly, stands in Theresa's mind. She shakes her head and concentrates on the jars before her.

Elli is in the barn. She has no idea why. They don't have any animals except for cats and mice. But Elli likes it in the barn. She finds it a peaceful place, her dad out in the fields, her mom somewhere else. These days, Elli likes to be far from her mother, because even when they are in different rooms, she can feel the hate. Elli stands in the middle of the barn, beneath the beams, which her father still obsesses about. She is biting her fingernail when the sharp pain drives her to the ground. She lets out a scream, which rises past the spiderwebs and silent, hanging blobs of sleeping bats, out the cracks and holes in the roof, where it mingles with Theresa's scream as she falls to the ground in the pantry, knocking over several jars that shatter on the floor—an explosion of red goo, which her husband, when he returns for supper, assumes is blood. He runs to get the phone, but she screams at him to help, so he kneels before her in the glass and fruit, and she screams the head and shoulders out. Later, she tells him it's jelly. He licks a finger but it tastes like blood. He helps her upstairs and tucks her into bed, the baby in the crib.

He looks everywhere for Elli, finally going to the barn where he barely sees her in the evening light. She is lying on the ground, surrounded by pools of jelly (he thinks, before he realizes, no, that can't be right). She looks at him with wild eyes, like his 4-H horse all those years ago when she broke her leg, and she cries. "Daddy? It's dead."

That's when he notices the small shape beside her. As he leans closer, she says, "Careful. They hurt." He doesn't know what she means until he sees the tiny bat wings spread across the small back. But that can't be right. He looks down at his daughter, horrified. "It's some kind of freak," she weeps. "Just get rid of it."

He picks the creature up, and only then notices its barely perceptible breathing. "Don't touch the wings," she says. He looks at her, his little girl who gave birth to such a thing. *Now she can get on with her life.*

"Get it out of here," she says.

He takes the shovel and walks out of the barn, bats flying overhead. Curiosity gets the best of him, and he touches the wings. The next thing he knows, he is standing in the cornfield, beneath the cold light of the moon, staring at his dark house, listening to screams. He looks around in confusion but he can't find the creature, or the shovel, or any sign that the ground has been turned. He runs to the barn.

He finds Elli surrounded by wild cats, and screaming. He hears a noise behind him, the snapping of gravel, and turns to see Theresa slowly making her way toward them. "Go back. Just go back in the house," he shouts. She stops, washed with white moonglow like a ghost. "You'll be in the way. Call 911."

Slowly, Theresa turns and walks toward the house.

He reaches between Elli's legs, relieved to feel a crown of head there. "It's all right. You're just having another one."

"I'm dying!" she screams.

"Push," he says, with no real idea if this is the right thing to do or not; he just wants it out. "Push, Elli."

She screams and bears down. He feels the head and shoulders. Squinting in the dark, he barely sees the cord. He's already forming a plan for suffocation, if it's like the other, but what comes out is a perfect baby boy that he tries to hand to Elli. She says she doesn't want it. He is pleading with her when the EMTs arrive. They help all three of them into the house, where Theresa sits in the dark living room, cradling her baby.

"Everything all right?" she asks.

Elli opens her mouth, but Pete speaks first. "Everything's fine," he says. "A boy."

"And a freak," Elli says.

"What?" Theresa speaks to Elli's back as she walks up the stairs, leaving the baby with the EMT who carried him inside. He hands the baby to Pete Ratcher, who thanks him for coming all that way "for nothing." He says it's his job, and not to worry, but Pete Ratcher watches the man walk down the driveway to the ambulance, shaking his head like a man who just received terrible news. Pete searches the sky for a long time before he realizes what he's looking for. "I have to take care of something," he says, and steps forward as though to hand the baby to Theresa.

She looks at him like he's nuts. "Give him to Elli. She's his mother."

He walks up the dark stairs and enters his daughter's room. "Elli? Honey?"

"Go away."

"I have to check on something. You know, the other one."

"Freak."

"Elli, these things happen. It's not your fault. And look, you have this one."

"I don't want him."

"God damn it, Elli."

He thinks that, all in all, he's handled everything well. It's been a hell of a night. He tries once more for a calm tone. "I have to go check on something. I'm going to put your baby right here, in the crib, but if he cries, you have to take care of him. You have to. Your mother is tired. Do you hear me, Elli?"

Elli mumbles something, which he takes for assent. He places the baby in the crib. It squirms, and he rubs its back. Only then does it occur to him that the baby is not diapered or clothed, not even *washed*, but still coated in the bloody slime of birth. He picks it up, and by the moonlight finds what he needs on the shelves of the changing table (a gift from Elli's high school teachers). He cleans the baby with several hand wipes, tossing them toward the plastic trash can, not troubling to make sure any of them actually land inside. Finally, he diapers the baby, wraps him tightly in a clean blanket and sets him in the crib. "Elli." She doesn't respond. "If he cries you have to take care of him. You have to feed him."

"I want Mom."

He realizes Elli doesn't understand that Theresa has given birth today too. He tells her this, saying, "You have a brother, a little baby brother. Your mom is too tired to help you right now."

When he closes the door, Elli gets up and walks across the room to stand at the window. After a minute, she sees him walking toward the cornfield. *What could he be doing out there?* she wonders. She turns away, shuffling like an old woman. She stands over the crib and touches the flat of the baby's back, places her hand on his soft cap of hair, then reaches in and picks him up. He cries softly. She says, "There, there." She jiggles him gently on her shoulder, but the soft cry turns into a wail. *Why are you crying?* she thinks. *I'm not going to hurt you.*

What is she supposed to do? She takes it back to bed with her, where she sits against the wall, jiggling it, saying, "There, there," over and over again, until she finally gets the idea of feeding it. She unbuttons her shirt and smashes its face against her breast. It cries and wiggles in her arms before latching on to her nipple and sucking until he finally falls asleep.

She would like to sleep with him, but she remembers hearing how mothers sometimes squash their babies by mistake. She thinks this is probably an exaggeration, but she isn't sure.

Eyes half-closed, she walks across the room, lays the baby in the crib, and shuffles back to bed. The next thing she knows, her mother is in the room in her nightgown, standing over the crib, and the baby is crying.

"Mom?"

"You have to feed him," Theresa says. "You can't just let him cry."

"I didn't hear it," Elli says.

"Him."

"What?"

"You didn't hear him, not it. You have to take care of this, Elli. I'm busy with your brother." Theresa picks the baby up and brings him to her. "Do you know where your father is?"

"He said he had to go take care of something."

"You have to feed him, Elli."

"In the cornfield. I *know*. Could I have some privacy, here?"

"I don't want to have to keep getting up for your baby, too."

"I didn't hear him. I'm *sorry*."

"You're going to *have* to hear him," Theresa says. "What's he doing in the cornfield?"

But Elli doesn't answer. She's turned her back and is unbuttoning her shirt.

"Can you hear *me*?" Theresa asks.

"I don't know what he's doing in the cornfield. It's *Dad*, all right?" She pokes her nipple into the baby's mouth.

Theresa walks out of her daughter's room, trying to stay calm, though she feels like screaming. She hears the baby crying and turns back, but Elli, who gives her a look as though she knew her mother had plotted this surprise return just to look at Elli's bare breasts, is nursing him. It takes a few seconds before Theresa realizes the crying is coming from her own baby. Suddenly life has gotten so strange: her daughter nursing a baby whose father she won't name; her husband out in the cornfield in the middle of the night; her own baby, whose lineage is uncertain, crying again, though it seems like only minutes since she fed him.

Voorhisville in June: those long, hot nights of weeping and wailing, diaper changing and feeding, those long days of exhaustion and weeping, wailing, diapering, and feeding.

Sylvia's roses grow limp from lack of care and—just as some dying people glow near the end—emit the *sweetest* odor. The scent is *too* sweet, and it's too *strong*. Everywhere the mothers go, it's like following in the footsteps of a woman with too much perfume on.

Emily continues baking, though she burns things now, the scorched scent mingling with the heavy perfume of roses and jasmine incense, which Shreve sets on a windowsill of the yoga studio.

"I have to do *something*," she says, when the mailman comments on it. "Have you noticed how smelly it is in Voorhisville lately?"

The mailman has noticed that all the mothers, women who had seemed perfectly reasonable just last year, are suddenly strange. He's just a mailman; it isn't really for him to say. But if he were to say, he'd say, *Something strange is happening to the mothers of Voorhisville.*

Maddy Melvern doesn't know any different; she thinks it's always been this way. She stares at her son, lying on a blanket under a tree in the park. She looks away for *one second* to watch the mailman walk past—not that there's anything interesting about him, because there isn't, but that just shows how bored she is—and when she turns back to JoJo, he's hovering over the blanket, six inches off the ground; flying. She holds him against her chest, frantic to see if anyone's noticed, but the park is filled with mothers holding infants, or bent over strollers, tightening straps. Everyone is too distracted to notice Maddy and her flying baby. "Holy shit, JoJo," she whispers, "you have to be careful with this stuff." Maddy isn't sure what would happen if anyone were to find out about JoJo's wings, but she's fairly certain it wouldn't be good. Even pressed against her chest as he is, she can feel them pulsing. She eases him away from her shoulders to get a view of his face.

He's laughing.

He has three dimples and a deep belly laugh. Maddy laughs with him; until suddenly she presses him tight against her heart. "Oh, my God, JoJo," she says. "I love you."

Tamara Singh has just secured little Ravi in the stroller—not wanting to hurt him, of course, but making sure the straps are tight enough to keep him from flying—when she sees Maddy Melvern laughing with her baby. *It just goes to show,* Tamara thinks, *that you never can tell.* Who would have guessed that the teenage unwed mother, the girl who'd done everything wrong, could be so happy, while Tamara, who'd done only one single wrong thing—the illicit sex thing—would be so miserable?

What is love? Tamara thinks as she stares at little Ravi, crying again, hungry for more. She parks the stroller by a bench and unbuttons her blouse. *Well, this is love,* she thinks—sitting there in the park, filling his hunger, holding down his pulsing wings; watching the ducks and the clouds and the other mothers (it certainly seems like there are a lot of newborns this summer) and thinking, *I would die to protect you; I would kill anyone who would hurt you.* Then wondering, *Where did that come from?*

But it was true.

The mothers were *lying.* They told each other and their loved ones about wellness visits, but none of the mothers actually took their son to a doctor. Because of the wings. Both pediatricians at St. John's were under the impression that they were losing patients to the other, and each harbored suspicions concerning the guerilla tactics being employed. The lying mothers became obsessed with their sons' health. Each cough or sneeze or runny nose was the source of much guilt. Nobody wanted to kill her child. That was the point, the reason they had stayed away from doctors: it wasn't about putting the babies at *risk*, it was about keeping them safe.

Friends and relatives concluded that the mothers were protective, coddling, suspicious, and overly secretive. The mothers even concluded this about *each other*, never suspecting they harbored the same secret.

"This is impossible," Theresa Ratcher murmurs to herself the first time she sees little Matthew's wings blossoming, like some sort of water flower, while she is bathing him in the sink. She touches one tip; feels the searing proof of hot pain; and the next thing she knows, she is standing in the cornfield. She runs to the house as though it is on fire, tumbles into the kitchen, where Elli sits feeding little Timmy. "Where's Matthew?" Theresa asks. Elli looks at her like she's nuts. Theresa glances at the sink, which is empty and dry.

"Did you lose him?" Elli asks. "How could you lose him?"

"Matthew!" Theresa runs upstairs. He is there, asleep in the crib. She pats his back, gently. It feels flat. Normal.

"What's wrong?" Elli stands in the door, Timmy in her arms. "Mom? Are you all right?"

"I had a bad dream."

"Outside? You fell asleep outside?" Elli asks. "Are you sick?"

Matthew cries. "I'm not sick," Theresa says, unbuttoning her blouse. "Before I forget: When is your doctor's appointment? Did you make that yet? I can't be keeping track of all this anymore."

"Don't worry about it, then," Elli says, walking down the hall to her room; but when she gets there, it smells like diapers, and flies buzz around the window. Still holding Timmy, Elli walks downstairs and onto the porch.

Her dad is in the cornfield with the boys he hired for the summer. They aren't boys Elli knows. They're from Caldore or Wauseega, her dad can't remember which. They come to the house for lunch most days and ignore her. Elli knows why. She walks over to the apple tree and spreads Timmy's blanket on the ground, which is littered with blossoms. She sets him down, then stares at the cornfield, trying to force herself to see it as a field, and not a cemetery. Was her dad nuts? Why'd he bury it out *there*? *Did he really think she'd be able to eat the corn this year?* Elli shakes her head. She looks at Timmy, who lies there grinning. "What's so funny?" she says, meanly, and then feels bad for it. It is just so hot, and she is so tired. Between the baby eating all the time, and the bad dreams she has of the other one flying into her room and hovering over her bed, she's exhausted.

She wakes with a dark shadow standing over her. Elli turns to the empty blanket; then, in a panic, looks up at Theresa, who is standing there, holding Timmy. "You can't do things like this anymore, Elli," she says. "You can't just forget about him. He's a *baby*."

"I didn't forget about him."

"Look." Theresa turns Timmy so that Elli can see his pink face. "He got sunburned." Elli looks down at her knees. She doesn't want to cry. Theresa leans down to hand Timmy to her. "I know this is hard, but—"

"Mom, there's something I have to tell you."

Theresa is not in the mood for teenage confessions. *Why is Elli doing this now?*

"There was another one, Mom."

"What do you mean? Another boy? Is that why you won't say who the father is?"

"No. Mom, I mean, another baby. I had two. Dad doesn't want me to say, 'cause, well, he was a freak, and he died. Dad buried him in the cornfield."

"What do you mean he was a freak?"

"Please don't tell anyone."

"Sweetie, I—"

"He had wings, okay?"

"Who had wings?"

"The other one. The one that died. Do you think it was something I did?"

Theresa cannot form a logical connection between her daughter's revelation and her own son's wings. Several things occur to her, but not even for a second does she consider that she might have shared a lover with her fifteen-year-old daughter. That notion comes later, with disastrous results. Instead, she thinks of the paper mill, or some kind of terrorist attack on their well, things like that.

"You didn't do anything wrong," Theresa says, "except have unprotected sex." Feeling like a hypocrite for saying it. "And if every woman who did that was punished with a dead baby, there wouldn't be anyone living at all."

"But it wasn't just dead, Mom. It had *wings*."

Theresa glances at the house, where she'd left Matthew resting in his crib. "How do we know that wasn't some kind of miracle? How do we know it was a sign of something bad happening, rather than something good?"

Elli sighs. "It's just a feeling I get. Remember 'We are the stuff that dreams are made on'?"

"What about it?" Theresa says, feeling tense at the topic hovering too close to the library, and Jeffrey.

"I don't know," Elli says. "It's just something I think of sometimes."

Theresa knows she's been distracted lately, perhaps not as supportive of Elli as she would have liked. She glances at the house again, trying to decide if Matthew could be flying through the rooms, banging into walls and ceilings. She doesn't know anything about raising a child with wings, except that it is hard enough to raise one without them.

"Try to think of it as a good thing, okay?"

Elli shrugs.

"Will you at least try?"

For three days, Elli tries to convince herself that her first baby was not a freak or a punishment for something she'd done, but a sign of something *good*. She almost convinces herself of it. But on the third day, while she has Timmy on the changing table, she watches in horror as dark wings sprout from his back.

That's when she knows. The stranger she had sex with was the devil. That explains everything. It even explains why she *did* it with him. She looks into Timmy's beautiful blue eyes. For once, he isn't crying. In fact, he is smiling.

Evil, Elli thinks, *can trick you.* She works the saliva in her mouth and spits. Timmy's face goes through a metamorphosis of expressions, as if trying to decide which one to employ—a slight smile, raised eyebrows, trembling lips—all while closely watching Elli. She begins to cry. He opens his mouth wide and joins her, the glop of phlegm dripping down his forehead. Elli wipes it with the blanket. "Oh, baby, I'm so sorry," she says, picking him up.

That's when Theresa walks into the room.

Elli, still crying, looks over the small dark points of her baby's wings at her mother, who puts her hand over her mouth and—turning on her heels—spins out of the room.

Theresa wheels down the hall like a drunken woman, and opens the door to her own room. Matthew lies there, damp curls matted at his forehead, his pretty pink lips pursed near his tiny fist. Gently, she rubs his back and feels the delicate bones there.

"Mom?" Elli stands in the doorway. "You *said* it could be good." Then she sobs and runs out of the room.

Matthew wakes with a wail. Theresa soothes him the best she can as she walks to the rocking chair. Sitting there, Theresa can see all the way out to the three figures working in the field. Matthew sucks at her breast while she stares at the blue sky and gently rocks, asking herself, "What does it mean? What does it mean? What does any of it mean?"

Of all the lying and confused families that summer, perhaps the Ratchers—with their strange convergence of mother, daughter, son, brother, grandson, grandmother, sister, husband, father, and grandfather, all embodied in one small triad—were the *most* confused, with the *biggest* web of secrets.

Pete Ratcher came home from his Saturday dart game at Skelley's Bar one hot night, with the news that Maddy Melvern, a year ahead of Elli in school, had given birth and also wasn't divulging the father's name. "What hot shot are these girls protecting?" he asked his wife, who tried to make all the right noises while she fed the little monster—that's how Pete thought of him, though he tried not to—who seemed to be hungry *all the time.*

Theresa tried to talk to Elli about it. "You know, Maddy Melvern had a baby too," she said. Elli rolled her eyes, the baby latching on her breast *again* as her mother stood there, *again* bothering her with ridiculous information (what did she care about *Maddy Melvern?*), when all she wanted was to be free, instead of trapped here with this baby and horrible dreams about that other one rising from the cornfield and flying over the house; trying to find her, to punish her for burying him out there, no better than one of the cats—though, really, it wasn't her fault. It was her dad who did it.

Meanwhile, Pete Ratcher spent more and more nights at Skelley's, because what was he supposed to stay home for? To watch his wife and daughter endlessly feed and rock the crying babies, which neither would let him hold? Like they didn't trust him or something? Christ, what was that about?

The regulars at Skelley's grew used to Pete Ratcher's complaints. The bartenders could wipe the counter, serve drinks, watch TV, and say, "Women these days," at just the right moment in Pete's lament; that's how predictable it was. The regulars were so tired of it they were careful not to sit next to him. That's how, on the night Raj came into Skelley's, blinking against the smoke, he happened to sit right next to Pete, who finally found a sympathetic listener.

Raj nodded and said, "I know, I know. He's my son, too. I *want* to be a part of his life. I *want* to change diapers and take him for walks. I don't understand why she won't let me do those things."

Tamara knew Raj was drinking. Frankly, she was shocked: it was not something she'd imagined he'd fall into. But only a week into this new bad habit of his, he ran into their bedroom to tell her he'd just seen the baby flying. She was able to convince him that he was so drunk he'd been hallucinating. "No, no. I don't drink that *much*," he said.

Tamara went into the nursery, and sure enough, Ravi was floating above the crib, hovering like a giant hummingbird. She had just plucked him to her chest when Raj returned to the room.

"And you get angry at *me* for not letting you hold him more? Look at you. How can I trust that he'd be safe with a father who drinks so much he thinks he sees flying babies?"

"I don't drink *that* much," Raj said. "And all this was happening before I was drinking."

"The baby was flying before you started drinking? Do you really expect me to believe this nonsense?"

"No, no. I mean *us*. We were already fighting about you not letting me near him."

Tamara, who, just a year ago, would never have believed she could hurt her husband, and, only five minutes ago, would have sworn that she'd never hurt her baby for any reason, now pinched Ravi's arm, hard, so that he broke into a loud cry. She turned to attend to his tears as Raj watched, helpless and confused. It was like watching a movie or television: his wife and son in a separate world, with no need of him at all.

The next night, when he came home from Skelley's, his pajamas and a pillow and blankets were on the couch, and the baby was sleeping with Tamara. Raj remembered hearing once about a woman who rolled onto her baby in her sleep and suffocated the newborn. He considered waking Tamara to warn her, but instead took off his shoes. He didn't bother changing into his pajamas before he lay down on the couch, vowing that tomorrow he wouldn't go to Skelley's. Tomorrow he would meditate and fast. Maybe he would even return to his yoga practice. How had he lost both himself and his marriage so swiftly?

Tamara heard him come home. She heard his breathing when he stood in the bedroom door and watched her. She was only *pretending* to be asleep. She heard him walk away, heard his shoes drop to the floor. Maybe she should tell him, she thought—but was this how he responded to stress? How would he respond to having a baby with wings? No, Tamara decided, she couldn't risk it. She was sure it was the right decision, but nonetheless fell asleep with tears in her eyes.

The tears were still in her eyes when she was awoken by the baby's crying. She brought him to her breast, which silenced him immediately. She fell asleep, but woke up throughout the night to feel the baby suckling. In the morning, she decided it had been her imagination—it was impossible that Ravi had been feeding all night long.

Elli could feel the way her mother was watching her. It was obvious that she did *not* think Timmy's wings were a sign of something good. Elli's dad (oblivious) tried to talk to her. He even brought up the subject of the beams. "Don't go in the barn anymore," he said. "Not until I do something about them."

Elli thought her dad was nuts. What did she care about the stupid *barn beams* when she had this baby with wings to take care of, and another one hunting her? She stared at her dad with his stick-out ears and the creases around his upraised eyebrows. He suddenly seemed like some kind of strange, mutant child himself. Elli shook her head and turned her attention to Timmy, without saying a word.

Theresa, sitting on the couch facing the TV and holding Matthew, observed all this: the way her husband tried to speak to Elli; the way she looked at him, appalled; then turned away as though she could not *bear* to speak to him. Theresa observed all this and she *knew.*

"I'm going out," Pete said. Neither Elli nor Theresa responded. *When did I become the enemy?* Pete wondered. Sometimes women were like this in the first months after giving birth. He'd *heard* about that. Pete remembered Raj saying, "Sometimes I feel so angry, but then I remember that I love her." Pete stood in the living room and tried to remember how much he loved them. It was actually sort of hard to do. It was hard to *feel* it.

June in Voorhisville. The leaves of oaks and elms and the famous chestnut tree on Main Street grow until the Voorhisville sun filters through a green canopy. Everything, from faces to flowers to food, appears tinged with a shade usually associated with alien masks or Halloween witches.

The mothers of Voorhisville are too busy to notice. There are diapers to change, endless feedings, tiny clothes to wash, and constant surveillance.

Cathy Vecker would like nothing better than to hire a nanny or let her mother and grandmother feed the baby, but she can't risk it.

"He's growing so fast," her mother says. "Are you sure he's normal?"

Cathy resists the urge to roll her eyes. "Look at Sylvia Lansmorth's baby," she says. "He was born around the same time as Raven. They're both the same size."

"Well, they say Americans are getting bigger. Are you sure the doctor doesn't want you to put him on a diet?"

As the tiny bumps on Raven's back sprout and flutter, the wings pushing against her hands like they have a will of their own, Cathy runs out the front door, ignoring her mother. "You have to stop," she whispers, though she doesn't expect him to understand. With a thrust as powerful as a man's hands, Raven's wings push against her, tearing through the train-patterned fabric of his little sleeper.

The next thing Cathy knows, she is standing in Sylvia Lansmorth's garden and Sylvia, dressed in something purple and flowing, is glaring at her. "You're standing on my roses," Sylvia says.

"Have you seen my baby?" Cathy looks around desperately, as though she expects to find Raven perched on a rose petal. *Well, who knows? Who knows what will happen next?*

"Your *baby?*" Sylvia asks. "How old is he?"

"Don't you know me?"

Sylvia shakes her head.

"I've known you my whole life," Cathy says.

Sylvia assumes she is talking to a mentally ill person. It's the only explanation. "Is there someone I can call?"

"We have to call the police." Cathy can't believe how calm she sounds. "I have to tell them everything."

Sylvia doesn't like the sound of that. "I'll call," she says. "You wait here."

Cathy takes a deep breath and almost passes out from the sweet rose scent. "There's something I have to tell you."

"Is this about your baby?"

"I tried to do the right thing. I did."

"Wait here," Sylvia says, glancing back at the house.

"I didn't mean to lose him."

"Of course you didn't."

"He flew right out of my hands."

"He *flew?*"

"You think I'm crazy."

Sylvia shakes her head.

"Of course you do. That's what I would think. Nobody's going to believe me. Unless they see the wings, and if that happens they'll call him a freak. The worst part is"—Cathy begins to cry—"I don't know where he is."

Sylvia puts her arm around Cathy's shoulder. "I believe you," she says. "Did you touch them?" She takes Cathy's hands in her own. "Look, you're all cut up. How did this happen?"

Cathy sniffs loudly. "The wings ripped right through his clothes and cut me when I was trying to hold on to him."

"Well, when this happens with my baby," Sylvia says, "I usually find him in his crib, sound asleep."

"You're just trying to make me feel better."

"No, it's true. But if you tell anyone, I'll deny it. Listen to me, honey: before you get all panicky, what you need to do is go home."

"Go home?"

"Yes. Go home and see if he's in his room."

"My mom and grandmother are there."

"Well, then you better hurry. You don't want them to find him floating over his crib or something, do you?"

Cathy has a stitch in her side by the time she gets home. She runs to the nursery, rushing into the room so loudly that the baby wakes. Cathy picks him up and holds him close. "Oh, I love you, I love you, I love you," she says, over and over again; thinking, *There's another one, there's another baby with wings, you aren't alone in the world, and neither am I.*

She takes off his tattered sleeper, shredded as if by some beast, and tosses it into the trash. The she places a gauze pad on his small back and binds it there with first aid tape.

The mothers of Voorhisville were using gauze and tape, plastic wrap (which caused sweating and a rash), thick layers of clothing, and bubble wrap. What to do about a child with wings? How to cope with the unpredictable thrust of them, the sear of pain, the strange disappearing babies? The flying! How to cope with that? Several mothers, and they are not proud of this, took to devising elaborate rope restraints. It is rumored that at least one mother suffered tragic results from this decision, reported as a crib death, but she is not here with us, so that remains speculation.

Many of the mothers describe the *isolation* of this time as having its own weight. "*I* felt tied down," Elli Ratcher says. "Knowing that my mom had the same problem didn't really help. I mean she was my *mom*, okay? What did she know about *my* life?"

Many of the mothers, when they hear Elli say this, walk toward her, intending to administer a motherly hug or at least pat her on the back, but something in Elli's expression causes them to stop, as though she is radioactive.

Theresa felt alone in the world. All that June *she knew* what Pete did, and tried to convince herself she did not. But it was the only explanation. She *knew*, and she had to do something about it.

Finally, one hot afternoon, she left Matthew with Elli, who said, "Well, okay, but you better hurry back. It's hard enough watching Timmy every second," and walked out to the cornfield, where Pete was working with the boys.

"Is something wrong?" he said. "Is Elli—"

"I *know*," Theresa said, loudly, angrily, as though she had only just figured it out.

"You know *what?*" Pete asked, looking at the boys, a quizzical women-are-going-to-confuse-you look on his face.

"I know what you did."

"Did to who?"

"To Elli."

Pete shook his head. "I don't know what . . ." His voice trailed off as he considered the baby lost in the cornfield. "Do you mean the other one? Is that what you're talking about? It was a freak, Theresa. It had wings, for God's sake."

Theresa dove at Pete with her fists. He ducked and weaved, and finally grabbed her wrists.

"How could you? How could you do such a thing? How could you fuck your own daughter?"

Pete dropped her wrists, stepped back as if struck. He gaped at Theresa, turned to the boys, who gaped at him, then stepped toward his wife. "I never—"

"I want you out! Don't you dare come near us again. I'll kill you. Do you understand me?"

Pete stood there, speechless.

"I don't care if you understand me or not," Theresa said. "You come anywhere near us, and I'll kill you. I don't fucking care if you understand, you monster."

Pete watched Theresa walk away from him, the awkward sway of her hips as she walked over the uneven ground. He turned to the boys, thinking to offer them an explanation of the mental illness some women suffer after childbirth, but neither one looked at him. He stood there until Theresa slammed the door behind her, then followed in her path, stepping slowly through the field, leaving the boys believing they were about to witness a murder.

Pete was a little worried about that as well. But there was no way around it. He had the keys to the Chevy in his pocket, and the Chevy was in the driveway. She didn't expect him to *walk*, did she?

How had this happened? Had Elli accused him of such a thing? Why? Standing by the car, he considered his options. He could go inside and try to straighten this out, or he could leave. The problem was the gun, which they kept in the basement and had only used for shooting squirrels when they infested the attic after all those traps had proven ineffective. It was an old gun. He didn't think Theresa knew how to use it, but maybe she did.

He arrived at Skelley's a great deal earlier than usual, and stayed until closing, at which point he realized he didn't have his wallet.

Doug, the bartender, told him he could pay the next time he came. "But no more drinks until then."

"You don't know of a place I could stay?" Pete asked.

Doug shrugged. "What about that friend of yours, that towel-head? Why don't you stay with him?"

In Pete's state, this seemed a perfectly reasonable suggestion. He reached for his keys, but Doug deftly scooped them up. "I'll take you," he said. "You can get your car in the morning."

Pete had no idea where Raj and Tamara lived, but Doug did. "Everyone in town knows," he said.

Pete slurred his thanks, then weaved up to the house, where he leaned on the bell until Raj opened the door. Tamara stood behind him, wearing a red robe and holding a crying baby.

"My wife kicked me out."

"I wonder why," Tamara said, then turned and walked down the dark hall.

"I don't mean to cause problems."

Raj put his hand on Pete's shoulder. "You look like you could use a drink, my friend."

Over tea, Pete told Raj what Theresa had accused him of.

"You need a lawyer," Raj said.

But by that time, Pete was crying. "I need my family."

Tamara woke up to the baby's crying. It seemed like he had only *just* gone to sleep. Then it stopped. She closed her eyes, but they popped right back open. That's when Raj burst into the room, holding the baby in front of him, extended at arm's length, the baby's wings rising and falling as gentle as breath, the strange man who had arrived in the night right behind Raj.

"He was flying! He was *flying!*" Raj said.

Tamara looked at her husband. "You're drunk."

"Tamara," Raj said, "I am not drunk. And neither are you." He opened his arms. Ravi rose into the air, his wings fully extended. He hovered, then flew higher and higher.

"Catch him," Tamara shouted.

Ravi laughed.

"Ravi Singh, you come down here this instant," Tamara shouted.

Laughing, dangerously close to the ceiling fan.

Tamara screamed. Raj leapt onto the bed and jumped, trying to catch Ravi by the foot. Instead, Raj grazed the baby's heel. That set him into a cartwheel, which luckily landed on the bed. Ravi lay crying, a strange bend to his shoulder, but Tamara kept screaming at the men not to touch him. They watched the dark wings shrivel until they were gone. Only then did Tamara scoop Ravi up, holding him close to her chest.

"I think we need to call the hospital," Raj said. "I think maybe his shoulder is broken."

"Oh, right," Tamara said. "And then what do we do? Tell them he fell from the sky?"

"That's what happened, Tamara. That's the truth."

Tamara looked from Raj to the man beside him. "Who *are* you?"

"Pete Ratcher."

"From the farm out by the old mill?"

Pete nodded.

"If you tell anybody what you saw, I'll kill you."

"Tamara!" Raj turned to Pete. "She doesn't mean it. She's hysterical."

Tamara didn't look hysterical. She looked like she meant it. It was the second murder threat Pete had received in twenty-four hours, and he felt he was becoming something of an expert.

"I'll call the doctor," Raj said.

"No," Tamara said. "I'm taking him in. I'll take him."

"I'll come with you," Raj said. "It's going to be all right. We can handle this, honey."

"Just stay here with your friend." She nodded toward Pete. "We'll talk when I get home. You stay here, okay?"

This was the kindest Tamara had been to Raj in so long that he agreed. "I'll call the doctor and let her know you're coming."

"Please," Tamara said. "She doesn't know you. She knows me. I'll call from the car."

Again, Raj agreed. He even helped pack the baby's bag, not thinking to wonder why Tamara needed so many diapers, so many sleepers, so much *stuff*. He was distracted, he would later tell the television reporter. It never even occurred to him that she was *lying*.

When Tamara left the house, she turned right out of the driveway, but circled around Caster Lane, heading west. Ravi, in his car seat, had stopped crying and looked at her with his beautiful blue eyes, while chewing on a teething ring. Of course he was way too young for teeth, but they were coming in. She'd seen them, and she'd felt them too, when he bit down on her nipple. "Okay, baby. We're going on a road trip, but first we're going to make a little stop at Mr. Ratcher's house.

I hear they have a new baby there. Let's see if we can make sure Mr. Ratcher has good reason never to tell anyone our secret."

Tamara would never hurt Pete Ratcher's baby. But he didn't know that. All she wanted to do was scare him. All she wanted to do was make sure he didn't hurt *her* baby. In a way, you could say her intentions were good.

It is just a little after four a.m. when Tamara Singh approaches the Ratcher driveway. She turns off the headlights, cuts the engine, and coasts in. What she's doing isn't *dangerous*—it's more on par with a high school prank—but Tamara thinks that maybe she now understands, just a little bit, what motivates a criminal. Beyond everything else there is this *thrill*.

When she unbuckles Ravi from the car seat, he is sound asleep; even touching his shoulder doesn't wake him. Tamara concludes they must have overreacted. She breathes a sigh of relief.

The air is heavy with the odor of manure, dirt, tomato plants, grass, and green corn stalks. Tamara walks across the gravel on tiptoe, but the noise breaks through the dark. In the distance, a dog barks. She walks to the back door, opens it, and enters the house. The Ratchers, like most of the residents of Voorhisville, do not lock their doors. Who can be bothered with keys, in this world that no one wants? Tamara wishes she had a sheet of paper so she could write that thought down.

The kitchen is lit by the stove light. The window over the sink is open, and the white curtains flutter slightly. Ravi stirs in her arms. Tamara leans her face close to his. "Shhh, baby," she whispers. Miraculously, he does. Tamara concludes that all the excitement must have worn him out. Suddenly she's aware of how tired *she* is. She tiptoes through the kitchen and into the living room.

The couch, plaid and sagging, faces a TV set with a small cactus on it. Between the couch and the TV, there is a coffee table littered with a parenting magazine, a paperback, unused diapers, a box of tissues, a half-filled glass of water, and an empty plate. On the TV wall stands the only nice piece of furniture in the room, an antique sideboard with a lace runner and two white taper candles in glass holders. Tamara lies down on the couch. As she falls asleep, she can hear the faint twittering of birds and—from upstairs—a baby's cry; the sound of footsteps.

When Pete woke up, feeling like he slept on rocks instead of a pullout couch, he found Raj sitting at the kitchen table, making designs with Cheerios. Pete didn't really have the energy to comfort Raj—after all, his wife accused him of molesting their daughter; he had serious problems of his own. The phone rang, but Raj continued rearranging Cheerios. "Should I get that?" Pete asked. He walked over to the phone. "Hello?"

"Is this Raj Singh?"

"Theresa?"

"Pete? What are you doing there?"

"Theresa, I never—"

"I need to talk to Raj Singh. Is he there?"

"Theresa, you have to believe me."

"I don't have time for this right now. Tamara Singh is here, and their baby is dead. Are you going to tell him, or should I?"

Pete watched Raj carefully place a Cheerio in between two others. "But what should I say? How should I say it?"

"Tell him his wife, for some reason, came here last night and fell asleep on the couch with the baby, and when she woke up, he was dead. Tell him not to call the doctor or the undertaker. His wife wants to bury him right here. Nothing formal. Just him and us. Tell him that's what she wants, so we're going to do it that way. Tell him the baby's wings are still out, and if anyone else sees them they'll probably want to take him, run tests and stuff. Tell him his wife could never live through that. Make sure he understands."

"That's what it was like with Elli's baby. The other one—the one that died."

"Tell him you'll bring him with you when you come home."

"Theresa? You don't still think—"

"I screwed up. Okay? I'm sorry, Pete. I've been under a lot of stress lately. What can I say? I'm sorry."

"But you *know*, right? You know I would never?"

"Are you going to tell him?"

"But how? I mean, how did it happen?"

"She said something about a fall, but I think she suffocated him by mistake. Just get here, okay? Don't let Raj call anyone."

"Theresa, did Elli say I did that to her?"

"No, it wasn't Elli. It was *me*. What do you want? I already apologized. It was a mistake, okay? Can we just move on, here? There's other stuff to deal with. Do you want to tell him, or do you want me to?"

"I'll tell him," Pete said, so loudly that Raj looked up from his Cheerios. Pete hung up the phone. "I have bad news," he said.

Raj nodded, as if—of course, naturally—it was just as he expected.

"Your baby's dead."

Raj collapsed across the kitchen table, scattering the Cheerios. Pete placed a hand on Raj's back, kept it there for a moment, and then walked out of the kitchen, through the living room, and out the front door.

Pete stood on the front porch, his head pounding. Crazy; it was just *crazy* that his wife thought he'd do such a thing. How could she ever have loved him if she thought he was capable of such evil? Pete knew that this was not the time to get angry at her, not when she realized her mistake, but he'd gotten drunk last night, and then there was all that business with the baby, and he'd been too distracted to feel it before.

The door popped open. Raj stood there with red eyes. "Tamara?"

"She's at my house. She stopped by to visit my wife, I guess."

"I have to make some calls—"

"No." Pete explained how Raj wasn't supposed to tell anyone, because of the wings, and how Tamara wanted the baby buried at the farm.

"I don't think that's legal."

Pete shrugged. "Theresa—and I guess your wife too—they think that if anyone finds out about the wings, they'll take the baby, and you know, run tests and stuff on him."

Raj considered this. "Okay. Give me a minute. And then you can drive me to your house?"

"We have to take your car. Mine is—"

Raj shut the door before Pete could finish.

Nobody knew that Raj had developed such a deep fondness for his yoga teacher, Shreve. Not even Shreve knew, until Raj called that morning, and, in a choked voice, explained that his baby had died. He wanted her to come and read from the Upanishads at the funeral out on the Ratcher farm.

"But don't tell anyone else, please," Raj said. "My wife is very worried because our baby had wings and she thinks it will cause problems if people find out."

"Your baby had wings?"

"I only just found out recently, myself."

After Shreve finished speaking to Raj, she called Emily and told her what happened. "Apparently he had wings."

"Wings?"

"Yep. What do you think about that?"

"I think maybe something like that might freak some people out," said Emily, choosing her words carefully, "but people are afraid of new things, you know? I mean who's to say . . . like, remember what we were talking about a while back? Who's to say it wasn't an angel?"

"There's something I have to tell you," Shreve said. "I'm nervous about doing this alone anyway. Do you think you could come with me to the Ratchers?"

Emily watched Gabriel doing a slow figure-eight pattern overhead, a sign that he was getting tired. "Actually, there's something I've been meaning to tell you as well," she said.

Mrs. Vecker, Cathy's mother, is in the grocery store when she overhears Emily Carr and Shreve Mahar having an animated conversation about what would be appropriate to bring to the Ratcher farm "at a time like this." She tells Cathy later that day. "It's all over town. Tracy Ragan's daughter's husband's best friend works with someone who is the father of a boy who was helping on the Ratcher farm, and he says Pete Ratcher is a child molester. You remember his daughter; that pretty red-haired girl? Well, she had a baby with wings—that's how Theresa Ratcher figured it out. Incest, you know, can create all sorts of problems. Theresa Ratcher kicked him out, and I guess the women are going there to see what they can do to help."

Sylvia and Jan Morris had just spent a couple hours together, talking poetry and mothering, when there was a knock at the door. Sylvia was happy to answer it, thinking it might be just the interruption needed to send Jan on her way. It was nice to have company for a *while,* but Sylvia was ready for a nap. She opened the door.

"Did you hear about the Ratchers?" Cathy asked in a rush, half into the room before she stopped. "Oh, I didn't know you had company. I didn't mean to *interrupt,*" she said, feeling oddly jealous.

"What about the Ratchers?" Jan asked.

"Pete Ratcher molested their daughter. She had a baby. They say it has wings."

"What do wings have to do with anything?" Jan asked.

"We have to help," Sylvia said.

It was decided that Cathy and Sylvia would drive in Cathy's BMW. They would meet Jan at the Ratchers'. Cathy and Sylvia stood by the roses and waved as she drove away.

"It doesn't mean he *wasn't* molesting her," Sylvia said.

"But . . . another baby with wings," said Cathy. "Don't you think this is getting kind of strange?"

Sylvia laughed. "*Getting* strange?"

As Pete Ratcher drove up to his house, he glanced at Raj. Pete felt bad for Raj, but Pete's overwhelming feeling was anger at Theresa. *How could she accuse him of such a thing? How could she believe him capable of such an act?*

"We should probably go in," Pete said.

"I did not know that your wife and my wife even knew each other."

Welcome to the club, Pete thought. *I didn't know that my wife thought I was some kind of monster.* The two men sat in the car, staring at the house.

Theresa watched from the kitchen window. She glanced at Tamara, who sat at the table, staring into space. "They're here," she said. "Your husband is here."

Theresa thought Tamara might have sighed, but the sound was so faint, she couldn't be sure.

When they came inside, Theresa gave Raj a hug. In just that brief encounter, she felt the weight of his sorrow. Raj walked over to Tamara and tried to hug her, but she just sat there. He turned to Theresa and said, "Where's my son? Can I see him?"

Tamara stood up so suddenly that the chair toppled. "I'll show you," she said and led him out of the kitchen to the living room, where Theresa had laid the baby on the sideboard with blankets all around him, the unlit candles at either end, like he was some kind of weird centerpiece.

Shreve and Emily park in front of the house, the engine off, the windows rolled down for air. "I'm glad we finally told each other," Emily says.

Shreve nods. "We have to figure out exactly what we need to know."

Emily twists in her seat to look at the two babies in the back. "We have to find out *how* he died—if it had anything to do with the wings."

"Or if it had something to do with Jeffrey, or the water, or something she ate."

"But how could Jeffrey have anything to do with Tamara Singh's baby?"

Shreve just smirks.

"Oh, come on," Emily says. "Us? And Tamara? I don't *think* so."

Shreve shrugs. "Remember, we're here to help bury a baby. We have to be discreet."

The thought of Tamara's dead baby casts a solemn shadow over them. Both women glance back at their children.

Elli watches from her bedroom window. It takes the mothers forever to unload the two babies, their diaper bags, a bouquet of flowers, and what looks like some kind of casserole or pie. Though both Timmy and Matthew are sleeping peacefully in the hot crib together, Elli keeps having a thought she doesn't want to have. She keeps thinking, *Why couldn't it have been Timmy?*, then hates herself for having this thought. She doesn't even want this thought, so she doesn't understand why it keeps popping into her head. She looks at the sleeping Timmy. *I would die if anything happened to you. (Why couldn't it have been you?)* It makes no sense. Elli watches the women walk to the back door. She hears the bell ring. *The mind*, Elli thinks, *is its own battleground* (like there's a war going on up there and she's just a spectator). The bell rings again. *Jesus Christ, would someone just answer it?* But it's too late; the babies wake up, crying.

What's she supposed to do? Pick both of them up? She picks up Timmy; pats him on the back, jiggling him. The next thing she knows, Matthew is flying out of the crib and heading for the open window. There's a screen on it, so naturally she thinks that at the worst he's going to get a little banged up, but when he hits the screen, he hits it *hard*; it falls right off the window, and Matthew flies out.

"Mom!" Elli screams.

Shreve rings the doorbell, waits for a while, and then rings again. Emily carries Gabriel's car seat in one hand and a plate of chocolate croissants in the other, the heavy diaper bag hanging from her shoulder. Shreve, who is similarly burdened, has to ring with the hand carrying the flowers, careful not to squash them. Inside, someone is screaming. "Sounds like they're taking it hard," she says.

A shadow passes overhead.

The door opens. Theresa stands there, her expression aghast.

"I'm Shreve Mahar," she begins, but Theresa runs right past her, brushing her shoulder, so that Shreve has to spin a half turn to maintain balance.

"Where? Where?" Theresa cries, staring up at the sky.

Shreve and Emily exchange a look. Elli Ratcher comes running out of the house, holding a screaming baby. "I'm sorry, Mom," she cries. "I'm sorry!"

"Matthew! Matthew!" Theresa Ratcher hollers.

Jan pulls into the driveway and surveys the scene before her. A barefoot woman stands, shouting, in the yard, her face craned to the sky.

Beside her stands the young red-haired girl, carrying a baby. On the porch is the dark-haired yoga teacher with a diaper bag, flowers, and a baby in a carrier. Standing at the foot of the stairs is a short woman who Jan thinks might be named Emma or Emily. Jan cranes her neck and looks up at the sky. She thinks they must have lost a pet bird, though the hysterical woman and the crying girl seem to be overreacting.

Jan is tempted to stay in the car, in the air-conditioning. She doesn't know any of these people. She should have come with Sylvia and Cathy. She realizes that the two women who are not looking at the sky are staring at her. She turns off the ignition. When she opens the door, she is hit by the heat and screams.

"Mom! I'm sorry! I'm sorry!" Elli screams, over and over again.

Theresa stands with her hand shielding her eyes, shouting Matthew's name.

Jan thinks she should get back in the car and turn around, but Jack gurgles at her from his car seat. She can't leave until she finds out whatever she can about the wings.

Theresa shouts for Matthew over and over again. She doesn't know what else to do.

Elli cries, holding Timmy against her chest. *Why couldn't it have been you?* she thinks.

Pete Ratcher comes out to the steps. Shreve begins to introduce herself, but Pete runs into the yard, grabs Theresa by the shoulders, and shakes her. Elli lunges to push him away with one hand, and Pete pushes her back. Not hard, they would later agree, but enough to cause Elli to lose her balance. As she tumbles, she opens her arms. All the women scream as Timmy falls, but the screams are abruptly cut short when dark wings sprout through the baby's little white t-shirt and he flies out of Elli's reach, over all of their heads.

"I thought he died," says Emily.

Shreve shrugs.

"Don't touch the wings," Jan shouts.

Shreve and Emily look at her and then at each other. "How does she know that?"

Little Timmy, laughing, flies in lazy circles and frightening dives, just out of reach of Elli and Theresa Ratcher, who jump at him as he passes. Pete Ratcher just stands there with his mouth hanging open. *I have been drinking too much*, he thinks. *This can't be happening.*

The Mothers

Even now, we the mothers find ourselves saying this can't be happening. This isn't real. Why, in the face of great proof otherwise, do we insist on the *dream* of a life few of us have ever known? The *dream* of happiness? The *dream* of love? Why, we wonder, did we believe in those dreams and not the truth? *We* are monsters. Why did we ever *think* we were anything else? Why do we think, for even a moment, that this is all a horrible mistake, instead of what it is: our lives?

Tamara

When Sylvia Lansmorth and Cathy Vecker drive up, they see Jan, Shreve, and Emily with their baby carriers, diaper bags, flowers, and foiled plate, Theresa and Elli Ratcher screaming, and Pete Ratcher, standing there, shaking his head.

"Is that him?" Sylvia asks. "He *looks* like a child molester."

Cathy points at the flying babies, swooping across the sky. "I *told* you things were getting strange."

"Matthew! Timmy! You come down here this instant!" Theresa shouts.

Pete turns and walks back to the house.

Emily sets her baby carrier gently on the ground and places the foiled plate beside it, then shrugs out of the diaper bag. She checks the straps on her baby's carrier, making sure they are tight before she walks over to Theresa Ratcher. "Try your breast." She has to say it a few times before Theresa hears her.

"What?"

"When I have this problem, I just take off my shirt. He always comes down for my breast."

Theresa hesitates only a second, trying to process the strange revelation of this woman she's never met acting as though losing a winged baby is a common concern. She pulls off her tank top and lets it drop to the ground.

"You have to take off your bra," Emily says. She turns to Elli. "Watch your mother. Do what she does."

Sylvia and Cathy sit in the car and watch in amazement as Theresa and Elli Ratcher take off their tops and unfasten their bras.

"Maybe we should come back later," Sylvia says, but another car pulls in behind them and they are blocked in the driveway.

Lara Bravemeen heard about the winged baby from the mailman, who heard about it from the senior Mrs. Vecker. When Lara drives up and sees the two women disrobing, the babies frolicking in the sky, she thinks she has found nirvana. She shuts off her engine, jumps out of the car, peels off her t-shirt, and unbuckles her bra.

"What the fuck is going on?" Cathy asks.

Theresa and Elli Ratcher stand with their arms spread, tilting their faces and breasts toward the sky. The babies begin a lazy glide toward them.

That's when the shot rings out.

Shreve jumps about a foot at the noise; turns and sees Pete Ratcher, standing there with a gun.

Emily looks from him to her baby, sitting in his carrier on the ground.

Theresa and Elli both turn, their mouths open in horror.

Pete Ratcher shoots again.

Shreve drops the flowers and runs with her baby.

The small body of Timmy Ratcher falls like a stone. Elli tries to catch him, but he crashes to the ground at her feet, and she falls over him, screaming. Matthew Ratcher stops his gentle glide and, wings beating furiously, shoots toward the sun.

Theresa Ratcher makes an inhuman sound. She runs at her husband, her fists raised.

Pete Ratcher watches her coming with his arms at his side, the gun hanging from his hand. Theresa dives at him and they both crash back into the house.

Tamara and Raj turn from their baby's corpse at the noise. They'd heard the screams and the gunshots, but were so absorbed by their grief they hadn't tried to process any of it. Now they see Theresa Ratcher, bare-breasted, straddling her husband, pounding him with her fists.

That's when Emily comes in, picks up the gun, and rests the muzzle against Pete Ratcher's head.

Raj steps toward them. Emily says, "Come any closer and I'll kill him." She turns to Theresa. "Got any rope?"

"It's in the barn," Pete says.

"Shut up." Emily presses the muzzle to his forehead.

Pete glances at Raj, who is standing in the doorway between the kitchen and the living room. Behind him stands his wife, but she doesn't look like she cares much about what is happening. Over her shoulder, Pete can see the dead baby; his small gray wings folded around his tiny shoulders.

Theresa comes back into the kitchen with a coil of rope. Several women with babies follow her. Cars pull into the driveway, the sound of crunching gravel audible even through Elli's screams.

"Who are all these—"

"Shut up," Emily says. "You"—she glances at Raj—"tie his wrists and ankles."

Raj opens his mouth to protest.

"Do it," says Emily, "or I'll shoot."

Emily is amazed anyone believes her. Pete Ratcher continues to lie there, though he is at least twice her size and actually knows how to use a gun.

"No," Emily says as Raj begins to wrap the rope around Pete's wrists, "tie them behind his back. Roll over. Slowly."

Pete makes a sound that might be a chuckle, but he rolls over, slowly.

The mothers heard it from their mothers, friends, even strangers. Lucy, of Lucy's Diner, heard about it from Brian Holandeigler, who'd heard it from Francis Kennedy, who'd heard it from Fred Wheeler, who said it was all over the canning factory. "Did I tell you we had a call there?" Francis said. "I knew something odd was going on in that house." Maddy Melvern heard about it from Mrs. Baylor, who had come over to talk to Mrs. Melvern about Melinda Baylor in Iraq. "At least my Mindy ain't gotta contend with no asshole like Pete Ratcher, who molested his daughter and gave her a baby with wings," she said. (Maddy made her repeat it twice.) Roddy Tyler heard it from Mrs. Vecker and Mrs. Vecker Senior, and when he walked to the post office that afternoon (in his duct-taped shoes), he told everyone about it. Maddy found Leanne and Stooker outside the drugstore, and after they oohed and ahhed at JoJo, she told them she needed a ride to the Ratchers'. "I didn't know you were friends with her," Leanne said. Vin Freedman heard it from Stooker's older brother, Tinny, and he told Mickey, who called up Elli, but nobody answered the phone there.

Everyone was talking about it. When one of the mothers heard, she could not pretend she hadn't. The Ratcher girl had a baby with *wings.* How could any one of them resist this revelation? The mothers packed diaper bags, left work, left home without explanation or offered a poor one, a scribbled note on the kitchen table, or attached to the refrigerator with a magnet. "Went out. Be back soon."

What they found was a bloodied, bare-breasted Elli Ratcher, kneeling in the dirt, holding her dead baby with his broken wings (right out there for anyone to see) and screaming, "No! No! I didn't mean it! No!"

The mothers were confused. *How long had she been doing this? When had this baby died? And what was all that blood about, anyway?*

The mothers, holding their own sons, approached Elli with caution. They circled her and said, "There, there," or "Everything's going to be all right." Some of them got close enough to pat her hot shoulder and get a good look at the baby. Definitely dead. Definitely wings.

When Theresa Ratcher came out of the house, the mothers—thinking she'd come for her daughter—parted. But Theresa only looked at Elli with a confused expression, then spread her arms and arched her back, her skin freckled at the throat but pure white on her breasts, which hung loosely toward her stomach. She stood there, her face upturned to the crows and the clouds and her eyes closed, until a shadow crossed the sun and came diving down. It was a baby, its gray wings pulled back, diving right for Theresa Ratcher, landing on her with arms spread like a hug. With a sob, Theresa's arms wrapped around him as he repositioned himself and began suckling. The mothers sighed. Theresa Ratcher, slowly, carefully, sank to the ground, kneeling in the dirt, smiling, and running her hand over her baby's hair, just five yards away from Elli, who keened over hers.

The Mothers

Everyone was at the funeral. Even Pete Ratcher, his wrists and ankles tied, though none of us are sure how he got there. We suspect Raj Singh helped him, though Raj should have been helping Tamara. Tamara has no memory of that day. From the time she fell asleep on the Ratchers' couch until after the trial, Tamara walked with open eyes, but remained in some kind of slumber. Perhaps Pete just hopped out there by himself—he hadn't been tied *to* anything, so it wouldn't have been impossible. We suppose that could have happened without any of us noticing. We were *busy.* There were two babies to bury, Ravi Singh and little Timmy Ratcher, plus all our own babies to attend to.

At that point we were still hiding the secret of the wings, which (we did not yet know) we shared, though several of us considered how much we should reveal about our own babies. If Theresa based her belief in Pete Ratcher's incestuous culpability solely on the evidence of *wings,* how much responsibility did we have for clarifying that wings weren't proof of incest? Still, we mothers—thoughtful, contemplative, responsible women—were not inclined to share our secret, even if it could save a family. Why save one family, if it would ruin our own?

Tamara

Carla Owens and Melinda Stevens fashioned caskets out of wooden crates they found in the barn, cutting the lids out of planks of wood Pete Ratcher had been using to shore up the beams.

Bridget Myer, who was such a fan of Martha Stewart that she *cried* when the homemaking diva went to prison, assembled a group of women who traipsed through the Ratchers' massive yard, picking dandelions, daisies, wild lilies, Queen Anne's lace, lilacs, and green stalks of corn for the altar—a card table covered by a white cloth and two white candles in the fake crystal candlesticks on either end.

It was just after noon. Elli Ratcher had washed off the blood and changed into a white sundress. Theresa Ratcher didn't change her clothes, though she'd put her shirt back on.

The crates were so small there was no need for pallbearers. Carla carried one to the front, set it on the altar, and Melinda carried the other. The lids were off at that point. The babies, cleaned and dressed by Shelly Tanning, Victoria Simmington, Gladiola Homely, and Margaret Satter, looked real sweet, surrounded by flowers.

Brenda Skyler, Audrey Newman, and Hannah Vorwinkski sang the opening song. They walked to the front and signaled when to start with little nods toward each other, but still didn't get it exactly right. They sang "Silent Night," because it's hard to find funeral songs with babies in them. They hasten to point out, in defense of their controversial choice, that there is no mention of the word *Christmas* in the entire carol. Also, instead of singing the word *virgin*, they hummed.

"I'd like any of you guys to think of a better song for a baby's funeral," Audrey says, if any of us mocks the choice. "And I don't count that Eric Clapton song. We ain't professionals, you know."

Shreve Mahar stepped to the front of the crowd. She glanced at Elli Ratcher, who looked like a bored but polite schoolgirl at assembly, and at Tamara Singh, who wept into her open hands. Theresa Ratcher rocked her baby in her arms, humming softly. Pete Ratcher, still tied at the wrists and ankles, leaned against the apple tree, close enough to follow the proceedings but not so close as to be a part of them.

Shreve opened the book to the previously marked page and read from the Upanishads.

> "In the center of the castle of Brahman, our own body, there is a small shrine in the form of a lotus-flower, and within can be found a small space. We should find who dwells there, and we should want to know her."

Shreve read the passage into a stunning silence, as if even the babies were listening. When she finished, Raj Singh stepped to the front.

"We are here today," he started, his voice breaking. He looked down at his feet, cleared his throat. "We are here. Today." Again, his voice broke. He took a deep breath. "We are here." He shook his head, raised his hands in a gesture of apology, and shuffled back to stand beside his weeping wife.

He did not notice how Elli Ratcher had snapped awake at his words. In the confused seconds after Raj's departure, she stepped forward, turned, and faced the mothers, glowing in the sun. "We are here today!" she said, in an excited voice. "That's it, isn't it? We are here! We are here!" She was quite giddy, as if she had only just discovered herself in her life. Eventually, Shreve escorted her back to stand beside Theresa. There was an uncomfortable period of uncertainty before everyone realized the funeral was over. Several mothers noticed flies gathering near the babies in their little wooden crates on the card table, and Shreve brushed them away.

Raj Singh spoke quietly to Theresa, then walked to Pete Ratcher and began to untie him. The mothers protested, but Theresa said, "He's not going to hurt anyone. They're going to dig the graves." Raj and Pete went into the barn together and came out with shovels. They walked over to the apple tree and began digging, as the mothers drifted back to the house.

The Mothers

We came to the Ratcher farm because of the rumors about a winged baby. We were determined not to leave that strange and unhappy place without some information. Tamara Singh was a wreck, and nobody could get anything out of her. She lay upstairs in Elli's bedroom while her husband and Pete Ratcher dug two tiny graves beneath the apple tree.

Elli was also of little use. "We are here," she kept repeating, her eyes wide.

"Grieving," some of us said. "Nuts," said others.

We did not mean it as judgment. We held our babies close and shuddered to guess how we would behave, should something so terrible happen to us.

"Her baby didn't just *die*," Emily said. "He was *murdered* by her own *father*."

It was a long day. We drifted in and out of conversations and emotions while the two men continued digging. We felt horrible for the mothers of the dead babies. We really did. But, also, we were there on a mission.

Tamara

When it was revealed that Elli and Theresa Ratcher's babies had been seen flying, the mothers (after dismissing Elli, with her "We are here" glassy-eyed uselessness) turned to Theresa. "Yes. So what?" she said to anyone who dared ask outright, did her baby *fly*? By Theresa's reasoning, this was no longer the point.

The mothers, most of whom had carried their heavy secrets for months, confided in Theresa Ratcher. By seven o'clock, the house was a riot of noisy babies; the plumbing just barely keeping up with the women's needs; the hot kitchen cluttered with fresh-baked casseroles, frozen pizza, and dishes in a constant state of being washed.

Finally, Theresa Ratcher called for everyone's attention. The mothers hushed the ornery babies, who, irritated from confinement, would not be hushed, and tried to listen to what Theresa was saying.

"You are all telling me the same thing. *All* the babies have wings."

At first, the mothers were horrified. Misunderstanding, they thought Theresa was not revealing a universal truth, but the deep secret they had confided in her. It was only after a few moments that someone realized what she'd said. "*All* the babies have wings?"

The mothers looked at each other. Nodding. Slowly smiling. Yes, it was true. There was a murmur, which quickly escalated into a babble of excitement, not funereal at all.

Theresa Ratcher opened her arms and Matthew broke free, diving and swooping overhead.

Soon babies were flying throughout the rooms, gleefully darting around each other. Some of the mothers, cut by babies' wings, drifted in a confused stupor, "awakening" (for lack of a better term) to the shock of a houseful of flying babies, but other mothers had grown so adept at avoiding the wings that they were able to explain what had occurred.

"All of them?" the stunned mothers asked.

"Yes. All."

Pete Ratcher and Raj Singh dug beneath the apple tree, the white blossoms only recently swallowed into tiny, bitter apples. They worked, accompanied by the buzzing of flies and bees, in mutual silence, until, just as the sun was leaning on the horizon, babies began flying out of the house. Both Pete and Raj stopped digging. "What can it mean?" Raj asked.

"It means the devil's come to Voorhisville," Pete replied, though Theresa and Elli both later said he was not a religious man.

Inside the house, Theresa once more quieted the women. "We have to make some decisions about how we're going to proceed," she said. "I mean, all of us sharing this secret."

Elli finally broke her spell of repeating "We are here" to cry, "My dad killed my baby!"

"We'll call the police." Cathy reached for her cell phone.

"Wait!" Shreve said. "What's going to happen if we call the police? They're going to want to see the body, right? And if they see the body, they're going to see the wings."

"But that doesn't mean anyone's going to guess about *our* babies," Maddy said.

Emily, who had slung the gun bandolier fashion across her chest (using one of Theresa's flowered scarves), sauntered to the front of the room. "I think probably all of us have had some close calls with our babies flying at inappropriate times, but right now nobody's exactly looking for babies with wings. If word gets out about the possibility, we might as fuckenwell call up *People* magazine ourselves, because someone is going to discover us. Sooner or later, someone is going to catch one of our babies flying, and then all hell is going to break loose. We need to take care of this ourselves. Also, for those of you who've been asking, I wrote down the recipe for the chocolate croissants. It's on the refrigerator."

Jan Morris stood up and introduced herself as a Realtor-poet. "I notice," she said, "that I am a bit older than most of you. I learned in my first marriage, which was a *disaster*, that you can tell how things are going to go by looking at how things went. We have two dead babies here. I don't think we have to look any further to see what chances our babies have in the world. We have all the information we need."

"It's like a painting," Lara said, "you know? That little bit of red in the corner, that little dot of color. You might not necessarily notice, but it's there and it affects everything. If you cover it up, it changes everything, but it's still there."

The mothers were silent, processing this, some more successfully than others.

"If we don't call the police, what do we do about *him*?" Cathy Vecker asked.

"Where is he, anyway?" Maddy said.

Sylvia stood up, so suddenly she knocked over her cup of tea. "He's out there! With our babies!"

Suddenly the mothers were frightened again, thinking of their babies *flying* over Pete Ratcher, who was untied and essentially free to commit murder again. The mothers ran outside, shouting. Upstairs in Elli's room, Tamara Singh wrapped a pillow around her head to try to muffle the noise.

Raj Singh stopped digging, but Pete Ratcher, after glancing up to see what all the fuss was about, continued.

Theresa took off her shirt. Emily did the same. Strangely, Elli did too, though of course Timmy was dead.

Matthew Ratcher flew to his mother's breasts, and Gabriel Carr flew to Emily's. The mothers, observing this, stopped shouting; took off their shirts, blouses, and bras; and offered their breasts to a darkening sky dotted with bats and babies, who dove to their mothers with delighted gurgles. It wasn't long at all before the yard and house were filled with mothers in the madonna position. Elli remained in the yard for a long time, bare-breasted and with empty arms. Nobody noticed when she returned to the house.

Raj stepped into the freshly dug holes, and Pete Ratcher handed the crates to him, then helped hoist him up. Pete immediately began refilling the holes with dirt. Raj tried to help, but was incapacitated by grief, so Pete Ratcher did this part alone. When he was finished, he left Raj standing there, beneath the apple tree, weeping.

Pete Ratcher walked back to his house, weaving around the nursing

women, guided by the fireflies' tiny lanterns. Theresa looked up from
her adoration of Matthew and said, "Get away from me, you monster."

"I'm not going anywhere," Pete Ratcher said, loud enough to get
everyone's attention. "I'm *his* father. I'm Elli's father. And I'm *your*
husband."

Theresa shrugged. "Well, you got two out of three right."

Pete Ratcher stood there, stunned. The women took advantage of
his state to tie him up again, while Emily pointed the gun at his dirty
forehead.

"You're under arrest," she said.

"Says who? You're no policeman."

But it didn't matter. We were the *mothers.*

Pete

We used to have animals on this farm. Cows. Chickens. An old
rooster. This was when I was a boy. We even had a horse for a while
there. Here's the thing: you gotta kill the ones born bad. I know, it's
not easy to do. Nobody ever said it was *easy.* You think I wanted to
kill my own *grandson?* You think I'm *happy* about that? But somebody
had to do something. These aren't babies that can grow up to be
regular men. You mothers are losing sight of that. Sure, they're cute
right now, most of them, but what's going to happen over time? You
can't carry them around forever. They're growing, and they're growing
unusually fast. Can't you see that? Come on, be realistic now. Just try
to step back for a while and consider what's happening. What do you
think's going to happen when they're grown? We have to take care of
this now, before it becomes a real problem. Think of it like Afghanistan or Iraq. I know you ladies voted to fight the wars there, right?
Well, Voorhisville is our Iraq. Don't you see? We have a responsibility. We have to take care of this mess. Here. Now. We *can* do this. We
should do this. Tonight. In the barn. I'll do it. Just say your good-byes
and I'll take care of the rest. I'm not saying it'll be easy—they do sort
of look like regular babies, but that's their trick. They're counting on
us to feel that way until they get strong enough to do God knows
what. We have a responsibility to the world. Do you think they're

going to stay all cute and cuddly, flapping around like sparrows? You have to ask yourselves the hard questions. You have to ask yourselves what they will become. You have to ask yourselves, seriously, what you are raising here. You might as well get it into your heads: I'm not going to be the only one who feels like this. You're the mothers, so it's only natural you want to protect them, but there are going to be others who feel the same as me. Lots of others. What are you going to do about them? You're not going to be able to keep ignoring this. You're not going to be able to tie everyone up. All I'm saying is that the world will not accept them. That's a given. All you have to decide is, do you make the hard choice now and get on with your lives, or do you just prolong their suffering because you can't cope with your own?

The Mothers

Afterward—before they started playing "Maggie May" 24/7, and before we were down to our meager rations of pickles and jelly, but after the windows had been boarded up with old barn wood—we had a little quiet time to think about what Pete Ratcher had said and came to the conclusion that he was probably right, but that didn't change anything.

We took him to the barn, and, though he was tied up, he seemed under the impression that we were taking his advice. "Don't worry," he said. "You ladies won't hear a thing. Well, maybe the shots, but no crying or anything. Timmy didn't cry but for thirty seconds at the most."

Elli went to her room, where she found Tamara and Raj Singh curled up in her bed, both still fully clothed but sleeping soundly. She eased in beside them, pressing against Raj the way he was pressed against Tamara.

Elli

I remember being in my bed with Tamara and Raj Singh. All three of us suffering like we were, it didn't even feel like we were three people, but more like one. The way I felt inside, I was Elli Ratcher, fifteen and on summer break, and I was a mommy with leaking breasts, and I was the monster who thought I wanted my baby to die, and I was a hundred years old like one of those women they show on TV in the black cape and hood, screaming over my dead baby, and I was the girl with the beautiful bones wrapped around the man with skin that smelled like dirt and I was the man who smelled like dirt and I was his wife dreaming the dead.

That saying kept going through my head. *We are such stuff as dreams are made on.* When I heard screaming, I thought it was a dream, and I thought *I* was a dream, peeling the girl I was away from the man lying there beside me. I walked my dream feet over to the window and the man got up and stood beside the girl and said, "What is that horrible noise?" I turned to that part of me, while the other part continued to sleep, and said, "It sounds like my father." That's when we noticed the babies flying out of the barn, swooping through the night sky. We watched the mothers, in a disarray of tangled hair and naked breasts. We heard their screams of blood as they ran into the house. I said, "This is not happening," and went back to bed. I heard the man saying, "Tamara, wake up, we must leave this place. Tamara, wake up," but as far as I know she didn't wake up until the morning.

Tamara

There are certain mornings in Voorhisville when the butterflies flit about like flower seraphs and the air is bright. Tamara woke up to just such a morning, taking several deep breaths scented with manure and the faintest hint of roses, all the way from town. *Sweet,* she thought, before she rolled over and saw the empty crib, which brought her back to the nightmare of her son's death and the other baby murdered by his own grandfather. It did not seem possible that such a reality could exist in this room, papered with tiny yellow flowers.

Tamara sat at the edge of the bed listening to the breathing of the girl who still slept there and the murmur of voices below, raised in argument, then hushed. She had to go to the bathroom. It did not seem possible that such a simple bodily function would take precedence over her sorrow, but it did. She shuffled to the door, the chair she had used to discourage visitors shoved to the side. She remembered Raj, pushing at the door, asking her to let him in. Vaguely, she remembered doing so. But where had he gone? She suddenly missed her husband, as if he had taken part of her with him, as if she suffered the ghost pain of a severed limb. She stepped into the hall, which was dim and hot.

The words "police," "reporters," "prison," "murder," "self-defense," "justice," "love," "fear," "danger," and "coffee" drifted up the stairs. Tamara stood in the hot hallway and listened.

Maddy

I got to the Ratcher farm right at the end of the funeral, which is okay, 'cause I'm not sure—even as solemn of a event as it was—that I could of kept a straight face through "Silent Night." Stooker dropped me off out by the road 'cause there was so many cars parked in the driveway and on the lawn.

"Looks like some kind of thing going on," he said. "You sure you wanna get out here, Maddy? We could go to the graveyard."

The graveyard, case you were confused by Elli Ratcher's spaced-out words (but what do you expect from a girl who tried to hang herself; I mean, it only makes sense there would be some brain damage, right?)—the graveyard is where kids in Voorhisville hang out, and if that don't give you the right idea about this shithole town, nothing will. Anyway, I got out of the car, and, like I said, got there right at the end part, where Elli was going, "We are here," like she was high or something. For all I know, maybe she was.

JoJo and me were there when Mr. Ratcher tried to convince us to let him kill our babies, like that was the *reasonable* thing to do, and I was one of them that voted to tie him up in the barn. That's as far as we got, I swear on my own brother's grave. So we all went out there, or I guess most of us did, and tied him to the center pole. He kept saying we were nuts. Back at the house, a bunch of the mothers called up husbands and kids and shit and said how they were at the Ratchers' and going to spend the night. I called my mom and told her me and JoJo was staying with Elli Ratcher. My mom goes, "Well, I suppose it would make sense you two girls would become friends."

We laid down on the floors in the living room and kitchen. I slept in the yard and some other mothers were out there too. We had our babies with us. Nobody slept upstairs 'cause nobody wanted to make Tamara or Raj or Elli have to hear the sound of a living baby. I would say that proves we were not evil, like some people say.

Mr. Ratcher was sort of upset. He kept saying he had to take a piss, so Mrs. Ratcher stayed behind to unzip him and hold him so he wouldn't wet himself. I was half asleep when she came back up to the house with Matthew. I didn't see no blood on her and that's something I would of remembered if I did, but it was dark. I told the mothers this. I told them the screams came later, *after* I saw Mrs. Ratcher come back to the house. The screams woke me up. I reached for JoJo, but he ain't anywhere around, and I think somehow that *monster*, Mr. Ratcher, got a hold of my baby, so I run out to the barn.

After my brother got killed in Afghanistan, I was amazed to find out that some people—and I am not just talking teenagers here— wanted to know *details*, like, was he shot or blown up, and what body parts did they send us?

Anyway, my point is, I ain't going to get into details about what happened in the barn for all you sick fucks that like to say you gotta know out of some sense of clearity, like that reporter said, and not because, let's face it, you get off on it somehow. But I will say this: I screamed really loud, and I am not someone who screams at scary movies and shit.

All of them were in the barn. Even the ones that had been in carriers. Somehow, they figured out how to unbuckle straps and shit. Just like that, they were no longer *babies*. We no longer had control over them. Some of the mothers say we probably never did, that they just fooled us for a while.

So the mothers come out and they see blood on the babies and they start undressing and the babies come swooping down and the mothers are screaming and everyone runs into the house and starts washing their babies—wiping the blood off, you know, to see where the *actual wound* is. I'm trying to tell them; I'm saying, "Mr. Ratcher is dead," but nobody pays attention. Some of them are screaming that they're going to kill him.

Then Mrs. Ratcher comes in and she's crying and screaming, "Who killed my husband?" and that's when she sees all the mothers wiping blood off their babies. She's all covered in blood herself, which she says was from trying to get him untied. "Give me a knife," she says. "I gotta get him untied."

Someone goes, "Theresa, you are better off. He was a child molester and a murderer and you are better off without him."

Mrs. Ratcher says, "He's no child molester—we had a misunderstanding, is all. And he's no murderer, either. Not usually."

The whole thing was so *horrible* I guess none of us could believe it. I mean, even now, after all this time, I still sort of expect to see Billy sitting on the couch, eating pistachios. I know how crazy a person's mind can get when something so terrible happens that you can't even believe it.

Mrs. Ratcher said, "Where's Elli? He didn't molest her. She can straighten this whole thing out."

But Elli was upstairs in bed—mourning, we assumed, her life and murdered child.

"My mother did the same thing," Evelyn Missenhoff said. "When I told her about my dad she said I was lying."

Mrs. Ratcher stood there, holding Matthew tight. In spite of all that day had brung—her grandson and husband both dead, not to mention the surprise of finding Tamara Singh asleep on her couch just that morning with her own dead baby—Mrs. Ratcher had a pretty face. She made a point of looking at each of us, shaking her head until that dirt-colored hair of hers brushed her freckled cheeks. "We have to call the police," she said.

A mother's love is a powerful thing. It can direct a person to behave in ways they never would of thought possible. When Billy got sent to Afghanistan, I overheard my mother telling him he didn't have to go.

"Yeah I do," he said.

"You could quit. You know Roddy Tyler? He got a honorable dis-
charge from Vietnam. Why don't you do that?"

"Ma, I wanna go."

"Well, if you *want* to."

I heard it in her voice, but didn't really understand until I had my
own child. Being a mother, I figure, is like going a little bit crazy all
the time.

The Mothers

The mothers want you to understand. We are not *bad* people, we are
mothers. When Mrs. Ratcher insisted we call the police, we saw it as a
threat, and did the only thing we knew to do: we took Matthew out
of her arms and tied her up to a pole in the barn—facing away from
her husband, 'cause we're not *evil.*

"Someone murdered Pete," she said. "And whoever did it is still
among you."

Did she *know?* It's hard to believe she didn't. But it's probably just
as difficult to understand how it is that we knew and didn't know at
the same time. Who could *believe* such a thing?

Later, when we heard the screams again, we tried to ignore them.
We rolled over. Closed our eyes. We tried to *believe* it was a dream. We
tried to believe we weren't even awake, but the screams pulled us back,
and we fell to the earth. And when we went to the barn, we saw all our
babies there, and Mrs. Ratcher, dead.

They flew out of the barn into the sky, up to the bright stars. We
weren't sure if we should call them back or not. We stood there, our
mouths hanging open, tears falling on our tongues.

Later, they came back, lunging at our breasts and drinking with
selfish, insistent sucks and tiny bites, until they finally fell asleep, and
we realized we had a problem.

Elli

I wake up on my birthday thinking about how I dreamt I had a baby.
With wings! And my mom did too! I dreamt almost all the mothers

came to our house for a funeral. I dreamt my dad killed my baby and the mothers tied my dad up in the barn. What's that saying? *We are such stuff as dreams are made on.*

When I open my eyes, the first thing I see is the empty crib. This nightmare is my life.

"Mom?" I call. "Mom?" She doesn't come. She's probably busy with Matthew. When I look at the crib, my breasts drip milk. What does it *mean*, anyway? "We are such stuff as dreams are made on." Does he mean the dreams of sleep, or the dreams of hope? And how are they made *on* us? Are we, like, scaffolding? I can't figure it out. I can't figure *anything* out. "Mom?" My breasts hurt. My arms hurt too. My whole body hurts. Maybe this is what happens to old people. Maybe it starts to take its toll, holding up all those dreams.

But I'm not old! Today is my sixteenth birthday! When I open the bedroom door, I can hear the voices of the mothers downstairs. Why aren't they gone? I can't decide how I feel about them tying my dad up in the barn, even though he killed Timmy. "Mom?" The voices go quiet. "Mom, could you come up here?" I don't want to see the mothers. I hate them. I don't want to see the babies, either. I hate them too.

"Elli?" someone says.

"Could you tell my mom I want to talk to her?"

There is all kinds of whispering, but I can't make out the words, before one of them hollers, "She's not here right now."

That figures, right? This is how my mom has been ever since Matthew was born. But then I think maybe she's out getting my presents or something. I feel better for about two seconds, until I remember Timmy is dead. I can't celebrate today. What is she thinking? "Could you get my dad for me then?" The whispering starts again. The mothers are really starting to get on my nerves.

I go downstairs. There are mothers everywhere—in the living room, in the kitchen. When I look out the window, I even see some in the yard. Babies are flying everywhere, too. One almost hits me in the head, and I have to clench my fists and hold my arms stiff so I don't hit it. The mothers sitting at the kitchen table look shocked to see me. "Your dad can't come right now, either," one of them says.

I don't know why, but I feel like I shouldn't let on that I know how strange this all is. I shrug like, okay, no big deal; and say, "We are such stuff as dreams are made on." This gets them looking at each other and raising eyebrows. Maybe it wasn't the right thing to say. I walk to the refrigerator and take out the orange juice. I open the cupboard, but all the glasses are gone. Then I see the dishes drying on the counter. I try to find my favorite glass—the one with Sponge-Bob SquarePants on it—but I don't see it anywhere. I finally take my mom's glass, the one with the painted flowers. I pour myself a tall orange juice. When I turn around, all the mothers are staring. I take a big drink. The mothers act like they aren't watching, but I can tell they are. When I put the glass down, they all pretend, real quick, to look at something else. "I think I'm going to go to Timmy's grave," I say. They look up at me, and then down, or at each other. They look away as if I am embarrassing. I shrug. I have to be careful, because I can tell that this shrugging thing could become a tick. Martha Allry, who is a year behind me in school, has a tick where she blinks her right eye a lot. People call her Winking Martha.

"Would you like me to come with you?" one of the mothers says.

She is a complete stranger. Even so, I hate her. She's one of the ones that tied up my dad in the barn. She's here when my mom is not. I say, "Thanks, but I'd rather be alone."

The mothers nod. They nod quite a bit, actually. I walk out of the kitchen. I don't have on shoes and I'm still wearing my nightgown. This is how we do things on the farm.

It's a beautiful morning. The birds are singing and some babies fly by, which is totally weird.

One of the mothers comes up to me and says, "Where are you going?" She sort of looks sideways at the barn when she thinks I'm not looking.

Right away I know my dad is still tied up. The mothers are not my friends.

"I'm going to Timmy's grave."

The mother's face turns into a bunch of Os—her eyes, her mouth, her whole face goes all round and sorry. I walk past her, already planning how I have to get into the barn and rescue my dad. I *think* I'm going to rescue him. I can't decide for sure. He's my dad, but he's also my baby's murderer. Maybe it was an accident. Maybe he was just trying to scare everyone. Maybe I hate him. I don't *know* what I feel, but I should have some say in this; it's my baby he killed.

I walk down to the apple tree where there are two mounds of dirt. No cross or anything. Nothing to tell me which one is Timmy. This makes me angry. It's like I get hit on the back of my shoulders, that's how it feels, and I just drop to my knees and start crying, right there in the dirt. I can't believe Timmy is dead. Nobody knows my horrible secret about how many times I wanted him to die. Nobody knows how evil I am. I am a very evil person. Nothing can change this. I wanted him to die and he did. That's the whole story. It doesn't matter that I'm sorry.

My breasts are dripping right through my nightgown. The apple tree is buzzing with bees. A plane flies overhead. My whole body hurts. It hurts to *breathe.* I can't stop crying. Will I ever stop crying?

Then, just like that, I stop crying.

The mothers are calling their babies. They are taking their tops off and spreading their arms and the babies are diving for their breasts. They go into the house. Some of them glance at me, and then, real quick, look away.

The yard is empty except for a couple of crows. I don't see anyone looking out the windows. The mothers have forgotten about me. I stand up, check the house again, and then walk, real fast, to the barn.

At first I can't really see, 'cause it's dark there. Not like middle-of-a-moonless-night dark, but shady, you know, and there's a strange smell. I can sort of see my dad, tied up to the pole; I can see the shape of him. "Dad?" I say, but he is totally quiet. I can't believe he fell asleep. I get a little closer. That's when I see what they did to him.

The mothers are evil; worse than me. He doesn't even look like my dad anymore. There are flies buzzing all over him. I try to shoo them away, but they are evil too.

We are such stuff as dreams are made on. I can't carry the dreams any-more. I can't hold them up. I am sinking under the weight. I can't look at him anymore. The mothers are monsters. I need my mom. She'll know what to do. She'll make the mothers go away.

I look at the beams my dad was always talking about. I look at the holes in the roof, showing bits of blue sky. I look at the tools by the door, the shovels, the hoe, the axe, nails, rope, Dad's old shirt, and Mom's gardening hat; I am spinning in a little circle waiting for Mom to find me, and that's when I find *her*: tied to the other pole, her back to my dad, but chewed up just like him.

I get the rope and the ladder. I make a noose in the rope and try to throw it over the beam that goes in between both of them, but it doesn't work until I weigh down one end with an old trowel my mom uses for tulip bulbs. A couple years ago I helped her plant red tulips all around the house. Afterward, we sat on the porch and drank root beer floats. We used to get along better.

I finally get the rope over the beam and twist the rope around it a few times. I have to be careful, 'cause that trowel swings back toward me. I know it doesn't make sense to be *careful*, considering, but the point is that I didn't want to feel pain. By the time I stand on the ladder and check the rope, my arms are really tired.

I pull on the rope and it holds tight. I put the noose around my neck and I don't like how it feels, but then I step off the ladder and kick it with my feet and I can feel the breath getting sucked right out of me, and there is this horrible noise like a bomb, and the next thing I know, I am free. Then I feel the weight of the world on me, and by the time I climb out of the wreckage, I know I have failed. The rope is around my neck, the barn collapsed, and all the mothers are staring at me, until the one with the gun says, "Well, all right; we can use this wood to board up the windows and doors."

The Mothers

We do not know how Tamara's husband snuck away. For a while he was quite a regular on the local news. He insisted we were not a cult. (We are *not* a cult.) He also denied allegations that we were some sort of militia group, though he did say he had no idea how many weapons we had. (We only have one gun.) We thought he was our friend until he started calling us monsters. "Tamara, honey," he said, looking right out of the TV screen at us, "I'm sorry I left you. I thought I'd get back in time. Please be careful. I'm here, waiting for you. You're not in trouble. I told the sheriff and the FBI and Homeland Security about your situation. They understand that you are being held against your will . . ." And on and on. We did not know that Raj, who had been so silent around all of us, could talk so much.

The mothers do not completely trust Tamara, and suspect she offered to be chronicler only to get our secrets. After all, she has nothing to lose. Her baby is already dead. We feel bad that we are reduced to such cold calculation, but our lives now depends on calculating. We also do not trust Elli Ratcher. We've been medicating her with various mood modifiers and enhancers that we pooled from our own supply. Though we started with a rather amazing amount of medication, the stash is dwindling at a suspicious rate. Several of us suspect Maddy Melvern of pilfering it for recreational purposes.

We cannot say we blame her. We pace about the house like restless animals in a cage. We *are* restless animals in a cage. We have played all the Ratcher games: checkers, Monopoly, Life, Candy Land.

We miss our babies terribly. We miss them with every breath; we miss them in our *blood.* For a long time we missed them with our leaking breasts. But we know we did the right thing. We think we did. We must have. We hope.

We were watching the morning news the first time we saw Raj, his dark eyes wide, his black hair like a rooster's, ranting about flying babies and murdering mothers. We hoped nobody would take him seriously, though it was unlikely that he would be completely ignored. "We need to fortify, and protect ourselves," Emily said.

That's when the barn came crashing down. We found Elli Ratcher climbing out of the rubble in her nightgown, a rope tied around her neck. She tried to run into the cornfield, but we brought her back to the house. We think that was the right thing to do. What was she going to do out there? Where was she going to run? This is her *home,* after all. Of course she objected, but that's how teenagers are. We try to take good care of Elli—and Maddy, of course—but they resist us. Perhaps we are overprotective, after what happened with our own children.

The hardest thing any of us ever had to do was release our babies.

We were not even finished nailing all the wood over the windows and doors when the first cars arrived. Pete Ratcher apparently had only one hammer; so there was that to contend with. We resorted to using books and shoes and other tools. We have to admit that not all of us pursued this task with equal vigor. Many of us weren't completely certain that Emily Carr hadn't also gone nuts. But we had bonded over the Ratcher deaths, as well as the revelation that all our babies had wings.

We had not yet figured out we were a *family*. It was only later, after Jan and Sylvia got in a fight over Scrabble and began throwing letter tiles at each other, when we had the discussion that eventually resulted in the remarkable revelation: Jeffrey had fucked us all.

The first car was full of high school kids. They drove by with their windows down, screaming nonsense. We continued to hammer wood over the windows and doors. The car stopped and the kids inside were silent. Then it made a squealing U-turn back toward town.

The next car was Mrs. Vecker's Ford Explorer, with its skylight and fancy hubcaps. It pulled over by the side of the road. Roddy Tyler stepped out, shading his eyes with his hand and squinting at the house. He walked over to the barn wreckage (in his duct-taped shoes) and started poking through the rubble. We are not sure what he was looking for, but he jerked back as though bitten by a black widow. He looked at the house again and then ran to the Ford, jumped in, and made a squealing U-turn, driving too fast.

We continued nailing. Perhaps with a bit more resolve.

Tamara

There is a certain scent in the Ratcher farmhouse now that its windows are boarded and the doors nailed shut. It is the scent of sweat and skin; and the sickly odor of bodies wasting away on a diet of jelly and pickles; and the pungent scent of pickles on breath made sour by slow starvation and the toothpaste long since eaten. Sometimes a vague perfume wafts in through the cracks and bullet holes. Elli

Ratcher has been discovered many times standing with her little freckled nose right in one of those holes, hogging that sweet air.

On just such an evening, Sylvia sat barefoot at the table, weeping. This was not the life she had imagined for herself: trapped in a farmhouse listening to Rod Stewart's scratchy voice over loudspeakers, eating grape and strawberry jelly while Homeland Security and FBI agents, reporters, and curious onlookers camped outside with bulletproof vests and guns and cameras. Once, before they shut the power off, she'd even seen on one of the news channels that someone was selling food from one of those trucks on the road in front of the house—hot dogs and nachos. She really didn't want to think about it.

Lara Bravemeen watched Sylvia, as she had many times before, and finally did the thing she had always wanted to do. She walked over to the weeping beauty, placed a hand on her shoulder, and, when Sylvia looked at her, leaned down and kissed her on the mouth— which, yes, was sour and pickled, raw with hunger, but also flavored with the vague taste of roses. Sylvia stopped crying, and Lara, desperate to paint, took a jar of jelly and began smearing it across the wall, though she knew she risked her life to do so—that's how serious the penalty was for wasting food.

Shreve Mahar told her to stop, but Lara just laughed. Shreve thought of her fiancé, who died before the world changed; and she thought of her little boy—released, as they all were, when the mothers realized what was coming; and she thought about Jeffrey. "Maybe we should just tell them that the babies are gone," she said.

That's when Jan Morris walked into the kitchen, with the petite body she had always wanted and the satisfaction that she had been right all along; it really did take starvation to achieve. "We're not telling them anything," she said. "What the fuck is she doing? Hey, is that our *jelly?*"

"It's like a poem," Sylvia said, "with color."

"Poems have words." Jan smirked.

"Not necessarily," said Shreve.

"Well, you better tell her to stop it or you-know-who is going to shoot her."

Sylvia and Shreve considered their options—tackling Lara to the ground or letting her continue her jelly painting, a death sentence for sure—and each of them, separately and without consultation, decided not to interrupt.

The Mothers

What was it about him? The mothers still cannot agree. Was it his blue eyes? The shape of his hands? The way he moved? Or was it something closer to what Elli said, something holy? Was it something evil? We simply do not know.

Tamara

Once, Tamara answered the house phone and spoke to a reporter.

"My name is Fort Todd. I wonder if you care to comment on some information I've uncovered about someone you might be interested in. He's a wanted man, you know."

"Who? My husband?"

"No, no, not him. Oxenhash. Jeffrey."

"I don't know who you're talking about," Tamara said.

"I've uncovered a great deal of information about these winged creatures."

"What winged creatures?"

"People mistake them for angels, but they aren't. Apparently this is one of the ages."

"I don't know what you're talking about."

"They're coming into fruition. There have always been some, but we live in a time where there are going to be thousands."

"What do they want?"

"I thought if we could talk—"

Tamara hung up, which she sometimes regrets. She often thinks of turning herself in. What does she have to lose? Her baby is dead, and her husband has abandoned her, saying things like, "Just walk out, honey; nobody will hurt you." How can he, despite all that has happened, remain so naïve? So she stays with the other mothers who share the secret the authorities have not yet figured out: the babies are gone.

Tamara stays with the mothers out of *choice.* She's given up her freedom, though not for them. It's for the children.

The Mothers

On this, all the mothers agree. As long as the authorities think the babies are in here with us, well, the babies are safe. We hope.

If you see one, his small wings mashed against his back, perhaps sleeping in your vegetable garden, or flying past your window, please consider raising him. We worry what will happen if they go wild. You don't need to be afraid. They are good babies, for the most part.

Tamara

Emily paces throughout the house with the gun slung between her breasts. Perhaps Shreve was right all along, Emily thinks, though their friendship has been strained lately. *Maybe it is all an illusion.* Certainly the men and women pointing guns at the house are under the impression that there are babies inside. Emily is convinced that that's the only reason why any of them are alive. "There ain't gonna be another Waco here, that's for sure," the sheriff said, when he was interviewed on Channel Six.

One night there was a special report about the standoff at Waco, Texas. The mothers sat and watched, for once not arguing about whose head was in the way, or who didn't put the lid back on the peanut butter jar, or who left the toilet paper roll almost empty and didn't bother to change it. (Thinking about this now, Tamara smiles at the quaint memory of toilet paper. *Wouldn't that be nice,* she thinks.)

When it got to the part where they showed the charred bodies— the tiny little bones of children's hands and feet, the blackened remains—the mothers wept and blew their noses. Some swore. Others prayed. It was up to Emily to point out what it meant. "They are not going to make that mistake again. As long as they think we still have the babies, we are safe. And so are our babies."

Before that night, Maddy didn't know a thing about Waco, Texas, and she's still not sure how it's connected to the mothers. But the mothers are convinced that they must stay locked behind boarded-up windows and doors; that this is the best thing they can do for the babies. Maddy isn't even convinced that the babies all got away, but she hopes they did. She walks through the house, trying to stay behind Emily, since she has the gun, keeping out of the way of Elli Ratcher, who sort of haunts the place—though she's not dead, of course.

Lately, Maddy has gotten so hungry she's begun eating the house. She pulls off little slivers of wood and chews them until they turn into pulp. She has to be careful to peel the slivers off just right. She's cut her tongue and lips several times. Maddy thinks she never would have guessed she'd start eating a house, but she never would have guessed she'd give birth to a baby with wings, either. When Maddy thinks about JoJo, she stops peeling a sliver of gray wood from the upstairs hallway and stares at the yellow flowers in the wallpaper, trying to remember his face. "Please," she whispers.

"It won't do any good to pray," Elli says.

Maddy jumps. Of all the people to find her talking to herself, why'd it have to be Elli Ratcher?

"I ain't praying," she says.

"That's good. 'Cause it won't help."

Elli stands there, staring at Maddy until she finally says, "What are you looking at?"

"Did you know I had *two* babies?"

Maddy shrugs.

Elli nods. "My dad killed *one* of them. And the other is in my closet."

"Well, it's been great to have you visiting us on Planet Earth for a while, but I got some stuff I gotta do."

"You better be careful. If Emily finds out you're eating the house, she's going to kill you."

"I ain't eating the house," Maddy says. "Besides, you're the one who should be careful. The mothers know you keep stealing the notebook."

"What notebook?"

Maddy rolls her eyes.

If Emily knew how afraid everyone was of her, she would be insulted. Even Shreve is nervous around Emily now. She didn't know, she honestly didn't *know*: if Emily found them in the kitchen, would she shoot all of them, or just Lara and Jan, who were the ones wasting the jelly? "Maybe you should put that away," Shreve said, but they ignored her. *It's like I'm not even real,* she thought. *It's like I'm the illusion.* Shreve wondered if this was what was meant by being enlightened. She looked at her surroundings: the dark little kitchen with the boarded-up windows and door, the bullet holes, Sylvia sitting in the straight-backed chair, Lara painting with jelly, and Jan Morris licking the wall in her wake, pausing once to say, "This is true art."

Maybe I have never *been here,* Shreve thought. *Maybe my entire life was an illusion: the death of my fiancé, the birth of my winged child, the couple who died in the barn, the babies, everything. Maybe everything is nothing at all, including me. Maybe I never existed.* She felt like she was being swallowed, but not by something dark and frightening, not by a beast, but more like something with wings, something innocent she'd always been a part of but only now recognized. She wanted to tell the others what she was feeling, but she worried that speaking would break the spell. Instead, she closed her eyes, until Cathy Vecker came into the room and said, "Have you all gone crazy? What do you think Emily's going to do when she finds out?"

When Emily walked past the kitchen, she quickly looked the other way. She hoped the mothers would get their act together and clean up the mess. The last thing she wanted was to have to confront the issue. If she did, they might wonder why she didn't shoot anyone, and that might cause them to become suspicious that there were no more bullets. She heard Cathy say, "We have to clean this up before Emily finds out. Do you want to *die*?" That got their attention. They all started talking at once about how, since the day Elli threw their babies out the window, they didn't really care if they lived or not.

———

Elli

We are such stuff as dreams are made on. That's what I whispered to each one, as though I was a fairy godmother, as I pushed them out the window, the mothers standing behind me, crying.

"You do it," they said. "Please. We can't."

"Why don't you ask Tamara? She's got a dead baby, too."

"She's writing about all this and interviewing everyone. She doesn't have time to actually *do* anything; she's too busy chronicling us."

"But I hate all of you."

"That's why it has to be you," they said, using their crazy mother-logic on me. "You won't let your emotions get in the way."

They were wrong. All those babies with Timmy's dimples, and Timmy's little round body, and Timmy's eyes looking at me. I saw him in every one of them, and I felt the strangest emotion of all: a combination of love, hate, envy, joy, and sorrow. The more I dropped Timmies out the window, watching them sprout wings and dart across the starry sky, the more I felt my own wings—small, fluttering, just a tremor at first—sprouting from my back. I kept waiting for the mothers to notice, but they were too busy holding their babies tight, kissing them all over, crying on them. More than once, the baby was soaked and slippery by the time he was handed to me. Even though I wore my mother's old winter gloves, there were several babies I did not toss, but dropped. They did not get to hear my blessing, though I whispered it into the air.

The mothers handed me their babies, sighing, weeping, blowing kisses; or the mothers had their babies ripped from their arms as they screamed or threw themselves to the floor or—in one case—down the stairs.

We are such stuff as dreams are made on. I whispered it into tiny pink ears shaped like peony blossoms. I whispered it into wailing wide-open mouths (with sharp white teeth, already formed), and I whispered it into the night. It was amazing how they seemed to understand; even those who were crying, even those who plummeted toward the earth before unfolding their wings and darting over the cornfield, following their brothers.

I breathed the dark air scented with apple, grass, and dirt, and I felt the air on my arms and face, and I was happy and sad and angry and loving and hateful, and I thought, as I tossed Timmies out the window, *We are such stuff as dreams are made on.*

Emily, with the gun hanging from the scarf my dad bought Mom last Christmas, handed her baby to me and said, "Maybe later we can bake cookies."

Sylvia handed her baby to me and said, "I hope he goes somewhere wonderful, like Alaska, don't you?"

Lara was one of the mothers who would not release her son. She stood there, crying and holding him, as the mothers reminded her how they had all agreed this was the best thing; the babies' best chance of survival. So far, this seemed to be true. No shots were heard. Even though Rod Stewart continued his singing, somehow the officials out there slept, or at least were not watching the sky at the back of the house. This was our chance. It was everything that had already been said and agreed on. But they still had to rip the baby from Lara's arms. She ran from the room, crying, and I thought, *Well, now you know how I feel.*

At least their Timmies had a chance. Mine had had none.

The last Timmy was Maddy's. She was hiding in the closet, actually. The mothers had to pull her out, and she was doing some serious screaming, let me tell you. She was also cussing everyone out. "I never agreed to this!" she yelled. "I hate all of you!" She held her baby so tight that he was screaming, too. You know, baby screams. Maddy looked right at me and said, "Don't do it. Please don't do it." Even though the mothers told her it's not like the babies were dying or anything; hopefully they were flying somewhere safe. I didn't answer her. That wasn't my job. Besides, I was sort of distracted by *my* wings. I couldn't *believe* no one had noticed them.

Maddy was the worst. They had to hold her shoulders and her legs, and then two other mothers had to pull on her arms to open them, and another mother was standing there to grab her Timmy. By the time she handed him to me, everyone was freaking. I held Maddy's Timmy out to the sky, like I did with all the others, and I opened my mouth to say, "We are such stuff as dreams are made on," but he tore away from me and flew straight to the cornfield. Just in time, because right then there was a shout and all the police guys came around to the window, screaming and pointing. I shouted and waved to distract them. The mothers pulled me away from the window, then put the boards up and nailed them shut.

Later, when I go to my room, I undress in front of the mirror. My body looks different now. My nipples are dark, I have a little sag in my belly, and my hips are huge. But the biggest change has got to be the wings. When I take my clothes off, they come out of their secret hiding place and spread behind me—not gray like the babies', but white and glowing. Unfortunately, they seem to be for cosmetic purposes only. I jump off my bed and try to think of myself as flying, but it doesn't work.

The mothers are crying. Rod Stewart sings louder, trying to get the eternally sleeping Maggie to wake up. Some man on the loud-speaker begs us to come out, and promises that they won't hurt our babies.

We are such stuff as dreams are made on.

I sit at the edge of my bed and think about how things have been going lately; my parents both dead, and my baby too.

We are such stuff as dreams are made on.

I lie back on the bed, which is sort of uncomfortable because of the wings, and stare at the pimply ceiling. I am having a strange déjà vu feeling, like I've figured this all out once before, but forgot. I hope I remember this time.

The Mothers

The worst days of our suffering were reports of winged children being captured and shot. We crowded into the dark living room and wept in front of the TV set; turned it on full volume, so we could hear the gloating of marksmen and hunters over Rod Stewart's singing.

Oh, our babies! Our little boys, shot down like pheasants, tracked like deer, hunted like Saddam Hussein.

The worst of these worst days were when the camera panned over the little corpses, lingered on the dark wings, always at some distance. Artful, you might say, but torture all the same, for us, the mothers.

We could not identify them. There was solace and madness in this fact. Sometimes a mother became certain that the baby was hers. For some, this happened many times. There are mothers here who have been absolutely sure on several occasions that their babies have just been killed. They walk about the house, weeping and breaking dishes. Other mothers haven't suffered a single fatality. These mothers are positive their sons have escaped, alive. They are the ones who insist we maintain this charade, though, frankly, the jig is almost up.

After the film of murdered babies and hunters grinning broadly beneath green caps, the news anchors raise neatly manicured eyebrows, smile with bright white teeth, joke, and shake their heads.

"What do you think, Lydia, about the standoff in Voorhisville? Do you think it's time for authorities to move in?"

"Well, Marv, I think this has gone on long enough. It's clear these mothers have been taking advantage of decent folks' good intentions. Who knows, perhaps they're even sending their babies out to be shot, hoping to generate more sympathy, though I would say their plan is backfiring. It seems to me that the authorities have taken every precaution to safeguard innocent civilians from being harmed. The fact is, even if there *are* children in that house, they are not innocent. We've seen the bodies with their dangerous wings. Homeland Security has taken several into custody. My understanding is that they are holding them on an island off of Georgia. My point being, these are not your average little babies, and we have a right to protect ourselves. The authorities need to go in there and deal with this mess before it drags on into Christmas. It would be nice if they could do it without anyone getting hurt, but that just might not be possible."

The house is getting smaller. Maddy Melvern is eating it. She thinks no one has noticed, but we have. Sylvia Lansmorth and Lara Bravemeen are having an affair. Cathy Vecker paces through the rooms, weeping and quoting Ophelia. Some of the mothers think she is trying to seduce Elli Ratcher, but the rest think not. At any rate, Elli does not seem to care about Cathy, or anyone.

We have noticed a strange smell coming from Elli's room. There are rumors that she nurses the decomposing corpse of her firstborn baby there.

We have let Elli keep her old bedroom all to herself. This is a tremendous act of generosity, given how the rest of us crowd into the small rooms of this old house, but we thought it was the least we could do, considering what happened to her family. None of us want to investigate the odor. It is getting worse. We know that soon we will have to deal with it. But for now, we simply hold our breath when we are upstairs; and, frankly, we go up there less and less.

They have shut the power off. We no longer know what anyone is saying about us. Those of us with husbands or lovers no longer get to watch them being interviewed and saying incredible things about how much they love us, or how they never loved us, or how they've had to get on with their lives.

We have lost track of the calendar. It is cold in the house all the time now. The apple tree, which can be viewed through the bullet holes in the left panel of wood over the kitchen window, is bare. Jan thinks she saw a snowflake yesterday, but she isn't sure.

We will not last the winter. We may not last the week. This could very well be our final day. We don't know if we've done enough. We hope we have. We hope it's enough, but doubt it is. We are disappointed in ourselves. We are proud of ourselves. We are in despair. We are exultant.

What we want for our babies is the same thing all mothers want. We want them to be happy, safe, and loved. We want them to have the opportunity to be the best selves they can be.

Rod Stewart no longer sings. The silence is torture. They are coming for us. We will die here. But if any babies, even one baby— and all of us hope that the one left is our own—was saved, it is . . . well, not enough, but at least something.

We do not know what our children will grow into. No mother can know that. But we know what we saw in them; something sweet and loving and innocent, no matter what the reporters say, no matter what happened to the Ratchers. We saw something in our children that we, the mothers, agree might even have been holy. After all, isn't there a little monster in everyone?

WE WANT TO WARN THE WORLD! Be careful what you do to them. They are growing (those who have not been murdered, at least). And, whether you like to think about it or not, they are being raised by you. Every child must be reined in, given direction, taught right from wrong. Loved.

If you are reading this, then the worst has already happened, and we can do no more.

They are your responsibility now.

You Have Never Been Here

You are on the train, considering the tips of your clean fingers against the dirty glass through which you watch the small shapes of bodies, the silhouettes on the street, hurrying past in long coats, clutching briefcases, or there, that one in jeans and a sweater, hunched shoulders beneath a backpack. Any one of them would do. You resist the temptation to look at faces because faces can be deceiving, faces can make you think there is such a thing as a person, the mass illusion everyone falls for until they learn what you have come to learn (too young, you are too young for such terrible knowledge), there are no people here, there are only bodies, separate from what they contain, husks. Useless, eventually.

Yours is useless now, or most nearly, though it doesn't feel like it, the Doctors have assured you it is true, your body is moving toward disintegration even as it sits here with you on this train, behaving normally, moving with your breath and at your will. See, there, you move your hand against the glass *because you decided to*, you wipe your eyes *because you wanted to* (and your eyes are tired, but that is not a matter of alarm, you were up all night, so of course your eyes are tired) you sink further into the vague cushion of the seat, you do that, or your body does that because you tell it to, so no wonder you fell for the illusion of a body that belongs to you, no wonder you believed it, no wonder you loved it. Oh! How you love it still!

You look out the dirty window, blinking away the tears that have so quickly formed. You are leaving the city now. What city is this anyway? You have lost track. Later, you'll ask someone. Where are we? And, not understanding, he will say, We're on a train. The edge of the city is littered with trash, the sharp scrawls of bright graffiti, houses with tiny lawns, laundry hanging on the line, Christmas lights strung across a porch, though it is too late or too early for that. You close your eyes. Let me sleep, you say to your body. Right? But no, you must admit, your body needs sleep so the body's eyes close and it swallows you, the way it's always done, the body says sleep so you sleep, just like that, you are gone.

The hospital, the Doctors say, has been here for a long time. It's one of those wonderful secrets, like the tiny, still undiscovered insects, like several sea creatures, like the rumored, but not proven, aliens from other planets, like angels, like God, the hospital is one of the mysteries, something many people know for a fact which others discount variously as illusion, indigestion, dreams, spiritual hunger, fantasy, science fiction, rumor, lies, insanity.

It is made of brick and stucco (architecturally unfortunate but a reflection of the need for expansion) and it has a staff of a hundred and fifty. With a population that large, the rotating roster of patients, the salespeople who wander in offering medical supplies (not understanding what they do to sick bodies here) the food vendors, the occasional lost traveler (never returned to the world in quite the same way), it is remarkable that the hospital remains a secret.

The patients come to the auditorium for an orientation. Some, naively, bring suitcases. The Doctors do nothing about this. There is a point in the process when the familiar clothes are discarded. It's not the same for everyone and the Doctors have learned that it's best not to rush things.

The Doctors appear to be watching with bored disinterest as the patients file in. But this is not, in fact, the case. The Doctors are taking notes. They don't need pen and paper to do this, of course. They have developed their skills of observation quite keenly. They remember you, when you come in, skulking at the back of the room, like the teenager you so recently were, sliding into the auditorium chair, and crouching over as though afraid you will be singled out as being too young to be here, but that is ridiculous as there are several children in the group flocking around that lady, the one with orangey-red hair and the red and yellow kimono draped loosely over purple blouse and pants, a long purple scarf wrapped around her bloody neck. For some reason she is laughing while everyone else is solemn, even the Doctors standing there in their white lab coats, their eyes hooded as though supremely bored. (Though you are wrong about this. The Doctors are never bored.)

The Doctors introduce themselves. They hope everyone had a good trip. They know there is some confusion and fear. That's okay. It's normal. It's okay if there is none as well. That's normal too. All the feelings are normal and no one should worry about them.

The Doctors explain that the doors are locked but anyone can leave at any time. Just ring the bell and we will let you out.

The orangey-red-haired lady with the bloody neck raises her hand and the Doctors nod. You have to lean over to hear her raspy voice.

How often does that happen? How often does someone leave without going through with the procedure?

The Doctors confer among themselves. Never, they say in unison. It never happens.

The Doctors pass out room assignments and a folder that contains information about the dining hall (open for breakfast from six to nine, lunch from eleven-thirty to two, and dinner from five-thirty to eight), the swimming pool (towels and suits provided), the chapel (various denominational services offered throughout the week). The folder contains a map that designates these areas as well as the site of the operating rooms (marked with giant red smiley faces) and the areas that house the Doctors, which are marked Private, though, the Doctors say, if there is an emergency it would be all right to enter the halls which, on the map, have thick black lines across them.

Finally, the Doctors say, there is an assignment. This is the first step in the operation. The procedure cannot go any further until the first step is complete. The Doctors glance at each other and nod. Don't be afraid, they say. Things are different here. Everything will be all right, and then, as an afterthought, almost as though they'd forgotten what they had been talking about, they say, find someone to love.

The auditorium is suddenly weirdly silent. As though the bodies have forgotten to breathe.

It's simple, really, the Doctors say. Love someone.

You look around. Are they nuts?

At the front of the room the Doctors are laughing. No one is sure what to do. You see everyone looking around nervously, you catch a couple people looking at you but they look away immediately. You're not insulted by this. You expect it even.

The bloody neck lady raises her hand again. The Doctors nod.

Just one? she rasps.

The Doctors say, no, no, it can be one. It can be many.

And what happens next?

The Doctors shrug. They are organizing their papers and making their own plans for the evening. Apparently the meeting is over. Several patients stand, staring at the map in their hands, squinting at the exit signs.

Excuse me? the lady says again.

You can't decide if you admire her persistence or find it annoying but you wish she'd do something about her throat, suck on a lozenge maybe.

The Doctors nod.

After we find people to love, what do we do?

The Doctors shrug. Love them, they say.

This seems to make perfect sense to her. She stands up. The children stand too. They leave in a group, like a kindergarten class, you think. Actually, you kind of want to go with them. But you can't. You look at the map in your hand. You find your exit and you walk toward it, only glancing up to avoid colliding with the others. Love someone? What's this shit all about? Love someone? Let someone love me, you think, angry at first and then, sadly. Let someone love me.

The bodies move down the long hallways, weaving around each other, pausing at doors with numbers and pictures on them. (Later, you find out the pictures are for the children who are too young to know their numbers.) The bodies open unlocked doors and the bodies see pleasant rooms painted yellow, wallpapered with roses, cream colored, pale blue, soft green, furnished with antiques and wicker. The bodies walk to the locked windows and stare out at the courtyard, a pleasant scene of grass and fountain, flowering fruit trees. The bodies open the closets filled with an odd assortment of clothes, plaid pants, striped shirts, flowery dresses, A-line skirts, knickers, hand-knit sweaters, and raincoats, all in various sizes. The bodies flick on the bathroom lights, which reveal toilets, sinks, tubs and showers, large white towels hanging from heated towel racks. The bodies look at the beds with feather pillows and down comforters. The bodies breathe, the bodies breathe, the bodies breathe. The bodies are perfect breathers. For now.

What if this is the strangest dream you ever had? What if none of this is true? The Doctors have not told you that your body has its own agenda, your mother has not held your hand and squeezed it tight, tears in her eyes, your father has never hugged you as though he thought you might suddenly float away, your hair has not fallen out, your skin become so dry it hurts, your swallowing blistered? What if all of this is only that you are having a strange dream? What if you aren't sick at all, only sleeping?

The Doctors eat pepperoni and discuss astronomy, bowling, liposuction, and who has been seen kissing when someone's spouse was away at a seminar. The Doctors drink red wine and eat pheasant stuffed with gooseberries and cornbread, a side of golden-hashed potatoes, green beans with slivered almonds and too much butter. They discuss spectral philosophy, spiritual monasticy, and biological relativism. They lean back in their chairs and loosen belts and buttons surreptitiously, burping behind hands or into napkins. Dessert is served on pink plates, chocolate cake with raspberry filling and chocolate frosting. Coffee and tea is served in individual pots. The Doctors say they couldn't possibly and then they pick up thin silver forks and slice into the cake, the raspberry gooing out. "What do you think they are doing now?"

someone says. "Oh, they are crying," several of the Doctors respond. The Doctors nod their knowledgeable heads. Yes. On this first night, the bodies are crying.

That first night is followed by other days and other nights and all around you life happens. There are barbecues, movies, tea parties and dances. The scent of seared meat, popcorn, and Earl Grey tea wafts through the halls. You are amazed to observe everyone behaving as if this is all just the usual thing. Even the children, sickly pale, more ears and feet than anything, seem to have relaxed into the spirit of their surroundings. They ride bicycles, scooters, and skateboards down the hall, shouting, Excuse me, mister! Excuse me! You can never walk in a line from one end to the other and this is how, distracted and mumbling under your breath, you come face to face with the strange orange-haired woman. She no longer wears the kimono but the scarf remains around her throat, bloodied purple silk trailing down a black, white, and yellow daisy dress. Her head, topped with a paper crown, is haloed with orange feathers, downy as those from a pillow.

Where you going in such a hurry? she wheezes.

Upon closer inspection you see they are not feathers at all, but wisps of hair, her scalp spotted with drops of blood.

Name's Renata; she thrusts her freckled fleshy hand toward you.

Excuse me! Excuse me!

You step aside to let a girl on a bicycle and a boy on roller skates pass. When you turn back to her, Renata is running after them, her bloodied scarf dangling down her back, feathers of orangey-red hair floating through the air behind her.

She's as loony as a tune, wouldn't you say?

You hadn't seen the young man approaching behind the bicycle child and the roller-skating one. You haven't seen him before at all. He stares at you with blue eyes, like a dog.

You don't got a cigarette, do you?

You shake your head vigorously. No. Of course not. It goes without saying.

In spite of his stunning white hair, he's no more than five years older than you. He leans closer. I do, he says. Come on.

He doesn't look back. You follow him, stepping aside occasionally for the racing children. You follow him through a labyrinth of halls. After awhile he begins to walk slowly, slinking almost. There are no children here, no noise at all. You follow his cue, pressing against the walls. You have an idea you have entered the forbidden area but what are they going to do anyway. Kill you? You snort and he turns those ghost-blue dog eyes on you as though with threat of attack.

You are a body following another body. Your heart is beating against your chest. Hard. Like the fist of a dying man. Let me out, let me out, let me out. You are a body and you are breathing but your breath is not your own.

The body in front of you quickly turns his head, left, right, looking down the long white hall. The body runs, and your body follows. Because he has your breath now.

What is love? The Doctors ponder this question in various meetings throughout the week. We have been discussing this for years, one of them points out, and still have come to no conclusion. The Doctors agree. There is no formula. No chemical examination. No certainty.

There's been a breech, the Doctor in charge of such matters reports.

The Doctors smile. Let me guess, one of them says, Farino?

But the others don't wait for a confirmation. They know it's Farino.

Who's he with?

They are surprised that it is you. Several of them say this.

The Doctors have a big debate. It lasts for several hours, but in the end, the pragmatists win out. They will not interfere. They must let things run their course. They end with the same question they began with. What is love?

———

It's quick as the strike of a match to flame. One minute you are a dying body, alone in all the world, and the next you are crouched in a small windowless room beside a boy whose blue eyes make you tremble, whose breathing, somehow, involves your own. Of course it isn't love. How could it be, so soon? But the possibility exists. He passes the cigarette to you and you hesitate but he says, Whatsa matter? Afraid you're going to get cancer? You place the cigarette between your lips, you draw breath. You do that. He watches you, his blue eyes clouded with smoke.

Thanks. You hand the cigarette back. He flicks the ash onto the floor. The floor is covered with ash. From wall to wall there is ash.

This isn't all mine, you know.

You nod. You don't want to look stupid so you nod. He hands the cigarette to you and your fingers touch momentarily. You are surprised by the thrill this sends through your body. I sing the body electric.

What's that?

You hadn't realized you'd spoken out loud. I sing the body electric, you say. It's from a poem.

You a fucking poet? he says.

You hand the cigarette back to him. Any moment now the Doctors could come and take you away. Any breath could be the last breath. His blue eyes remain locked on yours.

I mean, are you? A fucking poet? He doesn't look away, and you don't either.

You nod.

He grins. He crushes the precious cigarette into the ashy floor. He leans over and his lips meet your lips. He tastes like ash and smoke. The gray powder floats up in the tumble of tossed clothes and writhing bodies. The bodies are coated with a faint gray film and maybe this isn't love, maybe it's only desire, loneliness, infatuation, maybe it's just the body's need, maybe it isn't even happening, maybe you have already been cremated and you are bits of ash creating this strange dream but maybe you are really here, flesh to flesh, ash to ash, alive, breathing, in the possibility of love.

———

Later, you lie alone on the clean white sheets in your room. You are waiting. Either he will come for you or they will. You stare at the ceiling. It
is dimpled plaster dotted with specks of gold. You think it is beautiful.

Suddenly there is knocking on the door.

You open it but it isn't the Doctors or the police and it isn't him,
it's Renata.

Are you naked or dead? she says.

You slam the door. Your ash print remains on the bed, a silhouette of your body, or *the* body. She is knocking and knocking. You tell
her to go away but she won't. Exasperated, you grab your ash pants
from the floor, step into them, zip and button the fly, open the door.

She is almost entirely bald now, but she still wears that ridiculous
paper crown. She sees you looking at it. She reaches up to fondle the
point. One of the children made it for me. Behind her you see the
evidence of your indiscretion. Your ash footprints reveal your exact
course. The hallway is eerily empty.

Where are the children now?

They're gone, she croaks, stepping into the room, a few orange
hairs wisping around her. Haven't you noticed how quiet it is?

It is. It is very quiet. All you can hear is her breath, which is
surprisingly loud. This place . . . you say, but you don't continue.
You were going to say it gives you the creeps but then you remember
Farino. Where is he now? How can you hate this place when this is
where you found him? You may as well relax. Enjoy this while you can.
Soon you will be out there again. Just another dying body without any
more chances left.

She opens your closet and begins searching through it. Have you
seen my kimono? The one I was wearing when I arrived?

You tell her no. She steps out of the closet, shuts the door. They
say it's just like changing clothes, you know.

You nod. You've heard that as well, though you have your doubts.

She sighs. If you see it, will you let me know? She doesn't wait for
your reply. She just walks out the door.

You count to ten and then you look down the hall. There is only
one set of ash footprints, your own. Are you there? you whisper. Are
you there? Are you? Is anyone?

You cannot control the panic. It rises through your body of its own accord. Your throat tightens and suddenly it's as though you are breathing through a straw. Your heart beats wildly against your chest, Let me out, let me out. The body is screaming now. Anyone? Anyone? Is anyone here? But the hall remains empty except for your footprints, the silent ashy steps of your life, and this is when you realize you have not loved enough, you have not breathed enough, you have not even hated enough and just when you think, well, now it's over, the Doctors come for you, dressed in white smocks spotted with roses of blood and you are pleading with them not to send you back out there with this hopeless body and they murmur hush, hush, and don't worry. But, though they say the right things the words are cold.

They take you down the long white halls, following your footprints, which, you can only hope (is it possible?) they have not noticed, until, eventually, you pass the room your footprints come out of, smudged into a Rorschach of ash as though several people have walked over them.

Hush, hush. Don't worry. It won't hurt any more than life. That's a little joke. Okay, we're turning here. Yes, that's right. That door. Could you open it, please? No, no, don't back out now. The instruments are sharp but you will be asleep. When you wake up the worst will be over. Here, just lie down. How's that? Okay, now hold still. Don't let the straps alarm you. The body, you know, has its own will to survive. Is that too tight? It is? We don't want it too loose. Once, this was a long time ago, before we perfected the procedure, a body got up right in the middle of it. The body has a tremendous will to survive even when it goes against all reason. What's that? Let's just say it was a big mess and leave it at that. The cigarette? Yes, we know about that. Don't mind the noise, all right? We're just shaving your head. What? Why aren't we angry? Can you just turn this way a little bit? Not really much left here to shave, is there? We're not angry; you did your assignment. What's that? Oh, Farino. Of course we know about him. He's right there, didn't you notice? Oh, hey, hey, stop it. Don't be like that. He's fine. He just got here first. He's knocked out already. That's what we're going to do for you now. This might—look, you knew what you were getting into. You already agreed. What do you want? Life or death? You want Farino? Okay, then relax. You've got him.

You are on a train. Your whole body aches. The body is a wound. You groan as you turn your head away from the hard glass. The body is in agony. Your head throbs. You reach up and feel the bald scalp. Oh! The body! The dream of the body! The hope of the body for some miracle world where you will no longer suffer. You press your open palms against your face. You are not weeping. You are not breathing. You are not even here. Someone taps the body's shoulder.

You look up into the hound face of the train conductor. Ticket? he says.

I already gave it to you.

He shakes his head.

You search through your pockets and find a wallet. The wallet is filled with bills but there is no ticket. I seem to have lost it, you say, but look, here, I can pay you.

The conductor lifts the large walkie-talkie to his long mouth and says some words you don't listen to. Then he just stands there, looking at you. You realize he thinks he exists and you do too. The train screams to a long, slow stop. He escorts you off.

You can't just leave me here, you say. I'm not well.

Here's your ride now, he says.

The police cruiser comes to a halt. The policeman gets out. He tilts the brim of his hat at the conductor. When he gets close to you, he looks up with interest. Well, well, he says.

There's been some sort of mistake, you say. Please, I'm not well.

The conductor steps back onto the train. The windows are filled with the faces of passengers. A child with enormous ears points at you and waves. For a second you think you see yourself. But that isn't possible. Is it?

The policeman says, Put your hands behind your back.

These aren't my hands.

He slaps the cuffs on you. Too tight. You tell him they are too tight.

The whistle screams over your words. The train slowly moves away.

Aren't you going to read me my rights?

The policeman leans into your face with bratwurst breath. Just 'cause you shaved your head you think I don't know who you are, he says. He steers you to the cruiser. Places one hand on your head as you crouch to sit in the backseat.

I know my rights, you insist.

He radios the station. Hey, he says, I'm bringing something special.

You drive past cows and cornfields, farmhouses and old barns. The handcuffs burn into your wrists. The head hurts, the arms hurt, the whole body hurts. You groan.

Whatsa matter? The policeman looks at you in the rearview mirror.

I'm not well.

You sure do look beat up.

I've been in a hospital, you say.

Is that right?

You look out the window at an old white farmhouse on a distant hill. You wonder who loves there.

The station is a little brick building surrounded by scrubby brown grass and pastures. The policeman behind the desk and the policewoman pouring coffee both come over to look at you.

Fucken A, they say.

Can I make my phone call?

The policewoman takes off the handcuffs. She presses the thumb into a pad of ink. She tells you where to stand for your picture. Smile, she says, we got you now, Farino.

What?

What is this body doing with you? What has happened? They list the crimes he's committed. You insist it was never you. You never did those things. You are incapable of it. You tell them about the hospital, the Doctors, you tell them how Farino tricked you.

They tell you terrible things. They talk about fingerprints and blood.

But it wasn't me, you insist.

Farino, they say, cut this shit and confess. Maybe we can give you a deal, life, instead of death. How about that?

But I didn't, you say. I'm not like that.

You fucking monster! Why don't you show a little decency? Tell us what you did with the bodies.

I was in a hospital. He switched bodies with me. He tricked me.

Oh, fuck it. He's going for the fuckin' insanity shit, ain't he? Fuck it all anyway. How long he been here? Oh, fuck, give him the fuckin' phone call. Let him call his fuckin' lawyer, the fuckin' bastard.

You don't know who to call. They give you the public defender's number. No, you say, I have money. In my wallet.

That ain't your money to spend, you worthless piece of shit. That belonged to Renata King, okay?

Renata?

What? Is it coming back to you now? Your little amnesia starting to clear up?

How'd I end up with Renata's wallet?

You fuckin' ape. You know what you did.

But you don't. You only know that you want to live. You want to live more than you want anything else at all. You want life, you want life, you want life. All you want is life.

What if this is really happening? What if you are really here? What if out of all the bodies, all the possibilities, you are in this body and what if it has done terrible things?

Listen, you say. You look up at the three stern faces. They hate you, you think, but no, they hate this body. You are not this body. The stern faces turn away from you. What can you say anyway? How can you explain? You sit, waiting, as though this were an ordinary matter, this beautiful thing, this body, breathing. This body. This past. This terrible judgment. This wonderful knowledge. The body breathes. It breathes and it doesn't matter what you want, when the

Mary Rickert

body wants to, it breathes. It breathes in the hospital, it breathes in the jail, it breathes in your dreams and it breathes in your nightmares, it breathes in love and it breathes in hate and there's not much you can do about any of it, you are on a train, you are in an operating room, you are in a jail, you are innocent, you are guilty, you are not even here. None of this is about you, and it never was.

Acknowledgments

Thank you to Emma Powell, as soon as I saw your haunting photographs at emmapowellphotography.com I hoped you would allow a piece to be used for cover art; you did, and I couldn't be more pleased with the result. Thank you to my family, the Rickerts, Bauerbands, Vetters, Kenneys, McCanns, Dehecks, Dopkeens and Orths for cheering me on, sending thoughtful notes, attending readings, and hand selling my books. I am truly fortunate to have your love and support. Thank you also to the Lyons family, technically not mine, but I'm claiming you anyway. To my friends who have understood my need for solitude, even when it has been inconvenient to the friendship, thank you for loving me through my weird: Rietje Marie Angkuw, Cathy Barber, Kristen Barrows, Haddayr Copley-Woods, Karen Crandall, Kriscinda Lee Everitt, Marcia Gorra-Patek, Mary Leanord, Liz Musser, Sofia Samatar, Terry Shuster, and Vera Lisa Smetzer. Special thanks to Christopher Barzak, you have been my trusted companion through the challenges of a writing life, holding the lantern aloft for me. During my years as an apprentice writer I often struggled financially and benefitted from the kindness of others. I want to give a big thanks to Dr. Richard Dunham for your generosity when I needed compassion and dental work. Thank you also to Thomas Tunney for sharing your wisdom, expertise, and bagels! Thank you to my agent, Howard Morhaim, for working so hard on my behalf with class,

integrity, and intelligence; I am honored to have you as
my representative in the world. Over the years I have been
happy to meet, either in person or through email, many
people who have taken the time to tell me they enjoyed
something I wrote. These exchanges are some of the
highlights of my life. Thank you, dear readers, for being
a part of my story. Others have supported me with their
special talent for teaching, generously sharing the hard
lessons they learned so I might enjoy the benefit without the suffering. Thank you to Laurie Alberts, Karen
Joy Fowler, Douglas Glover, Joshilyn Jackson and David
Jauss. A special bow of gratitude to Ellen Lesser who
worked so tirelessly with me for two semesters, helping
me find my novel, and my passion for engagement with
critique, thus gifting me with that cherished experience
of a snowy night when I was so immersed in a great work
I momentarily forgot it was not my own. Thank you as
well to Vermont College of Fine Arts for accepting me
into the MFA program, in spite of the deficits I brought
to my application; it was a tremendous experience. Thank
you also to Meg Galaza of Yoga One Studio in Cedar-
burg, Wisconsin. When I think of the great teachers in
my life, I think of you. Thank you to Gavin J. Grant and
Kelly Link of Small Beer Press. As a young writer I often
imagined an idealized relationship between publishers,
editors and writers; it has been lovely to have such an
experience working with you. Finally, thank you to my
husband, Bill Bauerband for always leaving the tea kettle
on and the fire lit.

Publication History

These stories were previously published as follows: *The Magazine of Fantasy & Science Fiction:* "Memoir of a Deer Woman" (March 2007), "Journey into the Kingdom" (May 2006), "Cold Fires" (October/November 2004), "The Corpse Painter's Masterpiece" (September/October 2011), "The Christmas Witch" (December 2006), "The Chambered Fruit" (August 2003). *Subterranean Magazine:* "Holiday" (2007). SCIFICTION: "Anyway" (August 2005). Tor.com: "The Mothers of Voorhisville" (April 2014). *Feeling Very Strange: The Slipstream Anthology:* "You Have Never Been Here" (March 2006). "The Shipbuilder" appears here for the first time.

About the Author

Mary Rickert has worked as kindergarten teacher, barista, Disneyland balloon vendor, and in the personnel department of Sequoia National Park where she spent her time off hiking the wilderness. She is the author of two collections and a novel *The Memory Garden*. She has received the Crawford, World Fantasy, and Shirley Jackson awards for her writing. She lives in Wisconsin.